Jame

School Houses

Anatiposi

James Johonnot

School Houses

Reprint of the original, first published in 1871.

1st Edition 2023 | ISBN: 978-3-38212-752-7

Anatiposi Verlag is an imprint of Outlook Verlagsgesellschaft mbH.

Verlag (Publisher): Outlook Verlag GmbH, Zeilweg 44, 60439 Frankfurt, Deutschland
Vertretungsberechtigt (Authorized to represent): E. Roepke, Zeilweg 44, 60439 Frankfurt, Deutschland
Druck (Print): Books on Demand GmbH, In de Tarpen 42, 22848 Norderstedt, Deutschland

SCHOOL-HOUSES.

BY JAMES JOHONNOT.

ARCHITECTURAL DESIGNS

BY

S. E. HEWES.

NEW YORK:
J. W. SCHERMERHORN & CO.
1871.

Little, Rennie & Co.,
Stereotypers, Electrotypers, and Printers,
New York.

DEDICATION.

To Hon. Ezra Cornell,

Founder of Cornell University:

An Institution which, resting upon our Common School System, is its perfect supplement; which, discarding the narrow formalism of a single course of study, recognizes the activities and interests of every-day life as vital parts of its instruction; which makes culture wait upon use, and furnishes opportunity to multiform aspiration; and which proposes ultimately to furnish instruction to "any person in any study," making questions of race, color, or sex irrelevant and impertinent;—this work is respectfully inscribed by

The Author.

PREFACE.

THE work of the author upon "Country School-Houses," published in 1858, was the first effort made in this country to apply the principles of architectural science to the construction of school-houses. The reports received from State Superintendents, and from various other sources, show that this work has contributed materially to the improvement of school-house architecture within the past ten years.

The constantly increasing demand for a better class of school-houses in country districts has led to the preparation of the present volume. An endeavor has been made to make it as complete as possible, using all the best material of the former work and all the recent improvements in the construction of school-houses and school furniture.

It contains a great variety of plans and elevations, with full and accurate descriptions, so that varied tastes may be gratified, and any carpenter can construct a building precisely as described. It also contains a full description of the most approved school furniture and apparatus, so that a school may be supplied with everything necessary to its highest success without recourse to untried and costly experiments.

To make the work of greater value to every school district, hints and suggestions in regard to school arrangement, and the care and use of school furniture and apparatus, have been frequently interspersed through its pages.

With the hope that it may contribute to the improvement of our common schools, this work is respectfully submitted to teachers, school-officers, and all who are interested in the cause of education.

CONTENTS.

CHAPTER V.

HEATING AND VENTILATION.

CHAPTER VI.

GENERAL CONSTRUCTION.

CHAPTER VII.

PLANS AND ELEVATIONS.

CHAPTER VIII.

FURNITURE.

CHAPTER IX.

APPARATUS.

CHAPTER X.

OUT-BUILDINGS.

CHAPTER XI.

ARRANGING AND ORNAMENTING GROUNDS.

CHAPTER XII.

ARCHITECTURE AN EDUCATIONAL INFLUENCE.

APPENDIX.

CHAPTER I.

GRADED SCHOOLS.

CHAPTER II.

HEATING AND VENTILATION.

LIST OF ILLUSTRATIONS.

OUR SCHOOL-HOUSES.

CHAPTER I.

GENERAL SURVEY.

For the past few years architectural science has made rapid and decided progress. In nearly every kind of buildings, improvements have been made, both in regard to external appearance and internal arrangement. Evidences of this progress may be seen in the superior elegance of the modern public edifices and private residences of our cities and villages, and in the greater comfort and convenience of the later farm-houses in the country. The increase of architectural knowledge has correspondingly developed the general taste, which in its turn demands a greater knowledge. Thus one step in improvement leads to others still further in advance.

Fig. 1.

Of all buildings, however, the last to feel this progressive impulse were school-houses. In cities and large villages, where the necessity exists of erecting large and costly buildings, it is true that public attention has been turned in this direction, and there has been developed a distinctive architecture which applies the principles of science to the wants and necessities of the school. But in the rural districts generally too little attention has been given to the matter. The principles developed in the building of large union schools are not applicable to the wants of the smaller school districts.

Fig. 2.—LOG SCHOOL-HOUSE.

The old log school-houses can be remembered by most of the older inhabitants. It was a necessity of primitive times, and was on an equality with the dwellings of the people. A better kind of structure has succeeded it, though we find in the last report of the Superintendent of New York that one hundred and twenty log school-houses are still in existence in the Empire State.

The reports of the Superintendents of several States, within the past few years, show that an improvement has gone on in many sections, indicating a genuine educational revival. And yet a large proportion of the school-houses in the country are but illy adapted to meet the high requirements of modern educational ideas. Even the newer and costlier houses are often built without a proper knowledge of the wants and necessities of the school, while a very large number of the older houses are utterly unfit for human occupancy.

That good school-houses are indispensable to the very existence of good schools is a proposition that needs no demonstration. It is universally accepted by educators, and is beginning to be apprehended by the community at large. But with all the progress that has been made, school-houses are still deficient in the following respects:

1. THEY ARE UNSIGHTLY IN APPEARANCE. A traveller passing through a section of country can readily distinguish the school-house by these distinctions. It is situ-

Fig. 3.—OLD FASHIONED SCHOOL-HOUSE.

ated in a forlorn and lonely place. It exhibits every mark of neglect and dilapidation. It is entirely exposed to the depredations of stray cattle and unruly boys, by being situated in the street and not protected by a fence. It is unpainted, and nearly half unglazed. Its style is nondescript, being too small for a barn, too deficient in the elements of just proportion for a dwelling, and too much neglected for the out-buildings of a farm—in short, too repulsive in all respects, exhibiting too many marks of parsimony to be anything but a school-house.

It seems to have been erected simply for shelter, and with the smallest cost in the outset; to call it cheapness or economy would be a misnomer. It stands a vile offence against good taste, and an ugly excrescence upon the landscape. It makes no appeal to the higher sentiments, and, consequently, no effort can preserve the building or fixtures from disfigurement and ruin. Every teacher knows the difficulty of protecting the school-house and furniture from the ubiquitous Yankee jack-knife. The result is, that the building, unsightly when new, becomes more so through the rudeness which its very appearance stimulates. The busy fingers of time may soften its outlines and spread over its surface sober tints of brown; but the innate ugliness of the structure defies all efforts to make it other than a monstrosity.

2. THEY ARE POORLY BUILT. The foundations are often so imperfectly laid that they soon tumble, and the build-

Fig. 4.—DILAPIDATED SCHOOL-HOUSE.

ings are racked to pieces or stand askew. The frames and finish are of the cheapest kind, and soon the winds find their way through in every direction. The desks and benches are ingeniously inconvenient and uncomfortable, producing pains and aches innumerable. Most people of the present generation have a vivid and painful recollection of the seats of our old school-houses, without backs, and often too high to permit the feet to touch the floor. The suffering and uneasiness so produced were almost equal to the punishment of exposure at the pillory or confinement in the stocks, bestowed in olden times upon criminals. The whole construction of the building, both external and internal, were such that it merited and received no repair, and soon lapsed into a mass of ruins. Although great improvements have been made within the present generation, the ideas concerning the construction of school-houses are still crude in the extreme, and poor buildings are the rule rather than the exception.

3. THEY ARE NOT OF SUFFICIENT SIZE. The room is so confined that the pupils are forced into uncomfortable and inconvenient proximity to each other. Their work is interrupted and their personal rights are violated. The young, the weak, and the innocent are forced into the immediate atmosphere of coarseness and impurity, without a possibility of counteracting influences. Again, the ceilings are so low that there is an inadequate supply of fresh air, and, as a consequence of all this, physical as well as moral disease is engendered. Proper discipline in such schools is impossible, as the inexorable laws of nature oppose the teacher's work.

4. THEY ARE NOT PROPERLY VENTILATED. The quantity of air, limited at first, shortly becomes impure, and there are no means of changing it. A poisoning process then commences, the virulence of which is in direct ratio to the tightness of the room. A badly built or dilapidated school-house, under these circumstances, becomes a positive blessing, by preventing the exclusion of air from without. Besides the injury to health, the vitiated air of the school-room, by its

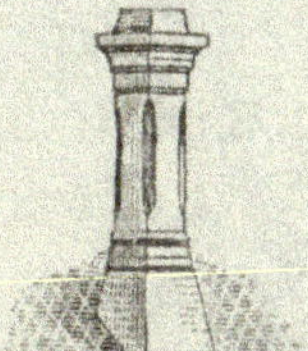

Fig. 5.

stupefying action on the brain, prevents intellectual action, and so defeats the purposes of the school.

5. THEY HAVE INADEQUATE YARDS AND PLAY-GROUNDS. Even in country places, where land is very cheap, the school-house is frequently placed directly on the line of the street, and generally at the corner where several roads meet. Not one inch of ground is set apart for the use of the pupils when out of the school-room. There is no place for recreation or privacy, all being exposed to the public eye. The street is the only play-ground, and filth, within doors and without, is the consequence. With such an arrangement, it is impossible to inculcate those lessons of neatness and refinement which are among the most important objects of education.

6. THEY ARE DESTITUTE OF THE NECESSARY OUT-BUILDINGS. In many cases there is no privy, and in many others there is at best but one for a large school of both sexes. A man in a Christian land, who would erect a house for his home and not provide a privy, would be considered worse than a heathen; yet, in multitudes of our country districts, this indispensable adjunct of civilization is altogether omitted, although in a school both sexes are brought together without the purifying and restraining influence which belongs to the household. Every feeling of refinement and decency is outraged by the exposure here indicated, and, in some measure, the same results ensue from having but one small exposed privy for a large school.

Fig. 6.

From these facts it will seem that there is a necessity for reform in the construction of school buildings. Indeed, it is the united testimony of superintendents, committees of investigation, and boards of school visitors, that in many sections of country the pupils in school are worse provided for in all things pertaining to comfort, convenience, and the cultivation of good manners and morals, than the inmates of our pauper-houses, or the prisoners in our penitentiaries.

An attention to these considerations is of primary importance in any scheme for the advancement and perfection of our school system. The idea is becoming quite prevalent that manners and conduct should receive due attention in a true system of education, and that the claims of these vastly outweigh those of any branch of mere rote instruction, or, indeed, of any science. This idea forms a basis for the criticism of the systems of instruction now in vogue, and is the key-note of the new education which the age demands. A large share of the neglect in these most vital of all departments of education is attributable to the want of attention to the physical comforts of pupils in the construction and furnishing of school-houses.

The remedy for these evils will be shown in the succeeding chapters.

Fig. 7.

CHAPTER II.

EXTERNAL ARRANGEMENTS.

In the construction and arrangements of school-houses, certain fundamental principles must be observed. These principles, in the order of importance, are HEALTH, COMFORT, CONVENIENCE, and COST. It requires no argument to show that when this order is inverted, and *cost* is made the first consideration, the higher interests of the school must be neglected and true progress rendered impossible.

Fig. 8.

The preservation of health should be considered of prime importance. Cost, comfort, and convenience should be subordinated to this. Unless our children can be educated in a way compatible with the preservation of their health, it were better at once to tear down our school-houses and abolish our school system.

The location.—The location of the school-house should be at a distance from all sources of malaria. The foul breath of decaying vegetation, or of stagnant water, becomes a fruitful source of disease and death. Unseen, it insidiously does its work, and spreads the atmosphere of the charnel-house as far as its influence extends. The diseases seeming to be epidemic, which sometimes break out in schools, may often be traced to some neighboring swamp or marsh or heap of decaying vegetables. Some manufactories generate disagreeable gases which, if breathed for any considerable time, are deleterious in the extreme. The school-house should be placed at a distance from all these sources of disease. It should also be situated away from the noise and dust of the street. There is scarcely anything more annoying or unwholesome than the clouds of dust which are driven along the highway. Let the location, if possible, be upon a hill-side, where it may be free from these annoyances, and where the purest air is supplied in unstinted measure. For the *moral* health of the pupils, let the school-house be placed at a distance from the places where scenes of brutality or debauchery are ever exhibited. If no natural obstacle oppose, the centre of the district would seem to be the best location for the school-house; this centre having reference, of course, to population as well as distance. If an acre of land is taken, perhaps it might most conveniently be laid out in a plot sixteen rods front and ten deep. Any other form might be adopted, and, under some circumstances, another might be preferable.

Fig. 9.

Of the situation of the lot, in reference to scenery, etc., more will be said in the chapter upon ornamental grounds.

The lot.—A large and commodious school-lot is of prime necessity. Without it, it is impossible to attain some of the most essential ends of education. A little attention on the part of trustees will secure an ample lot at very little expense. When public attention has been sufficiently turned to the importance of this subject, it will be comparatively easy to secure the donation of a school-lot, or, at least, the purchase of one at a small price. When the wants of the school, and the necessities of education are taken into consideration, one acre of land at least, is required for every school; and when such a lot can be obtained, a school-house should never be erected upon a smaller one.

It sometimes happens that the owners of land near the centre of the district refuse to sell for school purposes at any price. Such narrowness and illiberality is at present, in most of our States, without remedy. But we think, as popular education is now recognized as one of the functions of the State, it would be well to provide for taking the land at an appraisal by disinterested persons, as land for highways, railroads, and other public purposes is now taken. A law allowing the trustees of districts and the town authorities to locate the school-house lot, with or without the consent of the owner of the land, would be a highly salutary one, and would prevent strife, while rendering an important service to the schools.

A law substantially embodying the views given above has been enacted in the State of New York, and we believe in some of the other States, and the results have been beneficial. By this law the schools are placed beyond the caprice or obstinacy of those who may possess the land most desirable for the site of the school-house.

Position of the buildings.—In a lot sixteen rods by ten, the house should stand very nearly in the centre. This would be at a sufficient distance from the street to avoid noise and dust, with room enough in the rear for the necessary out-buildings. It would also divide the yard into two parts, for boys and girls. In any lot, the house should be placed in the middle as to width, and at a distance from the street, so that the out-buildings may be thrown into the back-ground.

Outside structure.—Buildings of small size, and consisting of but a single room, in these designs, admit of but little architectural display, within the limits of sound economy. In deciding upon the size and plan of the buildings, and the arrangement of the doors, windows, and roof, the first care should be to provide for health and comfort. Besides this primary consideration, due attention should be given to the durability of the structure, and to the observance of the laws of architecture in the proportion and arrangements of the building and its several parts.

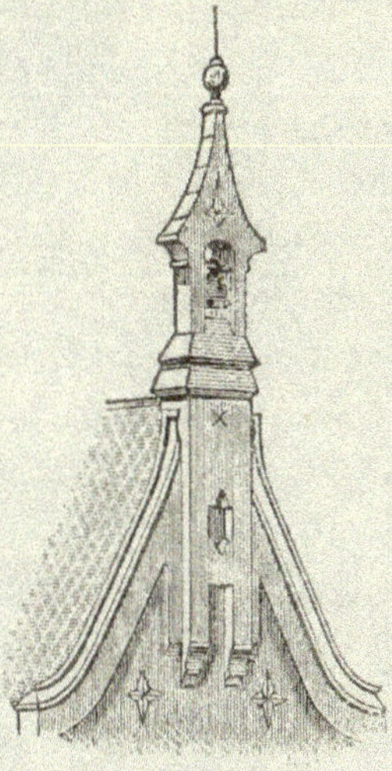

Fig. 10.

In the plans and details of this work an attempt has been made to carry these ideas into practical execution. A sufficient variety of elevations has been given to permit the exercise of different tastes. The parts have been arranged so as to meet the requirements of architectural law, but outside appearance has been subordinated to practical use.

In most cases it will be observed that separate entrances for boys and girls have been provided. This arrangement is regarded as highly important. It prevents improprieties between the sexes, while passing in and out of the school-room. The room in the lobby is also used for a clothes-room, at a manifest saving of expense.

Fig. 11.

In most of the plans proposed, the wood-house is placed directly in the rear, so that a portion of it may serve for a back hall. This arrangement contributes to harmony of external appearance, and prevents the out-door air from flowing directly into the school-room ; thus, serving a double purpose, the wood-house is very desirable. A basement, however, might be prepared for the storage of fuel.

WALKS.—That is a false economy which refuses or neglects to furnish the necessary walks in and about the school premises. Generally but a step removed from the carriage-path in the street, and without walks of any description anywhere in the vicinity, except a single path of the native soil, the wonder is that the school-house is not more rather than less offensive. During some seasons of the year the children must wade through mud and water to reach the school, and not one foot of dry space is provided where they can cleanse themselves until they enter the house itself.

The consequence is that dirt is everywhere, and tidiness is impossible. To remedy this, arrangements should be made to preclude the necessity of getting into the mud within the school-yard, and to enable the pupils to remove it from their shoes when coming in from the street. A plank or gravel path should be laid from the front gate to the front door. The steps at the door should be large and commodious. These steps, and perhaps also a portion of the walk, should be provided with scrapers. Plank walks should also extend from the back entrance to the privies, and perhaps around the sides of the school-house.

Fig. 12.

FENCE.—The school-lot can never be kept in order unless it is inclosed by a good and substantial fence ; this fence should be built of good materials, and put up in a substantial manner. A picket, or a post-and-rail fence, would answer every purpose. The gates should be built strong and heavy, and so arranged as to shut themselves. It might be well to set posts within the gates in such a manner that cattle could not get in, even if the gates should be left open. The fence that divides the yard should be of matched boards, and from eight to ten feet high, faced on the boys' side. The wood-house door should open into the boys' yard. In a succeeding chapter the subject of out-houses will be treated more at large.

Fig. 13.

CHAPTER III.

INTERNAL ARRANGEMENTS.

In the arrangement of the interior of the school-room the same principles should be considered as in the external structure, and in the same order, viz., health, comfort, convenience, and cost. A mistake made may not only in the end be exceedingly costly, but may go far to defeat the ends of education.

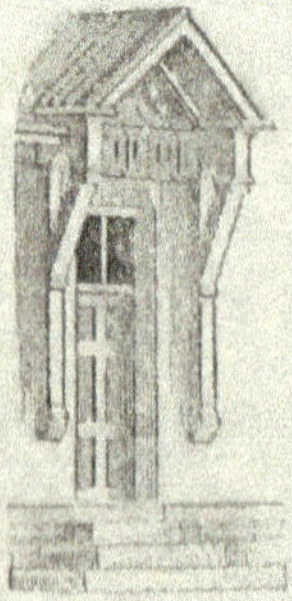

Fig. 11.

Size of the school-room.—This is a consideration of great importance. Every pupil should have sufficient room to sit and move without being confined or jostled. There should be sufficient space in the room for a large reservoir of air. Packing children close together, so that the breath and atmosphere of each is shared by his neighbors, is an unmitigated evil. Every child has a right to his own personality and his own share of uncontaminated air, and whatever deprives him of these becomes an outrage. This is often done, however, by the closeness of contact with others into which he is forced, and by the limited capacity of the apartment in which he is compelled to sit.

A school-room should also be sufficiently large to furnish each pupil with space enough for a desk and chair, and for free and unobstructed movement. There should also be room for the personal accommodation of the teacher, and for purposes of recitation. The height of the smallest school-room should never be less than twelve feet, and this should be increased to sixteen feet in the larger houses. Comfort and convenience in sitting and moving about depend upon the area of the room; the quantity of air, upon the area, and the height combined. In the plans furnished in this work, eighteen feet area, and nearly two hundred and fifty cubic feet of air, have been appropriated to each pupil.

SHAPE OF THE ROOM.—Of all rectangular forms, a square room will give the greatest amount of space, in proportion to the extent of outside walls. Many teachers, however, prefer a room one-fourth or one-fifth longer than its width; and probably no better form can be devised than this, or one between this and square.

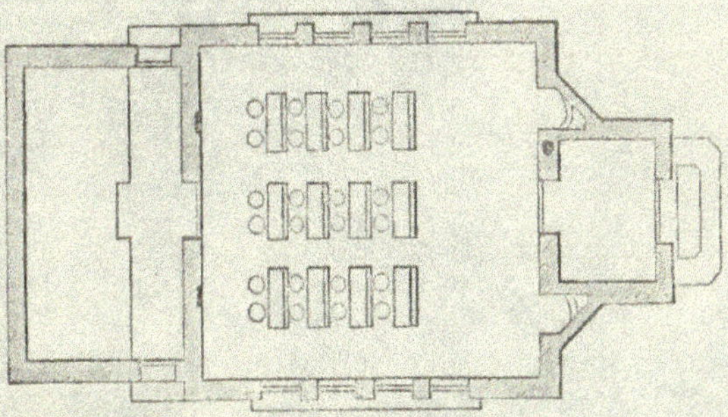

Fig. 15.

When the parallelogram is used, it will be found more convenient to leave the space for the teacher's desk, and recitation benches, upon the end, instead of the side. The octagonal form is thought by some to be peculiarly adapted to school purposes, and specimens have been presented in this work.

SEATS AND DESKS.—For the health and comfort of the pupil, the height of the seats should be so graduated as to enable him to set his feet squarely upon the floor. A contrary custom often produces suffering and a distortion of the lower limbs. Seats without backs are also to be deprecated. To relieve the overstrained muscles unnatural postures are assumed, and a crooked spine is the very probable consequence.

Fig. 16.—CORNELL PRIMARY SETTEE AND BOOK REST.

In a majority of the country schools the only seats used are wooden benches with flat surfaces and straight backs.

Fig. 17.—NEW AMERICAN SCHOOL DESK AND SETTEE.

They are furnished because they are cheap. No thought is given to the constant weariness and discomfort of the pupils who occupy them, nor to the annoyance which the uneasiness engendered occasions to the teacher and school. Yet no principle is more firmly established than that physical comfort is a necessary condition to the highest state of mental and moral improvement. The details of the form, size, and structure of seats and desks is given in the chapter on school furniture.

Many methods for seating school-houses have been proposed, and many experiments have been made to economize room and to secure the greatest convenience. It now seems to be generally conceded that the best arrangement is that of single or double desks, placed in parallel rows, with aisles between of sufficient width to permit passage. By this plan the pupils all face one way, and the teacher can see them all at a glance. When the seats are arranged upon the sides of the room, with the open space in the centre, this is impossible, and discipline is almost out of question. Double desks are more economical than single ones, as they cost less and take up less space in the room.

The desks should always be placed so that the pupils may face the entrance. The reasons for this arrangement are obvious. The entrance and exit of pupils or visitors will be sure to attract attention, and it is impossible to prevent this by any proper system of discipline. If the backs of the pupils are toward the entrance, they will turn about whenever the door opens or closes, presenting an unseemly appearance, as well as seriously

Fig. 18.—NEW AMERICAN SETTEE (FOLDING).

interfering with study and recitation. This habit of turning once formed, will be practiced upon other occasions, to the great annoyance of the teacher and the subversion of discipline. Again, when strangers or others visit the school, or call at the school-room for any purpose, the teacher is obliged to receive them at the rear end of the room, instead of the front, which is awkward and inconvenient. It is as though the entrance to the parlor of a dwelling should be made through the kitchen. With the pupils facing the entrance, when the doors open, a glance is sufficient, without a change of posture or suspension of business, to satisfy the most vagrant curiosity. The teacher can receive his visitors at once, and in the proper place, without parade and without difficulty. Finally, the door or doors leading to the wood-house or back yard should be in the rear of the room, and this can only be when the front of the room is next to the front entrance.

Fig. 19.

SIDE ROOMS.—In every school-house there should be a separate room for depositing hats, cloaks, etc., and in larger houses, another for library and apparatus. For the sake of economy and convenience, in the plans here given, the porch has been so arranged as to serve the double purpose of entry-way and clothes-room. In the smaller houses a single porch will be sufficient; but in the larger ones a double porch should be provided, so that there may be ample room for the uses to which it is to be put, and a complete separation of the sexes. These rooms should be well provided with hooks

Fig. 20.

and shelves. In the smaller houses a case for books and apparatus, answering every purpose, can be constructed upon one side of the school-room, in the place designated in the plans. In houses designed to accommodate more pupils than any one teacher can instruct, an additional room for recitation should be provided. A separate room for the teacher to occupy during recess and intermission, and to retire to when wearied and perplexed with the cares and duties of the day, is also very desirable; but we fear this reasonable luxury will not be realized until public sentiment is made more liberal in educational matters.

VENTILATION.—No school-room should be constructed without ample provision for the admission and circulation of pure air. This is habitually neglected, and, in consequence, the pupils suffer from a constant diminution of their vital energies as well as from positive disease. The cost of an entirely adequate system of ventilation is very inconsiderable, and no persons in the erection of school-houses can afford to neglect this most important arrangement. In the chapter upon ventilation the whole subject is discussed, and directions are given in detail for ventilation under all circumstances.

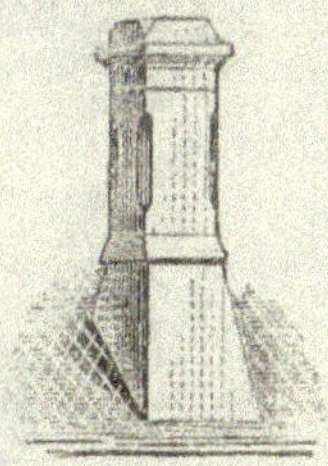

Fig. 21.

SPACES.—Pupils should not be crowded too much together, and so ample spaces are necessary in the school-room. The appearance of the room is greatly improved by wide spaces, and the health of the pupils is promoted by the greater supply of air. Roominess is also a necessary condition of quietude and orderly industry. The space in front of the desks should be sufficiently large for purposes of recitation; not less than ten or twelve feet in the smallest rooms.

A space of two or three feet should be left in the rear of the room for convenience of passage and for classes upon special occasions. The side aisles should be three or four feet wide; those between the rows of desks might vary from one and a half to two and a half feet.

CLEANLINESS.—It scarcely comes within the province of this work to descant upon the importance to health of keeping the person and clothing clean; yet it is a subject intimately connected with that of the wholesome ordering of

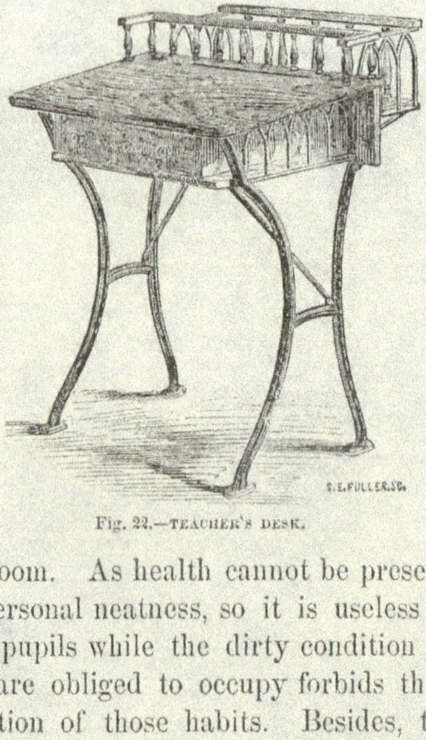

Fig. 22.—TEACHER'S DESK.

the school-room. As health cannot be preserved without habits of personal neatness, so it is useless to inculcate these upon pupils while the dirty condition of the rooms which they are obliged to occupy forbids the acquisition or preservation of those habits. Besides, the fine dust which accumulates in a school-room, and which is thrown into the air by every motion, is breathed into the lungs, and there acts mechanically upon the delicate little air-cells, producing irritation, which may end in inflammation and consumption.

In the construction of the school-room, cleanliness should be kept constantly in view. The floor should be well planed, smoothed, and matched, and carefully nailed. The blackboards should be provided with ample troughs to catch the chalk-dust. The desks and seats should be so constructed as to permit the floor to be easily swept and washed. The teacher's desk should be movable, while the recitation settees and extra seats for visitors should be movable or folding, for the same reason. Special apparatus for preserving cleanliness will be noticed in subsequent chapters.

Fig. 23.—THE NEW AMERICAN FOLDING SETTEE.

MISCELLANEOUS SUGGESTIONS.—The methods of ventilation recommended require the stoves to be placed in the front part of the room, and near the corners. The front, sides, and back of the room should be occupied by blackboards or black-walls. There is little danger of too much blackboard space. If a platform is used it should not be more than six or eight inches in height. In school-houses with a single room, an unbroken level floor is much better than any platform, as it allows a greater freedom of movement, and a greater amount of air in the room.

CHAPTER IV.

LIGHT.

Too little attention is given to admitting light into school-rooms. Windows are placed to be out of the way of the furniture, and at the conventional distance apart; but the thought that the admission of light exerts an important influence upon the health and comfort of pupils seems rarely to occur to the builders of school-houses.

Fig. 21.

In Germany, late scientific investigation has proved that a large proportion of the pupils of the intermediate and advanced schools have defective sight. In this country the same fact has been noticed. While this may be attributed in part to improper postures and the small type of books, much the greater part is the direct result of mismanagement in the admission of light.

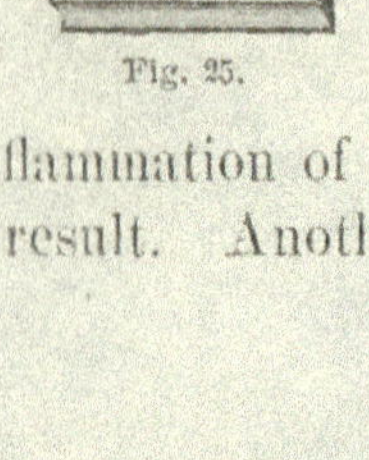

Fig. 25.

Defects of present systems.—In cities it often happens that school-houses are so shut in by other buildings that it is impossible to obtain sufficient light. In country places there is a want of light through negligence. In rooms dimly lighted the eye is unnaturally strained in endeavoring to read or to observe minute objects. Inflammation of the eyes, or near-sightedness, is often the result. Another defect is a glare of light that strikes directly into the eyes. Still another is the arrangement which produces cross-lights. Curtains, shades, and blinds are often omitted, so that there is no way to control the light. Windows are sometimes improperly constructed by being placed too low, so that the light comes in nearly on a level with the pupil; and sometimes they are too small. These defects can all be easily obviated.

Much has been said and written about the superiority of the north light and the skylight, and school-houses have sometimes been built so as to make use of light from these directions exclusively. But the wisdom of this course is seriously called in question. The north light is the most unvarying of all side lights, and the skylight is the strongest of all applications of light to interiors; but both exclude the direct rays of the sun. Sunshine is as necessary to health as air, and besides, it has a direct effect upon the nervous system, allaying irritability, and diffusing a happy spirit through the school, when its summer intensity is properly subdued by blinds or curtains.

Proper arrangement of light.—Windows should never be so placed that pupils will be compelled to sit with their faces to them. It makes an unpleasant glare of light, and sometimes induces "squint eyes." Windows should not be placed on two sides of a room, at right angles with each other, producing "cross-lights." The effect upon the eye is exceedingly unpleasant. When the muscles and lenses of the eye are adjusted for one light, they are out of focus for the other, and the eye becomes wearied and pained in its vain efforts to be in harmony with the two lights.

Fig. 26.

Height of windows.—Windows should always extend upward as far as is consistent with the proportions of the room, so that the light may come partially from above. They should be large enough in the aggregate to afford sufficient light in the darkest days, and then the light may be modified to suit the bright days. Light may with propriety be admitted in the rear of the room, but in case it is, it should be excluded from the sides, so as to avoid cross lights.

Fig. 27.

In the plans contained in this work, the windows are placed in the two opposite sides of the room, with a blank wall in front and rear of the pupils. In several of the series of elevations the windows are grouped together, so that a broad light, unbroken by shadows, fully illuminates the interior of the room. This arrangement is economical, affording the best possible admission of light, and at the same time gives opportunity for fine architectural effects.

BLINDS.—The windows should always be provided with blinds or curtains. Blinds are much to be preferred, and they should be placed inside. Outside blinds afford but little protection to the glass in any case, and none against malicious injury, while they are liable to be broken by the winds. Inside blinds are less liable to injury; they are more easily adjusted, and the light is more easily regulated. Window sills are sometimes placed so high as to be a deformity to the building. This may be intended to prevent pupils from looking out of the windows; but the real effect is to court the very evil which is sought to be avoided. School-boys and girls are bound to surmount all physical obstacles put in the way of their enjoyment of the largest liberty. The

Fig. 28.

Fig. 29.

vagrant gaze and curiosity of pupils can be much more easily restrained when the windows are placed in their proper places.

In the construction of windows, large panes of glass should be used rather than small, as the light is more uniform and unbroken. Select a good quality of glass, free from waves and imperfections.

The window is one of the most noticeable and effective of the architectural features of a building. It has about the same relation to the structure of which it forms a part, that the eye has to the human countenance. It can be made a perpetual deformity, or it can give beauty and expression to the whole building. Due attention should therefore be given to the form, the finish, and the situation of the windows, to the end that their appearance may be a source of continuous pleasure, and a contribution to the educational resources of the school. In the designs given in this work, the importance of windows in producing fine architectural effects has been fully considered, and an effort has been made to give suitable and satisfactory forms, and, at the same time, those that are simple and inexpensive.

Fig. 30.

CHAPTER V.

HEATING AND VENTILATION.

In devising methods for heating and ventilating rooms, three problems are presented, each of which must be satisfactorily solved before any system can be successful. These are economy in the use of fuel, equal distribution of heat through the room, and a plentiful supply of pure and properly tempered air. To solve these problems many costly experiments have been made, and a great variety of ingenious apparatus has been invented. Many of the systems which have been put in use have their good points, though none of them have come fully up to the required conditions; and nearly all of those are too costly for adoption in common schools.

Fig. 31.

Before entering upon a detailed examination of the various methods of heating and ventilation now in use, we will discuss the necessity of ventilation, with the principles upon which it is founded; and the nature of heat, with the laws of its transmission.

Composition of air.—Pure air contains 79 parts nitrogen, 21 parts oxygen, .0005 parts carbonic acid gas, and a variable quantity of water. The proportion of the constituent gases is very nearly uniform all over the world. Oxygen is the life-sustaining principle, while nitrogen seems to be merely a dilutent to render oxygen less active. Carbonic acid gas sustains vegetation, but de-

Fig. 1.

Fig. 2.

Fig. 3.

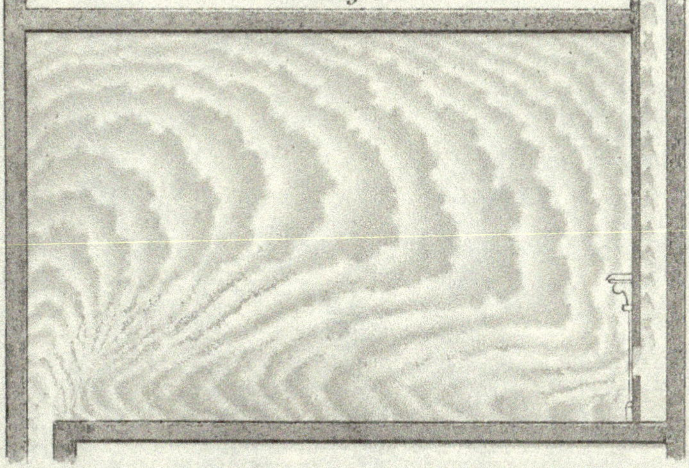

stroys animal life. The small amount found in the atmosphere is not dangerous; but when the proportion is sensibly increased, man and the higher animals are injuriously affected.

Fig. 32.

SOURCES OF CARBONIC ACID.—Carbonic acid gas is chiefly produced by combustion and by the breathing of animals. From these two sources thousands of tons of this deleterious gas are thrown out daily into the atmosphere in each of our great cities. But the currents which are constantly sweeping through this vast atmospheric ocean dissipate the poison as fast as it is generated, rendering it impossible for carbonic acid to accumulate to any considerable extent.*

When air is confined in rooms where combustion and breathing is going on, carbonic acid gas rapidly accumulates, and means must be devised for carrying it off, or the air is soon rendered unfit to sustain animal life.

SOURCE OF OTHER IMPURITIES.—Besides the carbonic acid a large quantity of effete matter is thrown off through the skin by insensible perspiration. The average amount of this decayed animal substance is about twenty ounces per day from each adult. When a number of persons are confined within a room, this becomes a fruitful source of impurity in the air. If not removed this

* In the city of Manchester, England, where more than two millions of tons of coal are consumed annually, and where the smoke hangs like a dark cloud over the city and adjacent country, the air was analyzed twenty-eight different times, and the greatest amount of carbonic acid found was respectively .0015, .0012, and .0010; while the average was about .0007, or but little more than the average of the entire atmosphere.

animal excretion is taken into the system through the lungs, producing disease. It is absorbed into the walls and ceiling of the room, whence it is given back to the air, causing the offensive odors so prevalent in ill ventilated apartments, even when not occupied.

Amount of air necessary.—It is stated upon the highest authority, that in breathing, an adult destroys the vitality of eight cubic feet of air every minute. In a school-room twenty by thirty, and ten feet high, forty pupils would render the six thousand cubic feet of air unfit to breathe in less than half an hour. The only reason why life is not destroyed in many of our school-houses is, that the buildings are so loosely constructed that there is constantly a kind of circulation of air. In a tight room, however, the air frequently becomes so poisonous that the pupils suffer both from a diminution of power and ability to work, and from positive disease.

Ventilation indispensable.—Frequent changes of air cannot be neglected with impunity. It is estimated by those who have given the subject most attention, that more than one-half of the diseases that afflict the human race can be directly traced to the breathing of foul air.

Fig. 33.

Fig. 34.

Proper attention to ventilation will go far to secure good health, while neglect will certainly produce disease to a greater or less extent. In the more modern treatment of disease, pure air is considered one of the most potent of the remedial agents; and the ravages of contagious diseases have been arrested by supplying it in unlimited quantities.*

* "One of the most striking illustrations of this, and perhaps one of the most wonderful cures of the cholera on record, was that of the New York workhouse, on Blackwell's Island. It lasted only nine

Responsibility for neglect.—In the construction of every school-house where ventilation is neglected, somebody is responsible for the vile odors which pervade the room; for the restlessness and nervous irritability of both teachers and pupils; for the headaches, bronchitis, and weak lungs so prevalent; for the sluggish vital action which robs the pupils of half their mental activity; and for the weariness and exhaustion of all the members of the school during the latter half of each day.

Before entering upon the subject of securing the simplest and most economic ventilation, it will be necessary to consider the nature of heat and its effect upon air.

Radiation of heat.—By radiation heat passes outward from a heated body in all directions. The intensity of radiated heat is inversely as the square of the distance traversed. Radiated heat does not raise the temperature of the air through which it passes. This is shown by the

---

days, but in that brief period one hundred and twenty out of eight hundred inmates died. I visited the building with Dr. Hamilton on the third day after its appearance, but the hospital then contained sixty or seventy patients, and some twenty-five or thirty had died within twenty-four hours. Dr. Hamilton attributed the rapid propagation and fatality of the disease, after it once had gained admission, mainly to confinement and crowding. It was observed that the cholera was confined for several days among the women, who had the smallest apartments, and were most crowded in their cells, while the men were mostly employed out of doors.

"The Doctor's prescription was very short and simple. A slight change was made in the diet, disinfectants were used, and at night a slight stimulant was given to each patient. But the great means that the Doctor relied upon for success was pure air all the time. The patients were kept out of doors from morning till night, and all the windows were kept open day and night. Although in the hot weather of summer, fire was made in the wards to insure a more perfect ventilation. In six days after the initiation of these simple hygienic measures the epidemic entirely disappeared." L. W. Leeds.

fact that the upper atmosphere is much colder than the stratum of air in immediate contact with the earth, whereas it would be warmer as we go toward the sun if the air was heated by radiation.

CONDUCTION OF HEAT.—By conduction heat is transmitted from a heated body to substances in immediate contact with it, which in turn transmit it to others, and so on, the intensity constantly diminishing as it passes away from the centre of action. Different bodies have the power of conducting heat in different degrees. Iron and the metals generally are good conductors, and clay, water, wood, and air are poor conductors. A good conductor both receives and gives off heat much more rapidly than a poor conductor. In the construction of the outward walls of buildings, a poor conductor of heat should always be used, to avoid the otherwise inevitable loss of heat.

CAPACITY OF BODIES TO RECEIVE HEAT.—The capacity of bodies to receive heat greatly varies. To raise a cubic foot of water to a given temperature requires seventeen hundred times the amount of heat that it does to raise a cubic foot of air to the same temperature. The capacity of air to receive heat is relatively small, and hence there is little loss of heat from a perfect system of ventilation.

HOW AIR IS HEATED.—Air is heated by being brought into immediate contact with a heated surface. The air of a room is heated in part by contact with the heating apparatus, and in part by contact with the walls, floor, and ceiling of the room. The parts of the room and the furniture are heated by direct radiation from the heating apparatus.

EFFECT OF HEAT UPON AIR.—Air, when heated, expands and becomes lighter. Owing to the derangement of equilibrium, the cooler and heavier air sinks and forces the warmer and lighter air upward. Whenever heat is more developed in one place than another, currents of air are always produced, and heat is distributed by this process, which is technically called CONVECTION.

MOVEMENT OF AIR IN A ROOM.—When confined in a room the cold air sinks to the bottom, and the warm air rises to the top. If the room is perfectly tight, and a small opening is made in either the top or bottom, no change takes place within the room, as there is no force to establish motion. If an opening is made in both the top and the bottom, the cold air flows in below and the warm air escapes above. If two openings are made above, or a single flue is divided into two parts, there will be an ascending current in one and a descending current in the other.

IMPURITIES IN A ROOM.—Carbonic acid gas is heavier than air, and when generated in considerable quantities at the same temperature of the air, it first sinks downward, but in a short time it becomes diffused through the air.

In a room at the temperature of 70° the carbonic acid of the breath at the temperature of about 90° rises, but, speedily giving off its extra heat, sinks again and accumulates at the floor. The carbonic acid generated by the burning of lamps, first rises to the top of the room, but the heat which carries it upward soon dissipates, and it then sinks downward. When air colder than the temperature of the room is admitted, it sinks to the floor, and the vitiated air lies in the stratum immediately above. But the tendency of gases is toward diffusion, and we may safely state that in rooms occupied by a large number of persons, the vitiated air will either be found well distributed through the room, or accumulated at the bottom. With these facts and principles before us, we are prepared to examine the different methods of heating and ventilation, and determine how far each goes to the solution of the problems which we named.

Fire-places.—With the open fire-place a current of air is always setting in toward the fire, making the ventilation very nearly perfect. The heat, however, is transmitted by radiation, and hence is unevenly distributed, and the current of hot air which constantly ascends through the chimney causes a great waste of heat.

Stoves.—By the use of stoves we have a greater economy of fuel, but the heat is still radiated, and consequently unevenly distributed, and there is no ventilation connected with the process of heating, except the very small current escaping through the draft of the stove.

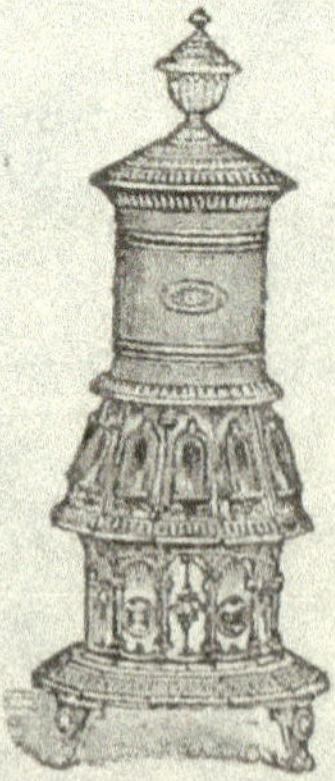

Fig. 35.

When stoves are used ventilation is sought to be accomplished in a great variety of independent methods.

Windows.—When windows are opened at the top for the admission of air, a cold current immediately flows in, which settles to the bottom of the room, where it serves to keep the feet of the pupils uncomfortably cold. On its way it strikes the unprotected necks and shoulders of the pupils who are seated near, causing colds in the head, rheumatic pains, and other forms of disease. The danger of sitting in draughts is abundantly set forth in the most elementary treatises upon hygienic science, and yet, to this day, people are found who contend that ventilation is sufficiently secured by the abominable practice of opening windows from the top.*

Fig. 36.

* Windows may be opened from the top just sufficient to allow the escape of hot air, but not to admit cold air, while pupils are exposed to the draught. While the children are seated care should be taken

OPENING IN THE CEILING.—A second method of independent ventilation is by having an opening in the ceiling. When the opening is merely into a room above, no currents are created and no ventilation is induced. But when the outlet is through a flue directly into the outer air, the hot air at the top of the room is drawn off, and the equally foul air below remains. This method changes the air but little, and causes great waste of heat.

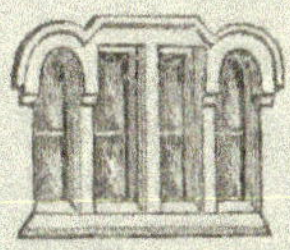

Fig. 37.

DOUBLE OPENINGS IN THE CEILING.—A more modern method of ventilation is to provide two separate flues from the ceiling, or to divide a single ventilating chimney into several parts. It is found that generally, while there is an ascending current through the one, there will be a descending current through another, causing a change of air throughout the room. This will always be the case when the room is perfectly tight, but when a door or window is opened the descending current at once ceases, while the hot air continues to escape. There is the same objection to this method of admitting cold air as to windows opened at the top, exposing pupils to draughts and to cold feet, and at the same time there is a great loss of heat.

These plans for the change of air in a room are all faulty, and so far stoves and good ventilation seem inconsistent with each other.

HOT-AIR FURNACES.—The most philosophic apparatus for heating which has yet been invented is probably the hot-air furnace. By its use the air is properly tempered before being admitted to the room, and cold draughts are rendered impossible. If adjusted so as to secure proper

---

to open the windows opposite the wind only. The windows may be opened at both the top and bottom at recess, and while the pupils are engaged in physical exercise.

distribution and an economic method of ventilation, it comes nearer to solving our three problems than any other.

MISTAKES IN ARRANGEMENT.—In the construction of the hot-air apparatus many amusing mistakes have been made. The cold-air box sometimes has been entirely omitted, and registers for the admission of hot air have been placed in the top of the room, or half-way down, instead of at the bottom, where they belong. The ventilating flues have sometimes been entirely omitted, and have sometimes been placed at the top of the room, when they served the purpose only of carrying off the hot air, and so wasting heat. The ventilating flue, when in its proper position at the bottom of the room, has often been placed so near the hot-air register that a limited circulation only was produced, and the heat was far from being evenly distributed.

THE BEST ARRANGEMENT.—From these mistakes, and a very long series of experiments, a most excellent arrangement has been devised. The hot air is admitted at the bottom of the room, and the ventilating registers are placed at the farthest distance from the hot-air registers also, and at the bottom of the room.

The flues from the ventilating registers are made to connect with the draught of the furnace, and the circulation is thus made complete. Hot-air furnaces, however, are too costly for use in common schools, and it remains for us to devise a system which shall be inexpensive and at the same time shall have all the excellences of the costly apparatus described. The details of the plan are as follows:

CHIMNEYS AND FLUES.—In rooms of considerable size, chimneys should be built in each of the front corners, commencing at the foundation. In smaller rooms a

Fig. 4.

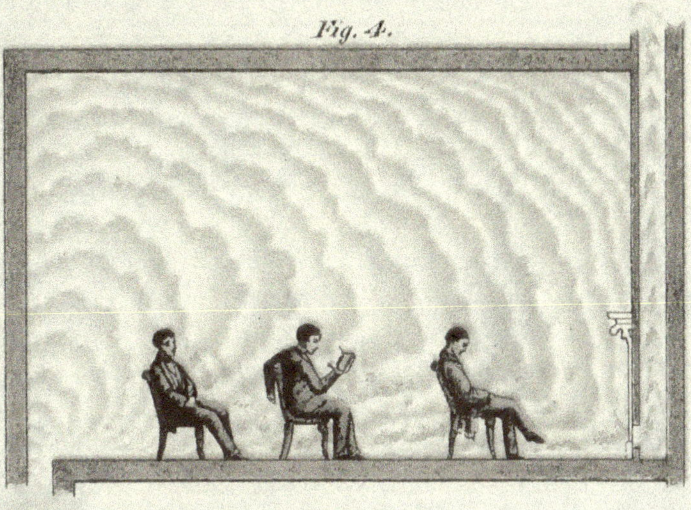

Fig. 5.

Fig. 6.

single chimney is sufficient. They are placed in front to avoid the long stove-pipe which otherwise would be necessary. These long pipes are disagreeable from the radiation of heat downward upon the heads of the pupils, and from their tendency to smoke, drip, and get out of place. Each chimney should have two flues, separated by the thinnest possible partition: one for smoke and the other for ventilation. The results sought by this arrangement can be effectively attained by having a pipe for the smoke carried up through the centre of the flue which is used for ventilation. From the ventilating flue of the chimneys air-tight horizontal tubes should be laid under the floor to the opposite sides of the room, terminating in registers opening through the floor or base-board.

Fig. 38.

STOVES.—The stoves used may be ordinary box stoves for wood, or upright cylinders for coal. When coal is used, the self-feeding stove should be obtained if possible. The stoves should be placed in the corners of the room, where they are most out of the way, and each one should be inclosed by a double case or jacket of sheet-iron, or some other material of like character, for the double purpose of preventing the intense primary radiation, and for providing space for the heating of air. A cold-air tube extending from the side of the building should be laid under the floor, and open directly beneath the stove.*

* A convenient and economic method of admitting cold air would be to place a partition or floor in the smoke flue of the chimney a little below the opening for the stove-pipe; make an opening from the outside into the flue below the partition; and to connect the flue below with the cold-air tube opening beneath the stove. This arrangement will secure a constant supply of air taken so far above

Operation of the stove and chimney.—When a fire is kindled in the stove, the heat escaping from the chimney raises the temperature in the adjacent ventilating flue and establishes a current upward. This causes a draught which acts upon the air of the room through the registers at the extremity of the ventilating tube, pumping the cold air from the bottom of the room.

Fig. 39.

Operation of the hot air.—The fire in the stove heats the stratum of air which surrounds it, and a hot current is produced, which enters the room next the floor, from between the outer and inner coats of the jacket, serving to keep the floor warm in the immediate vicinity, and affording a convenient place for warming feet. The hot air then rises to the top of the room, where it accumulates, and pressing downward upon the cold air, forces it out through the registers, thus directly aiding the draught of the ventilating flues.

Perfections of action.—The pure air, heated and properly tempered, soon has entire possession of the room. The ventilating registers attract it to the farthest part of the room, and the heat is evenly distributed. No warm air can escape from the room while there is any cold air in it, and so, no heat is wasted. The currents through the room are continuous, and the foul air is carried off as fast as generated. The whole system is brought directly under control by having adjustable registers at the opening into the ventilating tubes and in the cold-air tubes, and by proper dampers in the stove.

Moisture.—If the air is found too dry when it is

---

the surface as to be free from the impurities which often emanate from the ground.

admitted into the room, it may be properly tempered with moisture by having a basin of water placed beneath the jacket in such a manner that it can be filled from the outside. Great care should be taken that both the basin and the water are always clean.

CONCLUSION.—It is believed that the system of heating and ventilation here described fully meets the requirements demanded in the outset. The apparatus costs but little more than that in ordinary use. The extra cost of the jacket for the stove, and of the ventilating tubes, but a few dollars at the most, will be more than saved in fuel in a single winter. The use of fuel is more economic than that of the most approved air-tight stoves; for the necessity of opening doors and windows is entirely obviated. The distribution of heat is as perfect as that of the most approved hot-air furnaces, and the ventilation as thorough as with the old-fashioned fire-places. It has all the excellences of these several systems without their defects.

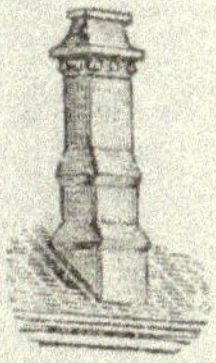

Fig. 40.

Fig. 41

CHAPTER VI.

GENERAL CONSTRUCTION.

THE terms Building and Architecture, though often used synonymously, are in meaning essentially different.

Fig. 42.

Building has reference to utility, while architecture aims to produce beauty. The object of building is accomplished when the ends of usefulness are attained; but architecture is not satisfied until it has created in the mind emotions of pleasure. The construction of walls, roofs, windows, and all the necessary parts of an edifice is the business of a builder; the office of the architect is to dispose and arrange these parts in the most harmonious and attractive manner.

The two most obvious uses in all buildings designed for the occupation of man are shelter and warmth. These conditions are found, by savage or barbarous nations, in natural or artificial caverns, in hollows of trees, and in rude huts of sticks and mud. At the very dawn of civilization the art of building began to receive attention. Rude at first, it gradually improved as the wants of man were developed, until it has reached a state of comparative perfection. In every stage of its progress, however, shelter and warmth have been the principal ends to be attained. We might class with these another scarcely less important, viz., durability. Hence, the strength and stability of walls, the tightness of roof, and outside covering, are matters of prime interest, and if neglected in the outset, no subsequent expenditure of skill or labor can provide a remedy.

MATERIALS.—The materials used should be excellent in quality. It is false economy that consents, under any circumstances, to use inferior materials. There may be, in the beginning, a small saving of cost, but the result will be premature decay, and consequent expense for rebuilding. The greatest care should be taken to procure bricks properly burned, straight-grained timber for frames, sound roof-boards and siding, floor-boards without knots, shingles of the first quality, and fresh-burned lime. These precautions cannot be too strongly urged. A single stick of bad timber will sometimes ruin a whole building; and many a brick wall has fallen in consequence of using lime which has been too long exposed. The money annually expended in repairs occasioned by the use of poor materials is more than triple that increase of the first cost, which would have entirely obviated the difficulty. Every part of the materials should be carefully examined by competent persons, and all, except the very best, should be rejected.

Fig. 43.

WORKMANSHIP.—The work should be well done. Job-work, as it is usually termed (often another name for work miserably performed), cannot be too earnestly deprecated. With the best of materials a careless or unskillful workman will construct a worthless building. Lumber of the best kind may be worse than wasted by a slovenly manner of framing and adjusting it. Shingles poorly laid will be followed by leaks, which must seriously damage the plaster and inside finish. Foundations insecurely built will rack and destroy every other part of the building. Window-frames imperfectly constructed, siding and floors loosely laid, and doors with yawning joints, all allow the entrance of cold and storms, and thus become the source of unnecessary expenditure for fuel, as well as of serious injury to the entire structure. Lath and plaster badly put on last but a short time, and constant patching presents an unsightly appearance, besides being a cause of annoyance and expense. Surely no further specification is needed to satisfy the most reluctant, that the truest economy demands such an expenditure for labor in the outset as shall secure the best possible construction. Faults in workmanship should be carefully provided against. Every part of the work should be subjected to the closest scrutiny.

Fig. 44.

Fig. 45.

But workmen are not alone to blame for improper construction. It is quite as often the result of false economy or parsimony on the part of owners. The estimates of mechanics are often cut down without an intelligent reason, upon the assumption that they are not made in good faith. In consequence, the workmen, who perhaps are forced by circumstances to undertake the job, are obliged to slight their work to save themselves from loss. The injury resulting does not end with the work imperfectly done. It impairs that confidence in man, which is the basis of all true humanity, and leads to a regular system of deception on the part of employer and workmen. Let those having charge of the construction of buildings, therefore, beware of offering a premium for *poor* work by paying less than *good* work is worth. Let them remember that "the laborer is worthy of his hire," and that to extort labor for less than its value is only a safe and legal species of robbery.

Architectural appearance.—The style of architecture in school-houses should receive its share of attention. Some general principles should be fixed as a guide for those intending to build. The old style, or, rather, no style, we put out of the question, as its whole object was to provide the cheapest possible shelter, without reference to true utility, and none whatever to beauty. What shall take its place is a question of present and pressing interest. Many styles have been proposed, but none as yet have been generally adopted. The two which have attracted the most attention, and which have most frequently been described in works upon the apparatus of education, are the Greek and the Gothic. These styles are now frequently found in places where considerable attention has been paid to improvement in schools, and they have been strongly recommended by those who have written upon the subject. Some inquiry into their respective claims may not be out of place here.

Fig. 46.

GREEK ARCHITECTURE.—When we speak of school-houses in the Greek style, we mean those in whose construction some features of the Greek architecture have been displayed. For example, we often see the Greek cornice extending around the building, with the tympanums upon the gables; pilasters, surmounted with capitals in imitation of the Greek columns; the Greek pitch to the roof; and, in many cases, the Greek portico. All these forms are beautiful in themselves, and, in their original combinations, unrivalled in architecture. But their adaptation to the purposes and uses of a school edifice may well be questioned.

Fig. 47.

The Greek architecture was developed chiefly in the construction of temples for religious worship, which were not designed so much for use as to please the eye. Only the outer and inner colonnade were covered; the god to whom the temple was dedicated was supposed not to need a roof, and hence none was provided. All the marvellous skill and energy of this remarkable people were employed in developing this style of architecture, and the result was very nearly perfection. The impression which such a building makes upon the mind is that of sublimity. But an indispensable element in this sublimity is magnitude. A diminutive structure can never call up the emotion of the sublime; and hence, when the Greek forms are used in the construction of small buildings, the old maxim is illustrated, that "there is but one step from the sublime to the ridiculous."

Not only were Greek temples roofless, but they were usually windowless; and when we reduce them to modern, every-day uses, we are obliged to depart from the model in these two important particulars. Originally, genius, labor, and treasure were all expended upon the colonnade; but little attention was given to the interior, and therefore it has been found impossible to adapt forms so developed to buildings in which the interior is the most important part. When the Greek temple is copied entire, it is found that the immense colonnade occupies a large share of the most valuable space, and hence the form is the very worst that can be devised for use. If only certain features are engrafted upon other forms, the results are defective and incongruous.

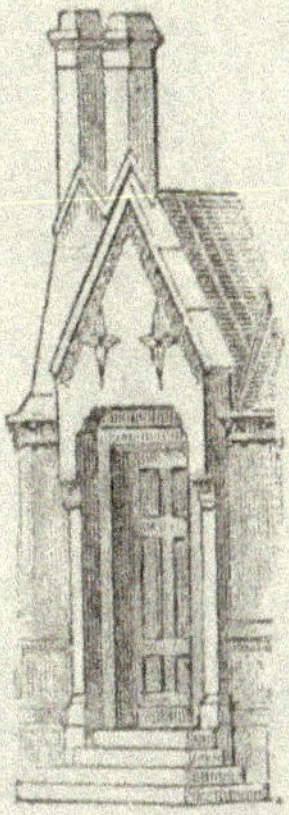

Fig. 48.

Another consequence is a great expenditure of labor and material, without any adequate return, either in convenience or beauty. For example, if the Greek cornice and tympanum are used with the ordinary pitch of roof, the laws of proportion are palpably violated; but if the original pitch is preserved, and shingles are used, the roof is too flat and soon decays. The horizontal cornice across the gable, which forms the base of the tympanum, is entirely useless, as are the capitals upon the pilasters. When any of these ornaments are used in the construction of ordinary school-houses, they always wear a pretentious appearance. We are inclined to adopt, as an incontrovertible principle, that Greek forms should never be used except in large and costly buildings. Their introduction into school-house architecture was unfortunate, and we trust the time is not far distant when they will fall into disuse.

Gothic architecture.—The full development of the Gothic architecture is found only in temples, where magnitude is an indispensable element. In the construction of these buildings the interior was considered of the most importance, and everything was subordinated to the perfection of its finish. The steep roof was thrown up to give opportunity for the high pointed arches inside, which, in the dim, shadowy light, excited emotions of solemnity and awe. When we interpose ceilings in Gothic structures we depart from the original idea, and the high meaning of the style is lost.

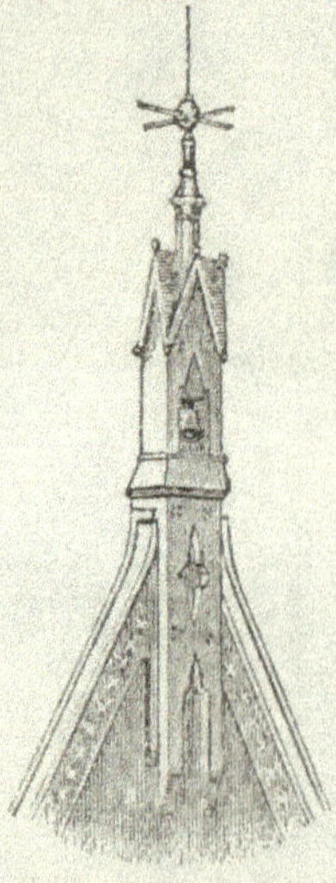
Fig. 49.

In modern times a great variety of small Gothic buildings have been constructed, peculiarly beautiful to the eye; but when the style has been Gothic throughout, the beautiful effect has been produced at the expense of economy and convenience. In the details of building, however, Gothic forms can be often used to advantage in combination with other architectural arrangements.

Modern architecture.—The best buildings constructed for modern use have usually a composite style. Beautiful forms are adapted from any of the classic styles, and all the combinations are arranged to meet the requirements of convenience. The architect can no longer follow the lead of sentiment and fancy, and create structures which excite astonishment and wonder, but he is bound by the laws of utility, and his work of fancy must be always subordinated to the useful.

Fig. 50.

The designs in this book have been constructed with this idea of utility constantly in mind. The comfort and convenience of the pupils have first been secured, and even the claims of so-called economy have been subordinated to these.

The next leading idea has been to secure the finest appearance at the least cost. With each of the plans a progressive series of designs have been given, commencing with the plainest and cheapest, and successively becoming more elaborate and costly.

No features have been added for the purpose of mere ornamentation, but beautiful appearance has been secured by the shaping and harmonious disposition of the necessary parts. The shape, size, and position of doors, windows, chimneys, gables, and cupolas have all been made to conduce to this end, and when one of the designs shall be selected, it should be carried out in the details, or otherwise the builders may be greatly disappointed. In the descriptions it will be noticed that certain features of different designs are interchangeable, but great care should be exercised in making changes, so that general effect shall not be incongruous.

Fig. 51.

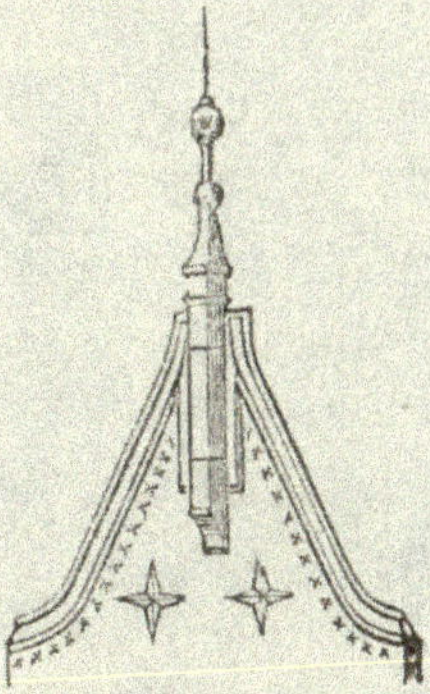

Fig. 52.

CHAPTER VII.

DESIGNS AND ELEVATIONS.

The plans and elevations in this work have been made with special reference to the present wants of district schools in the country and of primary schools in cities and villages. In size they are designed to accommodate all grades of schools consisting of from twenty-five to three hundred pupils. With each plan several elevations have been given, to allow selection in regard to taste and to conform to different ideas of economy.

Fig. 53.

In each series the cheaper elevations are as plain and economical in structure as is compatible with the health, comfort, and convenience of the pupils. Poorer and cheaper structures may be built, but they can never fully answer the purposes for which they are designed, and the efficiency of the school must suffer in consequence. In the long run it will be found that parsimony is not economy.

From the cheapest possible form the series rise in regular gradation to the more complex and ornamental. Beautiful forms in themselves are educational influences, and the rudeness of pupils may, in a great measure, be modified and subdued by a due attention to beauty in the school-house and furniture. Wherever the circumstances of the district will warrant the outlay, some of the more elaborate elevations should be chosen, and it will be found that the highest interests of the school will be served in the direct ratio to the expense incurred.

In all the designs sufficient size has been given to the rooms to afford an adequate supply of air, and to allow sufficient freedom of movement on the part of pupils. The shape of the rooms has been made to conform to the principles laid down in the chapter upon Internal Arrangement. The lighting and heating is according to the most advanced scientific knowledge upon these subjects.

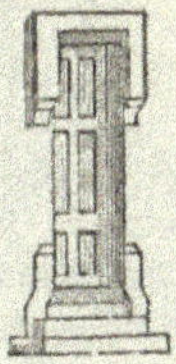

Fig. 54.

In regard to materials of construction, styles adapted to wood, brick, and stone, have been given. Most of the elevations may be constructed with either of these materials. Brick or stone is to be preferred to wood on many accounts. Houses of these materials, properly constructed, are warmer in winter, cooler in summer, and more durable than those built of wood.

Fig. 55.

DESIGN I.

In many parts of New England, and several other of the northern States, a popular form of a school-house is that of a building with a side to the street, with a smaller building used for a wood-house, extending along in a line with the main building directly upon the street. Usually, the entrance is through an open doorway into the wood-house, and thence directly into the school-room.

Fig. 56.

The advantages of the plan are cheapness of structure and convenience of access to the fuel. In regions where the storms of winter are severe and the snows are deep, the situation of the building directly upon the road-side, with but a single entrance to both the wood-house and the school-room, favors economy in the removing of snow and in the construction of paths. The wood-house also affords protection to the entrance of the school-room, and may be considered as an excuse for an entry-way.

But this arrangement is faulty in several particulars. The long, continuous roofs, or one gable falling beneath another, gives to it an unsightly appearance, and there is no visible outside door to the main building. There is but one entrance for the two sexes, and no lobby for depositing hats and outer garments. In the elevations given, an effort has been made to preserve the main features of this plan, but to so modify it in details as to correct some of the most obvious faults. At best, however, this can only

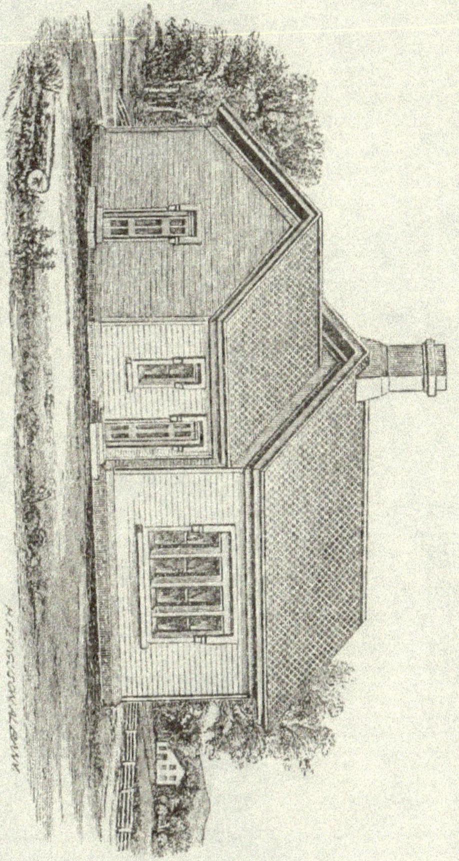

DESIGN 1.

ELEVATION 1.

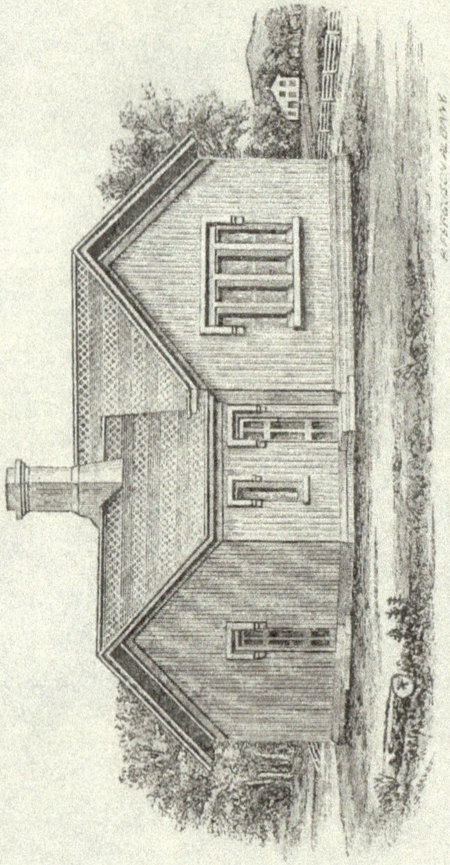

DESIGN 1. ELEVATION 2.

be done partially, as some of the most serious faults are essential parts of the plan.

In the plan given, Fig. 57, the wood-house is entirely inclosed, and a front door is constructed for a main entrance into the school-room, and a side door for the admission of wood. A partition has been made to extend

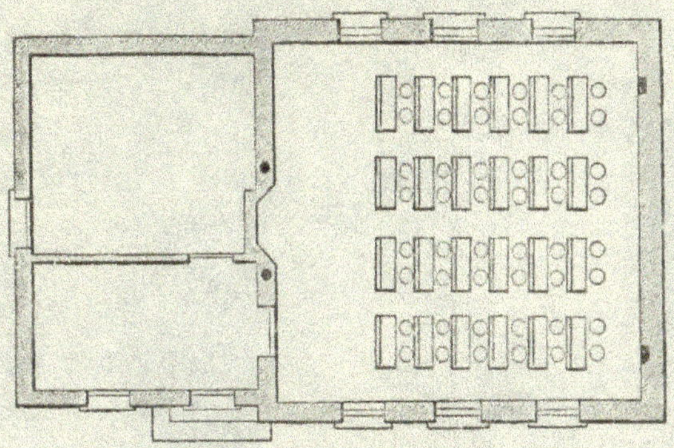

Fig. 57.

through the wood-house, cutting off the front part for an entry-way and a lobby for hats and cloaks. In the school-room a space has been left for a fire-place; but in case a stove is used it should be placed in the front corner farthest from the door. The wall in front, then, may be used as a blackboard.

The size of this building is immaterial, as the same general plan may be made to accommodate from twenty to one hundred pupils. For all but very small districts, the houses having two entrances are much to be preferred.

Elevation No. 1.—This is a very plain elevation of a wood structure furnished with clap-boards. The arrangement of the wood-house, narrower and lower than the main building, and the construction of the doors, give to the building an idea of proportion, and make it a great improvement upon the open wood-house style.

The windows in the main building are grouped together for the triple purpose of economy in construction, finer architectural appearance, and a better disposition of light. The separate windows, however, can be used if preferred. The large ornamental chimney is a feature which gives character to the whole structure, and which ought not to be omitted. Its large size is for the purpose of affording room for both smoke and ventilating flues.

ELEVATION No. 2.—The principal difference between this and No. 1 is that the roof of the main building is turned in the opposite direction, and is at right angles with the roof of the wood-house instead of parallel with it. Architecturally, this is a better arrangement, as one gable ought not to come directly beneath another. In the picture this building is finished with battens; but clapboards may be used if preferred. In case battens are used, the boards should all be narrow, not exceeding eight inches in width, and the battens only wide enough to cover the joint, and they should always be nailed through the middle.

ELEVATION No. 3.—In essential features it is like No. 2. The roof is of the same general description, but less steep. The cornices of the two buildings are upon the same level, and an ornamental cornice extends across the gables. The windows are represented as separate, but they may be grouped as in 1 and 2. The finish of this design is in brick, though either brick or wood may be used for either of the elevations. This design is specially adapted to a level country, where it is in harmony with the scenery.

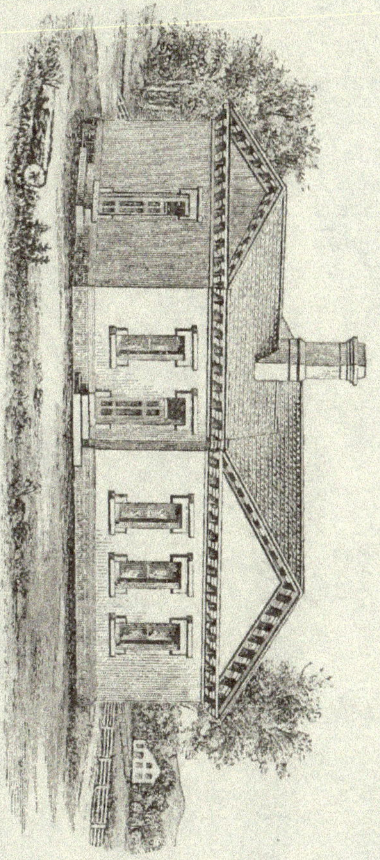

DESIGN I. ELEVATION 3.

DESIGN 2. — ELEVATION 1.

DESIGN II.

A small school may be well accommodated by a plan like that represented in Fig. 59. It consists of a school-room with a single porch in front, and a wood-house in the rear. The room represented contains seats for twenty-four pupils, but by increasing the length three feet there will be room for one more row of seats, and for thirty pupils, and by increasing its width four feet, it will contain still another row of desks, and seats for forty pupils.

Fig. 58.

The porch is a single room, but of sufficient size for a lobby for clothes. The stove is to be placed in one of the nitches in front, while the other nitch may be used for a closet. The ventilators in this, as in all the designs, are placed in the rear of the room, but each one is connected with the chimney by a tube under the floor.

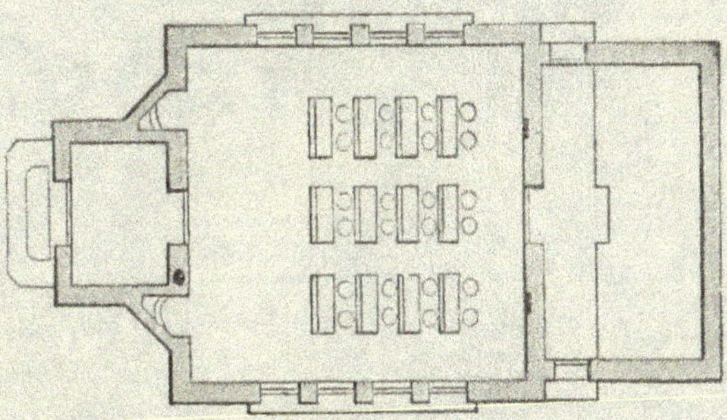

Fig. 59.

The wood-house in the rear serves the double purpose of back hall or entry-way and a place of storage for fuel.

The doors upon the sides should open respectively into the boys' and girls' play-grounds. The front part of the wood-house should be provided with a platform upon a level with the school-house floor, at least four feet wide.

This general plan is superior to Design I., by having back as well as front entrances, so that access may be had to the play-grounds and out-buildings without disturbance to classes, or to the general order of the school-room. The movements of pupils are not so conspicuous as they would be if, in their entrance and exit, they were always obliged to pass through the front door.

ELEVATION No. I.—This elevation is a simple and inexpensive building, with wide projecting eaves that give to it an appearance of comfort and solidity. The porch is finished with a tent-roof, to obviate the necessity of a gable under a gable. It is lighted by a small window upon the side, as the height of the roof would hardly admit of a head-window over the door. The windows are grouped together, and the whole design produces a very pleasing effect.

If a larger house is built upon this plan, the outside appearance may remain the same by simply increasing all the parts in proportion. If three feet be added to the length no other change need be made, but if the addition is made to the width the porch should be enlarged in proportion.

ELEVATION No. 2.—In this elevation the roof of the main building is placed at right angles with the roof of the porch and wood-house, giving a fine architectural effect to the group. The cornices of the three parts are upon the same level, and an ornamental cornice extends across the gable. This feature may be omitted, and the roofs may be arranged in the same manner as those in Elevation No. 2 of Design I. In case the gable cornice is

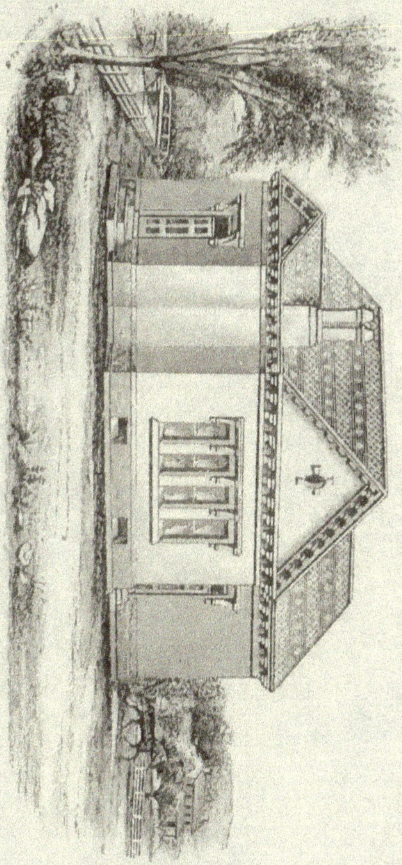

DESIGN 2. ELEVATION 2.

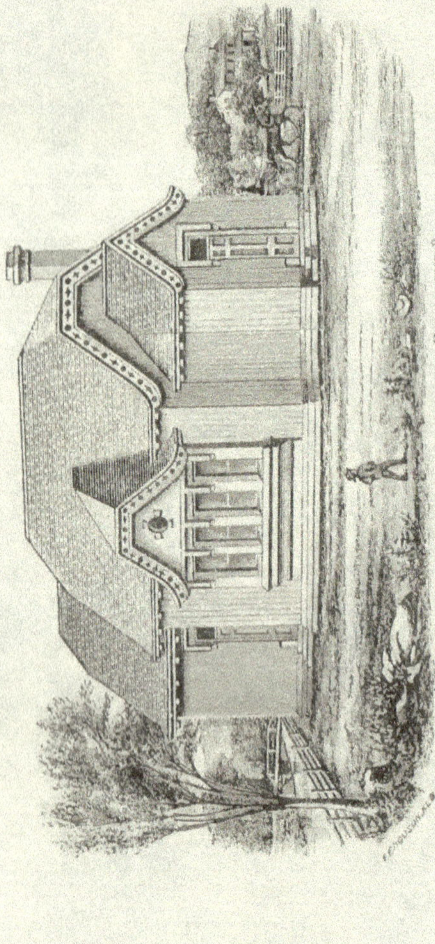

DESIGN 2. . . ELEVATION 3.

omitted the cornices of the porch and wood-house should drop below that of the main building. The porch is lighted by a head-light above the door. The materials of this building may be either brick or wood.

Elevation No. 3.—This elevation is more ornamental. The corners of the gable are cut off, and a small gable is erected over each of the large windows in the sides. The porch is finished with a common gable. The ornamental filigree work of the gables may be omitted, and the cornice made wide and plain, like that of Elevation No. 1. The only extra cost of this elevation is raising the gables over the windows, and in cutting down the corners of the roof, the whole of which ought not to exceed a few dollars. This elevation is represented as finished with battens, but clap-boards may be used, or the house may be built of brick. The superior appearance of this design will more than warrant the additional expense.

Elevation No. 4.—In villages and country places near cities, where the dwellings are of fine architectural appearance, the school-house should be in harmony with the surroundings, and there is a demand for ornamental designs. Elevation No. 4 has been prepared to meet this demand when a small school-house is wanted. The general features are Gothic, but the whole is chaste and neat and not excessively expensive. The steep gables all terminate in minarets or pinnacles. An ornamental bell-tower surmounts the front. The porch has an ornamental tent-roof, sloping down from the front gable. Gables are erected above the side windows, and a beautiful ornamental chimney extends upward from one side of the porch. The material may be brick or stone, the finish of the gables being a stone coping instead of a cornice. This coping may be made of wood with a covering of tin. This elevation might also be used as a session-room for a church, and for a variety of other public purposes. The roof should be covered with slate.

In some parts of the country the small number of pupils in the district is given as an excuse for a miserable school-house. The fact of a limited number of pupils may be a sufficient reason for the construction of a small school-house, but not for a poor one. The educational wants of a small district and of a small number of children are just as pressing as though the territory and the number were indefinitely increased, and a neglect to supply them is just as detrimental in the one case as in the other. If this excuse were a good one the State would be justified in withholding the public funds on the same ground.

But, again, it is argued that the smaller districts are often too poor to erect a respectable appearing and comfortable school-house. It may be that many of the districts are very poor, and in that case they are far too poor to subject their children to exposures and consequent disease, and so a good school-house becomes indispensable. Each district that partakes of the public money of the State is morally bound to provide all the appliances necessary for the proper expenditure of the money so obtained; and the poorer the district the greater is the necessity for all possible means for moral and physical advancement.

DESIGN 2. . . . ELEVATION 4.

DESIGN 3

ELEVATION 1.

DESIGN III.

Country schools generally need accommodations for from forty to eighty pupils. In the plan given for Design III., sixty seats are provided. The room is thirty-four by thirty-eight feet, and by slight changes in size it may be contracted or expanded. By adding three feet to the length space is given for ten additional seats, and by making the building four feet narrower there would still be sufficient room for four rows of desks, accommodating forty-eight pupils.

Fig. 60.

In this design two entrances are provided in front, each of which opens into a room which is at once an entry-way and a lobby for clothes. The space between the two entry-ways can be used for recitations, and a room may be finished in the basement, or added to the rear, for the storing of fuel.

This design is well adapted to districts in which the attendance is large during one portion of the year and small at other times. The recitation-room gives an opportunity for the employment of an extra teacher when the school is crowded. The front and back walls of the school-room, between the two doors, should be occupied by a blackboard. The stoves are placed in the front corners of the room and the ventilators in the opposite corners, in accordance with the principles laid down in the chapter upon heat and ventilation. This room is supplied with two back entrances opening respectively into the boys' and girls' play-grounds.

ELEVATION No. 1.—This elevation represents a plain but neat and substantial building of wood. The roof has

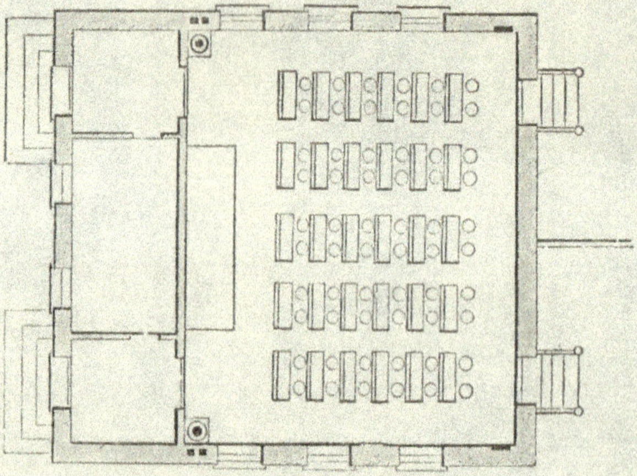

Fig. 61.

the plain, wide, projecting cornice and eaves which protect the walls of the building, and at the same time give it an appearance of comfort and solidity. The finish may be of battens, as in the engraving, or it may be of clap-boards, or substantially the same building may be made of brick. This elevation is represented as standing on a hill-side which slopes downward and backward from the house. In situations of this kind the back entrance may be omitted, and the basement may be fitted up for a wood-room. The nearly square form of this elevation, the perfectly plain finish, the arrangement of everything beneath a single roof, and the entire lack of ornamentation, render this one of the cheapest buildings which can be erected. If anything cheaper is attempted it will be by the use of poor materials, by scrimping just proportions, or by diminishing the size, so as to deprive pupils of

Design 8. - - Elevation 2.

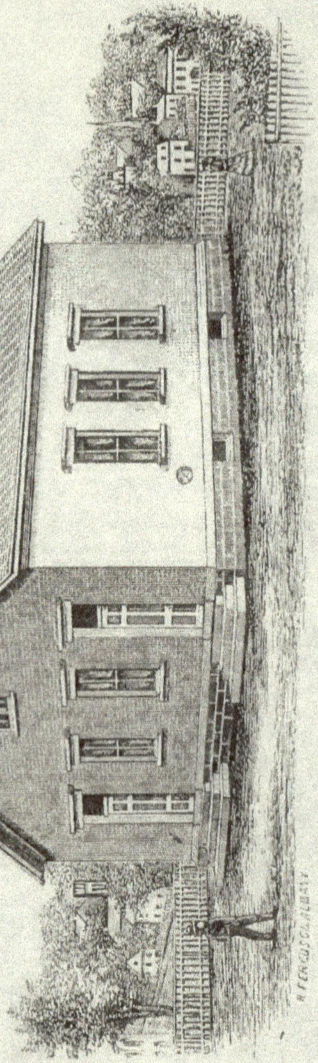

DESIGN 3. ELEVATION 3.

their due proportion of pure air, and of their freedom of movement. In either case the interests of the school will suffer, and present saving will be effected at a fearful future cost to the children.

ELEVATION No. 2.—This is another very plain and cheap structure of wood, finished with clap-boards. The bell-tower gives dignity to the building, but it may be omitted. The roof is the ordinary pitch and may be covered with slate or shingles.

In finishing wood structures in this manner, the clap-boards should be laid with but little exposure to the weather. This arrangement gives tighter joints, and makes the building much warmer. In some sections buildings designed for habitation are covered with a coating of tarred paper before the siding is laid, and this renders them almost air-tight. This covering is recommended for school-houses built in our northern climate, and in exposed locations. By its use the school-room will be made more comfortable, and a large saving in fuel will be made.

ELEVATION No. 3.—This building, in form, is but a slight variation from No. 2. The corners of the gables have been cut off and the form of the cupola changed; but otherwise it is substantially the same. The finish in the engraving is made to represent brick, but wood or stone may be used.

In the erection of brick walls care must be taken to have the walls hollow, or formed so that a space of air may be confined within them, otherwise the walls will be damp and the room unhealthy. The precaution should also be taken to have the foundation laid in hydraulic cement as high as the water-table to prevent the moisture of the ground from permeating the entire walls of the building. The effect of the moisture is not only deleterious to health, but, combined with the action of frost, it has a tendency to crack and destroy the walls of the building.

ELEVATION No. 4.—This elevation has been varied by the introduction of the arched windows and corner buttresses. These features give to the building a strong and substantial appearance. The cupola is a square structure supported by a projecting framework beneath, and in keeping with the general architecture of the house. The material represented in the picture is stone, though brick may be used.

The pointed arches in windows are always elegant, and may be much more commonly used in buildings to the manifest improvement of architecture. The window heads and sills should be of cut stone, but a fine effect may be produced by making the arches of brick and stone, or brick of two colors laid alternately. The string-course at the base of the window-caps may be omitted entirely, and the windows finished in the ordinary manner. The buttresses should always terminate in pinnacles, or otherwise the structure would appear bald and unfinished. In case brick is used in the erection of this building, a fine impression may be made by using common brick for the principal walls and pressed or Milwaukee brick for the buttresses and ornaments.

ELEVATION No. 5.—This elevation represents a stone building of quaint design, of fine appearance, and of cheap construction. The walls are made high and the roof steep. The front portion, containing the porches and recitation-room, has a lower wall and a roof which comes directly under the cornice of the main building and abuts against the gable. The angles of the main roof are cut off, and a plain stone cupola or bell-tower rises in front. The window-heads are circular arches, and may be constructed with cut stone or of the ordinary building stone

DESIGN 3. - ELEVATION 4.

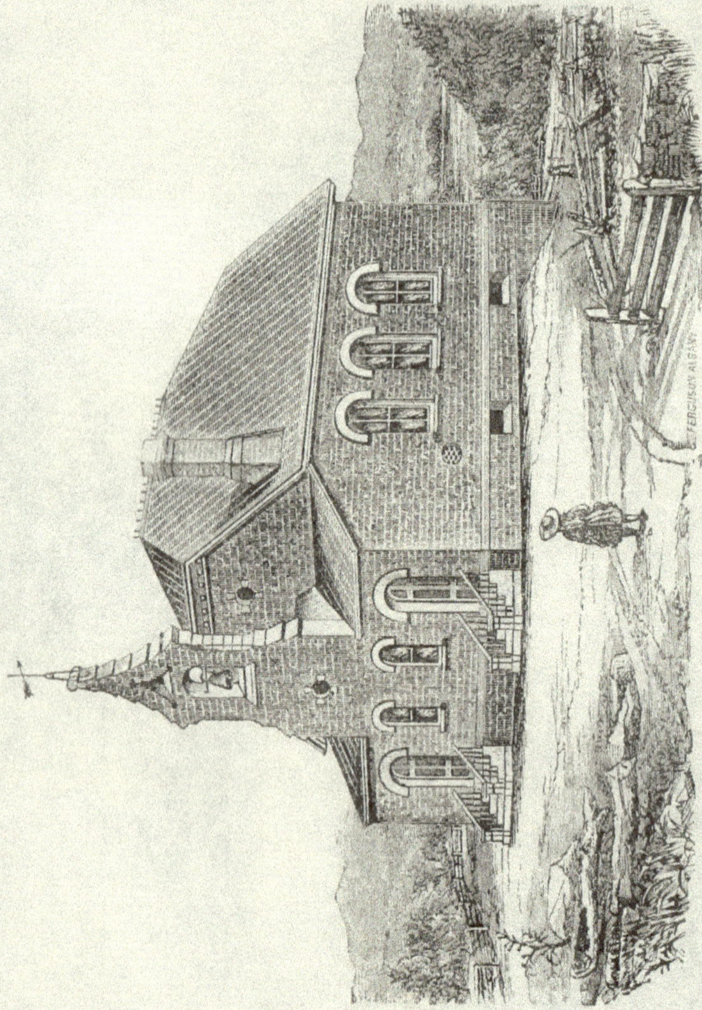

DESIGN 2. ELEVATION 5.

roughly fitted to its place. Courses of brick might be made to inclose the windows so as to produce a more picturesque effect.

In this design the fine appearance is entirely owing to the disposition of the several parts, each of which is necessary to the full effect. To give room for sufficient height in the porches, the main walls of the building must be carried up rather higher than usual; but the extra height of the school-room will be all the better for the pupils, as it affords them a greater amount of air. The bell-tower, though a simple wall of stone, with an opening for a bell, has a fine outline and is a necessary part of the building. Such a structure would be considered ornamental in any part of the country.

Wherever stone can be easily and cheaply obtained a building of this description may be put up at a moderate expense.

In constructing a stone building, extra care must be taken that the foundations are securely laid below the action of frost. The walls should be hollow or furred.

Elevations 4 and 5 would be appropriate designs for small churches, and be much more expressive in their architecture, while no more costly than many of the country churches now erected.

DESIGN IV.

The plan of this design represents another of the medium-sized school-houses. It is rectangular in form, and the school-room has seats for sixty pupils. By changes like that described in Design III., it may be made to accommodate more or less, according to the requirements. In the rear of the main building is a smaller structure, which may be used as a wood-room, recitation-room, or both. In it are the back entry-ways.

Fig. 62.

The windows are put into one group on each side, for reasons given in the description of Design II. The door in the front partition of the school-room may be omitted, and the entrance to the front recitation-room made through the front halls. The stoves and ventilating flues are arranged as in Design III. The recitation-room may be made wider by a slight increase in the length of the building.

We would call special attention to this design and the several elevations accompanying it. It perhaps combines more than any other the essential requisites of country school-houses. It is cheap. No room is lost, and no expense is wasted upon superfluous features. It is simple in construction, so that any carpenter can build it who has wit enough to put building materials together. It is exceedingly neat in appearance, as will be seen by referring to any of the elevations given; and this beauty will appear greatly enhanced when these elevations are

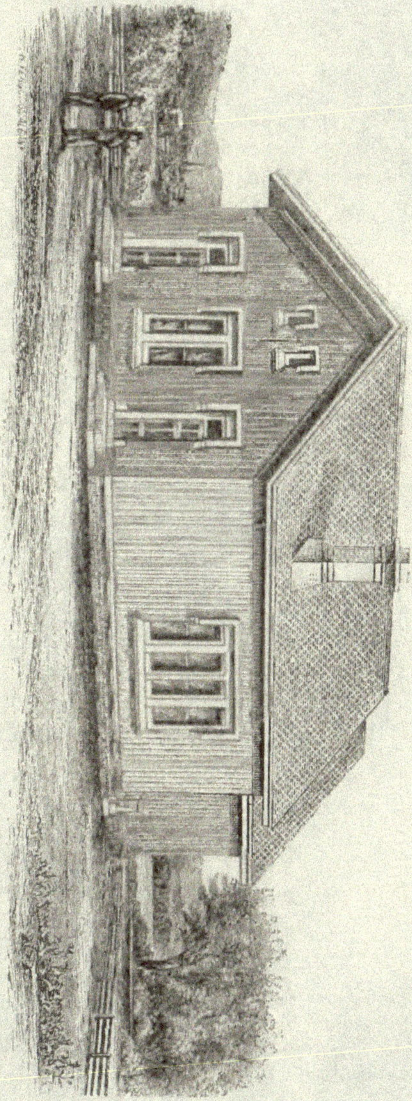

DESIGN 4. - - ELEVATION 1.

DESIGN 4. ELEVATION 2.

compared to the houses now ordinarily found in country places.

It affords ample accommodation for the school and freedom of movement for both teacher and pupil. It admits light in the most effective manner possible, and if properly furnished with adjustable inside blinds, the light can be properly tempered and distributed. Ample arrangements are made for a perfect system of ventilation, and an unlimited supply of fresh air in the disposition of

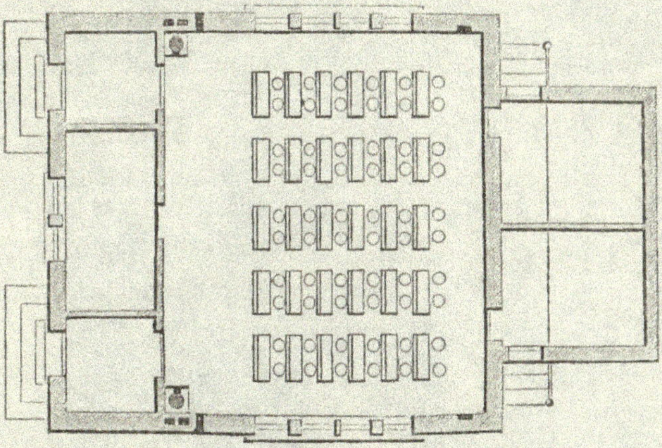

Fig. 63.

the stoves, chimneys, and ventilating tubes. If intelligent care is bestowed upon them, pupils need never suffer from the effects of foul air. Provision has also been made for ample summer ventilation in the large openings on the four sides of the house.

Again, by having an extra recitation-room the plan is an adjustable one, admitting of the employment of an extra teacher during the season when the school is most crowded. If either of the elevations of this design is adopted, and the building erected as described, it will last for several generations, and will afford ample and excellent accommodation for all.

One of the rooms in the rear or the recitation-room in front may be used for the district library, or it may be fitted up as a cabinet for the reception and preservation of such specimens of natural history as are beginning to be considered indispensable to the highest success of any school.

In making choice between the different elevations given, unless cheapness is considered the chief requisite, preference should be given to one of the more elaborate structures; and wherever a choice can be made in building materials, brick or stone should be used in preference to wood. A good stone house of this description, well furnished, would leave scarcely anything more to be desired in the form of school accommodation.

ELEVATION No. 1.—This is the plainest possible elevation of the plan of Design IV. It is a wood building, having a plain roof with the ordinary pitch, and wide projecting cornice. The finish may be battens or common siding; the former, however, is to be preferred on the score of appearance. The chimney is high and substantial, and in buildings of this kind, the chimney, being the only projection from the roof, should be built with care. The windows, which are grouped together in the elevation, may be arranged in the usual manner, in which case a side window would open into the porch, and the head-light above the door might be omitted.

ELEVATION No. 2.—This elevation, represented as finished in brick, may be built of wood. It is a modification of Elevation No. 1, with a change in the shape of the window-heads, the addition of a cupola, and the introduction of small mullion windows to light the porches. The finish is plain, and the general effect is good. The cupola may be omitted if desired, in which case the chimneys should be made broader.

ELEVATION No. 3.—This elevation is similar to the last,

Design 4. - - Elevation 3.

DESIGN 4. . . . ELEVATION 4.

the changes being mainly in detail. The window-heads are square instead of circular, and narrow ornamental hoods are placed above the windows and doors. The windows of No. 2 may be used, if preferred. The main feature of difference is the cupola, which in this design apparently grows out of the structure beneath, and hence is an integral part of it; while in No. 2 the cupola seems to be put on in such a way that it is not an essential part. The materials of the building should be brick, and it would appear much better to have the roof and base of the cupola covered with slate.

ELEVATION No. 4.—This is an ornamental design for village and suburban places. The cupola is light and elegant, and a gable is thrown up over the windows to give a greater architectural effect. The chimney is projected outside of the main wall, to break the monotony of the blank wall between the windows and the front corner of the building. The materials may be brick or stone. By the introduction of the gable over the windows, the walls are made lower, and the roof comes much nearer the ground than in the other designs. Instead of a cornice, the gables are finished with a coping of stone or of wood covered with tin.

This elevation would make an elegant design for a country church. Its fine architectural appearance is owing entirely to the general style of finish, the proportions observed, and the disposition of its several parts. No one feature has been added for mere ornament, though each of the necessary parts has been made ornamental. The roof should be of slate.

ELEVATION No. 5.—This elevation represents another ornamental brick or stone building, with a slate roof. The cupola, like that of No. 3, is made to grow out of the structure. The windows and doors have pointed Gothic arches, and over each of the side windows a gable has been erected. The whole grouping produces a very pleasant effect, and the design would make a most excellent school-house or a snug little church.

In erecting structures of this kind, great care must be taken to make the foundation secure. The underpinning should be laid upon concrete, and placed below the action of frost. The stone should be laid in hydraulic cement, and every care taken that the whole foundation should be of sufficient strength to support the weight which must rest upon it.

Objection is sometimes made to the erection of school-houses with cupolas and fine windows and doors, because they look so much like churches. This objection, however, is far from being a logical one. The school and the church are both engaged in the same work, and they are complementary rather than antagonistic. There is, therefore, no good reason why the fine forms invented to ornament places of worship should not be considered as legitimate when used to ornament places of instruction. As a work of art, and as an elevating influence in community, a fine architectural structure would be the same in either case; but in a school-house its beauty would have a more practical and enduring influence, as it would become intimately associated with the impressible hearts of childhood.

DESIGN 4. - ELEVATION 5.

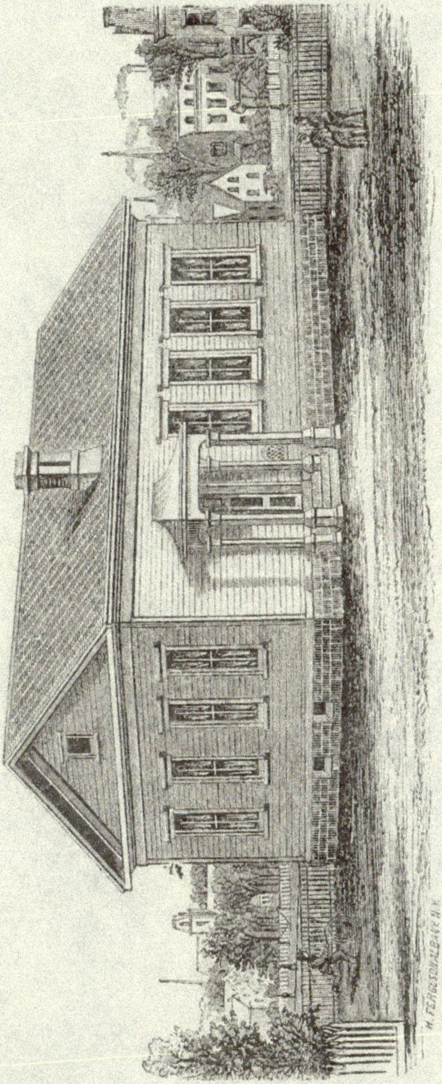

DESIGN 5.

ELEVATION 1.

DESIGN V.

The plan of this design represents a building somewhat larger than any of the preceding, and one approaching the size of the smaller Union Schools. As represented, the school-room has seats for seventy pupils, and by a slight addition to its length and breadth, may be made to accommodate from eighty to one hundred. The entrances are from the sides, and the two sides are finished exactly alike. This will give a large and commodious lobby for each sex, and a fine recitation-room for a second teacher. The entrance to the recitation-room may be from the porches, and the door in front of the school-room omitted, leaving the entire space directly in front for blackboard. The heating and ventilation of this room is like that already described. The rear doors may be omitted if thought best.

Fig. 64.

Elevation No. 1.—This elevation represents a plain wood building finished with ordinary siding. The windows are placed in the ordinary manner, the roof is made with as little pitch as is compatible with the use of shingles. No ornamental work has been admitted. The cornice is plain and substantial, and the building is as cheap as materials can be put together to answer the purpose of a good school-house. The small porch over the steps is a very desirable feature for the comfort of the pupils and for the cleanliness of the house. It affords protection from rains while the pupils are cleaning their feet, and at the same time it relieves in some measure the monotony of the architecture. A glance at the engraving

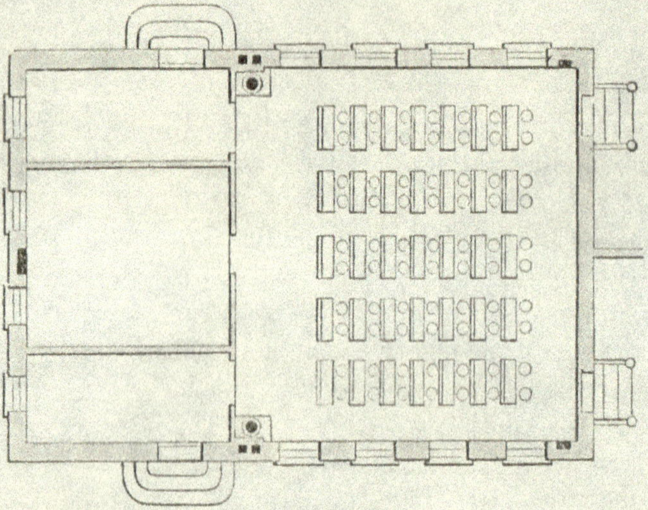

Fig. 65.

will show that, for just proportions, the roof of the porch is too low, and that when built, it should be elevated as far as the cornice permits.

In northern climates the foundations of buildings of this kind should be solid and continuous, both to give solidity to the structure and to prevent the circulation of cold air beneath the building. In the Southern States, however, it would be best to rest the building upon piers, to give a free circulation of air beneath the entire building. This will make the school-room cooler in warm weather, and will tend to preserve the timbers from decay. The piers should be firmly and securely built, or the building will be racked.

Elevation No. 2.—This elevation represents a wood building with a batten finish. An inexpensive hood is placed above the windows, and a cupola surmounts the roof. This last feature may be omitted, as it is not an

DESIGN 5. . . ELEVATION 2.

DESIGN 5. ELEVATION 3.

essential part of the building. The roof of the porch is thrown up into a gable, producing a fine effect at little cost. The roof has a plain projecting cornice of the cheapest form. The same form of building may be finished with clap-boards, or it may be built of brick.

ELEVATION No. 3.—This elevation represents the plainest form of a brick building. The roof is about the usual pitch for shingles, and the only extra feature is the cupola, which may be omitted.

ELEVATION No. 4.—In this elevation the roof is made steeper than the last, the cornice lighter, and the extension of the cornice across the gable has been omitted. The doorway is covered with a porch, which rises in the main roof in the form of a gable. The material may be brick, stone, or wood. The bell-tower is made smaller and lighter than that of No. 3.

ELEVATION No. 5.—This elevation in general form is like No. 4, but with several modifications in details. The pitch of the roof and the form of the cupolas are essentially the same. The corners of the gables are cut off, and the window-heads are rounded arches. In the engraving the finish is represented as brick or stone, with cut-stone groins, window-heads, and sills.

ELEVATION No. 6.—This is the most elaborate design of the series, and makes a highly ornamental school-building. It should be built of stone and have a slate roof. The doors and windows have pointed arches, and the roof and gables all terminate in similar arches. The corners of the roof are cut off, and the front is ornamented with a plain and substantial cupola. The stone porch over the door terminates in a gable, and all the gables are finished with stone copings. This elevation would make an admirable design for a small country church.

UNION SCHOOL-HOUSES.

The greatest need of the common schools of this country is a well-organized system of instruction. It is obvious to every one that a course of study adapted to the capacity of the more advanced pupils cannot be successfully pursued by the primary classes; and it ought to be just as obvious that the system of discipline, and the methods of imparting instruction in the two cases, should be different. Educators have long since demonstrated that certain fixed principles, both of instruction and discipline, are adapted to the different ages and development of pupils; and they have shown that a philosophical system of education will recognize these differences, and apply the principles in the arrangement of schools and in the construction of school-houses.

Fig. 66.

When pupils of all ages and states of advancement are brought together into one room for the purposes of education, as in our ordinary district schools, the work of instruction is very imperfectly performed. The quietness and attention to study necessary to the progress and highest success of an advanced school cannot be enforced in primary classes without seriously injuring the pupils, both physically and mentally; and conversely, the frequent change of position and noise incident thereon, indispensable to primary classes, cannot be permitted in a more

DESIGN 3. ELEVATION 4.

DESIGN 5. ELEVATION 5.

advanced school without a relaxation of discipline and an interference with study incompatible with its highest interests.

Again, the kind of instruction and the methods of imparting it are essentially different in the two cases. With primary classes the instruction should be confined principally to the elements of science objectively presented, and made interesting by appealing directly to the senses. The subject of instruction should be gradually developed, and the lessons principally oral. In the higher schools this system is changed. The primary knowledge having been gained, the expanding minds instinctively seek generalizations and principles. This requires quiet for thought, study, and reflection; and this quiet is not attainable in a room when primary instruction is properly going on. Our schools can never reach their highest state until these two incompatible states of discipline and instruction are finally and effectively separated.

Among the other faults of ungraded schools may be enumerated the following: 1st. The difficulty of having the school-room properly seated so as to accommodate all sizes of pupils. 2d. The great range of studies necessary to be pursued at the same time, rendering it difficult for the teacher to reach a high degree of excellence in the teaching of any. 3d. The great number of classes, allowing the teacher an entirely inadequate portion of time to each, and causing him to hurry from one to the other so rapidly that he cannot do justice to any. 4th. The confused and desultory manner in which instruction is carried on renders the school unattractive both to pupil and parent, and, consequently, there is little interest manifested in its welfare.

These difficulties will never be entirely removed until our schools are graded, and there has been developed and applied a complete and thorough system of instruction. This system should embrace, substantially, the whole course now pursued in our common schools, academies, and colleges, open to all, but allowing each individual to take only such portions of the advanced course as suits his inclination and circumstances. The application of the different portions of this system to the different grades of schools, and the nice adaptation of its progressive parts, are problems which demand the highest wisdom combined with the largest experience; but when once solved, they will be of incalculable benefit to education everywhere.

Fig. 67.

Fig. 68.

When such a system of instruction becomes established, the schools must be more efficient, and pupils will advance with greater rapidity. Teachers will not be left in doubt as to what course to pursue; for a specific work, arranged for each term and year, must be accomplished. Teaching will progress according to well-defined principles, instead of being left to individual caprice. The gradation, thorough system, and division of labor, will effect a saving of time equal to one-half of the entire period now allotted to the school-room, thereby doubling the educational advantages of our children. The means of a liberal education will be brought within the reach of all, at a cost but little greater than that of our present imperfect and inefficient course.

A full enumeration of the advantages of the proposed improvements, and of the changes necessary to effect it, would fill a volume. A very brief view of the main

DESIGN 5. - - ELEVATION 6.

features of the system, as far as they relate to the general organization of schools and the building of school-houses, is all that we need attempt here.

Fig. 69.

PRIMARY SCHOOLS.—Primary Schools should embrace a five years' course of study, extending from the age of five to ten years, with pupils of the average ability. They should take the place of the present District Schools, and be brought within the reach of every home in the land. The instruction should proceed in a regular course, and the pupils should be advanced, year by year, into higher classes, until the whole five years' course is thoroughly mastered.

INTERMEDIATE SCHOOLS.—Intermediate Schools should embrace a four years' course of study, continuing the work of instruction to the age of fourteen. They should be made up of a sufficient number of pupils from the Primary Schools to furnish the requisite number of a proper grade. The instruction here should be systematic, and the pupils advanced, year by year, as in the Primary Schools. The course of study in these schools would be about the same as that now pursued in our academies and in the higher classes of our common schools.

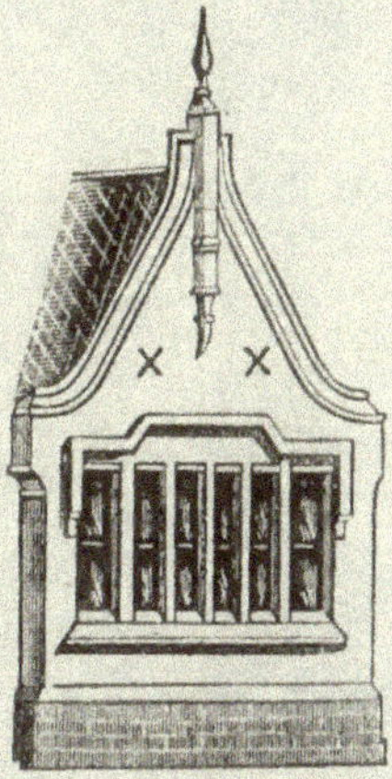

Fig. 70.

HIGH SCHOOLS.—High Schools should embrace a four years' course, carrying on instruction to the age of eighteen. Such schools might be composed of the pupils from a dozen or more intermediate districts. The instruction in these schools would be equivalent to that of our ordinary colleges, though perhaps of a more immediately practical character. This would complete the system of strictly public schools, though, beyond them, those of a special character would be established,—all necessary to the perfect development of a scheme of National education. Prominent among these would be the following:

Fig. 71.

THE UNIVERSITY.—The University should be devoted to professional instruction in the departments of Science, Language, General Literature, Law, Medicine, and Divinity. It should be the crowning glory of all, carrying instruction to the highest point attainable in our present civilization, and elevating civilization itself. It should present the golden opportunity to the scholar in pursuit of the highest culture, and prove the perpetual fountain from which knowledge would flow downward through all the grades of schools, until it reaches every inhabitant of the land, and elevates humanity to a higher level. The graduates of the University would naturally become the teachers of the High Schools, and from these last would come the great mass of the teachers of the Intermediate and Primary Schools.

Fig. 72.

NORMAL SCHOOLS.—Normal Schools, for the professional instruction of teachers, would find their appropriate place. Such persons only as had mastered the High School course should be admitted to the Normal Schools, and the two or three years spent in them should be devoted to the examination of the laws which underlie all systems of instruction, and the best methods of putting in practice the principles so developed. Then teaching would no longer be left to the caprice of ignorance, but would be intelligently and systematically carried on by persons masters of their profession.

WORK SCHOOLS.—All pupils should be obliged to take the course marked out for Primary and Intermediate Schools, but beyond this, entire freedom might be allowed. The great mass of pupils would probably not wish to obtain a liberal education, and would desire immediate entrance into some branch of industry. For the accommodation of this class, Work Schools should be established, in which they could obtain a knowledge of the fundamental principles of the business in which they are to be engaged. These Work Schools would include Mechanical, Agricultural, Mercantile, Manufactures, and Mining Schools, Schools of Design, etc.

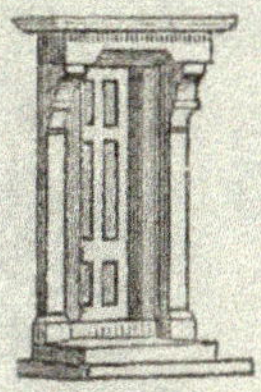
Fig. 73.

When this system of graded schools becomes the ruling policy, and there shall be established Professional and Work Schools to perfect it; when all these are consolidated and crystallized into a great national system, reaching from ocean to ocean, and so ubiquitous and Argus-eyed that no child in the Republic can evade its sight or escape its influence; then will labor, organized into system, be respected and honored by all men; then will each individual have the opportunity and all the necessary aids to secure the development of his peculiar talent in the direction that nature designed; and then we may expect a higher and more beneficent civilization.

In cities, villages, and the more thickly populated portions of the country, the systematic gradation of schools can be easily adopted, and the great advantages arising therefrom at once secured. Indeed, the system is now substantially adopted in most of our larger cities. In the more sparsely settled portions of the country it is difficult to establish any general system that is entirely unobjectionable; but even there, a steady policy of consolidating districts instead of dividing them would be beneficial, while the entire benefits of graded schools might be realized by the abolishment of districts and the substitution therefor of town schools. This matter is considered of such importance that an elaborate article upon the subject, from the very able report of the Secretary of the Vermont Board of Education, is inserted in the Appendix.

Fig. 74.

Where the gradation of schools has been established, two or more grades are often united in one building, under the distinctive name of "Union Schools;" and Union School-houses have become one of the "institutions" of the land. These houses, of necessity, must be larger and more costly than the common District School-houses; yet the cost must be far less than the aggregate cost of several separate houses affording the same accommodations. The lot, out-buildings, and general surroundings of a Union School-house will cost no more than those belonging to each of the smaller houses; so the argument, on the score of economy, is entirely in favor of Union School-houses.

The comparison is sometimes made between the cost of a large, well built, and commodious Union School-house, possessing all the modern improvements, and that of several of the old-fashioned, ill-constructed, and miserably-furnished houses, where children were packed almost to suffocation, and the balance has been in favor of the latter; but it is unnecessary to say that such a comparison is one-sided and unfair, and that to make it of any value, the same conditions must be preserved in the two cases.

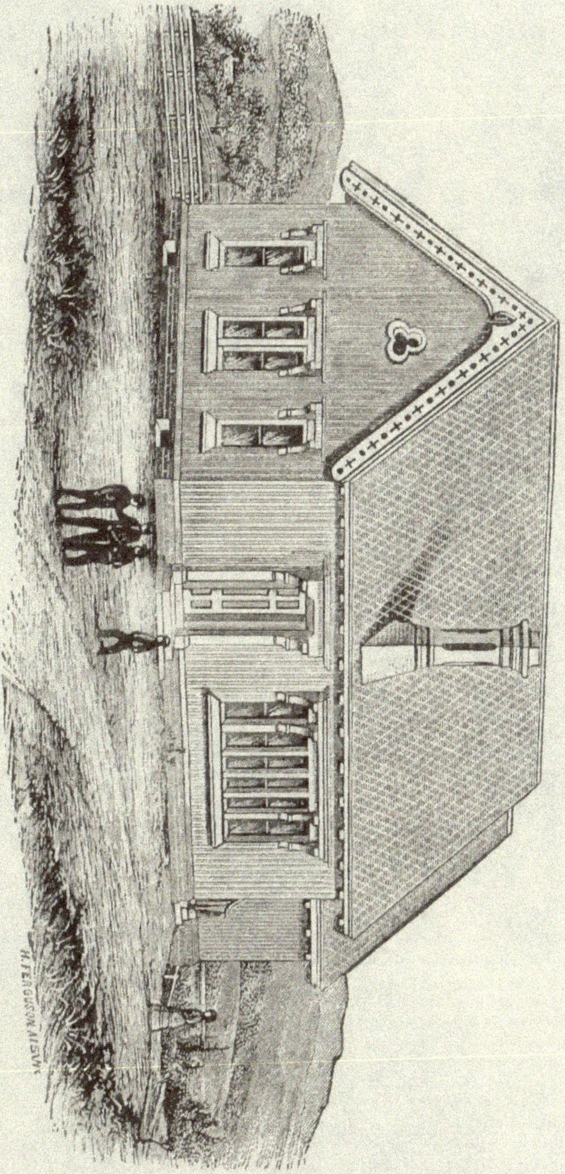

DESIGN 6. · · ELEVATION 1.

Several of the succeeding plans are well adapted to the wants of consolidated districts, and of Union Schools of two or more departments. No effort, however, has been made to give a complete series of Union School-houses, as such a series would be incompatible with the general design of this work. Plans for larger and more elaborate Union School-houses are left for a subsequent work, in which the whole subject of village and city school-house architecture shall be fully discussed. The series here given includes houses with accommodation for sufficient pupils to require the employment of from one to four or five teachers.

Fig. 75.

An effort has been made to present designs which will not only answer for immediate use, but will be permanent. In the construction of school-houses, it has too often been the case that present necessities alone have been provided for, and, in consequence, the structures have been of the most transient character, causing the whole school system to appear equally transient and unstable, and rendering necessary a heavy outlay for rebuilding.

In Massachusetts, where the old system of independent districts has been in operation for nearly two centuries, the schools of each town have recently been consolidated into a Union district with its primary, intermediate, and high schools. The result of the experiment has been satisfactory in the extreme. A genuine educational revival has taken place. Much more attention is paid to schools on the part of communities, a constant demand is made for better qualified teachers, and large numbers of new and improved school-houses have been erected. All parties interested unite in commendation of the new system, as greatly superior to the old in efficiency and in the economic expenditure of money.

DESIGN VI.

The plan of Design VI. is like that of Design V., with the addition of a building in the rear, and the grouping of the windows together. The school-room is thirty feet square, and has seats for seventy pupils. By increasing its length respectively three or six feet, it will be made to accommodate eighty or ninety pupils, and by increasing its length six feet and its width four feet, there will be room for one hundred and eight seats. The rear building may be used as a wood-room, or it may be made into one or two recitation-rooms.

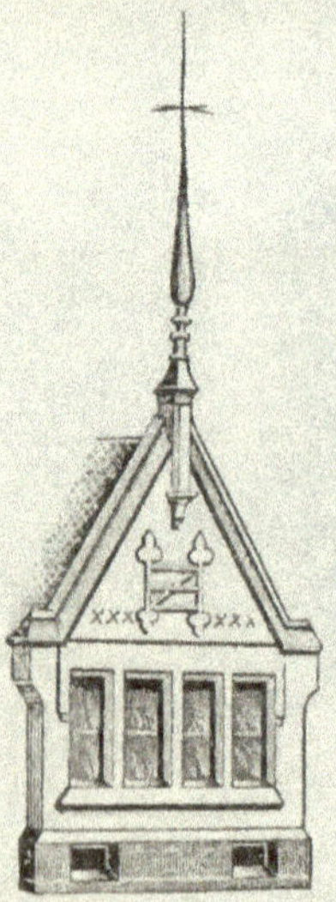

Fig. 76.

The entrance to the recitation-room may be from the school-room or from the halls. The recitation-room may be heated by a hot-air pipe, extending from one of the stoves in the school-room.

Once more special attention is called to the arrangements of the windows and the ventilation of this building. The windows are grouped together, and it is believed that this arrangement will be considered the best possible for a school-room, after it has received a fair trial. It furnishes a broad unbroken light, and in summer it will permit cooling draughts to circulate through the room whenever the air has any motion.

In winter the doors and windows must be kept closed, so that the air may be permitted to circulate in the channels provided for it. In this way the room will be kept

DESIGN 6. ELEVATION 2.

warm in every part, a strong current of pure air is constantly entering the room, and the foul air is as constantly flowing out. We cannot too often or too strongly urge the importance of providing for this perfect ventilation in the construction of school-houses.

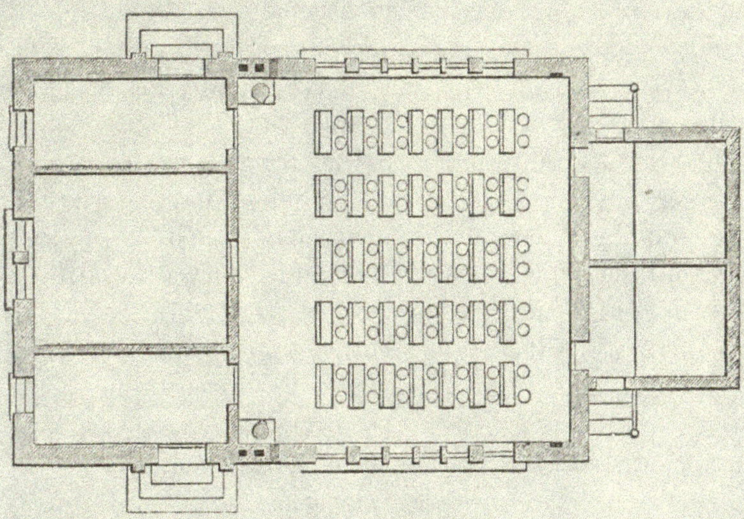

Fig. 77.

Designs V. and VI. each have two fronts, with separate entrances for the sexes, but one might be omitted if thought advisable, and the space of the entry-way might be used as a clothes-room or extra recitation-room. It would be better, however, to retain both entrances.

Elevation No. 1.—This elevation represents a plain wood building finished with battens. The roof is sufficiently steep for either slate or shingles. The plainness of the cornice has been relieved by ornamental scroll-work, which may be omitted. The windows are grouped together in the whole series, giving broad and continuous light.

The hoods over the doors and windows are simple, and they give an additional beauty to the structure. This building, with some simple changes, might be made of brick. If built of wood, it can be finished with the ordinary siding.

Elevation No. 2.—In this elevation we have a more ornamental design. A cupola has been added for a bell-tower, and gables have been erected over the doors and windows, to relieve the monotony of the outline. The gable over the door affords an opportunity for the construction of a very desirable open porch. The window-gable allows the window to be treated in an elegant manner, and the finish of both the sides and end gives to the building a very fine appearance. It will be noticed that, in the picture, the roof is slightly curved toward the eaves. This feature adds to the architectural beauty of the design, but it may be omitted, and still a good effect be produced. This design may be of wood, brick, or stone. If built of wood, the batten finish would be most in keeping with the general style of the structure.

Elevation No. 3.—This elevation in general resembles No. 2, but is changed in many of its details. The roof is straight, and comes down much lower. The windows and door-gables are elegant in design, and they are finished with simple stone copings. The cupola grows out of the structure, and is an integral part of it, which cannot be omitted without destroying the general symmetry of the design. The materials of this building should be brick or stone, and the roof should be slate. The pointed arches for the window-heads and doors give to the design a richness of appearance which fit it admirably for a village school, to occupy a prominent and sightly position.

Elevation No. 4.—This design is more elaborate and quaint than any of the preceding. It has several of the features of the older Gothic forms. The roofs are high

FERGUSON ALBANY.

DESIGN 6. ELEVATION 5.

and pointed, and each gable ends in a pinnacle. The pinnacle of the front gable forms the bell-tower, and this tower commences with a stone projection just above the window-heads. The gables are all finished with stone copings instead of cornices. The doors and windows are projected outward from the sides of the building, and the door-gable terminates in the chimney, the flues of which are carried up in the door-projection. The rear of the door-gable is carried up straight, like similar projections in this style of architecture. The roof comes down below the gable copings, making the walls of the building comparatively low.

ELEVATIONS NOS. 5 AND 6.—These elevations represent substantially the same kind of architecture as No. 4, with changes and modifications in details. They represent a later style of architecture, but still one quite ancient. The modifications of the gables, cupolas, door-ways, window-heads, and general style of finish are represented in the engraving, and need no verbal description.

These designs are more costly than the plain ones, but in districts where there is sufficient wealth to warrant the outlay, there can be no doubt in regard to the propriety of erecting buildings of this kind. They are ornaments to the village; they assist in educating the community to a higher appreciation of architectural forms, and of the beautiful in art; they are attractive places, and children are easily taught to take pride in them, and in their preservation. In No. 5 the pinnacles upon the gables have been omitted to show how important they are in the full development of the Gothic designs. The elevation appears bare and unfinished when compared with those in which the pinnacles are admitted. In Gothic forms the only proper way to avoid the use of pinnacles is to drop the corners of the roof, as in Elevation No. 3, Design III.

Either of the five preceding designs would make a fine country church, chapel, or session-room. The materials for the construction should be brick or stone, and the copings of the gables should be cut stone. In designs of this character no attempt should be made to reduce the cost, by changes of form, or by the use of cheap and poor materials. Where economy is essential, some of the cheaper forms of buildings should be adopted, and no effort wasted in endeavoring to build elaborate structures at little cost, or to produce fine architectural effects with inadequate materials. In each of these structures great care must be taken to have the foundation firm and secure. The roof, also, being a very prominent feature, should be accurately made, and, if possible, covered with slate.

In making choice between these different elevations, care should be taken to select such as will be found to harmonize best with the surrounding scenery. Pointed gables and pinnacles will generally be found best adapted to a hilly country, while the broad roofs and projecting eaves will be more in harmony with the scenery of a level region. Again, there will be ample opportunity for the display of taste in deciding upon fitness in regard to situation, whether upon the hill-side or valley, whether in the village or strictly rural region, and whether in an open exposed place or nestled in some sheltered woody nook.

Design 6. Elevation 6.

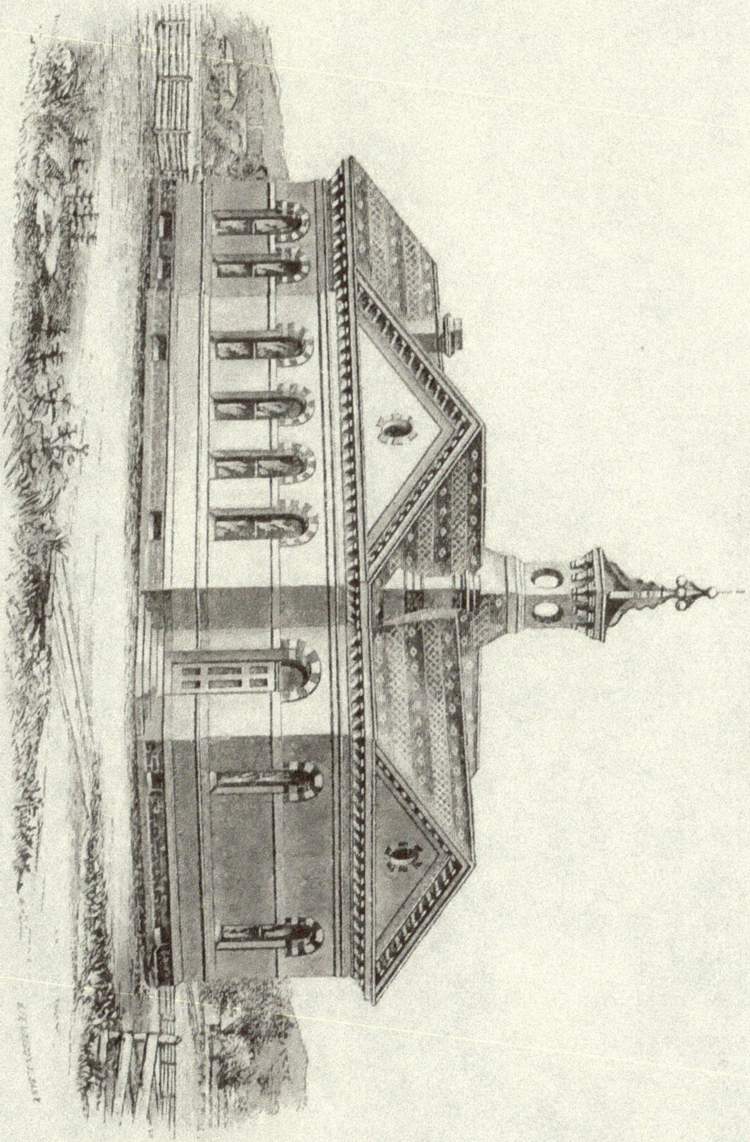

Design I. Elevation I.

DESIGN VII.

The plan of Design VII. represents a building with two school-rooms, and another large room which may be used as a single recitation-room, or divided into two. The school-rooms are separated by sliding doors, so that they may be thrown into one when occasion requires. Each room may be made to accommodate forty-two, fifty-six, or sixty-four pupils, without essentially changing the appearance of the building. The porches in front are ample for entry-ways and cloak-rooms. By a little addi-

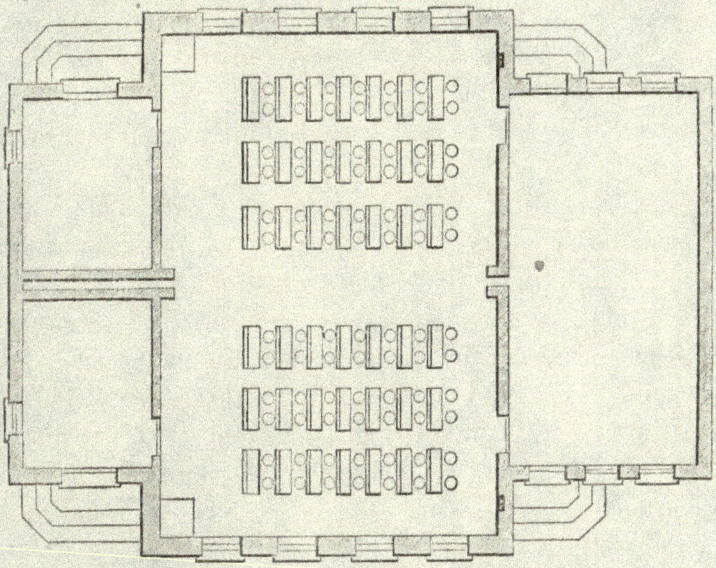

Fig. 78.

tion to the width of the front projection, room would be obtained for staircases, and the building might be made two stories in height.

Elevation No. 1.—The roof of the main building is

put on at right angles to the roofs of the front and rear projections, and all these are finished with gables. The

Fig. 79.

eaves of the three buildings are of the same height, and an ornamental cornice is made to extend across the gables. The cornices have a moderate projection and are finished with modillions. The pitch of the roof is as little as is compatible with the use of shingles. The window and door heads are rounded arches, and a string-course is made in the wall at the base of the window and door caps. These caps should be made of stone of two different colors, and cut to conform to the circle of the arch. A good effect may be produced by making these of brick and stone combined. The cupola is needed to give completeness to the building, but it may be omitted. The materials of this building should be brick or stone.

Elevation No. 2.—This elevation represents a very plain building, which may be built of wood, brick, or stone. The main building has a square hip-roof, and the projections have ordinary roofs with the corners cut off, and each side is relieved by a vertical projection. The cupola is a necessary part of the structure. The window-heads are square, to correspond with the general character of the elevation. If built of wood the finish might be of battens or clap-boards, but the former would best accord with the general style. The low roof, the bracketed cornice, and the general structure of this building admirably fits it for a prairie region.

Elevation No. 3.—This is a plain wooden structure, finished with battens. The projecting cornice is ornamented with filigree-work, which may be omitted. The

DESIGN 7. ELEVATION 2.

DESIGN 7. ELEVATION 3.

windows and doors are ornamented with simple projecting hoods, put on in the form of gables.

ELEVATION No. 4.—This elevation represents a structure with several features of the Gothic architecture. The roofs are all steep, and the gables terminate in pinnacles. The window and door heads are pointed arches, and the cupola is finished in similar forms. A sill-course extends around the building level with the window-sills. The materials should be brick or stone, and the roof should be slate.

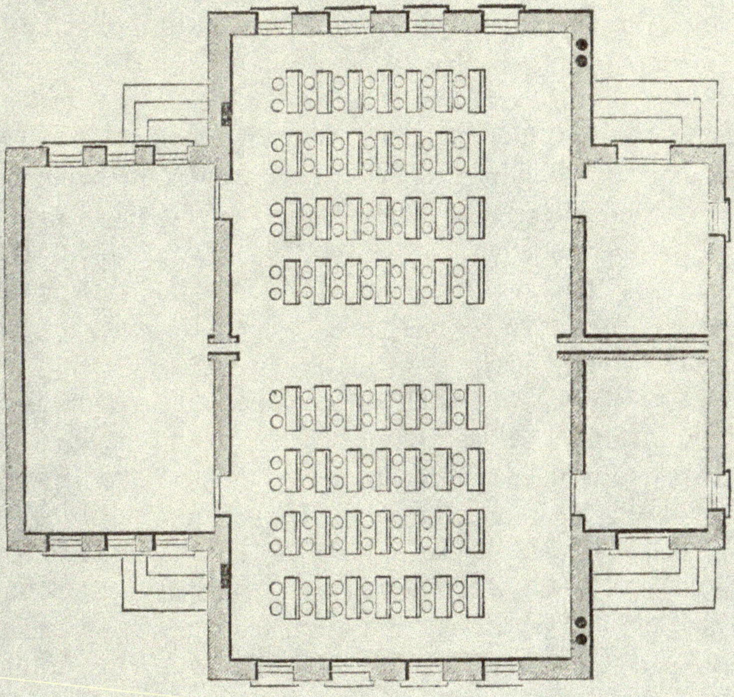

Fig. 80.

ELEVATION No. 5.—In this elevation we have another design with high steep roof and pointed gables. The window-heads, however, are square, and the gables are finished with a stone coping, which gives the structure a rich appearance. To break the monotony of the roof, little gables are projected over the doors and over the windows of the rear building. The cupola and ornamental chimneys are essential parts of the building. The materials should be brick or stone, and the window ornaments and copings should be cut stone. This elevation would be a fine design for a suburban or village dwelling, the only change necessary being in the inside structure.

ELEVATION No. 6.—This elevation represents a very plain and cheap structure of wood, the plainest form in which this general design can be represented. The finish is with battens. The roof has a plain and wide projecting cornice, giving a comfortable appearance to the design. The corners of the projections are made to fall below those of the main building for cheapness of structure and for variety in appearance. The windows of the school-rooms are grouped together. A bell-tower may be added to the centre of the roof if needed. This is a fine design for prairies and level country places, and it would by no means be considered out of place in a village.

ELEVATION No. 7.—This, the last of the series, is a very plain and substantial building. Its various features are happily blended, and its general appearance is fine. The roof is steep, but the gables, instead of terminating in pinnacles, are cut off, and the windows terminate in pointed arches. The large window in the principal gable is finished in a comparatively cheap form, yet it is so arranged as to become a prominent and beautiful feature in the building.

The materials should be brick or stone, though wood may be used. The cupola is an essential part of the building, and cannot be omitted.

FERGUSON, ALBANY

CONCRETE FOR BUILDING.

In erecting houses of considerable size and cost, due attention should be paid to durability. If the present generation leave as a legacy to their descendants excellent school buildings, the next generation may be supplied with the apparatus and physical appliances necessary to secure the highest success of the school. If, on the contrary, our children must be heavily taxed for school-houses, the era of school improvement in regard to methods, libraries, and cabinets, must be postponed for another generation.

Wood is the material most commonly used in the construction of school-houses, on account of its cheapness; and it answers a very good purpose for the building of small houses and for those that are designed to be temporary. Permanent houses, however, should be built of brick or stone; and this especially should be the case in the construction of the more elaborate elevations of the designs given in this work.

Stone is the best material for building which nature has furnished, and, in localities where it can be procured at little cost, it should always be used in the construction of school-houses. Walls of stone, well laid upon permanent foundations reaching below the action of frost, never crumble or crack, never shrink and shrivel in the rays of the sun, nor warp out of position; but they stand firm and erect, affording shelter and protection to many generations of children. Tender associations have time to cluster around such a building, and the spot where it stands becomes hallowed by the vivid and ineffaceable recollections of childhood. The clinging mosses and the gray lichens that clamber over its surface and nestle lovingly in every seam and crevice; and the sombre tints of brown that time spreads over its entire exterior, make it an object of admiration and an influence at once elevating and ennobling.

Brick may be used when good building stone cannot be procured, but it lacks the solidity, beauty, and durability of stone. When brick is used an effort should be made to relieve the dreary monotony of the color by the use of stone for door and window trimmings and for corners. Brick walls, however, left hollow or well furred out, afford a much better protection from the weather and are much more durable than wood.

In many country places building stone cannot be obtained and brick is too expensive for economic use. In such localities substantial walls may be made of cobblestone, gravel, and sand, which will be at once cheap and durable. Such walls are known as concrete, and when correctly built have all the solidity of the best stone.

When it is designed to build a concrete house, the site should be located near a bank of clean gravel, to lessen the expense of transporting materials. Excavations should then be made for the foundation walls below the action of frost. The concrete should be made of clean sand four parts and hydraulic cement one part, thoroughly mixed when dry, and then wet to the consistency of a thin mortar. In the use of coarse gravel, one part of cement should be used to ten parts of gravel. The excavation should be filled with this mixture, taking care to use enough of the sand mortar to fill all the interstices between the coarser materials. Stones of any size or shape may be used, only each should be thoroughly bedded in the mortar.

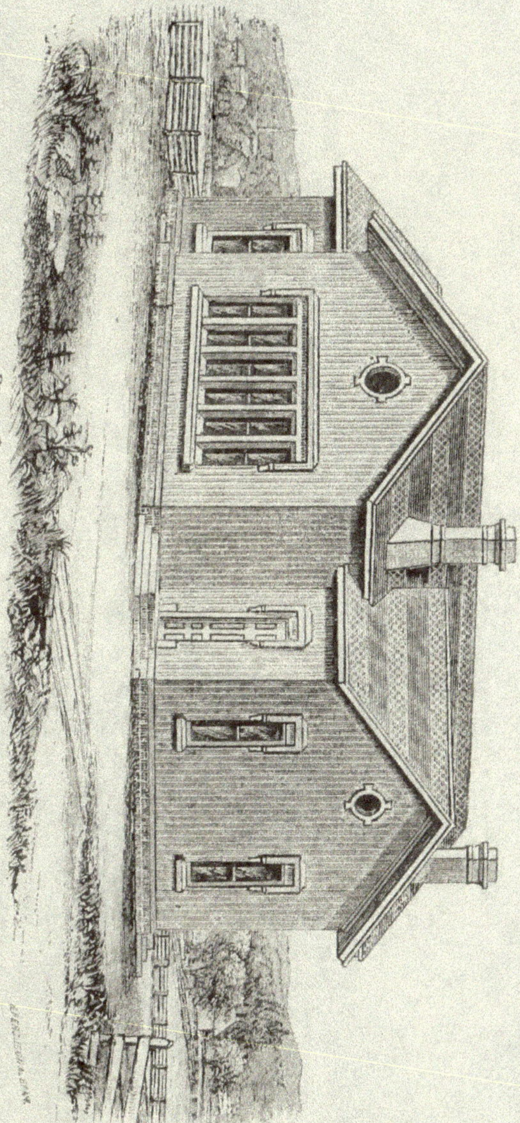

DESIGN 7. ELEVATION 6.

About one foot in height of this wall may be built per day in drying weather. From the surface upward curbs of plank, well stayed so as not to spring or warp, should be used; and, as each portion of the wall below sets, the curbs may be elevated to receive the new portion. The hydraulic cement should be used exclusively to a distance of one or two feet above the surface, after which cement and quick-lime should be mixed in equal proportions.

The door and window frames should be set in their proper places, and the concrete built around them as in ordinary stone or brick walls. Care should be taken to continually pack the mortar by tamping it with a stick prepared for the purpose, so that no openings will be left in the wall. Moulds of any form may be used for the window-sills, and for the window and door caps. Ornamental projections may also be made at the corners if desired.

As fast as the work progresses the outside should be covered with a thin coat of plaster, made of clean sand and hydraulic cement, so that all the little interstices may be filled and a smooth exterior finish secured. When the building is done it will be one solid stone from the foundation to the top, and if properly built will be almost indestructible.

In the use of concrete several cautions must be observed. The cement and lime used must be fresh and of good quality. The sand should be moderately coarse and clean. Neither with the sand nor gravel used should any dirt be admitted. The curbs should be moved with care, and the work built no faster than the mass below sets.

Where sand, gravel, and cobble-stone are easily obtained, a concrete building can be erected more cheaply than any other. The whole of the work may be done by unskilled laborers under the direction of one competent foreman.

The use of this material in building largely obtains in many parts of Europe. The late aqueducts and sewers of Paris have been made of stone manufactured in this manner, and the stone used in the construction of the Suez Canal was made from the sands of the desert through which it passes. In the vicinity of Paris a church has been erected of this material, which is one solid stone from the foundation to the top of the cross which surmounts the spire.

This concrete may also be used economically for a great variety of useful purposes. For drains and sewers it is as durable as the most costly and solid masonry. For floors to cellars and out-buildings, where solidity and protection against dampness are desirable, it is the best material that has yet been devised. It can be readily moulded into any desirable form for window and door caps and sills, and the ornamental stone-work of architecture. When made into blocks it may also receive any desired color; and in this manner the beautiful in form and variety in color can be secured at small cost.

Design 8. Elevation 1.

DESIGN VIII.

The plan of Design VIII. represents a large building, with two commodious school-rooms, and a large recitation-room, which may be divided into two. The halls in front are sufficiently spacious for wardrobes, and for staircases, if an extra story is needed. In front, opening into the front halls, are two small rooms, which may be used for fuel; they are so arranged that no dust need get into the rooms. The stoves are placed in niches in the front of the rooms, entirely out of the way. The ventilating flues are in the corners diagonally opposite. With due care in construction, the ventilation of these rooms will be perfect.

The light is admitted to the school-rooms upon one side only. In the rear of the school-rooms are two small rooms for apparatus, or, if there is a supply of running water, for water-closets. The small halls in the rear open both into the recitation and school-rooms. The large windows, properly supplied with blinds, will afford a strong and evenly distributed light, and one that can be tempered and controlled at will.

Elevation No. 1.—This elevation represents a plain substantial building, with steep roofs. The gables are plain and terminate in pinnacles. The cupola on the centre is all that is strictly ornamental, and even this may be omitted, though the building will appear much better with it. The doors and windows terminate in round arches. The group of windows, opening into the school-room, gives a fine architectural appearance to that side of the house. In front, the blank wall is relieved by blank windows. The materials for the building may be wood, brick, or stone. If wood is used the finish should be

12

with battens, so that the lines may be vertical. If brick, the ornamental work around the windows and doors should be of cut stone, of at least two different colors, or of brick and stone. The roof should be of slate, though shingles may be used.

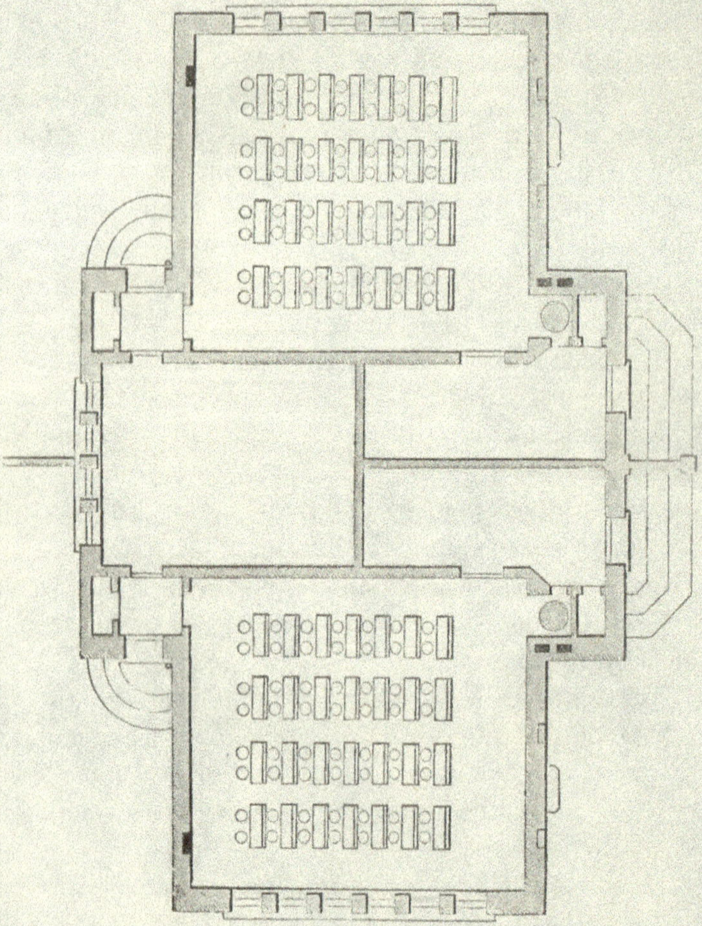

Fig. 81.

ELEVATION No. 2.—This is another very plain and satisfactory design. The roof has a steep pitch, but the corners of the gables are cut down, avoiding the necessity of using pinnacles. The front is ornamented by the two

DESIGN 8. ELEVATION 2.

DESIGN 8. ELEVATION 3.

stately doorways, which terminate in pointed arches, and the blank side-walls are broken by the projection of the chimneys. The large window in the side is a combination of fine forms, and the whole design is chaste and elegant. The cupola and ornamental chimney-tops are necessary parts of the building.

It should be built of brick or stone, though wood may be used. With brick as the material, the windows and doors should be finished with cut stone of different colors, or of stone and brick alternately, as represented in the engraving.

A fine effect would be produced by using stone in a rough state for the walls, and ornamenting the windows, doors, and corners by projections, the courses alternately of different-colored cut stone. It may be built of wood, in which case the finish should be with battens. The fine effect of this building is owing to the judicious arrangements of the parts, as it is exceedingly simple, and would cost but little more than the plainest form that can be devised. The extra cost is in the roof and window-heads.

Elevation No. 3.—This elevation represents Design VIII., finished with a French or Mansard roof. In the centre a square hip-roof terminates in a cupola, and on the sides the steep French roof comes down to the cornice. The top of the steep portion is surmounted by an ornamental open balustrade. The walls, windows, and doors are like those of Elevation No. 1.

The French roof, in general, is not well adapted to buildings of one story, but this design would be an admirable one for a level country, or for hot climates, where it is necessary to have considerable space between the room occupied and the direct rays of the sun. If an extra story should be given to this building, the French roof would appear to better advantage, and the design would prove admirable.

DESIGN IX.

In some sections of the country the octagonal form of buildings is popular, chiefly on account of economy. The same amount of walls and roof, in an octagon, will inclose a greater area than any rectangular form. The great objection to this building is its unsightly appearance, and indeed, an octagon, with a plain hip-roof, and no projections to relieve the dead monotony of its walls, has about as much architectural beauty as a joint of stove-pipe set upright. In the elevations given, an effort has been made to obviate the difficulty by varying the outline by projections, and by carrying the roof up in gables. The plan is

Fig. 82.

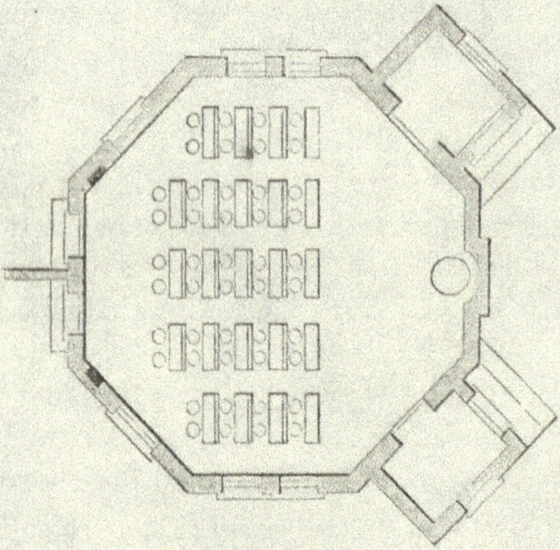

Fig. 83.

admirably adapted to the wants of a small school. The room is compact, well lighted, and easily ventilated. In

DESIGN 9.

warm weather, the windows and doors can be opened upon seven sides, insuring a circulation of air. Upon two sides, porches for entrances have been built, and the doors to these are on the sides rather than in front.

The elevation of this design is so placed that we stand directly in front of one of the porches, and have a view of the front of the building and the door of the other porch. The chimney is projected from the wall so as to relieve the blank space, and the top is finished for a bell-tower. The materials may be of wood, brick, or stone, and the finish of any kind that is used in architecture. The only special caution necessary in constructing this building is that the roof shall be well made. The gutters must be lined with metal, which should be held in its place by the projecting ends of the shingles, but *not nailed*. If nailed, water will find its way through the nail holes, and the frost will tear the metal asunder.

Fig. 84.

DESIGN X.

This design represents an octagon with a projecting front. The walls are sixteen feet, and the room has ample accommodations for sixty pupils. In the front are two fine porches, and in the rear is a large recitation-room and two small triangular back passage-ways. The room is admirably lighted by the windows upon the two sides, and in every way is convenient for a school.

Fig. 85.

The elevation of this design represents the four opposite sides thrown up into gables, all ending in pinnacles. The corners of the gables may be cut down as in Elevation No. 7, of Design VIII., if desired. The materials may be wood or

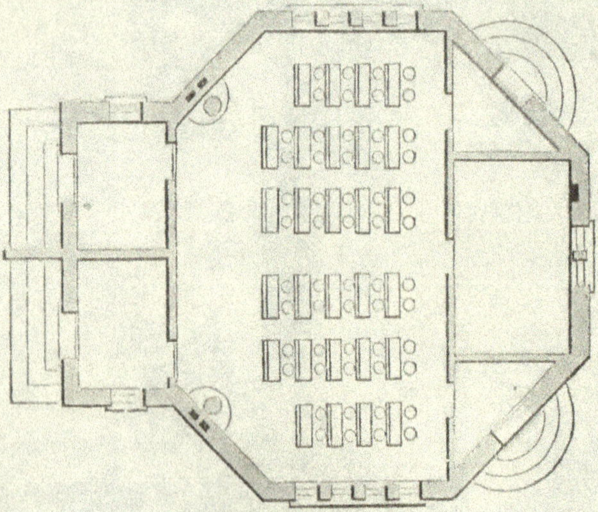

Fig. 86.

brick. If wood is used, the finish should be with battens. If brick, the window-sills should be cut stone, and the

Design 19.

window-caps, stone, or projecting brick arches. The cupola is a necessary part of this building, and should not be omitted.

An examination of this plan and elevation will show that it is admirably adapted to the purposes of a school. The school-room is sufficiently commodious to accommodate a sufficient number of pupils to give employment to one or two teachers. It is well lighted and ventilated. The arrangement of seats, blackboards, stoves, and passage-ways secures at once comfort and convenience. The ventilating ducts are placed at the farthest extremity of the recitation-rooms, and openings are left in the partition at the bottom so that both rooms are heated and ventilated by the same apparatus.

The elevation will admit of many changes in details. The window and door caps may be finished in pointed arches, and the cupola may be made more open, like some of the preceding designs. In the construction of octagon buildings, relatively a greater saving can be effected by using concrete than in any other form. The curbs used for the walls can be as easily fitted for the corners as though they were right angles; while by the use of brick or stone a considerable expense would be incurred by the extra mason-work in shaping the corners.

DESIGN XI.

The plan of this design is very much like that of Design VIII., but with the front halls broadened so as to admit

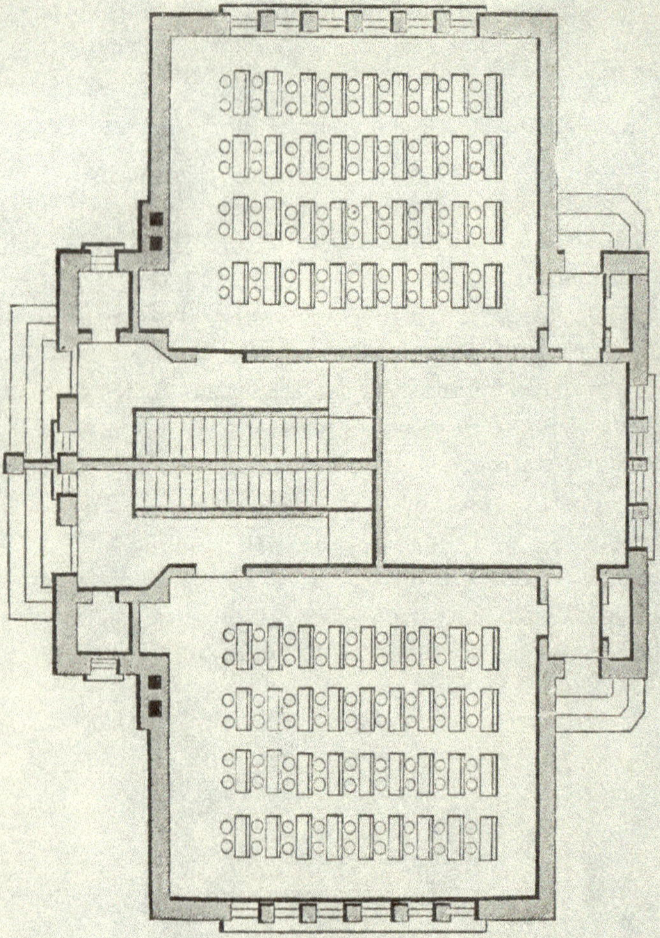

Fig. 87.

of the construction of a staircase in each, in case a two-story building should be needed.

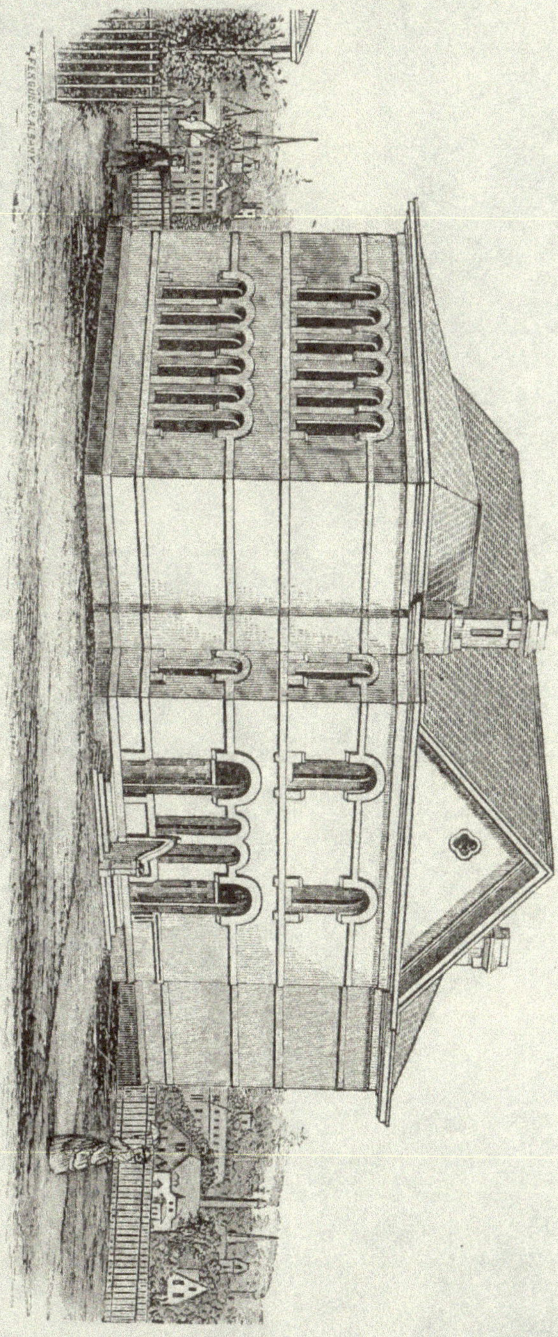

DESIGN 11.

Each floor consists of two large school-rooms, and a recitation-room, which may be divided into two if necessary. The broad light coming in upon one side only is in accordance with the latest scientific authority, and the ventilating apparatus will furnish fresh air continually and in abundance.

The elevation of this design is a cheap affair, and is given rather as a hint than as a design to be copied. For a building of the size a plainer finish could scarcely be devised. Should a more elaborate roof and finish be desired, either of the three elevations of Design VIII. might be copied. The Mansard roof of Elevation No. 3, Design VIII., would appear much better on a two-story building like Design XI.

This elevation is the last of the series in this work, and it serves as a connecting link between the smaller houses adapted to country districts and the more elaborate and varied architecture demanded by village and union schools.

In most villages where two or three teachers are constantly employed, a two-story house much larger than is required for the daily needs of the school should be erected. The lower floor of this edifice should be devoted to the schools, and the upper floor should be made into a public hall. In this manner provision can be made at little expense for the accommodation of school exhibitions, public lectures, and the like, and the whole would be under the control of the school trustees, and would thus become a part of the educational influences of the community. The profits arising from letting the hall, in most cases, would pay the interest on the money invested, and in a series of years would supply the school with apparatus and a library.

CHAPTER VIII.

FURNITURE.

All effort at reform in the building of school-houses will fall far short of accomplishing its object, unless it comprehends a radical change in school-house furniture. In a great majority of our country districts the furniture used is of the very rudest description, and does not answer the purposes of its construction. Even in sections of the country where education has received considerable attention, and the appearance and condition of the school-house have been improved, the old desks and benches are too often retained. We have already alluded to the positive evils resulting from this state of things. Not only are the pupils rendered physically uncomfortable, but their bodies are often permanently injured, and their mental improvement seriously retarded.

The whole philosophy of this subject seems to lie in the proposition, "That the furniture of the school-house should be such as will conduce to the health and comfort of the pupils, and to the general convenience of the whole school." Anything less than this would be a positive wrong, and ought never to be tolerated. It is also very desirable to take one step farther, and make the whole so attractive that it will have a direct tendency to cultivate good taste and refinement.

School-house furniture is of two kinds, the general and the special: the former comprehending all the articles needed for preserving order and cleanliness, and the latter including that which is peculiar to the school-room, such as desks, seats, tables, and the like.

GENERAL FURNITURE.

By general furniture we mean all the apparatus necessary for convenience and cleanliness, but which is not necessarily peculiar to the school-room. Were it not for an almost culpable negligence on the part of school officers generally, it would not be necessary to speak of these matters in a work of this kind ; but teachers and pupils are often seriously incommoded, and schools materially injured, by inattention and neglect in such little things. All of the following articles are absolutely indispensable to the highest interests of the school.

SCRAPERS.—For the purpose of affording facilities for removing mud from the feet, plank or stone walks should be constructed, and steps of like materials should be put up at all outside doors. These walks and steps should be supplied with scrapers, so that a large number of pupils can use them at the same time. A strip of band-iron securely nailed to the edge of a plank, so that the edge of the iron may rise half an inch above the surface of the plank, will make an excellent and economical scraper. A great variety of portable scrapers are manufactured, and can be easily and cheaply procured by those who prefer them.

MATS.—Every outside door should be provided with one or more coarse mats, and the inside doors with those of a finer character. Mats made of the husks of maize are well adapted to the former situation, and pieces of rag-carpet, or something of the kind, would answer well for the latter. Coarse rope matting is more costly, but more durable than husks. In school-houses of more than one story, it would be well to carpet the staircases with rope matting to deaden the sound of passing feet.

Brooms and brushes.—Having taken measures to prevent the accumulation of dirt in a school-room, there next should be provided means for removing that which will collect in spite of all precautions. Every school-room should be thoroughly swept every day, and the floor should be well scrubbed at least once a week. For these purposes a broom, a floor brush, and scrubbing-brush or mop should be provided. A small floor brush is indispensable in removing the dirt from under the seats and desks.

Pails.—A mop-pail must necessarily accompany the mop or scrubbing-brush; and there should also be provided a pail and cups, for the purpose of furnishing the pupils with drinking-water when necessary.

Wash-basins, etc.—In the back hall there should be a sink or bench, furnished with wash-basins and towels. As personal cleanliness is a cardinal virtue, and as children cannot always avoid becoming dirty while at school, the means for removing the dirt becomes a matter of prime necessity. With these facilities, teachers need never allow pupils to enter the school-room with dirty hands and faces; and the result of efforts bestowed in this direction will be fixed habits of personal neatness, which will not only add to individual health, but to public morality.

Umbrella stands.—A water-tight box, or half of a tight barrel, should be placed in each of the front halls to receive umbrellas, and to prevent the annoyance arising from their dripping upon the floor.

Clothes-hooks.—Pupils should never be allowed to bring their hats, bonnets, and extra clothing into the school-room when the school-house contains a hall. In this hall substantial clothes-hooks should be placed to afford ample accommodation. These hooks should be numbered, so as to prevent the confusion arising from having several claimants for one hook. Pins made of hard wood might be used for clothes-hooks; and, indeed, such pins would be much better than the common iron hooks, which are too easily broken.

Fire apparatus.—Besides the stove, several other fire utensils are necessary for convenience and safety. When wood is used, there should always be furnished a shovel, pair of tongs, and a sheet-iron ash-pail. When coal is used, a scuttle, poker, and screen, in addition to the above. An iron ash-pail is indispensable to afford protection against fire. Many a school-house has been burned in consequence of storing ashes in barrels or other vessel of wood.

Clock.—All system in school operations must depend upon the proper observance of time, and hence a good time-piece should be provided. A clock placed in sight of all the pupils is much preferable to a watch in the hands of the teacher. The cost of a good clock is inconsiderable, and no good reason can be assigned for not providing one for every school-house in the land.

Programme clock.—A school clock has lately been invented and brought into use, so constructed that it may be set to strike at any times desired. When the teacher has made out his programme, he can set his clock to strike at the close of each exercise. Teachers and pupils are thus automatically reminded of the school order, and no one is obliged to watch the time, and so have his attention diverted from the work on hand. This clock would be a desirable acquisition in any school.

Thermometer.—For the preservation of health, a nearly

uniform temperature should be preserved. But our own sensations of heat and cold cannot be depended upon, as they are seriously affected by our physical condition. A thermometer should be provided as a guide, and to prevent the alternate broilings and freezings to which children are so frequently subjected.

In most cases the teacher can succeed in obtaining these articles of general furniture by properly presenting the matter to the trustees or committee. He can also see that they are all put to their proper use. In the matter of cleanliness, especially, he can produce radical and much needed reforms by a little care and attention. By precept and example he can create a public sentiment in his school, so that an end will be made of that filthiness which is so common in our country school-houses, and lasting habits of neatness may be formed by his pupils.

Another important lesson in connection with furniture may be enforced by the teacher, viz., that useful articles should be used and not abused. The destructive propensities of children should be checked at an early period, and they should be taught to take care of everything provided for their education. Indeed, this care becomes an important element of education, leading to wise economies and habits of self-restraint. Children at quite an early age may be taught that saving is as important as earning, and that economy is a virtue that can be always shown in thoughtful care.

SPECIAL FURNITURE.

In the construction of seats and desks the following general principles should be observed:

First: They should be substantial, not easily broken or disarranged. The furniture of a school-room, of necessity, is subjected to comparatively rough usage, and if made weak, its frail appearance invites and stimulates the rudeness which destroys it. Strength, then, is a necessary condition, not only to preserve it from ruin, but to repress the element which is usually precociously developed in children.

Second: They should be easy and comfortable. Churches are usually furnished with cushioned seats, although occupied but a limited portion of one day in the week, while the school-house, which is occupied five days in the week, is supplied with rough, ill-shaped benches. This custom, to say the least, is not philosophical. There is no good reason why the seats in our school-houses should not be more comfortable than those in our churches. This general rule of comfort would preclude the use of seats without backs of suitable form. The spines of children have often become distorted from lack of support while sitting in the school-room. The sufferings which those little frames have undergone would cast in the shade the horrors of the "middle passage."

Third: The seats should be graded to the different sizes of pupils. This principle is often practically violated, and school-rooms are provided with seats all of the same size. In consequence, either the larger pupils are seated much too low for comfort, or the smaller ones are perched so high that their feet cannot touch the floor, and they are obliged to maintain a constant watchfulness lest they should fall from their dizzy eminence. With this latter class, "to sit" becomes an exceedingly active verb, and restlessness, aches, and distortions often result.

Fourth: They should be constructed so as to afford accommodation to the pupil and to all his educational apparatus. A shelf should be provided for packing away books, slates, maps, etc., and a permanent inkstand, to prevent the frequent injury and disfigurement resulting from overturning the ink.

Fifth: They should be neatly finished, so as to be ornamental as well as useful. In this case beauty serves the strictly utilitarian purpose of protecting from injury as well as a higher and perhaps more important one. The rude furniture of the olden time was soon covered with ink-spots, cuts, and scratches innumerable. Elaborate jack-knife carvings overlaid each other every term, until the original form and complexion was entirely obliterated. Whenever poorly made or unpainted furniture is used, a like result must follow. Well-finished and elegant furniture, on the contrary, has often been in constant use for years, without receiving a single scratch, the beauty preserving it, as well as serving to inculcate habits of order and carefulness. School furniture should be finished like fine cabinet-work.

In their arrangement the seats and desks should be so placed that each pupil can freely pass to and from his seat without disturbing others, and so that every part of the room is accessible to both pupil and teacher.

To meet all these requirements, single or double desks are generally used. The former are preferable on many accounts, but as they are more costly and occupy more room than the latter, they will probably not come into general use. Double desks answer all the demands of education, are more economical, and will therefore be usually adopted. In the seating of all the designs in this work the double desk has been used, and all calculations in regard to the number of pupils which each room will accommodate have been made with reference to them.

DIRECTIONS FOR CONSTRUCTING DESKS.

Clear, well-seasoned, hard wood, like birch, or cherry, or ash, or Connecticut Valley and Canada chestnut, second growth, is the best material of which to construct desks, as it is firm and solid, and readily admits of a beautiful finish. Desks made of pine or other soft wood are too easily scratched and damaged.

Double desks should be three feet to four feet long, and from ten to twenty inches wide, depending on the size of the pupils to be accommodated.

All edges and corners should be carefully rounded, and all the work should be smoothed and well finished.

About two and one-half inches of the farther side of the top should be level, and the rest slightly inclined.

A groove should extend across the level surface to prevent pencils, etc., from rolling off, and provision should be made for the insertion of a permanent inkstand. An opening in the farther edge has been sometimes made for the purpose of receiving a slate, but of late this arrangement has been abandoned, as no practical good results, and the appearance of the room is injured.

About five inches below the top of the desk a shelf should be placed, two-thirds as wide as the top, and slightly inclined backward.

The standard that supports the desk may be wood or iron, and the peculiar manner of constructing each will be fully illustrated in the diagrams found in the Appendix. Wood is cheaper, but iron more durable and less liable to get out of repair.

A modern style of seat and desk is made to fold up, to

allow free passage between the desks, to permit pupils to rise immediately in their places, and to afford a better opportunity for sweeping. This desk will be more particularly described hereafter.

The following table shows the height of the seats and desks of the different grades as adopted by most of the school-furniture manufacturers :

			Height of Desk.	*Width of Desk.*	*Height of Seat.*
(1) Children's Desk	and	Settee	18 in.	10½ in.	9½ in.
(2) Small Primary	"	"	20 "	10½ "	11 "
(3) Primary	"	"	22½ "	12 "	12 "
(4) Intermediate	"	"	25 "	15 "	13½ "
(5) Grammar School	"	"	26½ "	15 "	15 "
(6) High School	"	"	27½ "	15 "	16½ "
(7) Academic	"	"	29½ "	15 "	17 "

The desk height is measured at *front*—back edge should be one and a half inches higher. Seat height is measured at *front*—pitch of seat should be one and a quarter inches.

Lengths of desks to seat two pupils of the Primary and Intermediate grades should be three feet, and for the higher grades they should be three feet and six inches. Too much care cannot be taken to avoid having the seats too high. This is a common fault, and is very injurious to children.

In the Supplement to this volume we shall give elaborate illustrated descriptions of the best modern school-furniture.

CHAPTER IX.

APPARATUS.

In country districts the opinion is quite too frequently entertained that when a school-house has been constructed and furnished with seats sufficient to accommodate the pupils, nothing more is needed to insure the success of the school. The necessity and importance of apparatus, for the purpose of establishing facts and illustrating principles, is so little understood and appreciated that the majority of schools are as destitute of these appliances of instruction as though no advance had been made for the last hundred years.

On the other hand, teachers, and sometimes trustees, with more zeal than discretion, purchase indiscriminately everything that offers in the form of apparatus, and so waste money in useless articles. It is a mistaken notion that a large amount of costly apparatus is necessary to the success of a school. In our academic institutions quantities of different articles are frequently found which have cost large sums of money, and are useless from not being complete or from misuse and neglect.

These extremes are to be avoided. No money should be wasted in the purchase of useless articles in incomplete sets, but the things essential should always be furnished. Fortunately most of the indispensable apparatus is inexpensive and within the reach of all. The ingenious teacher will usually explain and illustrate his lessons by the aid of such common things as can be readily obtained. He can also do an excellent work by so presenting the subject that the pupils themselves will be induced to make their own experiments with apparatus of their own devising.

GENERAL APPARATUS.

Blackboards.—The first article of general apparatus indispensable in every school-room is a blackboard. There is scarcely a single exercise in the school but may be made more clear and interesting by the use of the blackboard and chalk. With it large classes are taught with as much facility as individuals are without it, and there is not a moment in the day when its aid may not be required to elucidate some difficult point, or to teach to the eye what the mind does not distinctly comprehend through the avenue of the ear. A teacher who understands drawing can make it compensate in a great measure for the lack of almost every other kind of apparatus. We look upon the blackboard as a school-house fixture almost as important as the roof or foundation-stones; and in this age of the world there is scarcely a corner of the country so benighted where an effort would be made to dispense with its use.

The blackboards should be sufficient in number and in size to permit all the members of an ordinary class to work at the same time. They should be about five feet wide, placed two feet above the floor, and should extend entirely around the walls of the rooms. A trough should always be placed beneath the board to catch the dust and to serve as a shelf for chalk and wipers. In all the designs given in this work, the blackboard surface has been intended to occupy all the available space not taken up by doors and windows. The very best and cheapest blackboard surface is made by applying the Eureka Liquid Slating to a thoroughly well made and smooth hard-finished wall. Care should be taken to have a firm, substantial, smooth, and dry wall. The Rival Liquid Slating answers about the same purpose and is somewhat cheaper. In the Supplement will be found descriptions of blackboards and all the necessary accessories.

Globes.—The next indispensable article of general apparatus is a globe. Without a globe a teacher cannot succeed in explaining to the comprehension of children the peculiarities of the earth upon which they live, or the ordinary phenomena resulting from the earth's shape and motions. With its aid he can accomplish all this, and can also clearly illustrate and define such geographical terms as children very seldom understand, and can correct errors which almost inevitably result from the exclusive use of maps. A comparatively small and cheap globe, with the full outline of the natural divisions of the earth, will answer in the absence of one of the larger and more expensive globes.

APPARATUS FOR PRIMARY SCHOOLS.

That facts must precede principles, and that the object of primary instruction should be mainly to awaken the attention and develop the powers of observation, is beginning to be fully recognized by modern educators. The old system of commencing the process of instruction by forcing children to learn mere abstractions, is well-nigh exploded. It is now considered by all who have given much attention to this subject, that it is much more important that a child should be able to observe all that he sees, hears, or feels, than that he should be able to repeat by rote all the text-books used in the school. In cultivating the powers of perception and observation, it is much more effectual to speak to the eye than to the ear; and by children, experiments and ocular demonstrations are much more easily comprehended than any statement of principles or processes of logical reasoning.

To carry out a system founded upon these principles, it will be necessary to change the course of instruction at present adopted for our primary classes, and to furnish our rooms with such tangible objects as will convey important lessons, and furnish the proper foundation for a philosophical course of education. Nature has furnished these objects of sense in lavish profusion, and there is no district in the country too poor to have a bountiful supply of them. But here the labor of the teacher is indispensable, for nature never betrays her secrets unless they are sought for, and the minds of children need directing until they are sufficiently developed to investigate and experiment without aid.

We might, with propriety, denominate this system of instruction, "The education of the senses by means of lessons drawn from real objects." To make it at once intelligible and practical, we will examine it under the following heads, viz.:

FORM.—Almost the first thing that the child perceives and comprehends is difference in form, and the primary room should be furnished with a great quantity of apparatus to illustrate these differences. Forms very dissimilar should first be taken, and the pupils should be gradually introduced to those more nearly alike, until they are able to accurately discriminate between those that have but very slight differences. They will always be interested in these exercises, as the idea is taught through the sense of sight, and can be fully comprehended without any reasoning process. Care should be taken to insure perfect accuracy of observation during every step of this process, and the scientific names should be given to each of the different forms. Apparatus for the teaching of form might consist, 1st, of blocks representing geometric solids; 2d, different specimens of the animal kingdom; 3d, the different forms of the stalks, leaves, and seeds of plants; and 4th, of the different forms assumed by minerals and crystals.

The use of the geometric solids will introduce the facts and first principles of geometry; and where that science is taken up as a study, the pupil will be already familiar with the terms used, and will look upon it as an old friend rather than a new acquaintance. The inspection of the different specimens of the animal kingdom will excite an interest in the subject of natural history, and the transition would be easy from an observation of the forms of animals to that of their habits and peculiarities. The examination of the forms of plants, while exceedingly interesting in itself, and presenting a great variety of useful information, will lead directly to the study of botany, in which is enfolded the whole science of the vegetable kingdom. To understand the peculiar forms of minerals and crystals requires a higher development of the powers of observation and a more mature judgment; but the subject can be easily taught if rightly presented, and the pupil will at once become interested in mineralogy. By this system the child, in time, will become perfectly familiar with all kinds of forms, and will be able to accurately describe the shape of anything that he sees.

SIZE.—Nearly the same objects that are used to illustrate form may also be used to illustrate size, and the results will be nearly the same. At this stage there should be introduced the conventional standards of measure, and the pupils should be taught the tables of measure practically and inductively. The apparatus necessary would consist of an inch, foot, and yard rule for long measure, blocks representing a square inch and foot for square measure, cubical blocks for solid measure, and a variety of measures, like gill, pint, and quart cups, gallon, peck, and bushel measures, etc.

The tables should then be taught in the following manner: An inch measure is put into the hands of a child, and he is required to draw a line upon the blackboard just as long as the measure, then to the end of this he is to add another inch, and repeat the process till he has drawn a line twelve inches in length. He is then instructed to call this whole measure a foot; and with a foot as a basis, he can then measure a yard, rod, etc. So with each one of the measures, take the least denomination as a basis, and teach its name, use, and the number of times it is to be taken to make one of the next higher denomination before the name of that denomination is given. A box or barrel of clean sand should be furnished to experiment with in the measures of capacity. After becoming acquainted with the denominations and tables of measure in this practical manner, the pupils should be encouraged to continually apply their knowledge in the measurement of everything within their reach. They might measure the dimensions of the school-house, the lengths of the neighboring fence rails and posts; and in time they might measure the distance from the school-room to their respective homes, and the distance around farm lots, thus taking the first practical lessons in surveying.

WEIGHT.—The difference in the weight of objects should next be considered. In this, as in form and size, almost every natural object, from the pebbles in the street to the most delicate organization, can be used for illustrations and experiments. Conventional weights and the tables should also be introduced, and a balance should be procured as an article of apparatus. The pupils should be taught the denominations inductively, as in the tables of measure; and they should experiment, by weighing everything in the balance, and lifting it to judge of its weight, until the muscles would be educated to determine the weight of any object with a considerable degree of accuracy.

COLOR.—The differences in the color of objects should receive early attention, and every school-room should be furnished with apparatus illustrating the primary colors, the intermediate shades, and the neutral tints. In all the seasons but winter, objects illustrating all the endless varieties of shades of color may be obtained from among leaves and flowers; and by their aid not only would the senses be educated, but a taste for the beautiful would be cultivated.

ORDER.—Order can be systematically taught by the use of objects already enumerated. Every variety of thing may be classified in regard to form, size, weight, and color, and each class may be put in its appropriate place. Exercises of this kind will cultivate habits of external order, and will lay the foundation of that systematic arrangement of ideas indispensable to the highest progress in science and art.

A child thus trained to habits of observation will see and hear much more than one educated in a different manner; and when are added habits of critical investigation into the origin, uses, relations, and causes of things, there is little more to accomplish. He will then be able to enter into a series of original and independent examinations, and he can see

> "Books in the running brooks,
> Sermons in stones, and good in everything."

There is not an object in all art or nature but for him will have its lessons of wisdom.

CABINET.—A cabinet of curiosities and common things should be collected to form a never-failing reservoir of objects from which important lessons may be derived. This cabinet should contain specimens of the different metals, such as iron, lead, copper, tin, and zinc; of the principal minerals which enter into the composition of the rocks, such as quartz, mica, hornblende, limestone, and gypsum; of the most common chemical products, such as salt, saltpetre, copperas, alum, and soda; of all the minerals in the neighborhood, such as pebbles, fragments of the rocks, clay, sand, and especially such rocks as contain fossils; of the vegetable world, consisting of the leaves and flowers of all the plants and trees of the vicinity; the different kinds of wood, both with and without bark; the different grains, like corn, wheat, rye, oats, barley, and rice; other articles of food, like sago, tapioca, Irish moss, capers, etc.; and the different articles for household use, like flax, hemp, cotton, gums, spices, and fruits; of the products of the sea, such as shells, sponges, coral, whalebone, and a great variety of other articles; of the most common animal products, such as wool, hair, wax, bones, ivory, etc.; and of manufactured articles, as silk, linen and cotton fabrics, leather, paper, parchment, crockery, porcelain and glass ware, and, indeed, everything used in the domestic arts and in common household operations.

The lessons to be derived from the specimens of the metals and minerals might include an examination of their peculiar properties and qualities: how the members of the different classes differ from each other; where they are obtained, the process of obtaining them, and the agents necessary to effect this object; their relative value, and their several uses in the economy of the world and in science and art. The examination of vegetable and animal products would include the peculiarities of organization, the conditions of life and growth, the geographical distribution of plants and animals, their origin and history, a description of the processes of both nature and art in collecting and preparing them, and their uses to the world. The lessons to be derived from manufactured goods would lead to the examination of still higher subjects, and would include much of geography, history, mechanics, chemistry, and the like. It will be seen that in every school there can be collected a cabinet of this kind at little or no expense, which will furnish an inexhaustible fund of information, requiring only an intelligent teacher to elucidate and make it available.

Slates.—Besides the articles which have here been enumerated, each pupil in a primary room should be provided with a slate. This will afford unfailing amusement, and the pupil, if properly instructed, can acquire by its aid the first rudiments of drawing. There is scarcely an exercise in the school in which it cannot be used to advantage, and it becomes a source of great relief to a child from the wearisome monotony of a school day. Slates with attachments containing drawing and writing lessons have lately been prepared, and are most excellent for use in primary rooms. It is very desirable that slates should be supplied with rubber corners, to prevent noise and scratching of desks.

PAPER SLATES.—In many respects the paper slates lately introduced into our schools are a great improvement. They are light, noiseless, and not easily broken. They can be shut up and carried inside of a book, and in almost every particular they are more convenient than the stone slate. It is also claimed for them that they are tolerably durable and comparatively cheap.

PLAYTHINGS.—The primary room should also be supplied with a variety of articles properly termed "playthings." These might consist of dissected maps, objects for counting, blocks, and a great variety of things of like character. Blocks four inches long, two inches wide, and one inch thick, would perhaps be the most convenient of any for the building of houses and the like. All these should be arranged in a proper place, and the little children should be permitted to use them when tired of sitting still, or when not engaged in specific school duties. There is scarcely anything that the intelligent teacher may not make available to amuse, interest, and instruct his pupils.

CARDS.—A great variety of cards are now prepared for the use of schools, and many of them are valuable. The alphabet, the elementary sounds of the language, and the elements of reading may be profitably taught by the use of cards. The classification of science and of natural history may also be taught in a similar manner, and in nearly every branch of instruction cards may be made useful.

PICTURES.—In objective teaching, when the object itself cannot be obtained, pictures are indispensable. They convey instruction through the eye as well as the ear. Geographical and historical information especially can be illustrated and made instructive by the use of well-selected pictures.

The appearance of natural scenery, such as mountains, glaciers, rocky ravines, volcanoes, cataracts, tropical fruits, and a great number of other things of like character, can be understood better through pictorial illustrations than through elaborate descriptions. Pictures should be chosen with care, and such only taken for use as represent something important. In the study of natural history pictures become indispensable, for scarcely any idea of the peculiar shape and appearance of animals can be gained from mere description. In selecting pictures for schools, avoid the coarse, cheap lithographs of the shops, for they will have a tendency to deprave taste rather than elevate it.

STEREOSCOPIC VIEWS.—A series of stereoscopic views would be of the greatest value in teaching many branches now imperfectly taught or entirely neglected. A few characteristic views of the natural features of each country, of works of art, and of the costumes of the people, would give more accurate and vivid geographical knowledge than can be obtained from any verbal description. The principles of architecture and of natural science can be illustrated in the same manner, and the driest of studies can be made interesting.

NUMERICAL FRAME.—A small frame, known as the "numerical frame," consisting of ten rows of little balls, and ten balls in each row, strung upon wires, on which they move easily, is a valuable auxiliary to the teacher in giving instruction in the first principles of numbers. The simple rules of arithmetic, and many things of a more complicated character, can be readily illustrated by it, and the whole class can be instructed at once.

SPECIAL APPARATUS.

MAPS.—Every school-room should be supplied with a map of the town, county, and State in which it is situated, as well as with the maps representing the grand divisions of the globe. The first real knowledge of geography is derived from those objects in nature which are known to the pupil, and this is followed by making a map of this known portion of the earth. From the special map the pupil becomes familiar with maps in general, and is able to understand the relative position of places. For use in the school-room, outline maps, in which physical features are represented by color, and political divisions by faint outlines, are much to be preferred to those that contain names in full. Maps or charts upon which is given a map and a picture of each of the natural divisions of land and water, are of great value in primary schools.

CHARTS.—Variety is rest. The active-minded pupil finds relief from study, not in blank idleness, but in seeing and thinking about something else, something different from the arithmetic or grammar of which he is weary. As affording the best available material for turning this necessary diversion of mind into recreative study, charts make the most appropriate as well as most useful decorations that can be introduced into the school-room. They relieve the dead blankness of naked walls, and instruct while they adorn. Silent yet entertaining, they are the most efficient helps that the teacher can call around him. Affording legitimate relief from study, they prevent the pupil's activity from overflowing into illegitimate courses, as mischief; thus they are aids to discipline as well as instructors. No room is complete *as a school-room* without them.

Philosophical apparatus.—Much costly apparatus has been prepared for illustrating principles of natural philosophy, which may be very good in its way; but from its costliness is beyond the reach of country school-districts. Almost every necessary experiment can be performed with articles that the teacher can procure at little or no expense. For example, the mechanical powers can be illustrated by such machinery as can be obtained at any farm-house. The lever, the compound lever, the pulley, the wheel and axle, the inclined plane, the wedge and the screw, are all easily obtained. The common steelyard and a couple of pulley-blocks, a wheel or two from an old clock and a wooden screw, which can be procured at any carpenter's shop, are all that are really necessary for this purpose. Hydrostatics and hydraulics can also be illustrated by apparatus equally simple. A few tin tubes or bits of lead pipe, and vessels of wood or tin will do, if the teacher has zeal and a little genius. We have not space for all the details of the use of common things in the illustration of principles; but will close by repeating that all necessary experiments can be made by the use of apparatus that is cheap and within the reach of all.

Miscellaneous.—The following articles would be found useful and convenient: a tellurian to illustrate the revolutions of the earth and its relation to the sun and moon, the changes of the seasons, the phenomena of day and night, the ebb and flow of the tides; a magnet and small galvanic battery, to illustrate magnetism and electricity; and an orrery to show the relative size of each of the planets in the solar system, the periods of their revolution, and their respective distances from the sun. A few lenses and mirrors, plane, concave, and convex, and a prism, which can be procured at little cost, are desirable to assist in simplifying the abstruse subject of optics.

The school should always be supplied with fixtures to make the apparatus available, and to preserve it from injury. Hooks should be placed upon the walls, upon which maps and charts may be suspended, and pointers should be provided for recitations upon maps and blackboards. A closet should be provided for preserving the apparatus when not in use.

Fig. 88.

CHAPTER X.

OUT-BUILDINGS.

The general form and location of all the out-buildings necessary to a school have already been described, and nothing more need be added in regard to the porch, wood-house, etc. Privies have also been briefly noticed, but, in consequence of a general apathy upon this subject, we devote this entire chapter to the further consideration of their character, location, and arrangement.

Fig. 89.

We are fully persuaded that, in consequence of a culpable neglect in this direction, all efforts for the improvement of the social and moral condition of our schools are, in a great measure, neutralized, and that from the same source arises much of the disinclination that parents have to sending their children to the public schools.

In some districts, even at the present day, there is no privy! The following extract from the annual report of Hon. John C. Spencer, Superintendent of the Common Schools of New York, to the Legislature, in 1840, very forcibly shows the folly, wickedness, and brutality of this practice:

"A man who should build a good dwelling-house, but provide no place for retirement when performing the most private offices of nature, would be thought to give the clearest evidence of a coarse and brutal mind. Yet respectable parents allow their children to go to a school where this is the case, and where the evil is greatly aggravated by the fact that numbers of both sexes are collected, and that, too, at an age of extreme levity, and when the youthful mind is prone to the indulgence of a prurient imagination. Says one of the school visitors, 'In most cases in this town the scholars, male and female, are turned promiscuously and simultaneously into the public highway, without the shelter of so much as a *stump* for a covert to the calls of nature. The baneful effects of this barbarous custom on the young and pliant sensibilities are truly lamentable.'"

The Superintendent of the Common Schools of Connecticut, in 1850, holds the following language: "An appalling chapter might be written on the evils, the almost inevitable results of neglecting to provide these indispensable appendages to school-houses in our State. Who can duly estimate the final consequences of the first shock given to female delicacy from the necessary exposure to which the girls in the public schools are inevitably subjected; and what must be the legitimate results of these frequent exposures during the school-going years of youth? What quenchless fires of passion have been kindled within the bosoms of the young of both sexes by these exposures; fires that have raged to the consuming of personal happiness, to the prevention of scholastic improvement, and to the destruction of personal character? Again, what disgust has been created in both sexes by not having the appropriate retirements which nature imperiously demands? And, finally, may not the disinclination, the aversion of large numbers of families, of mothers especially, to sending their daughters to the public schools, have been created by the sufferings they themselves have endured from the above cause; and an unwillingness to subject the delicacy of their daughters to the obnoxious trial?"

The evils here so vividly and truthfully pointed out are not confined to the districts where no privies are built, but they apply in an almost equal degree to country districts where there is only one small, mere apology for a privy. In a majority of cases, a slight building, made of rough boards, is erected, of such a character that it answers no purpose of privacy, and is only useful as a very poor and inadequate screen. It is usually situated directly upon the highway, in close proximity to the school-house, and is completely exposed to public observation. Only one building is furnished for the accommodation of the two sexes, so that there can be no surety that the delicacy of young girls will not be outraged by the contact of grossness and brutality. Again, it is usually built with a very shallow vault, with no conveniences and no guards against abuses, and it soon becomes the most offensive and disgusting object in itself that it is possible to conceive, and a positive nuisance to the school and neighborhood. We believe that the picture here given of the condition of our country districts, and the evils resulting from that condition, are not overdrawn, and that they are of such a character as to demand immediate attention.

In arranging privies for a school, the following principles should always be observed. They should be commodious, and constructed so as to avoid offensive odors. They should be placed at a sufficient distance, so that they could never become offensive to the school. They should be screened from public observation. It will be seen at once that a school-lot is necessary to afford a decent location for a privy. As long as school-buildings are erected in the street, or upon a lot large enough to contain only the school-house, it will be impossible to bring about reform. There can be no place protected from observation, or where the building itself will not constantly be liable to abuses. In a lot containing an acre, the school-house should be placed in its centre, and a high, tight board fence should extend from the centre of the rear of the building to the farther edge of the lot, dividing the rear yard into two parts. The privies should be situated near the centre of the back part of the re-

Fig. 90.

spective yards, carefully guarded by screens of wood, or by living hedge. They should be supplied with large, well-stoned vaults, at least six feet deep. If possible, a drain should lead from the vault to a distance, and a stream of running water should be permitted to flow through it. The buildings themselves should be well plastered and painted, and finished in the same general style of architecture as the school-house. The seats should be provided with lids hung with butts, and all the walls should be left hollow, opening into a ventilating chimney above to carry off the gases. The plaster should be left very rough, and a heavy coat of coarse sand should be mixed with the paint to render scribbling and obscene figures impossible.

Great care should be taken to so construct the seats that defilement becomes almost impossible. In this matter, however, reference need only be made to that provided for boys, because girls' privies are seldom abused in this way. Besides the lids hung with butts, which should be placed in all privies, in that of the boys a strong brace of plank should be firmly affixed to the frame of the building, so that the covers cannot be opened beyond an angle of sixty degrees, thus rendering it impossible to stand upon the seat. Fig. 91 represents a privy suitable for the girls' yard. It consists of one apartment, furnished with the requisite number of seats. The size of the building must depend upon the size of the school. This building should be neatly finished and painted.

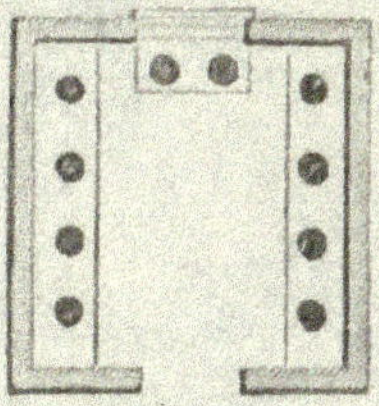
Fig. 91.

The privy for the boys is more troublesome. The difficulty of keeping them clean is well known to every teacher. We apprehend that this trouble arises principally from the fact that urinals are not provided, and consequently the seats are often wet, and thus rendered unfit to sit upon. Fig. 92 represents a privy for boys, arranged to guard against this evil. It is fourteen feet by ten feet, and divided into two apartments by a close partition. The part A is supplied with seats separated by partitions; and the part B with a trough, divided into stalls by partitions, in a manner similar to A. This arrangement is such that there cannot be the slightest

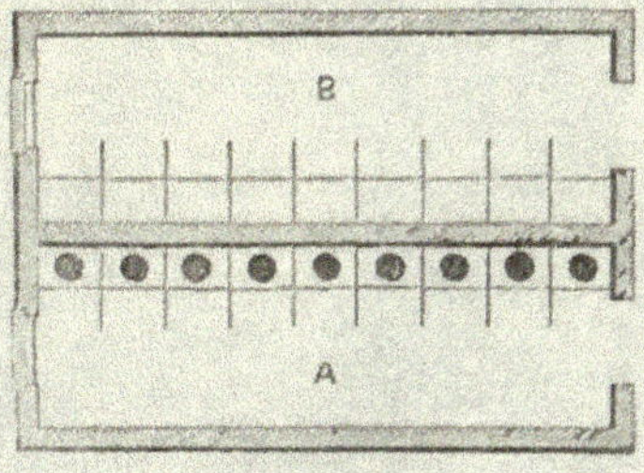

Fig. 92.

excuse for any abuse of any part of the building, and teachers would have very little difficulty in keeping it scrupulously neat, and free from every kind of defilement and injury.

Locks should be placed upon all the doors of privies, so that they cannot be entered except during hours when the teacher can have them under his own personal supervision. When privies are thus perfectly constructed, the teacher should always be held responsible for keeping them in good order. He can do this very easily by personally inspecting the buildings every day, and promptly noticing the very first violation of the rules of decency. Thus the teacher may accomplish a great good, by teaching habits of decency and modesty, and by repressing all exhibitions of grossness. He may also inculcate important hygienic laws in this connection, which will be of the greatest importance to the pupil through life. It is the custom of many excellent teachers, principals of some of our most noted union schools, to frequently look into the privy while the boys are in it, thus rendering the abuse very difficult, and its detection almost certain. In this way all the out-buildings of the school are kept as fastidiously neat as those connected with our best dwellings. Let all interested in schools contrast such a state of things with that usually found in country districts, and decide whether the advantages gained would not outweigh the expense incurred.

CHAPTER XI.

ARRANGING AND ORNAMENTING GROUNDS.

Ample school-grounds are needed for a great variety of purposes; and when the philosophy of instruction shall be fully understood, large yards will be considered indispensable as affording opportunities for physical exercise, and for displaying the beauties of nature. Physical education is now too often neglected, and, indeed, the circumstances and surroundings of the majority of our schools are such that a regular course of physical discipline is impossible. The necessity and importance of exercise are forcibly expressed in the following extract from the *Family Gymnasium*, by Dr. Trall:

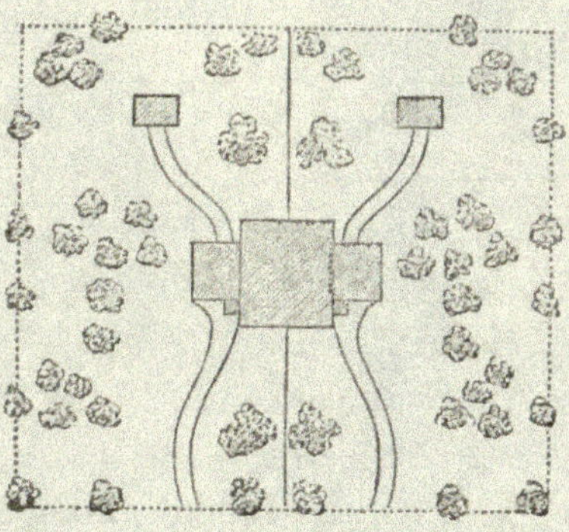

Fig. 93.

"It is as natural for a child to exercise as to breathe. When unrestrained, nearly all children are distinguished for restless activity. Nature bids them exercise, and they obey the mandate, often in spite of ignorant parents, nurses, and teachers, who scold and whip them for restlessness. Teachers are often more disposed to consult their own convenience than to study the laws of nature as applicable to their young charge; and, by dint of praising quietness and blaming activity, the poor child's nature is smothered; and pale cheeks, diminutive muscular development, weakness, dyspepsia, consumption, and death are the fruits of the oft-repeated command, 'Keep quiet.'

"Exercise is as essential to development as air is to life. No person can acquire a large, compact, muscular organization without it.

"'But you would not have girls run and romp over hill and dale, and laugh boisterously, like boys?' Let us examine the subject, and see what Nature, the great teacher, will say concerning it. Do young female animals frisk, jump, and play like males? and do little girls instinctively laugh loudly, and run and play like boys? If so, we may safely infer that Nature has established the same general law of exercise—not for animals merely, but for both sexes of the human race.

"Rousseau observes: 'If you wish to develop the mind of a pupil, develop the power which mind has to govern—exercise his body, make him healthy and strong, that you may make him prudent and reasonable.'

"Systematic gymnastic exercises, which give energy and precision to muscular movements, are not only useful in the development of bodily vigor, but are also efficient auxiliaries in mental education by inducing habits of order, exactness, and directness in the mental operations."

To render this systematic exercise possible, there must be considerable space; and it will be seen that this space is not designed for mere amusements, but in reality becomes one of the most important educational auxiliaries. The ground devoted to play and exercise should be free from obstructions, and hence trees, flower-beds, etc., would be out of place in that portion of the school-yard. Different kinds of gymnastic apparatus should be provided for these yards, so as to give variety to exercise, and to develop every muscle of the body. Teachers should understand the science and art of physical development, so as to be able to encourage the adoption of such plays as will be most likely to secure the desired result.

Having made the best possible disposition of the school-buildings, and secured the desired open spaces for play-grounds, the subject next to consider is that of "ornament." While answering strictly utilitarian purposes, the whole grounds may be so arranged as to become educational influences; first, by being attractive to the pupils; second, by affording them constant pleasure during their school-days; and third, by cultivating in them a taste for the beautiful in nature. For the purposes of ornament, trees are at once the most beautiful and the most enduring. They can be procured at a very trifling cost, wherever school-houses are built, and, unlike most of things connected with schools, they increase in value and beauty each successive year, nature assuming the cost, and lavishing upon them her rarest beauties of color and form. A. J. Downing, the great lover of nature, in his work upon "Landscape Gardening," thus speaks of trees, and of their influence upon the mind:

"A tree, undoubtedly, is one of the most beautiful objects in nature. Airy and delicate in its youth, luxuriant and majestic in its prime, venerable and picturesque in its old age, it constitutes in its various forms, sizes, and developments, the greatest charm and beauty of the earth in all countries. The most varied outline of surface, the finest combination of picturesque materials, the stateliest country house would be comparatively tame and spiritless without the inimitable accompaniment of foliage. Let those who have passed their whole lives in a richly-wooded country—whose daily visions are of deep, leafy glens, forest-clad hills, and plains luxuriantly shaded—transport themselves for a moment to the desert, where but a few stunted bushes raise their heads above the earth; or to those wild steppes where the eye wanders in vain for some 'leafy garniture'—where the sun strikes down with parching heat, or the wind sweeps over with unbroken fury, and they may, perhaps, estimate, by contrast, their beauty and value.

"Wood, in its many shapes, is then one of the greatest sources of interest and character in landscapes. Variety, which we need scarcely allude to as a fertile source of beauty, is created in a wonderful degree by a natural arrangement of trees. To a pile of buildings, or even of ruins, to a group of rocks or animals, they communicate new life and spirit, by their irregular outlines, which by partially concealing some portions, and throwing others into stronger light, contribute greatly to produce intricacy and variety, and confer an expression which, without these latter qualities, might, in a great measure, be wanting. By shutting out some parts and inclosing others, they divide the extent embraced by the eye into a hundred different landscapes, instead of one tame scene bounded by the horizon.

"The different seasons of the year, too, are inseparably connected in our minds with the effects produced by them on woodland scenery. Spring is joyous and enlivening to us, as nature then puts on her fresh livery of green, and the trees bud and blossom with a renewed beauty that speaks with a mute and gentle eloquence to the heart. In summer they offer us a grateful shelter under their umbrageous arms and leafy branches, and whisper unwritten music to the passing breeze. In autumn we feel a melancholy thoughtfulness as

'We stand among the falling leaves,'

and gaze upon their dying glories. And in winter we see in them the silent rest of nature, and behold in their leafless sprays and seemingly dead limbs an annual type of that deeper mystery—the deathless sleep of all being.

"By the judicious employment of trees, we may effect the greatest alterations and improvements within the scope of landscape gardening. Buildings which are tame, insipid, or even mean in appearance, may be made interesting, and even picturesque, by a proper disposition of trees. Edifices, or parts of them, that are unsightly, or which it is desirable partly or wholly to conceal, can readily be hidden or improved by wood; and walks and roads, which otherwise would be but simple ways of approach from one point to another, are, by an elegant arrangement of trees on their margin, or adjacent to them, made the most interesting and pleasing portions of the residence."

There is an opportunity for the exercise of a great diversity of tastes, both in selecting and in arranging trees for ornamenting school-grounds. In selecting, the following principles should be taken as guides: First, such trees should be chosen as will harmonize with the general features of the landscape. For example: in a hilly or very broken region the tall, spiry-topped trees, like the pine, fir, spruce, and hemlock, would be in keeping with the natural scenery, but upon a wide, extended plain, they would appear comparatively mean and incongruous. The round-topped and symmetrical trees, like the oak, maple, and beech, are much better adapted to the quiet scenery of a level region than to the irregular outlines of a rough, mountainous surface. Second, the different varieties of trees selected should harmonize with each other. Although a variety is always desirable, yet the different kinds chosen for any given spot or group should be somewhat similar in shape, so as not to present too great a contrast. For example, a group consisting of a maple, beech, and oak would be harmonious, while one consisting of a Lombardy poplar, weeping-willow, and fir would be incongruous.

For different purposes, also, different trees are to be chosen. Some are selected to border an avenue or path, and some for mere shade; some are to be placed singly, and some disposed in groups; and different varieties of trees are particularly adapted to each case. For single trees, where there is to be left sufficient space for their entire expansion, in a level or moderately hilly region, there is no tree in grace or beauty can surpass the drooping elm. The maple is a noble tree, and is admirably adapted for either a situation as a single tree, or as a member of a group. The oak and chestnut are among the largest and noblest of all our trees, and either may be taken for the central object of a group. The weeping-willow appears best as a single tree, and in a level tract of country. The spruce, hemlock, ash, and beech, from our common forests, all make beautiful shade trees. Among other shade trees that can be easily procured in some sections of the country are the horse-chestnut, locust, and hickory, the magnolia and cottonwood of the Southern States, and the buckeye and black walnut of the West. The soft maple is highly valued as an ornamental tree, on account of its red blossoms of early spring, its dense green foliage in summer, and its beautiful

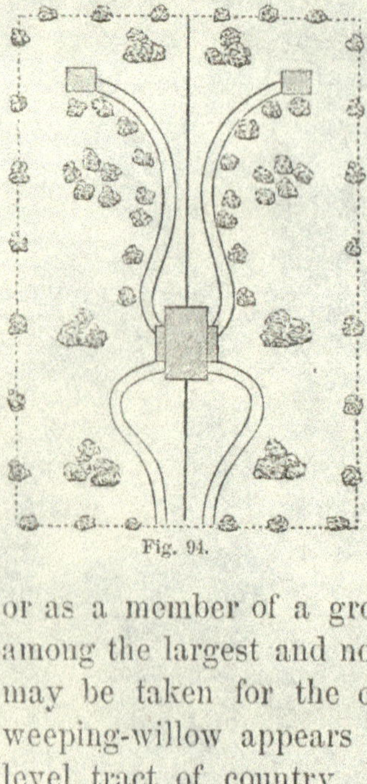

Fig. 94.

dress of deep crimson after the first frost of autumn. To conclude, there is scarcely a tree of our forests that would not become a beautiful ornament, if transplanted and nurtured with proper care.

The arrangement of trees should be the subject of careful study. They are usually set out in straight rows, without any regard to beauty of grouping, and effecting no result except that of furnishing shade. The stiff formality of their position goes far to destroy the effect of their beautiful outlines, and thus the most important objects of their culture are lost. When we bring into immediate contrast the stateliness and formality of an estate planted with trees in straight rows, with a natural landscape, with trees and groves promiscuously scattered over it, we can at once appreciate the immeasurably superior beauty of the latter scene over the former.

Trees should be planted singly or in groups. Single trees should be such as have a graceful and beautiful outline, and convey to the mind the feeling of completeness, as the drooping elm, weeping-willow, and horse-chestnut. Groups may consist of several kinds of trees, that are harmonious in character, planted so closely together that at a little distance they have the appearance of a single object. They should always be composed of one principal tree, larger and taller than the rest, with the others grouped around it as subordinates.

These single trees and groups should be so disposed about the school premises as not to interfere with the play-grounds, and at the same time to produce as great a variety as possible in the appearance of the landscape. If the situation is a fine one, openings should be left to afford views of distant objects, such as a lake, river, or mountain, all of which objects will appear much more beautiful seen through a vista, bounded by the shifting foliage and waving branches of the trees.

Shrubs that are commonly used for hedges should also be thickly planted in gracefully curved lines, in such a manner as to completely screen the approach to the out-buildings, and to cover up such portions of the buildings as should not be exposed to public gaze. Flowers might also be cultivated to a limited extent, but, as a general thing, they would not receive sufficient attention in our country districts to insure their successful culture.

School-grounds arranged in this manner would become great powers of refinement and important influences for good. When trees are once planted, the winds, the sun, and the rains carefully and assiduously nurture them, supplying their every want, and converting their puny stalks into giant forms, until

> "They stand massy, and tall, and dark,
> Fit shrine for humble worshipper to hold
> Communion with his Maker."

The first school impressions of childhood would be associated with their graceful outlines, the waving of their branches, and the struggling of light down through green leaves. Lessons of wisdom and beauty, which would endure forever, could be continually gathered from their trunks, their leaves, and their blossoms. The men that planted them would perform a work directly aiding in the elevation of humanity, and long after their forms have mouldered in the dust, whole generations of children would "rise up and call them blessed."

CHAPTER XII.

ARCHITECTURE AN EDUCATIONAL INFLUENCE.

ORDINARY use is not the only value of buildings. They may be so constructed as to appeal to the higher sentiments, and render important aid in developing the better and finer feelings of our nature. This is the proper province of architecture, and the work of the architect is to so fashion our buildings and arrange their details, that while they answer the purposes of their erection, they may, at the same time, satisfy that love of the beautiful, the symmetrical, and the harmonious.

Fig. 95.

In this country too little attention has yet been given to those things which elevate and refine. The entire energies of our people were early and exclusively devoted to subduing the wilderness and providing the necessaries of life. They could bestow no time on pursuits which did not directly conduce to the simplest ends of human existence. Consequently, their descendants are a prompt, resolute, and vigorous race. But the arts of refinement which were, at first, through absolute necessity, neglected, are now habitually despised or disregarded. No people on earth who have attained to an equal degree of intellectual and moral culture, evince so little taste and refinement.

We begin, however, to discern the dawning of a better day. We begin to feel that there are wants in our nature that are not to be satisfied by mere material appliances. We begin to appreciate the beautiful, and its influence in developing our higher powers. Evidences of this change of public sentiment may be found in the attention now paid to art, in the patronage bestowed upon artists, and in the improvement of the architecture of public buildings and private residences in many parts of the country. The results of this improved sentiment react upon the community, softening the sharp features of our national character, multiplying those little amenities which give grace, beauty, and dignity to our life, and even aiding to develop the Christian virtues of faith and charity.

Numerous and potent are the influences furnished by literature for the cultivation of the taste; but impressions more vivid and lasting may be made by the presentation to the senses of sublime or beautiful objects, such as natural scenery, landscape improved by art, and the best productions of sculpture, painting, and architecture.

Of the various influences which tend to mature and refine the taste, we have occasion, in this work, to refer only to those of architecture. The importance and necessity of this art to the great work of education we shall endeavor to show.

Fig. 96.

Architecture, primarily, deals only with forms which address the eye. It embodies ideas of proportion, symmetry, variety, harmony, and unity.

By Proportion is meant that due relation which should exist between the different dimensions of a building, in order to convey the idea of correctness. We frequently see buildings in which this principle is violated, and are pained at the want of taste so prominently displayed. Buildings too long for their height, too high for their length, or too wide for either, appear to be the "rule," rather than the "exception;" yet a well-proportioned structure is immediately and almost universally recognized as such, and cannot fail to afford general satisfaction and delight.

SYMMETRY requires a proper balance of parts. The regular placing of doors and windows, and the disposal of all the details, so that none shall seem out of place, are in obedience to this principle.

VARIETY is the opposite of monotony, and would induce us to relieve blank walls in some manner, and to break up long horizontal lines, so as to produce an agreeable effect, like that made by a diversified landscape, or a number of views in nature, each differing from the other. This would lead us also to obviate sameness in a range of buildings, and, within certain limits, to give diversity to details. It would forbid the erection of those vast square or oblong piles of brick and mortar, which now so frequently burden, without adorning, the face of the earth.

HARMONY may be defined as the limit of variety. It is that peculiar relation which all the parts should have to each other, producing in the mind a sense of completeness and adaptation. It allows no incongruities, and indulges in no conceits. Harmony in architecture, as in music, so arranges and blends the different parts, that each seems an indispensable element of a perfect whole.

UNITY refers to the evident design which pervades the structure; the one idea, which has not only harmonized the parts with each other, but adapted the whole to its uses. In accordance with this principle, while all the other laws of taste in architecture should be observed, they should be subordinated to the object of the construction.

As the mind becomes familiar with beautiful objects, and with the laws of beauty, its sensibility to moral excellence is cultivated, the manners are conformed to the principles of harmony, and the effects produced upon the whole man are of the most beneficial and lasting character. The influence ascribed by Plato, in his *Republic*, to a musical education, may be predicated with equal truth of a judicious culture in this department of art. It is essential, he says, "because it makes rhythm and harmony to settle deeply in the inner soul, and take strong hold of it, carrying with them comeliness, and making a man comely-minded. Also, because one so nurtured will have the quickest perception of all faults and imperfections in art or nature, and, regarding them with just aversion, will admire and love the beautiful. This he will receive with joy into his soul, will feed on it, and assimilate his own nature to its beauty, will learn to censure and hate deformity, *even in early youth, while yet incapable of understanding the reason why*, and when the reason comes, will embrace it gladly, as a familiar thing."

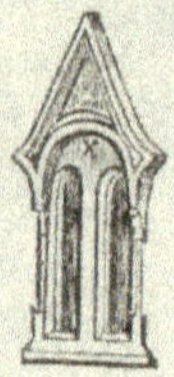
Fig. 97.

In those countries where architecture has reached its highest development, taste and refinement exert their greatest influence. As an instance of the refining effect of beautiful objects, the fact might be mentioned that, in many of the old countries, sculptured decorations in architecture have remained for ages uninjured, save by the elements; and that even after the edifices they once adorned have fallen into ruin, veneration seems to have shielded these trophies of art from profanation. In our more logical and practical communities, the destructive passion would be restrained by no such sentiment; and not twenty-four hours would elapse after an old building of celebrity had been abandoned, before fragments would be chipped off for mementoes, or pounded to pieces, to satisfy the analytical spirit of some ruthless traveller. Beauty of form, however, seems, in some measure, to afford protection. An old or mean-looking building, deserted or unoccupied, is a target for boys, and even for children of a larger growth; and every one feels an instinctive desire to rid the earth of such deformity. But a complete and beautiful structure generally enjoys a longer, if not an entire, exemption from injury. When taste is really and universally cultivated, there will be no danger of the wanton desecration of beautiful objects.

In the erection of every school-house particular care should be taken to observe the rules of taste as regards form. In our country districts, where a small and plain building only is demanded, we need to consider proportion and symmetry alone; the other principles of architecture applying chiefly to larger and more pretending structures. If this is done, if our school-houses all conform to these two fundamental laws, they cannot fail to become strong educational influences. The advantages of obeying the principles of architecture in the construction of school-houses may be summed up in a few words:

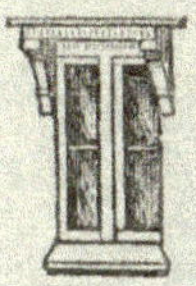

Fig. 98.

1. If the building is an object of beauty, the very sight of it inspires emotions of pleasure.

2. It adorns and beautifies the landscape of which it forms a part.

3. It becomes an attractive place to children, and does not repel them by its deformity.

4. It practically teaches ideas of proportion and symmetry, and new and exalted conceptions of beauty of form.

5. It throws over property the shield of beauty, and so checks, and finally eradicates the rudeness which is stimulated by deformity.

6. It forms one of those influences which have most power over the heart and affections, directly aiding the teacher in the most difficult and important part of his work.

Let this principle be remembered by all: "That school-houses, however small, should never be built without conforming to those general principles of taste which are universally recognized by cultivated people," so that if they do not exert a positive influence in elevating taste, at least they will have the negative excellence of not violating it. The work of education in those higher departments, which recognizes beauty both of form and morals, and the subtile and mysterious relations which exist between the two, at best, is an onerous and difficult one, and every external influence which assists in forwarding it becomes a positive benefit.

Fig. 99.

APPENDIX.

GRADED SCHOOLS.

The general consolidation of separate districts into town schools must give a renewed impulse to the building of school-houses. The supervision of schools passing into the hands of more experienced and thoughtful men cannot fail to exert a beneficial influence in this direction. The following extracts, from the report of the Hon. A. E. Rankin, Secretary of the Vermont Board of Education, in 1869, contain unanswerable arguments in favor of the abolishment of the old, isolated district system. Although designed specially for Vermont, the same arguments will apply to other parts of the country as well.

TOWN SYSTEM VERSUS DISTRICT SYSTEM.

While we strive assiduously so to economize as not to increase the expense of our educational system, we do not take proper pains that the money which is annually expended shall be so applied as to secure the largest return.

Let me enumerate some of the prominent obstacles which are in the way of the greater efficiency of our schools:

1. Total lack of or insufficient supervision.
2. Constant change of supervision.
3. Poorly qualified teachers.
4. Constant change of teachers.
5. Lack of interest in schools on the part of patrons.
6. Employment of relatives and favorites without regard to qualifications.
7. Too small schools in many districts.

8. Too short schools in small districts.
9. Employment of immature and incompetent teachers in small districts.
10. Poor school-houses.
11. Irregular attendance.
12. General lack of facilities to aid the teacher.
13. No schools at all in many districts.
14. Lack of proper classification.
15. Pupils study what they choose, and not what they ought.

These twice seven and one plagues of our common-school system will be recognized by every one who has had any experience in connection with the public schools of the State.

If it could be shown that this nest of evils which so impairs the efficiency of our schools could in some measure be removed by a radical change of system, no one surely would oppose such change. I am confident that these evils may in very great measure be alleviated by a change in our system of public schools. I believe that the adoption of what is called the *town system*, in contradistinction from the *district system*, would tend largely to diminish them.

I know there are obstacles in the way of the consummation of so desirable an end as the reduction of the number of schools. But if it can satisfactorily be shown that there can be not only a large saving in expense, but that our schools can be increased in efficiency, I doubt not these obstacles can be removed. Let us, in a somewhat general way, discuss some of the disadvantages which result from the present system.

Teachers understand how impossible it is to secure in a small school, or in a small class, that healthful and proper stimulus which is almost an incident to the large school or the large class. One who has himself ever been an entire class, or one of two or three constituting a class, will remember how difficult it was to create in himself any such measure of interest as would make the labor of preparation other than a dreary task. And this evil extends to the teacher as well as to the pupil. He, too, needs stimulus.

The small district fails to secure that aggregate of interest on the part of the inhabitants toward the school which is essential to make it successful. This aggregate of interest is the sum total ot individual interest. Five families have less interest in a school than have ten, ten less than fifteen, and so on. The teacher thus receives less stimulus from his surroundings in small than in large districts. So with the pupils.

A careful examination of the statute will disclose the fact that the duties imposed upon the school committee are the most important duties committed to the citizens of the State; that in their keeping are the highest interests of the State. Properly to discharge the duties of this office, one should possess high moral character, great natural endowments, large measure of mental discipline, an unusual degree of intelligence, good practical common sense, broad and liberal views, sound judgment, and a fervent love for the welfare of the State, quickened by the recognition of the fact that its permanence and security depend upon the efficiency of its schools.

Under the present system, the educational interests of the town are in the keeping of from thirty to one hundred officials, consisting of prudential committee, district clerks, the town clerk, and the superintendent. What town in the State can furnish this maximum number of men, competent to hold this important trust? How many of the two hundred and forty-three towns of the State could furnish the maximum number? How many could not furnish five men who, by native gifts and acquirements, are fitted for these duties?

Is not our present system defective in that it requires too many officers? The average number of individuals in each town, who are the school officers of the town, will be found to be from fifty to sixty, if we estimate three prudential committees to each district; the whole number of school officers in the State, something more than twelve thousand. Such an army ought to do the work well, we say. Yet, who does not believe that one-fifth the number would do it far better? This gives one school officer for every seven school children. What an absurdity! Who believes in this multiplicity of supervisors, which almost inevitably results in no supervision at all? Why not elect a board of selectmen, fifty in number? Who would care to live in a town thus supervised? Is it not that three men are found better than fifty, that three are elected? Six men competent for the duties of the school department of the town would be infinitely more efficient than fifty, even if it were possible to secure fifty men as competent as the six.

But this large number of school officers necessitates the selection of incompetent men, many of whom have little interest and less ability. The average ability of six of the best men of a town is, let us say, twice as great as the average ability of the best twelve, and four times as great as the average ability of the best twenty-four, and eight times as great as that of the best forty-eight. This is not perhaps the exact ratio, but it illustrates what is meant, that within certain limits, just in proportion as you increase the size of your board, just in that proportion do you diminish its aggregate of ability and efficiency. Six men of inferior ability, associated with six men of superior ability, give for a resultant a mean between the two; this is when they are properly disposed and work with some degree of harmony; when not so disposed, the former may and often do neutralize the efficiency of the latter. I believe, then, in this regard, that our system is radically defective, that it necessitates a train of evils which cannot be averted while it exists; that in no other department of the government can be found such inefficiency, misjudgment, mismanagement, and general demoralization. It may seem presumptuous in me to attack a system which has been in operation for so many years, and to which the people have become attached, which has resulted in so great good to the State, and has given Vermont a prestige in which her sons may well feel an honest pride. But it is unwise to allow the success of the public schools of the past to blind us to the defects of our system. We must not forget that the position of the State, like that of the individual, is relative. While our sister States were reaping a lesser percentage of profit than the percentage which, by the faithfulness of the friends of education, was secured to Vermont, in spite of our monstrous and hydra-headed system, we held a position of honor and eminence. But to-day, when other States, by abolishing or modifying old systems, and thereby utilizing a larger percentage of their working power, that very position which was but just now one of superiority has become one of inferiority.

The State is a *unit*, for certain purposes. The county is a *unit*, for certain purposes. The town is a *unit*, for certain other purposes. For the purposes of education the district has been regarded as a *unit*. For almost every other purpose the town has been found to be the *true unit*. Indeed, in several respects, in the educational department even, the town district system prevails. Would it not be wiser to make the town a unit for educational purposes? This question merits further discussion.

It is quite natural to think that a teacher who can be secured for a small stipend will answer for a "small school," so that small schools will in general be taught by teachers who could not secure situations in larger ones, and would fail if they did.

Small districts will be likely to have poor school-houses. The expense of building and repairing falls heavily upon ten or a dozen tax-payers. And the old school-houses, many of them unfit even for stalled cattle, will have to serve till that time when we have grown wiser and adopted a new order of things; for there is no hope under the present system that the future will afford relief. The population, except at business centres, is year by year gradually growing less.

Small districts are far less likely to furnish those facilities for illustration and reference so necessary to the teacher. Indeed, everything which involves an expenditure is likely to remain undone. The committee-man feels like being very economical when he reflects that he will be assessed one-tenth of any expenditure; so that globes, dictionaries, and maps, and all school-apparatus, are excluded from the school.

Change from the district to the town system would result in a more efficient supervision. Almost every town can select a board of men competent to look after the interests of the public school. This is not true of one-half of the districts of the State. A choice from ten men gives poorer chance of proper supervision than a choice from three or five hundred.

Such change would result in a more permanent supervision. Small communities are more severely democratic than larger ones. Every man must have his share of the honor, and take his turn at the wheel, without regard to competency.

Making one central board of supervision would render possible competitive examinations, which are now practically impossible. Such examinations would immediately shut out the most incompetent of our teachers. They would discourage girls, scarcely beyond the age which the law designates as *infancy*, from seeking places in our schools as teachers, when they should be there as pupils.

Fewer daughters, and nieces, and wives' sisters would be employed. Even when they are thoroughly competent, their employment is often seen to awaken such spirit of antagonism as will impair the efficiency of the school. Nepotism is as baneful an evil in the politics of the school district as in the broader field of the State and the nation.

Again, a better class of teachers would be secured in the smaller districts. It could not be expected that all the schools of a town would be of equal size. The larger ones, the village schools, as now, would secure the best teachers without regard to expense. The lesser communities, noticing that they were obliged to help support good schools and pay large prices to the teachers of the larger schools, would very soon begin to feel that if they were obliged to help support good schools for their townsmen, it would be wise for them to compel their townsmen to help sustain good schools for them.

This change of supervision would tend to remove the evil of a constant change of teachers. Permanency of supervision would result in permanency of teachers. The frequency of change in teachers is a most alarming evil with us. It breaks up all connection between one term and another. Each teacher has his own ways, and it takes some time to get out of the old ways and into the new, and quite a portion of each term is spent in getting started. It thus often happens that a term is one-third spent before the work is well begun. It requires a term of ordinary length for a teacher to become familiar with the peculiar characteristics of his pupils. No very efficient work can be done till this is known. He has first to learn their needs and their capacities before he can adapt his instruction to the necessities of each pupil. An ordinary teacher, who has taught a school for one term, will do more for that school than one of superior endowments and acquirements who is an entire stranger to the wants of the school. Perpetual change of teachers and inspectors of schools utterly ignores the value of experience. I can conceive of no remedy for these evils which will be likely to prove so efficient as this change of system.

Again, this change would result in a democratic equalization of the burden of supporting schools. It now costs each tax-payer in a small district more to support a poor school than it costs the tax-payer in the larger district to support a good school. Statistics show that the expense per pupil increases in the inverse ratio as the size of the school diminishes.

Why should not taxation for the support of schools be equalized? Equity demands that it should. Every reason which can be urged in favor of good schools demands that it should.

The district system stands in the way of the introduction of the graded system. I make this statement upon the supposition that there is no probability that district lines will be changed until some other than the district system is adopted. True, this might be done. Districts might be reorganized and their geographical boundaries changed; but they never will be while the old system remains.

No one, I suppose, at this day assumes to doubt the wisdom of the application of the principle of division of labor, as applied to the mechanical pursuits. The manufacturer who should require each workman to make all parts of a watch, would find that he could not compete with his rival who put each workman upon a single piece. Even in the manufacture of boots and shoes, where no great mechanical genius is required, it is found to be economy to allow each man to do a distinct part, so that the boot or shoe is not the work of one hand, but of several. Confined to one class of work, the workman becomes more skillful, and turns off work more rapidly; his tools are fewer and ready at hand, and there is no loss of time in changing from one piece to another. If this be economy in the mechanical pursuits, how much more apparent is the wisdom of applying this principle to the more delicate and responsible work of developing and training the human mind?

Now this is the principle upon which the graded school is based. It is found that the teacher who teaches a few branches, and concentrates all his time and efforts upon these branches, can give more efficient instruction than the one who attempts to teach all. It is upon this principle, in part, that each college professor has his distinct department. To this may be added the reasonable expectation that if one has to teach but one department or grade, he will be likely to work in that department or grade where he can work with the most ease to himself, and consequently with the greatest profit to the school. Teachers who are eminently successful in one grade, are oftentimes eminently unsuccessful in another grade of the same department; so that they, like other workmen, soon ascertain what their special province is, and adapt themselves to it.

This, however, is not the most substantial argument in favor of grading schools. A graded school is simply a classified school. Every one knows, who is at all familiar with schools, that their success depends very largely upon their classification. It requires just as much time to instruct one individual as to instruct a class —just as long to instruct a class of three as a class of twenty. If your school has as many classes as individuals, and this often happens in small schools, the teacher's time is frittered away to little purpose. No school whose curriculum comprises all the studies from the A B C to the highest branches taught in the common school, can be thoroughly classified without having more classes than the teacher can well instruct.

If your district has one hundred and twenty-five pupils, it is evidently good economy, instead of dividing them without regard to advancement, and thus making the curriculum of each school as comprehensive as the curriculum of the whole would have been, to divide them with reference to advancement, thereby diminishing the number of classes in each department to one-third or one-fourth the number which would otherwise be required. And probably it will be found that the number of pupils which would require four teachers without proper classification, would, when classified, be well taught by three teachers, at a saving of one-fourth the expense, and with far better results.

Every teacher knows how difficult it is to make an impression upon a heterogeneous mass grouped together and called a class—made up of pupils pursuing the same studies, indeed—but of diverse age, diverse capacity, and diverse acquirement, as is usual in an ungraded school.

The more gifted and accomplished are held back, while those of lesser gifts and acquirements are dragged on beyond their strength. The former grow lazy and indifferent; the latter discouraged and disgusted. The former acquire an overweening confidence in their own abilities; the latter fail to cultivate that healthful self-appreciation essential to success, which is naturally developed by association with one's peers. Thus it happens that all stimulus, both to the bright and the dull, is removed.

Besides, it is impossible for any teacher to adapt his instruction to the varied capacities and diverse accomplishments of unclassified classes. This is difficult enough in a class which has been selected and grouped with reference to like capacities and similar acquirements. If he adapts his instruction to the more advanced, it will be beyond the comprehension of those less advanced. If, on the other hand, it is adapted to the needs of those less gifted, it becomes tedious and uninstructive to the others. Thus will all the interest be dissipated, while, if well classified, each individual spirits the other. Mutual labor and mutual sympathy are powerful stimulants, especially to the young. Each spurs and supports the other, and industry and diligence is secured in all.

Again, the graded school furnishes additional inducement to effort in this way: Each class has its specific work, and no advancement to a higher grade can be secured until that work is done. Each grade is a position which cannot be reached except by passing step by step all the intermediate ground. The pupils in each grade have the perpetual incitement of their more advanced associates. From one grade to another is to them a long stride. It seems a thing worthy to strive for. Now these stimulants are especially needed by slow and not over-gifted minds, and to this class a majority of children belong. The result is that progress is far more rapid and thorough in a graded than in an ungraded school.

Still, again, the graded system secures a systematic course of education. Each pupil does not for himself, nor can his parents for him, elect this study or that, as whim or caprice may dictate. He must take each in due time and order. That course of study is prescribed which will secure the best and most symmetrical mental development, embracing those studies a knowledge of which is likely to prove of the most practical benefit to the pupil in the business pursuits of after-life.

People sometimes wonder that academies do not flourish as they did years ago. They are not only dying out in Vermont, but all over the country. Massachusetts has but few left, and these are for the most part *graded academies.* The same process is going on in New York. Within the last few years one-third of the academies in this State have become extinct. The truth is, the old academic system is dead, and the sooner it is buried beyond resurrection, the better. It served in its day and generation, but belongs to the past. While we honor it for the good it has done, if we are wise, we shall lay it away in a napkin. It has been supplanted by something which is better. I speak only of ungraded academies.

The material difference between the academy and the graded high-school is, that the latter is classified, while the former, gathering its pupils as it does from a large circuit, and changing in its elements from term to term, cannot be classified.

The graded school has also this other advantage, that it is *democratic.* All must contribute to its support, and all may avail themselves of its advantages.

These graded schools have been established in many of the large towns of Vermont. There are many other towns which desire and are working to secure them. A large proportion of the villages of the State have, within a radius of a mile and a half, pupils in sufficient numbers to make from two to four grades. The obstacles in the way are the old district lines. They are held in a sort of reverence. I don't know but the people somehow connect them with that passage of Holy Writ which pronounces maledictions upon those who remove ancient landmarks. It would be about as easy to remove the equator as to disturb one of these ancient lines. Vermonters seem to hate everything which savors of innovation. But we must not forget that dislike of innovation is often a serious obstacle to progress. The people will be slow to move in this direction. It is the duty of the legislature to step in and take the responsibility, if it can be seen to be a measure which should be secured.

It is thought that these schools are more expensive. But a greater percentage of profit is often secured by a greater expenditure. And it must not be forgotten that there is an element of profit which cannot be directly and positively estimated. It is that influence which a good school has upon the prosperity of a place. It is often of more material advantage than a manufacturing company.

It may be doubted if the aggregate of expenditure for educational purposes is greater in a village where there is a well-organized and judiciously-managed graded school, than in a village of the same size where the old system exists. For, from the expense of the graded school, if it be what it should be, may be deducted the expenditure of the support of a dozen, and oftentimes more, children, who from lack of proper educational facilities at home, are compelled to go abroad. And beyond doubt, home is the place to educate children. Besides, a good graded school has an income secured by the attendance of pupils from abroad. We must also, in this connection, remember that the many whose means will not allow them to send their children away to better schools, are abridged in the privileges which they might enjoy, had they all the facilities they are entitled to at home.

This is the material view of the case. Go into any of our towns which have been blessed with a good school for forty or fifty years, and you will find the aggregate of intelligence to be far greater than in those towns which have enjoyed less educational facilities. Is the intelligence of its inhabitants nothing to a town? Is not the expenditure which shall secure this a good investment? True, we cannot estimate it in greenbacks; yet it is an investment that will make its return in kind. It is an invariable rule that the percentage of increase of valuation of property in any community is in the direct ratio of the increase of intelligence and virtue.

Every citizen of extraordinary intelligence, or extraordinary virtue, enhances the value of all property of the town in which he lives. By just so much as you add to the virtue and intelligence of the inhabitants of the town, do you add to the value of its acres. It is thus that it is true that "every man's sin is every other man's business." It is just as true that every man's ignorance is every other man's business.

Hon. Henry Barnard thus sets forth the evils that result from the lack of proper classification of schools:

"From the number of class and individual recitations, to be attended to during each half-day, these exercises are brief, hurried, and of little practical value. They consist, for the most part, of senseless repetitions of the words of a book. Instead of being the time and place where the real business of teaching is done, where the ploughshare of interrogation is driven down into the acquirements of each pupil, and his ability to comprehend clearly is cultivated and tested; where the difficult principles of each lesson are developed and illustrated, and additional information imparted, and the mind of the teacher brought in direct contact with the mind of each pupil, to arouse, interest, and direct its opening powers;

instead of all this and more, the brief period passed in recitation, consists, on the part of each teacher, of hearing each individual and class, in regular order and quick succession, repeat words from a book, and on the part of the pupils, of *saying their lessons*, as the operation is most significantly described by most teachers, when they summon the class to the stand. In the mean time the order of the school must be maintained, and the general business must go forward. Little children, without any authorized employment for their eyes and hands, and ever active curiosity, must be made to sit still, while every muscle is aching from suppressed activity; problems must be solved, excuses for tardiness or absence received, questions answered, whisperings allowed or suppressed, and more or less of extempore discipline administered. Were it not a most ruinous waste of precious time,—did it not involve the deadening, crushing, distorting, dwarfing of immortal faculties and noble sensibilities,—were it not an utter perversion of the noble objects for which schools are instituted, it would be difficult to conceive of a more diverting farce than an ordinary session of a large public school, whose chaotic and discordant elements have not been reduced to system by proper classification. The teacher, at least the conscientious teacher, thinks it anything but a farce to him. Compelled to hurry from one study to another, requiring a knowledge of methods altogether distinct; from one recitation to another, equally brief and unsatisfactory, one requiring a liveliness of manner that he does not feel and cannot assume, and the other closeness of attention and abstraction of thought, which he cannot give amid the multiplicity and variety of cares; from one case of discipline to another pressing on him at the same time—he goes through the same circuit, day after day, with a dizzy brain and aching heart, and brings his school to a close with a feeling that with all his diligence and fidelity he has accomplished but little good."

It may be urged against the abrogation of this old system, that the people will not willingly surrender these powers which the statute has conferred upon them,—the controlling of their own schools. But they surrender no power. It still remains in their hands. The only difference is that they act upon the matter in a larger assemblage, and under certain restraints which will be likely to insure better results.

A small minority in a district meeting often, by preconcerted action, can prevent the having schools at all, or limit them to the shortest possible time, or impair their usefulness when in operation. Now these ends could not be obtained in the town meeting.

It is far more likely that wise and judicious measures will be adopted in a town than in a district meeting, both on account of the healthful counterbalance which is always found in a larger assemblage, made up of many who have no personal and direct interest in the matter upon which they act, as well as from the fact that the controlling minds in the former are likely to be wiser and of greater experience. I think it is true, as Mr. Boutwell suggests in a paper which I append, that the district system is thoroughly anti-republican. It may secure what *is thought* to be the greatest good to the greatest number, but it often utterly fails to secure the greatest aggregate of good to all, which is the end that true republicanism aims to secure.

It may be objected that it would not be right to compel children to go so far to school, as would be necessary if districts were consolidated. It certainly would be right if thereby greater good would come to the State. The State certainly has the right to regulate and control in all matters upon which the efficiency of its schools depends. Nor is it simply a right; it is a sacred duty. Which is better for the child, that he shall go a half-mile to a poor school, or that he should go twice or thrice that distance to a good school? It would be far cheaper for those residing in the remote parts of a district to carry their children—each taking his turn, or together hiring some one to do this—than to support a school by themselves.

The following remarks upon this point, which I have chanced upon since writing the above, from the Report of the Agent of the Board of Education for Massachusetts for the year 1869, are worthy of perusal:

"In one district a school has been kept for a single scholar at an expense of between $60 and $70. In almost every town that I have visited I am satisfied this difficulty could be remedied, without great inconvenience, by reducing the number of schools, thus giving to each a larger number of pupils, and with no more, but perhaps even less, money than has heretofore been annually appropriated, securing for them all a longer period of instruction and a better class of teachers. It was said very truthfully, a few years since, by the committee of a town in Franklin County,—the one to which I have referred as quite recently manifesting such opposition to the legal requirement,—in which, with one hundred and twenty-three school children, there were ten districts, some containing 'not more than four or five scholars,' such a 'town ought to appropriate more money, or reduce the number of districts.' 'Reducing the number of schools from ten to six, which we think might be done without great inconvenience to the people, would save the expense of maintaining four schools, and the schools would in our opinion be greatly improved, a better class of teachers employed, and the intellectual, social, and moral condition of the schools would be promoted. It will be said that in a sparse population like ours, the trouble of collecting all our scholars into six schools would more than balance the advantages, especially in winter. This objection is more specious than solid. In almost all the districts, those who have female scholars attending, convey them to and from school in their sleighs or sleds, and when the horse is harnessed it makes but little difference whether you drive him one mile or two; at the same time you are beating the snow and opening good roads to the traveller, and bettering the social condition of your neighborhood. But one practical truth is more convincing than many theories. How do we act when the money is drawn directly from our own pockets, as it is in supporting private or select schools? Would the town sustain ten private schools to save travel? Do they not devise 'ways and means' to get to school beyond the limits of their own districts? Suppose there were fifty scholars in town to attend those schools, would any one think it worth while to have five schools, because it might save a little travel or other inconvenience? Why should we be more careful of money when we pay it voluntarily, than when it is drawn from us in the form of taxes?"

Now I assume that every tax-payer of Vermont has a direct interest in any change which will insure the best possible schools at the least expense, and will not refuse to countenance and encourage any change which will secure better schools at a less cost; for we are proverbially a thrifty people.

Wise men learn from the experience of others. If the experience of others is less impressive than our own, it has at least the advantage of being far cheaper.

Several of our sister States, which had formerly a district system similar to our own, have abolished that system and substituted therefor the system of town supervision, which places the schools of the town under the control of a town board, elected by the town. In some instances this change has been secured gradually —legislatures authorizing towns to change when they vote so to do. Of course this gradual change is slow. I cannot ascertain that any State which has once inaugurated the movement has been willing to go back to the old order of things. And it is stated by Secretary Boutwell that no town in Massachusetts, that had tried the new order for two years, ever turned to the old. These facts are significant.

I append an extract from one of Mr. Boutwell's annual reports, made to the Massachusetts Board of Education when he was Secretary of that body. These remarks were thought so conclusive and of such value that they were printed by themselves as a circular and distributed throughout the State. I am glad to append them, because I am compelled to treat the subject altogether in a general way and upon general principles, being entirely without experience or observation. I feel that the opinion of Mr. Boutwell, based as it is upon thorough knowledge of the results of both systems as they were tried side by side, will have greater weight than any arguments I can urge:

"The laws of 1859, abolishing the district system and transferring the duty of selecting teachers from the prudential to the superintending committees, having been repealed by the same legislature, at its autumn session, there has been but little opportunity for testing the new system. The history of the proceedings of the legislature of 1859 furnishes abundant evidence of a desire to promote the interests of learning, and the passage of the measures in question was in harmony with that desire.

"When the committee on education were considering the expediency of abolishing the district system, I expressed the opinion that the people were not prepared to accept the change without serious opposition in some counties. I was myself unwilling to make an educational measure the subject of public controversy in the State, and much more unwilling to connect our educational policy, as a Commonwealth, with the fortunes of any political party. Under these circumstances, I could not advise the passage of the law, yet I did not for a moment doubt the patriotic and laudable purposes of the committee, or the real wisdom of the change contemplated, if the people were prepared to accept it. And I am now constrained to declare, as the result of extensive correspondence and interchange of sentiment with the people of the State, that their attachment to the district system is not as strong as I formerly supposed, and that a large majority are prepared to accept its unqualified abolition. It may not, however, be wise to legislate upon the subject immediately; but I deem this a fit occasion to invite the inhabitants of the towns where districts still exist to take the matter into their own hands, and reconstruct their school system upon a basis which will admit of economy, progress, and efficiency. I entered upon the duties of the office I now hold with some faith in the district system; my observation and experience have destroyed that faith entirely. It is a system admirably calculated to secure poor schools, incompetent teachers, consequent waste of public money, and yet neither committees, nor districts, nor towns be responsible therefor.

"It is unquestionably true that the best schools are found where the district system does not exist; and the charge, in a few instances made or suggested, that there has been no improvement for twenty-five years, is limited in its origin and in its truthful application to those towns which are divided into districts. Whenever a town has established the municipal system, and adhered to it for two years, there has never within my knowledge been a serious effort in favor of the restoration of the district system. These facts are so encouraging and so conclusive, that they ought, without argument, to convince the most skeptical. The great object of the people is the establishment of good schools at the least cost, and they have no interest in the district system when it fails to secure these ends.

"Practically, the district system denies the value of experience. Each year sees a new prudential committee-man, and each term a new teacher. The experience of a year is rendered valueless by the election of a new committee; and the teacher labors for a single term, commencing without a knowledge of what the pupils have previously accomplished, and ending without an interest in their future.

"Under these circumstances, it is not strange that district schools are kept, term after term, and year after year, without an appreciable increase of power.

"The quality of the school depends upon the character of the teacher; and the character of the teacher depends upon accident, or the caprice, prejudices, or convenience of the committee-man. Each teacher brings into the school his own ideas of teaching, and after two, three, or four months, he goes away, and his place is taken by a stranger, who introduces new methods, without the judgment of anybody concerning their relative value. The successive terms of school in the same district have not, usually, any personal or educational connection with each other. Each term is an experiment which proves nothing but its own failure or comparative success; and it does not even furnish, either in its failure or its success, a basis for future operations.

"The district itself is a questionable organization. More frequently than otherwise it has no legal existence; and whenever a vote authorizing the levy of a tax is resisted, the courts usually find it difficult to sustain the proceedings of the district.

"There are in the cities and towns of Massachusetts three distinct school systems. First, the municipal system. Where this exists the towns erect and support the school-houses, and confide to the superintending committees the selection of teachers. This system exists in eighty or a hundred cities and towns, which together probably contain more than one-half of the population of the State, and, in the character of their schools, they are far in advance of the rest of the Commonwealth.

"In the second class, about fifty in number, the town erect and support the school-houses, but the territory is divided into districts, and the power to select teachers is confided to prudential committees.

"The third class comprises those towns whose territory is divided into districts, and in which each district is charged with the duty of selecting its teachers and providing a school-house.

"In most towns where this system exists, the districts are too numerous, the school-houses are poor and inconvenient, and the number of pupils is insufficient to constitute a good school. Districts containing less than twelve pupils each, may be enumerated by the hundred. It is quite likely that in the sparsely peopled sections of the State, a necessity for small districts occasionally exists; but it is a manifest public right to require pupils to travel from one to two miles to school, according to circumstances, rather than incur the expense of sustaining small, and, of course, poor schools. Moreover, the interest of the family is the same. A good school, even though the distance be considerable, is infinitely more important than the immediate neighborhood of a poor school. These small districts are tenacious of existence, and the only means by which they can be destroyed is for the towns to assume exclusive jurisdiction, including the burden of the houses, and then, from time to time, as occasions arise, pass judgment upon the expediency of continuing schools for the accommodation of a small number of persons who may often enjoy better educational advantages elsewhere. And in behalf of weak districts, whose pecuniary means are inadequate to the erection of suitable school-houses, I appeal to the towns, and ask them to reassume a burden which they ought never to have thrown off. To the town the erection of a school-house is usually a small matter; to a weak district it is often a burden far greater than all its other public contributions combined.

"The district system is an obstacle to the establishment of graded schools. There are many villages, in towns where the district system exists, that are divided into districts, which, if united, would furnish pupils for a school of two, three, or four departments. In all these cases there is great waste of money and of teaching force. The object of our school system is to get a competent teacher into every school; but the district and the prudential committee systems are the best security which the public can take that that object shall never be attained. Admit that all the inhabitants of a district are disposed to do what is right and proper, and what are the chances of success? Rotation in office is the law of their public action. This is often a necessity. Each citizen feels the burden of the duties, and he therefore claims that others shall bear their share. Often there is a public sentiment which at once demands for and concedes to every man the right to hold the office in turn. In either case the one all-essential requisite of experience is wanting. And though the prudential committee may be a good citizen, a good farmer, a good mechanic, or a professional man in regular standing, he yet lacks knowledge of the business which he is to transact. His acquaintance with teachers also is limited; and he finds, moreover, that the towns in which the prudential system does not exist, having always a committee competent to make contracts for a year in advance, have secured the services of the most competent persons. Thus, by the unnecessary multiplication of districts and schools in the sparsely peopled towns, the small number of pupils in each school, the lack of experience in prudential committees, and, on the other hand, the existence of superior schools, the payment of higher wages, the larger experience of committees where the municipal system exists, there has arisen a difference between the towns of the Commonwealth which admits of no other explanation than that suggested in this report. Nor ought the statement of the fact to be omitted, that the course pursued occasionally, where the district system exists, is open to the gravest objections. District meetings are not generally attended by even a majority of the voters. It therefore happens that it is possible for a minority to elect the officers and control the policy of the district. Hence it is true of nearly every town, that once at least in its history, the organization of a district has been seized by a small number of men who entertained schemes inconsistent with the welfare of the schools. Assembled by concert, in the shades of evening, in a dimly lighted house, they have proceeded, without serious opposition, to consummate their schemes; and a prudential committee, in their interest, has been elected, who at once makes a contract with a relative, friend, or favorite, without regard to the intellectual or moral welfare of the children who are to be members of the school.

"Nor, under such circumstances, is it often in the province of the superintending committee to resist the scheme, or to redress the grievance. These evils come from the exceptional and anti-republican character of our school districts. There is no other department of government in the Commonwealth, or under its authority, in which it is possible for a single person, acting in the name of the people, to proceed without consultation, without deliberation, without agreement, and bind his constituency in matters affecting their nearest rights and dearest privileges, and all without regard to any influence or opinion but such as proceeds from his own whims, passions, prejudices, or errors.

"Nor can it be assumed that the district system is, even in the least degree, a promoter of popular liberty. It does nothing for education that might not be better done by other agencies; and, as a system, it exerts no influence, not even in the most remote degree, over the civil or political fortunes of the people. Experience is a great teacher, and neither the district system nor any system analogous to it, exists in the larger number of American States, and yet popular liberty is not confined to Massachusetts. Moreover, at least half of the people of the State have voluntarily abandoned the district system, and are not aware of any loss of liberty.

"Nor is it true that more interest in schools is manifested where the district system exists, but the greater interest is observed where good schools are found. The quality of the schools and the interest of the people act and react upon each other. A generous and intelligent public interest renders the establishment of good schools necessary and easy, and good schools are calculated to widen, strengthen, and deepen the interest of the people. Therefore it is absurd in reasoning, and false in history, to assume that a system under which poor schools are the rule, and good ones the exception, is adapted to increase the interest of the people in learning, or in the institutions thereof.

"In concluding this part of my report, I earnestly invite the inhabitants of the towns where the district system still exists, to make faithful trial of the municipal system for the period of two or three years. And be it everywhere understood, that the abolition of the district system, whether by a law of the State, or the action of the towns themselves, works no concentration of power in the hands of any body outside of the respective municipalities interested. The legislature takes nothing, the Board of Education takes nothing, but the towns reclaim and exercise certain authorities, and perform certain duties, primarily, originally, and always their own, until they saw fit to transfer them temporarily and for certain purposes, to the districts, whose existence even was due to and always dependent upon the action of the towns. The reassumption of these duties and authorities is entirely consistent with the original policy of the Commonwealth, which regarded the towns as the responsible managers of the common schools. Nor can there be any safer depository of this power. If anywhere under the canopy of heaven, and among men, there is a perfect democracy, it is in a New England, a Massachusetts town meeting. There, in the light of day, and in the presence of the world, where the power of each man, without regard to social, sectarian, pecuniary, or industrial distinctions, is equal to that of any other man, the people proceed to legislate upon all their municipal concerns. And is there one of higher moment than the management of their public schools? And is there danger to popular liberty when the power to take the initiative in the selection of a teacher is transferred from the evening meeting of a minority of a school district, to the inhabitants of a whole town, assembled in the light of day to legislate upon all matters of local and municipal importance?

"It is a principle in our government, that whoever contributes to the public burdens has a right to be heard by himself, or by his representative, in the expenditure of the public money; and it therefore follows that as long as the schools of a town are supported by the taxation of all its citizens, each citizen has a right to a voice in the expenditure of money for educational purposes. This voice must be heard in the choice of a committee authorized to select the teachers, or it cannot be heard at all. The superintending committees are chosen by the people, one-third each year, and therefore there is annually an opportunity for the expression of public sentiment. Under the municipal system the entire responsibility is upon the committee, and under the pressure of this responsibility, with a large and constantly enlarging experience, there can be but little doubt of their disposition or their ability to meet every reasonable expectation. Led to retain those teachers who have succeeded, and forced to put aside those who are comparatively incompetent, the standard of qualifications would be gradually elevated, and the schools proportionately improved.

"I have been thus earnest and minute in this exposition of the district system, in the hope that the inhabitants of those towns where it still exists may be led to make a trial of the municipal system, which, I am persuaded, will render their schools at once more valuable and more economical. It is practicable for many, even of the smaller towns, to consolidate their most populous districts, establish graded schools with two or three departments, the higher of which shall furnish training equivalent to that usually given in good English High-Schools, without much addition to their present appropriations."

Let us now see if we can gather up some of the results that would grow out of this change which is advocated.

1. It would secure just as many schools as the necessities of the community demand, each being an integral part of one central organization, and adapted to the wants of each individual community.

2. It would dispense with a large number of school officers.

3. It would establish a uniform rate of taxation.

4. It would furnish more uniform and equal advantages and privileges to every citizen.

5. It would allow the child to attend school where his own interests would be best conserved, with no restraint save what the general interests might require.

6. It would prevent strife about district lines.

7. It would diminish the aggregate expenditure for schools.

8. It would secure a more efficient system of school inspection and supervision.

9. It would secure permanency of supervision.

10. It would secure greater permanency of teachers.

11. It would secure a better class of teachers.

12. It would secure better compensation to competent teachers, and less employment for incompetent ones.

13. It will secure better school-houses.

14. It will secure greater facilities to teachers for reference and illustration.

15. It will enable towns to establish graded schools.

16. It will secure uniformity of text-books in the same town.

17. It will result in more uniform methods of teaching.

18. It will secure the establishment of a course of study, and will tend to keep pupils longer in school.

19. It will secure to the State department more reliable statistics.

20. It will insure schools in every district, and prevent a bare majority from depriving a respectable minority of school privileges.

21. It will tend to diminish neighborhood quarrels.

22. It would insure the employment of fewer nephews and nieces, sisters and sisters-in-law.

23. It would insure a larger aggregate of interest on the part of the community in each school.

24. It would render possible competitive examinations.

It may be asked, would not this radical change in our school system interfere with their present and immediate usefulness? Would it not so disorganize and break up the system that the schools would be impaired for some time to come?

I think not. The material change would be simply the substitution of a town board of school managers in place of the various district boards. This substitution need cause no break in the working of our schools—scarcely a jostle. The prudential committee would continue to discharge their duties until the election of the town boards, at which time all district supervision would cease; all school property would come into the possession of the town upon such conditions as the statute should provide.

Not a school need be closed or interrupted, not a teacher discharged, not a contract vitiated or annulled. The educational machine would work right on without obstruction, but more smoothly and with greater efficiency, because of the greater simplicity and unity of the new system, and its better supervision. Without shock, without confusion, almost without attracting observation, the change would be wrought, and we should wake up some morning and find ourselves possessed of a more compact, more simple, and more efficient, though less expensive, school organization. One need scarcely be reminded of change, save as it is suggested by the munificence of the blessings it secures.

It may be asked what shall be done with the school property which now belongs to the districts. It would pass to the possession of the town, each district being credited with the amount of its valuation on appraisal, less the amount of indebtedness of said district. That is, the town would practically purchase the school property of each district and assume its indebtedness.

CHAPTER II.

VENTILATION.

The following extracts from the works of Mr. L. W. Leeds upon ventilation are of great value. The chapter upon Heating and Ventilation in this work, with slight modifications, is the embodiment of principles which Mr. Leeds so ably advocates. The modifications are necessary to secure an apparatus at once cheap and adapted to the wants of common schools.

VENTILATION AND WARMING.

"That great American institution, the cast-iron stove, is in disgrace. It has been, we think, unjustly and unmercifully persecuted. There is a strenuous effort being made to exonerate ourselves from just censure merited by our many sins of omission and commission, by endeavoring to cast the blame upon this most faithful servant of almost every laboring man's home.

"That great and successful laborer for the improvement of American homes, A. J. Downing, devoted no stinted portion of the brilliant delineations of his gifted pen to the unmeasured condemnation of this peculiar American institution. Charles Dickens's fertile brain seems almost exhausted in gathering up expressive adjectives of condemnation to hurl at that 'eternal, accursed, suffocating, red-hot demon of a stove, so commonly found in America.'

"This Dr. Harris quotes approvingly, and thinks the better health of the foundling hospitals of Paris is because this 'accursed stove' is unknown in those public institutions.

"Catharine E. Beecher, and an unnumbered host of other very able writers, strive not to be outdone in condemning the poor object that they suppose to be the great source and cause of those foul-air diseases that seem to have increased so fearfully of late and are causing such devastation in our modern American homes.

Now, add to all this Dr. Derby's very able arguments intended to call attention to the great harm probably arising from the escape of that intense poison, carbonic oxide, from burning anthracite coal, and the very learned discussions and experiments of the French Academy of Sciences, showing that the virulent poison pays no attention to the simple, crude attempts to confine it by cast-iron, but passes through such obstructions at will, with almost as much ease as a squirrel would through a post-and-rail fence; and after all this, one can scarcely perceive what will be the result of attempting to plead its cause, to advocate the general or almost universal use of this despised and persecuted article, the American stove.

"But we will do it, not in the interest of the stove manufacturers—for we have no friend in the business, and the stove is too much in disgrace to afford to pay for its advocacy in that way—nor yet from mere compassion, as many take the part of any persecuted object, but from sincere conviction of its intrinsic worth, because it is our belief that its universal use, if used properly—not abused—would be of inestimable value to the American people. We believe that they are of much more value to us than all the gold mines of California and Nevada. The value of the shipping that sails from our ports and dots the ocean in every clime is but a drop in the bucket compared with the value to us of the proper use of our American stoves. Now, we will endeavor to give our reasons for entertaining an opinion so singular and unpopular.

"Accepting as a truth that saying of the great Dr. Franklin, that 'Public Health is Public Wealth,' and which an eminent hygienist of England lately said should be inscribed in letters of gold over every school-house and public building throughout the land, it becomes a question of the gravest importance as to how the best conditions of public health can be obtained.

"We must not take a casual and superficial glance only at a few of the prominent members of society, who by their wealth and position may be able to attract more attention from the public than a whole factory full of men and women who labor from seven in the morning until six at night; because these wealthy men, if they lose an hour, or a day, or even a month, by sickness, have no fear of losing their situations and the entire support of a dependent family. But it is the men and women upon whose strong muscles the country is dependent for all its manual labor whose health must be looked after and preserved—it is the health of these that forms the great wealth of a nation.

"Now, one of the great fundamental conditions of our existence is, that we maintain a uniform temperature of our body, the standard of which is commonly much above that of the surrounding atmosphere; and this must be secured at all times, or existence itself ceases. Upon the manner of supplying this artifical heat, and the supply of fresh air which more or less accompanies it, depend the health, wealth, prosperity, and happiness of the nation on one hand, and the sickness, poverty, and wretchedness of it on the other. In the early settlement of a country, when wood is very abundant, the open wood-fire is not only the cheapest and simplest form of obtaining the required artificial heat, but it is in many respects the most advantageous to health of any known means. But in large cities and thickly-settled countries, wood is too expensive for ordinary use for a large majority of the people—and the wealthy even neglect to use wood-fires, from ignorance, propably, of their real sanitary value. Fires of coal in open grates are the next most simple arrangement, and although not without their inconveniences, yet they have some excellent sanitary qualities; and it is our opinion it would add greatly to the health and happiness of many families, even in moderate circumstances, to have an open fire to sit by, should they have to substitute an old-fashioned rag-carpet to cover the floor instead of a more expensive one.

"But notwithstanding the many advantages of the open fires of wood and coal, yet they are expensive, as they consume from three to five times as much coal to produce the same amount of heat in a room as can be produced by a good stove. The question is not so much, Shall the laboring classes use stoves, or shall they have open fires? as it is, Shall they have stoves, or shall they go without artificial heat altogether? If Charles Dickens were to visit the forty thousand paupers said to dwell in one portion only of London, he would not, to be sure, find them crowded around that 'peculiar American institution,' the 'infernal red-hot stove;' but, *far worse*, he would find them crowded together in some cold, damp, chilly room, perhaps a few hovering over same smoking embers, but the majority huddled together in a corner, covered by all the old rags they had left after calking all the cracks of the doors and windows, to keep out, if possible, any breath of air.

"Heat is a great and valuable sanitary agent, and if it can be made available more cheaply by the use of the stove than in any other way, it is the duty of the sanitarian to teach the people how to use that, and not to spend his time in abusing it simply for the faults resulting from its misuse. The want of a proper supply of fresh air when heating by the stove is one great cause of this hue and cry against the poor stove. It does, of course, allow a small room to be shut up almost air-tight, and if crowded with filthy people, with a kerosene lamp smoking in the room, there is no doubt whatever that a very foul and offensive atmosphere may be thus manufactured. A bright, open fire scarcely allows of this abuse. But it is the simplest thing in the world to remedy all this, and it can be done with the stove much cheaper, and frequently with more satisfaction, than with the open fire. All that is required is to bring in a good supply of fresh air from out of doors, and discharge it on the top of the stove.

"But in attempting to do this it is quite strange how many very intelligent persons will commit the fatal error of supposing that all that is necessary is to cut a hole through the floor, and the fresh air will flow up around the stove itself, instead of which it will simply flow out over the floor, being heavier than the air in the room. It must always be conducted to, and discharged on top of the stove, and then it simply falls down and mingles with the heated air arising around the stove. This introduction of fresh air around the stove was very fully explained by Dr. Franklin and most enthusiastically advocated by him, and he introduced it largely during his lifetime through the world-renowned 'Franklin stove;' yet owing to the stupidity, or ignorance, or whatever we must call it, of the people as to the value of or necessity for fresh air, this valuable feature of this celebrated stove—in fact, all the *Franklin*—was omitted, and the simple skeleton, without the spirit, handed down with his name.

"We have taken much pains to inquire of recent prominent writers who have urged the use of the 'Franklin stove' if they knew what a 'Franklin stove' was? They are apt to be quite indignant at the suspicion of such ignorance; but on inquiring how they propose supplying the fresh, external air to their stove, they want to know what is meant. We have found scarcely a single writer thus questioned who had the correct idea of a Franklin stove. There was a large number of these Franklin or ventilating-stoves used during the war, and when, to the liberal supply of fresh air was added an abundant supply of moisture, an artificial atmosphere was produced which for genial warmth, freshness, and purity could scarcely be excelled by any artificial means of heating now known. The success of this manner of warming the hospitals during our late war has given a great impetus to the reintroduction of Franklin stoves. Their introduction into the hospitals and barracks of England is urged by the surgeons and inspectors. The Sanitary Committee of the Paris Exposition spoke in the highest terms of this system of heating and ventilation as adopted in the United States.

"Owing to the necessity in schools of the children sitting very close to the stove, most of those made for such positions are entirely surrounded by the casing, thus forming an air-chamber around the whole stove. This greatly obstructs that portion of the heat that gives the great superiority to open fires and stoves over hot-air furnaces. We mean the direct radiation. The effects of heating by direct radiation and by currents of circulating warmed air are very different. You may be sitting in front of an open fire from which the *rays* of heat will be thrown out so strong that you will be kept comfortably warm, and at the same time there may be a *current* of air surrounding you, and from which you are breathing, which passes by you into the fire at a temperature many degrees below that indicated by the thermometer.

"On the contrary, in a room heated exclusively by hot-air currents you are surrounded by and breathing air heated hotter than indicated by the thermometer; because the cold walls and cold windows are constantly absorbing the heat of the solid bodies in the room by radiation.

"When we consider how much more active and vigorous the system is when breathing the cold, bracing air of winter than when breathing the warm debilitating air of summer, we can readily understand how much more wholesome would be an atmosphere in which a large proportion of heat would be derived from the direct radiation of a hot stove or open fire, than where all the air was vitiated by overheating for the purpose of securing the required warmth in that way.

"The loud and universal complaints against all hot-air furnaces have fully demonstrated the entire impossibility of producing a comfortable and satisfactory atmosphere in a room by that means only. With the open fire, the highly heated and vitiated air is carried directly up the chimney. Much heat is thus wasted, of course; but this may be far better than the wasting of the health by attempting to breathe it. In heating by the stove, the air that comes in contact with the hot sides, and is thus heated and consequently vitiated, is frequently retained in the room; this makes a stove-heated room more unpleasant than when warmed by the open fire. But suppose there should be sufficient ventilation to carry out of the room directly this warmed and vitiated air, and depend mostly upon the radiation from the stove for heating, that would be still much cheaper than the open fire, and far more wholesome than the heat from a miserable hot-air furnace.

"To continue our comments still further upon this topic, we may remark that the radiation from the hot-air stove would act in all directions equally—one must remember the rays of heat are thrown as much to the floor as to the ceiling; it is only the currents of warmed and vitiated air that rush to the ceiling, while the currents of cold, and generally purer, air flow along the floor. But if the pure external air is brought in on top of the hot stove and falls over it, the radiation from the stove is sufficient to keep up an equal temperature over the whole room; and if the supply of air by the stove is sufficient to fill the room and allow for what is carried off for ventilation, there will be no cold air sucking in under the door and around the windows, which creates those cold, unpleasant draughts so much complained of. Now a word about that dreadful poison, 'carbonic oxide,' that passes through the iron stove so easily. It is our belief that many hundreds and thousands die every year from the escape of this gas; but practically the amount that escapes through the solid iron is probably a very small fraction compared with what escapes, or rather is expelled, through the open joints of stoves and furnaces, or from open fires, by badly constructed flues. Here is the great trouble with most of our heating arrangements. We believe that poorly constructed and entirely choked flues are the cause of more sickness and deaths in the United States than cholera, yellow fever, and small-pox combined. Few persons who have not made a general investigation of this subject have any conception of the very large number of flues in daily use that are either entirely choked or totally inadequate to carry off the gases and smoke from the fires which they are intended thus to relieve; hence the very frequent annoyance from gas and smoke daily met with."

VENTILATION AND WARMING.

"A kind of chronic confusion and bewilderment seems to have taken possession of the public mind in regard to ventilation. The disappointment consequent upon the failure to realize the wonderful results anticipated by the sanguine inventors of many new contrivances for ventilation, seems to have cooled the ardor of not a few of the young and enthusiastic advocates of that science. Older and more indifferent ones have quietly closed up all openings that produced so many draughts, and seemed to have supposed, like the bird of the desert, that by hiding their eyes to their great enemy, they could thus escape his attacks. The results are related in every morning's paper in the record of the large number of deaths resulting from foul air. There have been so many failures in what might be termed scientific ventilation, or special schemes and contrivances of theoretical men, that any modest, industrious man, though of good ordinary intelligence, shrinks from a proposition to investigate the mysteries of this subject with as genuine a shudder as he would from a request to explain the wonders of spirit-rapping.

"Now, the first thing that presents itself to the utilitarian mind, when asked to step out of or beyond the regular routine of daily life, is, "Will it pay, or is it necessary?" then, "How can it be done, and what will it cost?" That there is need of some improvement in the ventilation of most of our buildings is now very generally acknowledged; but a willingness to spend the necessary money to secure good results, and a belief that such expenditure will pay, are still generally wanting. There seems to be a prevailing belief that what is needed is some new invention that is going to supply all the time, summer and winter, pure fresh air, without any further thought in regard to the matter. This is a very erroneous supposition. It is also a very unfortunate one, because, while it is impossible that it should ever be realized, its constant anticipation prevents that care and attention to the proper use of the appliances for ventilation which are accessible to all. If, therefore, the public were to cease altogether from looking for new inventions, and wasting money on them, and each one were to devote his whole attention to making the best use of whatever he had for ventilation and warming, real progress would soon be made on a good and substantial foundation. This popular longing for new things has taught many utterly to despise all arrangements heretofore in use, because, as they are expecting that the true theory of ventilation is yet to be discovered, and that it will be entirely different from anything they have ever thought of, therefore, whatever they have seen before must necessarily be good for nothing. Instead of this, to-day, all the essential means of ventilation and warming likely to be developed for a long time to come are really at hand. Improvements will consist in increased knowledge as to the use of them to the best advantage.

"While it is very true that there are many exceedingly uncomfortable buildings, and that the atmosphere in most modern houses and public buildings is very unwholesome, yet it is equally true that there are, even at the present time, many well-ventilated and well-warmed buildings. One of the first things to learn is to be able to tell when a building is properly ventilated and warmed, and when it is not. The perfection of ventilation consists in the unconscious satisfaction of all the inmates—a condition in which they think nothing about it. The contrary, however—that is to say, a constant complaining of a want of proper ventilation in a public room—by no means proves that those complaints are just. One often finds attending the same services of a Sabbath, persons of exceedingly different habits and constitutions. Not unfrequently a young lady may be observed entering with glowing countenance and in the full bloom of health. Accustomed to be in the open air, taking her ride, walk, or skating every day—rain or shine, sleet, snow, or hail—and accustomed as well to sleep in a perfectly cold room, with windows open all winter—as the strong, pure blood courses through her veins, there is a pleasure and a delight in her very appearance. To enter a room at a temperature of 70° Fahrenheit is to her oppressive; and she throws back her furs, commences fanning, and begs the sexton please give them a little fresh air, or she will certainly smother. But, perhaps, on the very next seat behind her may be seated a poor, emaciated victim of foul air—a lawyer, perhaps, or the secretary of some life insurance company—whose poor, thin blood has almost ceased to perform its legitimate function, and whose deep cough and short breath but too plainly indicate his long abuse of the great fundamental principle of all healthy existence—an abundant supply of pure air. The very sight of him sends a cold, creeping ague over you. He has scarcely taken his seat when he buttons up his coat and wants to know if they intend to freeze everybody to death; concluding with the remark that, if they cannot manage to keep the building warm, he will have to quit attending, as it is impossible to avoid taking a severe cold every time he ventures there. This is the very common experience of every one who has ever had the care of any large public building.

"Now, it would be quite difficult so to warm and ventilate a building as perfectly to satisfy both these extremes. The great value to be derived from a thorough personal knowledge of the theory and practice of ventilation is the ability to adapt one's self to the conditions that necessarily surround us.

"If the young lady directly in front of you in a railroad car insists on having the window open with the thermometer at zero, of course it would be utterly useless to attempt to explain to her that it is not necessary. It is, therefore, better to put on your overcoat, wrap your shawl around your feet, and endeavor to find a seat in front of her. Or, if you have been so foolish as to attempt to deprive your poor body of a good night's rest by taking a berth in a sleeping-car, and have been waked up after half an hour's restless sleep just in the middle of some horrid dream, raise your window a little and put your folded newspaper under it, and draw the blinds down over it to prevent its being discovered by the attendant. Then, by putting your face close to the opening, even if it is small, you will have sufficient pure air to give you a good night's rest, perhaps, if not too much disturbed by the awful snoring and growling of your fellow-passengers, tossing about in the foul atmosphere of other parts of the car. Thus, there are many very simple ways of securing good ventilation, no matter how unfavorable the surrounding conditions may be. But it is entirely impossible—this word *impossible* should be used with caution—that one should be always surrounded with conditions not admitting of the advantageous use of a little correct knowledge of the general principles of ventilation and warming.

"Perhaps the very best patent that could be obtained for anything connected with this subject would be the application of a little common sense to the use of our ordinary contrivances. This certainly would be sufficiently novel to secure the granting of the patent at once. One of the very common causes of failure with many of the contrivances for ventilation, is the neglect of those adopting them to take a full, complete, and comprehensive view of all the circumstances surrounding them. They fail to comprehend the force and power of the ever-varying currents of the external atmosphere. The pressure of a strong wind amounts to many tons on the side of an ordinary building. Now, the whole of this pressure may be exerted one moment, and almost entirely withdrawn the very next. Or, it may be pressing on one side of the building one hour, creating a partial vacuum on the other, and the next hour both the pressure and vacuum may be reversed. These are great controlling conditions; and yet one sees, daily and almost hourly, in the offices and rooms of persons of good ordinary intelligence, a lamp or a gas-light burning in one corner of a large apartment, which, it is confidently expected, will thoroughly ventilate the whole building. Or, perhaps, a little toy-wheel, at times whirling around in the window-pane, and at other times motionless, is designed to answer the same purpose. The little woolly lap-dog, as he bellows out at the express-train with all the energy and force of his little lungs, scarcely presents a more ludicrous waste and misapplication of power. One must first learn to comprehend these great controlling natural forces; and, whenever it is possible, work with them instead of attempting to oppose them. It will be seen at a glance, however, that all contrivances for ventilation must necessarily be varied frequently, owing to the constantly altering conditions with which one is surrounded. An open window is very agreeable on a warm spring morning, but quite the contrary when admitting the keen, piercing wind of a cold winter's day. Windows and doors are our great natural ventilators; and many persons, in speaking of ventilation, overlook the important part they really play in the ventilation of buildings. Occupants exercise considerable thought and care in opening and closing these according to the ever-shifting conditions of the atmosphere, and ought to exercise the same intelligence in regulating other contrivances for ventilation. The difficulty is, that many persons seem to be anticipating the discovery of some system of ventilation that will require no thought and no intelligence to regulate. When they can control the external temperature, and keep it forever at one uniform standard, and cause the wind to blow forever with the same force and in one direction, this may be done, but not before.

"Important as windows and doors are for general ventilation, yet, in every building, and in almost every room, it is very desirable to have some other provision for ventilation—some contrivance that may be frequently and easily regulated according to the veering of the wind and the alteration of temperature, as well as according to the relative temperature of the external atmosphere and that of the room.

"When the public shall have comprehended that one breathes more than ten times the number of pounds of air that one eats of food, and that it is of ten times the importance to have pure air than it is to have pure food; and further, when the public shall have determined to make a liberal expenditure of time, money, and thought to procure this constant supply of pure air, then it will be in a condition to examine critically the many contrivances offered for that purpose, and will probably soon learn that there has been an exceedingly small amount of common sense applied to the accomplishment of the object aimed at. At the same time, considerable valuable ingenuity has been wasted for want of taking an enlarged, clear, and comprehensive view of the whole subject before starting."

SUNSHINE

"Sunshine, the great motive power of atmospheric movements, is *the* motive power of natural ventilation. It is also Nature's great disinfectant; and if there is one place more than another in which its influence cannot be dispensed with, that place is the school-room.

"From the disregard of sunlight—direct sunlight—so noticeable in the construction, not only of school-houses but dwellings, it is to be feared that few persons realize how soon the walls, carpets, and other porous objects in a room become foul by the absorption of effete matter exhaled from the bodies of the occupants. A free circulation of air is of great value, as well for removing these exhalations before they can be deposited as for supplying fresh air for breathing. But mere change of air is not sufficient: a more powerful agent is required. Every lady knows, unfortunately, how soon direct sunlight fades the bright colors of her carpets and upholstery. Too few appear to know that the same blessed agent is equally energetic in dissipating the fever-breeding, consumption-causing air that pervades and clings to her carefully-shaded furniture. We want fewer heavy curtains and closed shutters, and more sunshine in our public and private apartments.

"Many attempts have been made to secure the thorough ventilation of buildings by currents of air produced by artificial means, to the entire neglect of natural ventilation; but always with disappointment. Ventilating engineers are apt to commence by calculating first how much each person will inhale or exhale in a minute, and then, by making what seems to be a liberal allowance for the contamination of the surrounding air, endeavor to provide for the requisite supply of pure air. The results obtained almost invariably fall short of what is actually required. Especially in mild or close weather do these artificial arrangements fail. Then nothing short of the full sweep of the external air will answer. For rooms in which large numbers of persons are to be collected, it is a primary requirement that there be openings on every side, so that any outside currents of air, from whatever direction, may be made use of.

"Objections may be made to our arrangement of windows because of the great amount of light that would enter at them. That, of course, could be regulated by means of blinds. The direction of the light that strikes the pupils' books can be regulated in the same way. Blinds should be used on all the windows, because they are far superior to curtains in admitting a free circulation of air, while excluding the direct rays of the sun; and the blinds should be *green*, because that is the color most agreeable to the eyes. At intermissions, and before and after school, the blinds should be opened to admit direct sunlight, the purifying effect of which is absolutely indispensable in keeping the school-room wholesome.

"The only objection that we can see to our school-house thus overflowed with sunshine and fresh air, is that the children would so luxuriate in these essentials of physical health and vivacity, that they would be as restless and mischievous as the boys and girls of an old-fashioned country school kept in an over-ventilated log-house. They would need a very different treatment, it is true, from that required to spur into activity the poor, pale-faced, automatic dolls that go through the routine performances of many of our public schools; yet we must confess a strong liking for the *spirit* of the country school-boy."

SCHOOL MATERIAL—Part I.

SCHOOL DESKS etc

CONTENTS.

Important to all who Use, Buy, Sell, or Manufacture School Furniture.

Know all Men by these Presents, That I, Aaron H. Allen, of Boston, Massachusetts, in consideration of, and pursuant to, an Indenture made and executed on the Sixteenth day of September, 1869, by me and J. W. Schermerhorn & Co., of the City, County, and State of New York, do declare that I have granted to them the sole right and privilege of Manufacturing and Selling School Furniture, made according to Letters Patent of the United States, for Tilting Seats supported by the Lever, granted to me on the 5th day of December, 1854.—Re-issued on the 15th day of January, 1861,—and extended *seven* years from the 5th day of December, 1868, and subject to the terms and conditions in said Indenture contained.

In witness whereof, I have hereunto set my hand and seal, this Eighteenth day of September, A.D. 1869. { L.S. }

(Signed) A. H. ALLEN.

(Witnessed)

The undersigned **CAUTION** all persons against the use of infringements of the above-named Patents—which, we believe, cover all the Folding-seat School Furniture now in use, supported directly or remotely on the Lever principle. All who may use the same without license from us are liable for damages.

We respectfully solicit the names of persons who are using infringements, without our license, and shall cheerfully pay for such information.

We do not desire to annoy school officers and others who may have innocently purchased violations of our patents; and yet it is our plain duty to protect our rights under the patent laws. We have secured **Allen's Opera-seat Patents,** at great expense, **for our own trade;** and we must insist upon our rights.

Suits against the Cities of New York and Brooklyn are now pending, and preliminary proceedings are in progress in several other cases.

J. W. Schermerhorn & Co., *Proprietors*

Of Allen's Opera-Seat Patents,

(As applied to School Furniture).

INTRODUCTION.

Too many of our schools have rude, unsightly, and uncomfortable furniture; and yet Americans may congratulate themselves upon having their schools supplied with better furniture than the schools of any other country. The school furniture of Great Britain is to-day not superior to ours a quarter of a century ago, and England's school furniture is somewhat better than we find in most European countries.

A contemporary seriously describes school furniture consisting of "a bench with legs long at the one end and short at the other. The large scholars sat upon the higher end, and the smaller were graded down to the lower end." We have never seen any furniture like this, and must confess that the contemporary dates farther back than we can. We do, however, distinctly remember the old-fashioned "bench," hastily constructed from a pine slab, fresh from the neighboring saw-mill. The flat, unplaned side was considered good enough for the seats of the urchins of those days. Cuttings from a sapling were inserted, bracingly, for supports. There was nothing to rest the wearied backs of the boys and girls of that period. "Writing and ciphering" facilities for the larger pupils were made by arranging boards slopingly around the walls of the house. A "slab bench" was placed under the edge of this writing-desk, and those occupying the same would "face to the wall" when at work, and "face about" when the teacher wanted to lecture them, or display them to "the committee." This arrangement had its advantages as well as its disadvantages. If active-minded pupils were intent upon "eating apples," reading story-books, or making caricatures of the watchful schoolmaster, they might be "caught" by that individual approaching quietly from the rear.

That style has now passed away, giving place to modern school furniture. Even our rural schools are demanding furniture of the better kinds. And our manufacturers of school material have been compelled to fall out of the ranks, or intelligently study the construction of school furniture as "a fine art."

Absolute Requisites for Good School Furniture.

First—COMFORT.

The seats and backs must be curved to precisely fit the natural curves of the bodies of the pupils. An indifferently curved *seat* is not enough—both *seat and back* must be curved, and *properly curved.*

Second—FOLDING SEATS.

Pupils must be able to *take and leave their seats without difficulty and disturbance;* the teacher must know that he can *call up every pupil promptly*, at a given signal; the school-room must *have capacity for* light gymnastics; *free passages across the room* must be allowed, with ample opportunity for *cleaning the floors.*

Third—DURABILITY.

This quality must be secured by the use of the *best material, skilled workmen,* and *correct construction.*

Fourth—GOOD APPEARANCE.

This quality, besides making the school-room attractive, will protect the furniture from the attacks of penknives and other destructive instruments. Good appearance is necessary to aid in educating taste.

Fifth—COMFORT, First and Last.

Correct physiological principles must be observed in the construction of all modern school furniture.

Besides these absolute requisites, school furniture should be (1) economical as to price—the best need not be the most expensive: (2) *readily taken apart,* for safe and cheap transportation—the patented manner of "dove-tailing" the several parts permits this, besides rendering the *effects of shrinking, swelling, and warping impossible.*

Sizes.

The **sizes** of all our **styles** of **School Furniture** are **uniform,** as shown in the following table. The lengths are for desks and settees for **two pupils,** and are commonly called **Double Desks and Settees.** The furniture called **"Children's,"** is adapted to pupils in infant schools; that called **"Small Primary,"** is adapted to pupils aged from 5 to 7 years; **"Primary,"** to those aged 7 to 10 years; **"Intermediate,"** 10 to 13; **"Grammar,"** 12 to 15; **"High School,"** 15 to 19; **"Academic,"** to adults. Due allowance should be made for the variable sizes of children in different latitudes. Great care should be used to avoid selecting sizes **too large** for the grade of the pupils. This mistake occurs more frequently than that of grading the desks and settees too low. We all know that **we rest better in a low chair** than in a high one.

	LENGTH.	HEIGHT OF DESK.	WIDTH OF DESK.	HEIGHT OF SEAT.
Children's,	36 inches.	18 inches.	10½ inches.	9½ inches.
Small Primary,	36 "	20 "	10 "	11 "
Primary,	36 "	22½ "	12 "	12 "
Intermediate,	36 "	25 "	15 "	13½ "
Grammar School,	42 "	26½ "	15 "	15 "
High School,	42 "	27½ "	15 "	16½ "
Academic,	42 "	29½ "	15 "	17 "

Settees for rear rows—any size, to match the desks.

Desk height is measured at *front*—back edge is 1½ inches higher. Seat height is measured at *front*, with a comfortable pitch of about 1½ inches

Single Desks intended for **one** pupil, have same dimensions as double desks, except **length,** which varies from 18 to 24 inches.

The average space required on the floor of the school-room for **Children's, Small Primary, Primary, and Intermediate** sizes, is 25 by 36 inches.

The **Grammar, High School, and Academic,** require about 28 by 42 inches.

The width of the aisles must depend upon circumstances. **Folding** seats require less waste of space for aisles than fixed seats. 18 to 24 inches is ample.

Of each style of desks and seats we have the sizes named at the bottom of the page on which the said style is described.

Price Lists will be sent on application with stamp. In calling for price lists, it is well to mention **the number and grade of pupils requiring furniture.**

SCHOOL FURNITURE.

STYLE A.

The American Settees, with Slate-Rests and Book-Boxes.

1. The "Cornell" Settee, for Primary and Intermediate Classes.

The men and women of to-day can readily recall the aches and pains inflicted upon them by the ill-shaped furniture of thirty years ago. The school officers of that period were apt to consider anything good enough for "the smaller scholars," and to act with disregard to the comfort of children, which has done more to create positive "hatred of school" than any other one cause.

The style illustrated in the cut is as easy and comfortable as it is possible to construct school furniture. The shape of the seat and back is precisely adapted to fit the natural outlines of the persons of pupils. This shape, together with the proper pitch of the seat, tends to compel an *erect* posture, which is sure to induce better health and habits than can be expected when uncomfortable furniture is used.

Style A is intended more especially for those in the children's and primary departments, and for those in the intermediate department who have not yet attained to the "copy-book" degree. The arm, or "slate-rest," is sufficient for supporting the books and slates of the children, who can rest upon it when they lean forward. The book-boxes beneath the seat are ample for putting away books, slates, etc., when not in use.

This style is economical as to price and as to space required. It is constructed under the dove-tailed patent, hence is very substantial, and being easily taken apart ("knocked down"), may be cheaply shipped, and readily put together at its destination.

It is made of *three heights*—**1**, Children's; **2**, Primary; and **3**, Intermediate; in lengths of 3 ft., 4½ ft., 6 ft., 7½ ft., and 9 ft., with slate-rests for two, three, four, five, or six pupils respectively.

Popular School Desks and Settees.

STYLE B.

(*Munger's Patents, and Allen's Opera Seat Patents.*)

The inventor of THE NEW AMERICAN SCHOOL DESKS AND SETTEES, which have become so widely famous, devised this style in response to the demands of school officers who want good school furniture at *cheaper rates than any heretofore made.* At the same time, in this cheaper style many of the superior points of the original invention have been preserved, substantial wood ends being used in place of the expensive iron frames.

They are *comfortable*—the backs and seats having the proper curve. They have the indispensable *folding seats.* They are constructed under the "dove-tailing" patent, and hence may be *shipped flat,* and readily put together by unskilled persons. No more substantial desks than these are made. Some may object to the wood ends, which certainly are not as light and graceful as the iron frames. In many sections, however, they have found great favor, and are pronounced as good as the more expensive furniture.

The following are the regular sizes by name and by number; the dimensions in detail are given in another place:

4. Children's Desk and Settee—for two Pupils.
5. Primary, " "
6. Intermediate, " "
7. Grammar, " "
8. High School, " "
9. Academic, " "
10. Settees for Rear Rows " "

4½. Children's D. and S.—for *one* Pupil.
5½. Primary, " "
6½. Intermediate, " "
7½. Grammar, " "
8½. High School, " "
9½. Academic, " "
10½. Settees for Rear Rows " "

STYLE C.

The New England School Desks,

WITH FOLDING CHAIRS.

This style is so called because School Desks of similar appearance have long been popular in many parts of New England.

The desk, simple and economical in construction, has its several parts joined on the "dove-tailed" plan, so that it may be packed entirely flat, and put up at its destination. Hence its transportation is exceedingly cheap. The several parts fit perfectly, and the application of a little glue to the dove-tailing parts when they are put together, makes them perfectly firm and substantial.

The Folding Chair is a Novelty, which gratifies the wants of those who demand the *individual* as well as the *folding* seat. The curves of the backs and seats are the same as those of our "New American Desks and Settees."

These chairs are made *folding*, under the patents of A. H. Allen, the inventor of the famous Opera Seat. We have purchased the exclusive use of his patents, in their application to school furniture, at a great expense. Teachers and school officers who have most carefully and intelligently studied the wants of modern schools, demand Folding Seats.

Style C may be recommended for general utility and *economy*, but not for beauty. Though better, in appearance, than the cut represents, yet it cannot be depended upon to improve the taste of the rising generation.

There are five sizes, for two pupils:—**11**. Primary,—**12**. Intermediate,—**13**. Grammar,—**14**. High School, and **15**. Academic. Also five sizes, for *one* pupil:—**11½**. Primary,—**12½**. Intermediate,—**13½**. Grammar,—**14½**. High School,—**15½**. Academic. The dimensions are the same as appear in the table of standard sizes.

STYLE D.

The Accommodation School Desks,

WITH THE WILCOX FOLDING CHAIRS.

THIS style (*D*) is a considerable improvement on style *C*, and is somewhat more expensive.

The DESK has strong iron frames, which give it a light and graceful appearance. All the iron parts dovetail into the wood-work, making it convenient to pack it *flat*, and put it together at its destination. This manner of joining the parts strengthens the desk, as the wood and iron mutually brace and stiffen each other.

The CHAIR, devised by Mr. Wilcox, is a success. It has the proper comfortable shape—both back and seat being curved; it affords independent seats for each pupil—which some teachers prefer; and its appearance is GOOD.

Its merits, compared with the "pedestal chair," need not be seriously discussed. Pedestal chairs invariably become loose because of the severe strain upon the screws which (at first) fasten them to the floor. Their construction permits this—and they then prove very noisy and annoying. The Wilcox chair can have no difficulty of this kind. Its construction renders it absolutely firm under all circumstances. It is well balanced, and even without screws, it will do quite as well as ordinary household chairs. Moreover, it is FOLDING—the many advantages of which need not be named here. *Well-informed educators everywhere demand folding seats.*

Of this style there are the following, whose dimensions are given in the "table of standard sizes."

16. Primary Desk and Chairs—for *two* Pupils.
17. Intermediate, " "
18. Grammar, " "
19. High School, " "
20. Academic, " "

16½. Primary D. and Chair—for *one* Pupil.
17½. Intermediate, " "
18½. Grammar, " "
19½. High School, " "
20½. Academic, " "

STYLES E & F.

The New American School Desks and Settees.

(Munger's Patents, with Allen's Opera-Seat Patent.)

E. Combined Desk and Settee. **F.** Independent Desk and Settee.

The exact physiological curvature of the seat and back has not been easy to find.—Much time was spent in gradual approaches to this curve. Different models were subjected to the criticism of teachers and school-children, and the still severer test of use. The faults of each form were carefully noted and corrected, until their various and often obscure defects were eliminated and the proper curve determined. That it was no easy task to discover the shape universally adapted to the persons of old and young—which would support the body just where it needs supporting, and leave it free at every other point—is well attested by the almost universal failure of cabinet-makers and upholsterers to devise a chair, settee, car-seat, or church-pew that one can sit on half an hour without positive discomfort. The commonest faults (where a curve is attempted) are too great a curvature, or a misplaced one—a curve that strikes the back too high up, gouging the sitter under the shoulder-blades, or one bearing upon the shoulders like a yoke. Fig. *x* represents a seat, curiously contrived to miss the end intended. It is a copy of a portion of the engraved illustration of a certain "Sofa-backed" school seat. A more elaborate contrivance for forcing children to sit on the small of the back would be hard to find. Every one of the curves is just the reverse of what it should be. We have seen School Furniture with a boasted "curved back," having the edges of the back rudely "rounded off" a little, regardless of the natural outlines of the bodies of the pupils. That, however, is a farce which can hardly satisfy the enlightened wants of the educators of the present day.

Fig. *x* (Bad Form).

The curves of the backs and seats of Styles E and F are faultless. [OVER]

The folding seat is the nicest adaptation of Allen's Opera-seat patent yet conceived of. It is perfectly simple and noiseless. The lever works in a mortise, inaccessible to the fingers or dress of the children. And whether the seat is down, or folded up, it rests upon rubber cushions, which, besides making it **noiseless,** yield a grateful spring to the occupants. It is difficult to show on paper the nice points of this folding seat. The accompanying cut may perhaps give some idea of it; but the thing itself must be seen and used to be perfectly understood and appreciated.

Independent Settee, with Book-Box.

The dove-tailing patent is used for attaching the wood and iron. This prevents all warping or checking of the wood, and allows the furniture to be readily taken apart and safely packed for shipment, at about one-fifth of the usual freight charges on set-up furniture.

Style **E** is **the best Combined Desk and Settee made.** Its great width of base; the perfect balance of all its parts, rendering it steady even without the use of floor screws; and the rigid union of the wood and iron, make it so strong and firm that the chief, if not the only objection to **combined** desks and settees, liability to "joggle," is reduced to almost nothing.

Style **F** has been prepared for those who have insuperable objections to combined desks and settees. Such persons will recognize a special triumph in the **Independent Desks and Settees.** These will give the same appearance to the School Room as Style E. The Desks and Settees stand close together, are perfectly symmetrical, and yet are entirely distinct. No space is wasted, and no desk and settee touch each other.

In Styles **E** and **F** the space for books is ample on a shelf beneath the desk-top. In the double desks this shelf is divided in the middle by a partition. The ends of the desks are open-work to permit easy inspection by the teacher, and prevent the introduction of contraband articles.

These styles are considered complete to the minutest details. **They are careful and artistic combinations of all the absolute requisites of perfect School Furniture. They are unrivalled in comfort, in strength and durability, in finished workmanship, and in graceful and elegant appearance.**

Men of the best mechanical ideas and those who have given most study to modern School Furniture are the loudest in their praises.

The **Combined** has the following dimensions in "table of standard sizes:"

21. Children's Desk and Settee—for *two* Pupils.	**21½.** Children's D. and S.—for *one* Pupil.
22. Primary, " "	**22½.** Primary, " "
23. Intermediate, " "	**23½.** Intermediate, " "
24. Grammar, " "	**24½.** Grammar, " "
25. High School, " "	**25½.** High School, " "
26. Academic, " "	**26½.** Academic, " "
27. Settees for Rear Rows, "	**27½.** Settees for Rear Rows, "
28. Ditto with Book-Box, "	**28½.** Ditto with Book-Book, "

The **Independent:**

29. Primary Desk and Chairs—for *two* Pupils.	**29½.** Primary D. and Chair—for *one* Pupil.
30. Intermediate, " "	**30½.** Intermediate, " "
31. Grammar, " "	**31½.** Grammar, " "
32. High School, " "	**32½.** High School, " "
33. Academic, " "	**33½.** Academic, " "
34. Settees for Rear Rows, "	**34½.** Settees for Rear Rows, "
35. Ditto with Book-Box, "	**35½.** Ditto with Book-Box, "

STYLE G.

Assembly-Room Desks and Settees.

(Munger's Patents with Allen's Opera-Seat Patent.)

It is often necessary that the School-room be used for a general Assembly-room—for Sunday-school, Public Lectures, and other purposes. Hence Furniture which will permit **the School-room to be readily transformed into an Assembly-room,** has long been desired. Inventors in this Country and in Great Britain have tried their skill; but with clumsy and expensive results. The achievement illustrated in the cuts is a decided success.

Economy of cost and space; strength and simplicity of construction; ease and rapidity of changing a School-room of Desks into an **Assembly-room of Settees:** all have been considered and accomplished. With this Furniture it is easy for the School-room to serve the double purpose of School and Public Hall.

The top is easily let down by the pupils, while seated in their places. The book-boxes are located as shown at A A A, extending the entire length of the Desks, giving ample book and slate room. When the Desks are folded the book-boxes are closed, keeping out the dust. Book-boxes may also be attached beneath the seats—as shown on Settees on another page. When desired they may be supplied with locks.

When Desk and Seat are both folded, less than one foot in width is occupied, leaving ample space for gymnastic exercises, passages, etc. (See Cut.)

The *folding Seat* (Allen's Opera-seat patent), with the *Comfortable Curves* of both back and seat, which have made the **New American School Desks and Settees** so widely famous, do good service in this style.

The **Assembly Desks and Settees** have five sizes, see table of standard sizes:

36. Primary Desk and Settee—for *two* Pupils.	**36½.** Primary D. and Settee—for *one* Pupil.
37. Intermediate, " "	**37½.** Intermediate, " "
38. Grammar, " "	**38½.** Grammar, " "
39. High School, " "	**39½.** High School, " "
40. Academic, " "	**40½.** Academic, " "
41. Settees for Rear Rows, "	**41½.** Settees for Rear Rows, "
42. Ditto with Book-box, "	**42½.** Ditto with Book-box, "

STYLE H.

"Old Style" Desks and Chairs.

We are ready to supply the "Old Style" Desks and Chairs, though we do not care to recommend the uncomfortable and inconvenient chairs, and do not deny that distant customers will find the transportation expenses a very important item. Yet, many School Officers have long endured this style of Furniture, and many others may find no insuperable objections to it: and sometimes, for special reasons, may prefer it.

Circular Back Pedestal Chair.

The iron-work is strong and plain, having no points nor angles to tear the dress and catch the dust.

Besides the chairs which appear in the cut above, the "Circular Back Pedestal" chairs, and the "Extra School" chairs are appropriate for use with these desks. The three styles are about the same price.

Extra School Chair.

[Sometimes we have of this and similar styles *second-hand lots*, but little used, and "as good as new," which we can supply "at bargains." School Officers desiring to exchange them for modern styles, place them in storage for us to dispose of at "a sacrifice." We will not attempt to sell them to customers who cannot call and examine them for themselves.]

There are five sizes:

43. Primary Desk and Chairs—for *two* Pupils.	**43½**. Primary D. and Chair—for *one* Pupil.
44. Intermediate, " "	**44½**. Intermediate, " "
45. Grammar, " "	**45½**. Grammar, " "
46. High School, " "	**46½**. High School, " "
47. Academic, " "	**47½**. Academic, " "

STYLE I.

Box Desks with Lids.

This style is an old favorite, yet in fair demand. It suits certain tastes, and meets tl requirements of certain circumstances which other styles may not seem to satisfy.

We make these desks as handsomely as their construction will permit. The iron su ports are substantial and plain—entirely without angles and points to tear the dress an afford lodgement for dust. They are fitted to screw fast to the floor, though they may l used without the floor-screws. They are well braced—(our artist has not clearly show the braces in the cut).

The box part is well made of thoroughly seasoned wood. The lids have brass hing and close on rubber cushions to avoid noise.

The book-box beneath the lids is divided into two compartments in the double desk each of which is supplied with a little shelf for pens, pencils, etc, and each lid has a bra for holding it when open. The top is properly inclined for writing. The level part of tl top is grooved for pens and pencils, and is bored for inkwells.

The Lids are made plain, and finished in the usual manner, or they are covered wi **green enamelled cloth**, as may be ordered.

Any chairs, movable, fixed, or folding, may be used with these desks. Chairs are so separately.

There are **five sizes**—heights are given in table of standard sizes

48. Primary Box D. with Lids—for *two* Pupils.
49. Intermediate, " "
50. Grammar, " "
51. High School, " "
52. Academic, " "

48½. Primary B. D. with Lids—for *one* Pup
49½. Intermediate, " "
50½. Grammar, " "
51½. High School, " "
52½. Academic, " "

STYLE I—(CONTINUED).

Single Box Desks with Lids.

The cut represents the Box Desks with Lids adapted to **one** pupil. They are constructed precisely like those intended for two pupils, with same dimensions except as to length. Any kind of chairs may be used with these desks:—we have chairs to suit all tastes, and all purses.

New American Chair.

Most educators appreciate the varied advantages of the **folding** chairs, and insist on having them. Of these there are two kinds—the **new American folding chair** and the **Wilcox folding chair**—both of which are made under the **Allen Opera-Seat Patents.**

Five sizes of these desks and chairs, uniform with heights in table of standard sizes.

Wilcox Chair.

[Chairs appearing on these two pages (representing Box Desks with Lids) are named as follows—we enumerate them in the order in which they appear: **(a) Circular Back, Cane seat; (b) Circular Back, Wood seat; (c) Extra School; (d) Curved Back, Cane seat; (e) New American Folding; (f) Wilcox Folding.**]

53. Primary B. D. with Lid—for *one* Pupil.
54. Intermediate, " "
55. Grammar, " "
56. High School B. D. with Lid—for *one* Pupil.
57. Academic, " "

Single Desks, like Style D, with Chairs.

Economy of cost and space, and sometimes other considerations, induce school offic and teachers generally to purchase **double desks**, to accommodate two pupils. Howev desks for single pupils are frequently called for. Hence, all of the desks shown in t catalogue are made **single, for one pupil,** as well as **double, for two pupils.**

It is not necessary to occupy our pages to show the several styles of single desks, sin the views which we give of the double desks are sufficient to give correct impressions of t appearance of the desks when made for one pupil instead of two—the difference being length only.

The above cut represents the single desk of Style D, shown on page 11.

Any style of chairs to suit the requirements of the case may be used. We have alrea illustrated several kinds of **movable, fixed, and folding chairs**—to which we wou now refer. Sizes are uniform with Style D.

STYLE J.

Wall Desks.

Desks like that shown in the accompanying cut are occasionally very convenient for placing around the walls of the school-room, or in spaces which may sometimes be required to be cleared for aisles. The top readily folds **down,** like the tops of the "Assembly-Desks," to make a free passage when required. The top, in folding down, incloses the book-box A. They are made to order in any required lengths.

There are five sizes:

58. Primary.
59. Intermediate.
60. Grammar.
61. High School.
62. Academic.

STYLE K.

The New York Desk-Settee.

The Patent Desk-Settees, illustrated above, are used very extensively in the **Public Schools of New York City.** They have been in use since 1864, and have been very severely and satisfactorily tested.

They have two seats--the upper seat being arranged to turn up and over to form a desk, the lower seat being occupied by the pupil when writing, and the upper seat when the top is folded down, to **convert the desks into settees.**

This cut gives the same desks in another position, and shows the sliding frame for holding books, slates, or copies for drawing, etc., etc. When not in use, the frame is passed down behind the seat. They all have book-boxes beneath the seat, book-racks attached to the backs, inkwells, etc.

They are very substantially constructed. When desired, they will be supplied with plain backs, in place of the balluster backs shown in the cuts. There are the usual sizes for all grades of schools :

63, Primary; **64,** Intermediate; **65,** Grammar; **66,** High School; **67,** Academic.

Normal and Collegiate Desks.

68. Plain Box Desk, with Lid and Brace for holding it open,

Substantial iron supports, thoroughly braced. The top is grooved for pencils and pens and is bored for ink-wells. It is made of ash or cherry, with plain or cloth top as may b desired.

The Chair shown in the cut is **Oak, Curved Top, Cane Seat.**

69. Similar to 68, with more elaborate iron supports. Same price. It is expected tha chairs will be selected to suit the wants of the purchaser. These desks are quite as we adapted to one style of chair as another.

The Chair shown in the cut is the **Wilcox Folding Chair.**

Normal and Collegiate Desks.

70. Turned Post, Box Desk,

With lid and brace, enamelled cloth top. It is usually made of Black Walnut, but will be supplied in Ash or Cherry, when desired. It is specially desirable when the desks are required to be *movable*. The Chair shown is the **Extra School.**

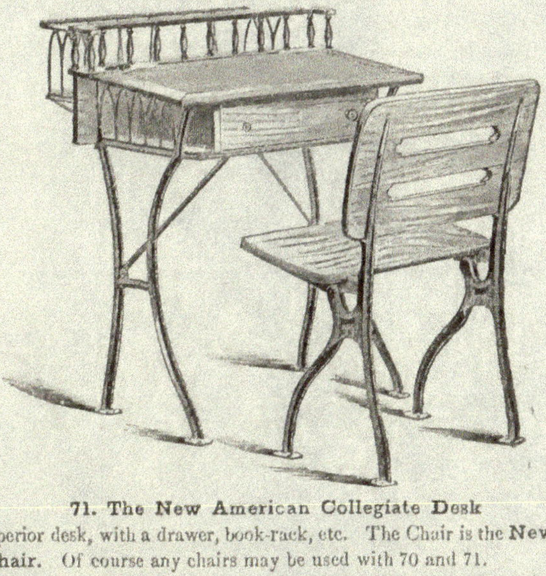

71. The New American Collegiate Desk

Is a very superior desk, with a drawer, book-rack, etc. The Chair is the **New American Folding Chair.** Of course any chairs may be used with 70 and 71.

The four preceding desks, Nos. 68, 69, 70, and 71, are supplied double, for two pupils, as well as single, as shown in the cuts.

Besides the desks here enumerated, all of our many styles are made large enough to adapt them to Normal and Collegiate uses.

Lecture-Room Settees for Seminaries, Colleges,

NORMAL SCHOOLS, AND UNIVERSITIES.

72. The Cornell Lecture-Room Settee

Was originally devised and constructed for Cornell University. Its use there has been highly approved by the president, faculty, students, and visitors. And it is in most satisfactory use in several of the first Colleges, Theological Seminaries, Normal Schools, and other prominent institutions.

The settee itself is the same as our New American Settee. To this is attached, at intervals to suit the circumstances of the case, desks, suitable for students' use in taking notes. These are strongly supported by ornamental cast-iron brackets, front and rear.

Settees are estimated by the foot at prices shown in our price list. When book-box is attached (as in cut) **20** cents per foot additional is charged. Writing desks (with brackets) for each student, **$1.00.**

They are shipped *flat*, or "knocked down," making transportation expenses scarcely one-tenth of that on ordinary settees.

73. The Cornell Examination Table

Was constructed at the suggestion of Hon. A. D. White, President of Cornell University. It contains no drawer for the concealment of papers, and folds flat for compact storage when not required for examination purposes. A hundred may be put away in a moderate size closet.

READING STANDS.

36.

37.

The Cuts 36 and 37 illustrate Stagg's Patent Revolving Reading Stands.

Cut 36 shows a stand entirely folded up. It is thus adapted to a variety of school, library, office, or household uses.

37 shows it with book-rack elevated and occupied by a book. The top serves as a brace, as well as a sloping desk on which the reader may make his notes and memoranda. The book is held open by nicely-adapted fingers. **Price, $10.00.**

38.

The Lecturer's Reading Stand (38)

Is a complete book-rest for the public reader. It is readily adjusted to any height, and to any inclination of desk. It has elastic fingers to retain the book or manuscript. It is substantial in construction and elegant in appearance. It is a useful and ornamental article for the private and public library.

In the public schools of New York city it is used as a Bible stand. For general utility it has no equal.

For use in Sunday-schools, lecture-rooms, and public halls there is nothing to equal this reading stand. It has had fair trial, with satisfaction.

The feet are of iron, shaped to give great stability to the stand, even when occupied by a heavy book.

For shipment the feet are readily taken off to render transportation safe and cheap.

Price of Lecturer's Reading Stand, $15.00.

Adjustable Stand

FOR

Artists, Draughtsmen, and Students.

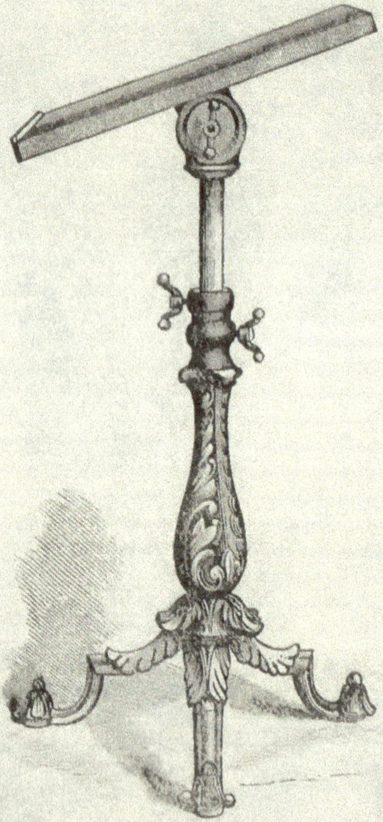

This Stand can be adjusted to any required height. Its top can be set at any inclination, and by turning back the screw at the right, it is allowed to rotate to bring either side in front. All adjustments are easily made, thus allowing it to be used when **sitting** or **standing,** with equal facility, as artist's easel, draughtsman's stand, or study table. It is good for holding large books of reference.

It is the best thing for draughtsmen, because it enables them to turn or incline their work at pleasure. And it is *a most complete artist's easel*, for, by a touch, the light on the picture may be entirely changed.

It is made almost entirely of iron, with substantial wood top, and its tasteful appearance makes it equally acceptable in the office, counting-room, library, or school-room.

PRICES, ETC.

Pine Top, stained, 21x21, plain.................................$10 00
Black Walnut Top, 22x26, casters.................................11 00
Black Walnut Top, 22x26, moulded edge, castings richly bronzed........13 50
Black Walnut Top, 22x26, moulded edge, gold bronzed and ornamented..15 00

Settees for Recitation Rooms, Sunday Schools,

PUBLIC HALLS, &c.

82. Common Wood, Plain Seat, Settee—Stump Arm.

83. Turned Spindle Back, Scooped Seat, Settee—Scroll Arm.

84. Flat Spindle Back, Fancy Rail, Double Rounds, Scooped Seat, Settee—Fancy Brace Arm.

Settees for Recitation Rooms, Sunday Schools,

PUBLIC HALLS, &c.

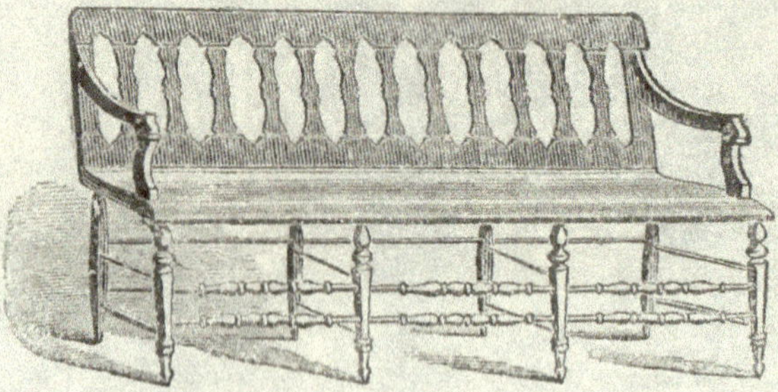

85 Fancy Flat Baluster Back, Double Fancy Turned Rounds, Scooped Seat, Settee—Fancy Brace Arm.

86. Slat Back, Cane Seat, Settee—Scroll Brace Arm.

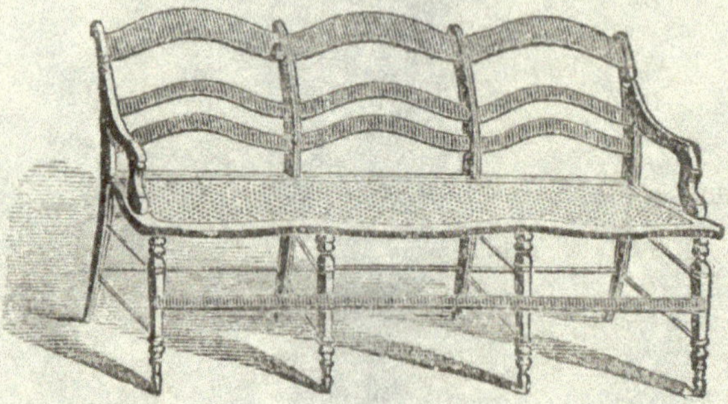

87. Grecian, Cane Seat, Flat Front Brace, Settee—Fancy Brace Arm.

Settees for Recitation Rooms, Sunday Schools,

PUBLIC HALLS, &c.

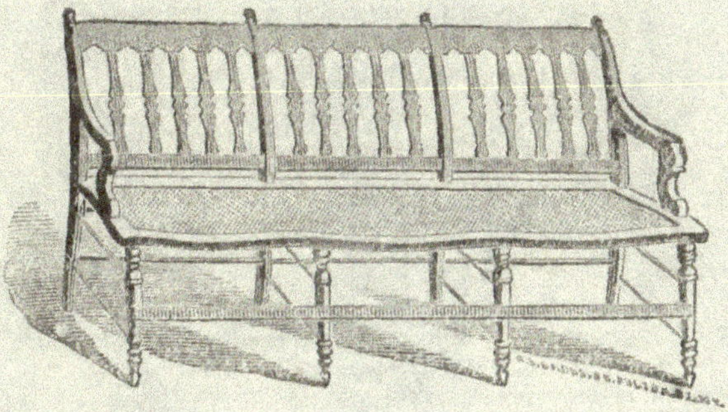

88. Flat Fancy Baluster and Rail, Cane Seat, Settee—Fancy Brace Arm.

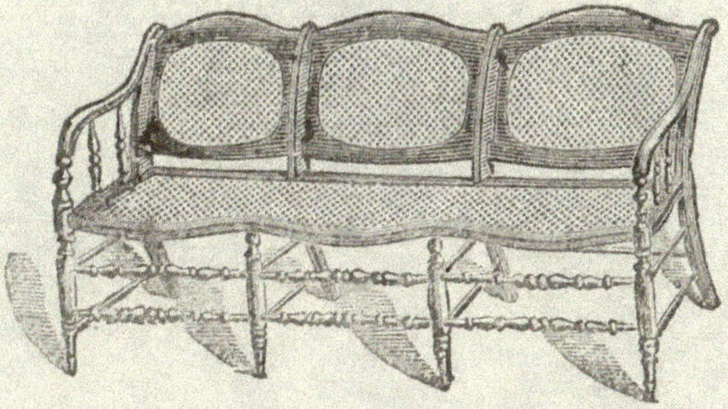

89. Fancy Cane Back and Seat, Square Rear Posts—Fancy Turned Double Rounds, Settee, Spindled Arm.

90. Flat Baluster Back, Scooped Seat, Settee—Bent Arm, Spindled; with Folding Book-Shelf attached.

Settees for Recitation Rooms, Sunday Schools, PUBLIC HALLS, &c.

91. Reversible, or Railroad Plain Spindle Back, Plain Seat, Settee—Bent Arm, Spindled.

92. Reversible, Turned Spindle, Scooped Seat, Settee—Iron supports and Arms.

93. Reversible, Flat Baluster, Plain Seat, Fancy Turned Posts, Settee—Bent Arms, Spindled.

Settees for Recitation Rooms, Sunday Schools,

PUBLIC HALLS, &c.

94. Reversible, Curved Slat Back, Curved Seat, Settee—Iron Arms and Supports. Style to correspond with the New American Settee.

SETTEES with reversible backs, enabling the occupants to face either way, are not uncommon. They are known in the lecture-room, and in the Sunday-school, and more particularly in the railway car. But, hitherto, they have not been constructed with *adjustable seats*, as well as backs. It is undeniable, that a seat, to be *comfortable*, must pitch downward from the front edge. Comfort and physiological considerations alike demand this.

No. 95.

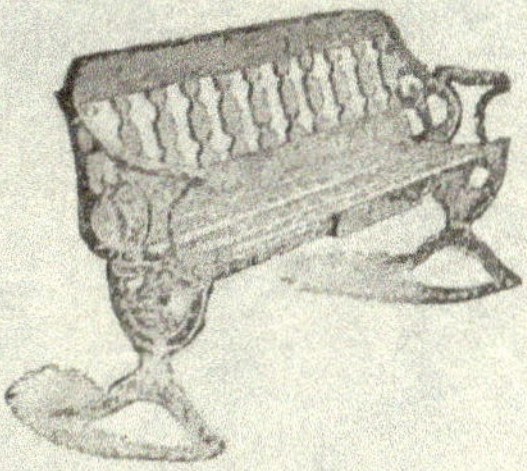

No. 96.

95. Joeckel's Reversible, Spindle Back, Pitching Slat Seat, Settee—Iron Arms and Supports.

96. Joeckel's Reversible, Baluster Back, Pitching Slat Seat, Settee—Iron Arms and Supports, with Book-Box.

MR. JOECKEL'S PATENT SETTEES have this advantage besides the back is reversed without turning it over. It is suspended on a pivot, like a pendulum, and is easily changed, at the same time giving the seat the proper pitch, and holding it securely in position. Strength and elegance have not been overlooked.

Settees for Recitation Rooms, Sunday Schools,

PUBLIC HALLS, &c.

97. **The Wilcox Settee has a Folding Seat,** (under Allen's Opera-seat patent), curved slat back and iron supports. It is a cheaper form of the **New American Settee** described in another place. It has the same general advantages as the New American, and can be shipped—"knocked down"—just as safely, and cheaply.

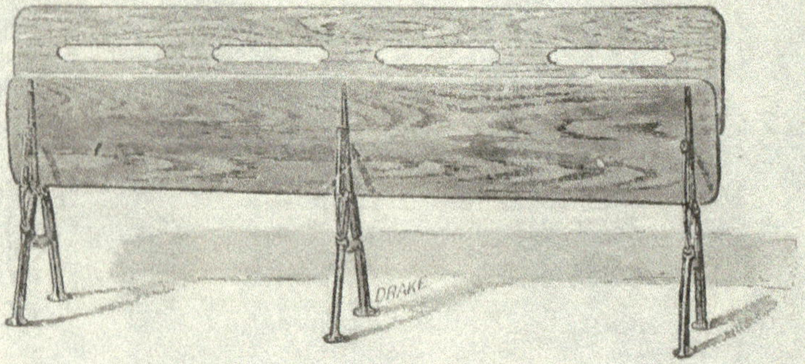

New American Settee—Seat folded up.

The Wilcox Settee folds just as compactly as the New American shown in the cut, giving ample space for standing, or for passages, sweeping, etc.

And again, if the hall is to be cleared of settees for any special purposes, these settees may be most compactly stored, each settee requiring only two inches of space in width.

The Wilcox Settee, and the New American Settee are graded to suit children and adults of all sizes. The regular lengths of these settees are 6 feet, 7 feet, 8 feet, 9 feet, and 10 feet. All other lengths made to order.

Settees for Recitation Rooms, Sunday Schools,

PUBLIC HALLS, &c.

98. **The New American Settee** has a curved fancy slat back, and a curved seat—the curve being the same as that which has made the New American School Desks and Settees so widely famous for their comfort. The wood and iron are dove-tailed together under Mr. Munger's patents—the advantages of which are obvious. **The seat is folding, under Allen's Opera-seat patent.**

The several peculiar advantages of this settee make it without an equal, and greatly superior for many purposes.

The lever device for folding, as now constructed, is more clearly shown in the accompanying enlarged cuts. The lever is pivoted on a strong bolt, and works noiselessly in a mortise, inaccessible to the fingers or dress: and whether the seat is up or down it rests on rubber cushions.

New American Settee for Primary Schools,

ALSO SETTEE WITH FOLDING ARMS.

99. New American Settee, Primary, Folding Seat, Book-Box.

For primary schools these frequently supply a convenient, comfortable, and economical purpose. Sometimes a book-rack is attached to the back of the settee.

100. New American Settee, Folding Seat, and Folding Arms.

This style was constructed at the suggestion of William Ballantyne, Esq., of Washington, D. C. It has peculiar advantages for those who want a **Folding Settee with Arms which readily fold with the Seat.**

SCHOOL MATERIAL,—PART II.

TEACHERS' DESKS, Etc.

CONTENTS.

TEACHERS' CHAIRS.

1. Common Windsor, Wood Seat.
(Too common and cheap for regular school use.)

2. Windsor, Wood Seat.
(Somewhat better than No. 1, but not *recommended.*)

3. Bent Top, Wood Seat.
(A cheap and strong chair.)

4. "Extra School."
(A well-known chair improved.)

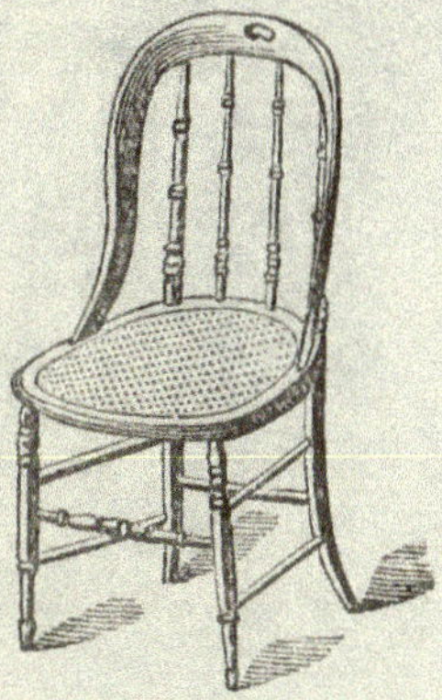

5. **Curved Top, Cane Seat.**
(A very good chair, much used in schools.)

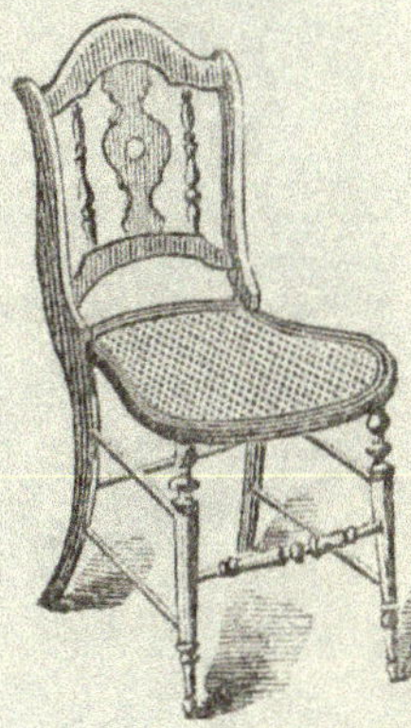

6. **"Bell" Bannister.**
(Similar to No. 5, costing a little more.)

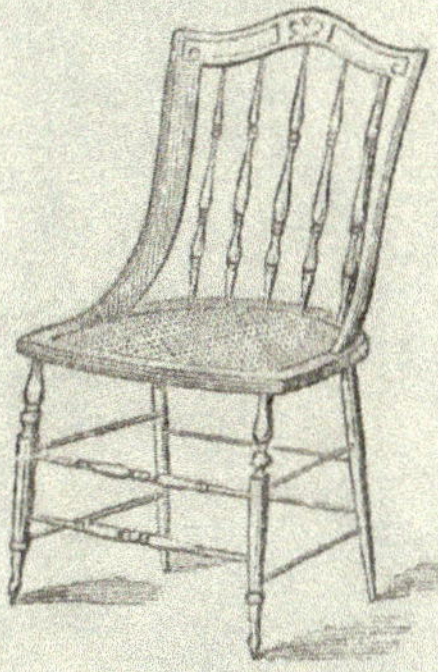

7. **"Square" Top, Cane Seat.**
(Somewhat better than Nos. 5 and 6.)

8. **Wood Seat, Bent Arms, with Rods.**
(A style not preferred by ladies.)

9. **English Cottage.**

10. **Cane Seat, Bent Arms, with Rods.**
(Similar in style to No. 8.)

11. Grecian, Half Arms.

12. Continental, Wood Seat.
(A durable and comfortable chair.)

13. Continental, Cane Seat.

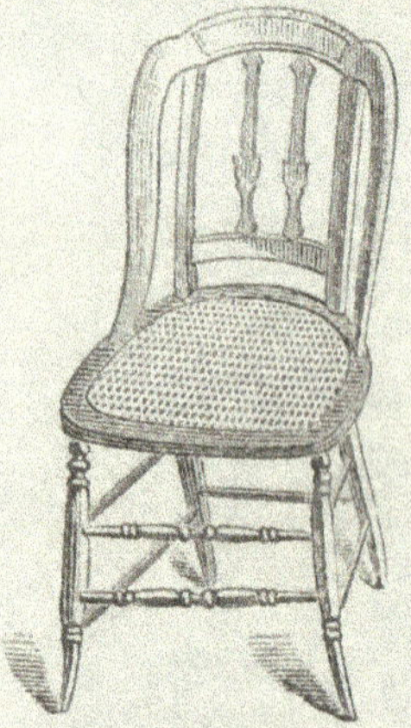

14. Banister.

15. Prescott Arm-Chair.
(A favorite in New York City schools.)

16. Brace Arm.
(A good chair for ladies.)

17. Library, Flat Spindle.

18. Library, New Style.

19. Common Arm, Wood Seat.
(Revolving pivot.)

20. Douglas, Bent Arms.
(Revolving pivot.)

21. Library, Cane Seat and Back.
(Revolving screw.)

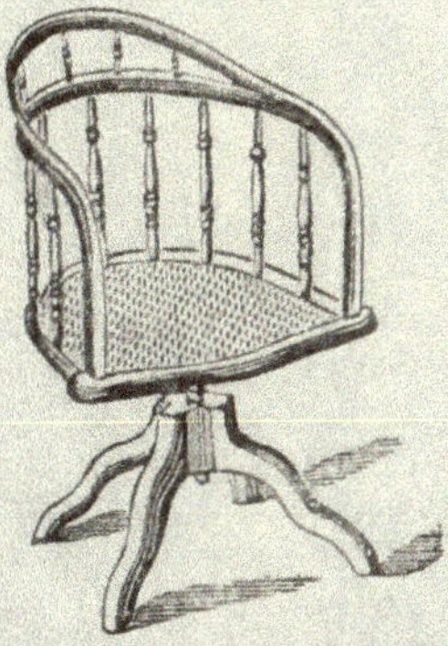
22. Crescent Cane Seat, Spindle Back.
(Revolving screw.)

Teachers' and Students' Chairs, etc.

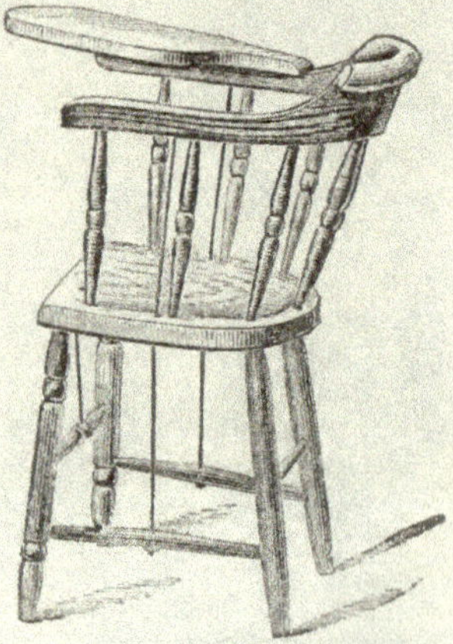

23. Student's Chair.

24. Student's Classical Chair.

23 is an old favorite, made in a very thorough and substantial manner.

24 has a wider and larger desk attached, which moves on a bolt passing through the arm of the chair. It is intended to hold a lexicon, grammar, and another book or two, and will be found specially convenient for students studying classics.

25. "Cornell" Chair.

26. Waste Paper Basket.

25 is a very strong chair, with desk attached. It may be screwed to the floor; but will stand well without the screws. For shipping it can be taken apart, and packed flat.

It will be found useful as a Teacher's Chair in the School Room, a Study Chair at home, or a Student's Chair in the College or University Lecture Room. In lengths for several students it is used with great satisfaction in Cornell University, in Rutgers College, in several Theological Seminaries, and in other first-class Educational Institutions.

26. The Waste Paper Basket is a necessary companion to the desk of teachers and others who value tidiness. The cut illustrates only one style, made of "round willow, crossbar work, plain"—several sizes—price . . . . .60 to .75.

There are elaborate fancy styles and shapes, colored, varying in price **$2.00** to **$5.00**.

TEACHERS' DESKS.

1. Maydo Desk, Plain Top.
(Size, 18 in. by 24 inches.)

2. Maydo Desk, Cloth Top.
(Size, 18 in. by 24 inches.)

These are the smallest, plainest, and cheapest desks made for teachers. The supports may be taken off for shipment, making transportation cheap. They are recommended only in cases where the argument of economy *must* prevail.

3. Black Walnut, Turned Supports.
(Size, 22 in. by 32 inches.)

This is a neat desk, with more capacity than Nos. 1 and 2, and yet very cheap. However, every teacher should have a larger desk than this.

4. New American, Small Size, One Drawer.

(Size, 25 in. by 27 inches.)

This is specially adapted for use in small class-rooms. It occupies very little space, and has unusual capacity, considering its size. It is thoroughly braced, and stands very firmly. It is precisely like No. 5, fully described below, except that it is shorter, having only one drawer, while No. 5 has *two*. The discrepancy in the appearance of the two arises from the fact that No. 5 is drawn on a smaller scale.

5. New American, Regular Size, Two Drawers.

(Size, 25 in. by 42 inches.)

An excellent desk *for the class-room*. The book-rack is original, simple, and convenient. It allows the teacher reference books at hand, yet never in the way, while globe and call-bell, and the indispensable Dictionary, have places within easy reach. Drawers, with locks and keys, afford security for private papers, stationery, records, etc. It is provided with two ink-wells, one for black and one for red ink, so placed that ink cannot get from them into the drawers. This desk has met with general favor in the schools of New York City and elsewhere. It is economically packed for shipping. It has been patented.

6. The Guilford Desk.
(Size, 24 in. by 45 inches.)

This is a very convenient and graceful desk, with fair capacity. It contains two drawers and a book-box. It has all the necessary qualities of a good desk, and can be recommended for the purpose to which it is adapted. Its iron supports can be readily taken off for safe and cheap shipment.

7. The Todd Desk. Two Drawers and Book-box.
(Size, 24 in. by 45 inches.)

This desk has two drawers and a book-box of unusual capacity beneath the lid. Besides the two drawers and pigeon-holes shown in the cut, the book-box is divided into small compartments under the level part of the top, for putting away papers, etc. It is an excellent desk for school purposes, and has had large demand.

8. **The Model Desk. Four Drawers and Book-Box.**

(Size, 24 in. by 52 inches.)

This is a handsome desk. It is made of ash, trimmed with black walnut, finished in panels, front, rear, and ends, having a remarkably graceful and lively appearance. It has four drawers, wide book-box beneath the lid, with ample space for books and papers on both sides of the writing surface.

9. **The New Model Desk.**

It has the size and capacity, with the general appearance, of No. 8, though plainer and stronger. For this reason it will generally be preferred.

10. **The New Model Desk, made of Black Walnut.**

11. Teacher's Desk, with Flat Top, Eight Drawers.
(Size, 24 in. by 52 inches.)

This is an elaborately finished desk, intended for the principal's platform, the side to the school being inclosed. It is made of beautiful grained ash, trimmed with black walnut, and panelled in front and at the ends with fine black walnut trimmings. It has eight drawers, of varied sizes, while the flat top gives ample space for papers, etc. Enamelled cloth covers the top.

12. The Same, made of Black Walnut, Billiard Cloth Top.

13. The Brewer Desk.
(Size, 24 in. by 60 inches.)

This desk can be shipped in three sections. It seems complete in all the essential requisites of a first-class principal's desk. It is made of ash, tastefully panelled and trimmed with fine black walnut mouldings.

14. The Same, made of Black Walnut.

15. Tremont Principal's Platform Desk.

(Size, 36 in. by 108 inches.)

This is an elaborate and elegant desk, of very great capacity. Its size is about three feet wide by nine feet long. The front contains closets for storing the books of the pupils, thus supplying the place of book-cases for an entire school. The doors of these closets are so nicely arranged that when closed they will not be observed.

It was originally designed and constructed for the schools of Tremont, N. Y., credit being due to Mr. William Herring, of the School Board, and Mr. George H. Albro, Principal of School No. 1.

It is made of finely grained ash, panelled and trimmed with black walnut.

The bright color and beautiful grain of the ash, which is used in constructing most of our teachers' desks, show to extra advantage in this desk. It is finished, as usual with all our work, in shellac, and grows brighter and harder with age. No person of good taste will be likely to select for school furniture such woods as grow dark and sombre.

Rear view of No. 15.

Besides the ten drawers and the middle place for records, which show in the cut, there are two large book-boxes under the lids. For the purposes intended we think this desk has no equal. Its appearance would be creditable to any first-class school-room, and would harmonize with the best modern ideas of school furniture.

16. The Same, made of Black Walnut or Mahogany.

17. Desk for "State Department of Instruction," Office of Board of Education, or Trustees' Room.

18. Same, of Black Walnut, Billiard Cloth Top.

This extensive desk is required in cities and in large towns. It is built for occupation on both sides. It has many compartments and drawers to accommodate vast business, with ample places for putting away records and account-books, and filing many papers. It is constructed in five parts, for convenience in shipping and in setting up. Being made to order, its size will be varied to suit the demand.

19. "Commissioner's" Desk, Carved Black Walnut, Enamelled Cloth Top.

(Size, 23 in. by 25 inches.)

20. Same. Carved Black Walnut, French Polished, Cloth Top, with Gilt Border.

This desk is an improvement on a desk which has been greatly admired. It is a beautiful and convenient article of office or household furniture. It has a capacious box under the lid for books and papers, and a closet on each side, with shelves, etc. It is panelled on all sides.

21. The Class-room Library Case.

Size, four feet high above the brackets, three feet four inches wide, with movable shelves for books. Panelled doors.

Other sizes and styles made to order, at reasonable prices.

22. The Library Table.

Size, three feet by five feet. Four drawers. Made of selected ash, black walnut trimmings, octagon legs.

23. Same, made of Black Walnut, Billiard Cloth Top.

Other sizes and styles made to order.

24. Teacher's Table. Plain Top, no Drawer.
(Size, 20 in. by 28 inches.)

25. Teacher's Table. Plain Top, One Drawer
(Size, 24 in. by 36 inches.)

26. Teacher's Table. Enamelled Cloth Top, One Drawer, with Lock and Key (like Cut).
(Size, 24 in. by 36 inches.)

27. Same, in Black Walnut, Enamelled Cloth Top, with Gilt Border.

28. Teacher's Table. Plain Top, Two Drawers, with good Locks and Keys.
(Size, 24 in. by 42 inches.)

29. Teacher's Table. Cloth Top, Two Drawers, with Locks and Keys (like Cut).
(Size, 24 in. by 42 inches.)

30. Teacher's Table. Cloth Top, Two Drawers, Black Walnut.
(Size, 26 in. by 36 inches.)

Any size or style to order, at proportionate prices.

Home Desks for Children and Adults.

31

33

31. A neat Home Desk for Children, black walnut, with Lock and Key.
32. Ditto, larger, size between 31 and 33 which the cuts illustrate.
33. For Young Ladies—large, with interior Compartments.

34

35

34. Is a pretty and convenient desk, with large drawer in lower part. The upper part contains two little drawers, and several compartments for books, writing materials, etc. The top has two shelves for books, ornaments, etc. The lid is hinged, and closes upward like 35.

35. Is larger and more elaborate, having in addition a closet underneath, with nicely panelled doors. Both these desks are ornamental as well as useful, and are highly appreciated by ladies.

The Desk Organ,

(PATENTED.)

36. **Complete Teacher's Desk and Double-Reed Organ............ $110.00.**

THIS Teacher's Desk has a Double Reed ORGAN attached, so that it does not interfere with the uses of the Desk, occupying no space appropriated to books, papers, etc., while the Organ, by turning a key, can be drawn out all ready for use, as shown in the cut.

Its advantages are: 1. Economy of Space, no more being required than for the desk alone 2. Economy of cost; the price shows this.

The Organ is made by Mason & Hamlin.

Any of Mason & Hamlin's School, Household, and Church Organs, at manufacturers' best rates.. **$55.00** to **$750.00.**

Illustrated Circular, with prices, sent on application, with stamp.

37. **Academy, School, and Church BELLS,**

in great variety, from the best Bell Foundry in the country. Illustrated Catalogue sent on application with stamp.

Portable Book Shelves.

I. The Gardner Patent Book Racks, Walnut, Plain Ends.

No. 2.	Size—Width 12 inches,	Height 12 inches,	2 Shelves—Price	$0.70
3.	" " 15 "	" 15 "	2 " "	1.00
4.	" " 18 "	" 18 "	3 " "	1.50
5.	" " 21 "	" 21 "	3 " "	1.80
6.	" " 24 "	" 24 "	3 " "	2.20
7.	" " 27 "	" 27 "	3 " "	2.85
8.	" " 30 "	" 30 "	3 " "	3.65
9.	" " 36 "	" 36 "	4 " "	5.20
10.	" " 34 "	" 48 "	5 " "	6.45
11.	" " 36 "	" 64 "	6 " "	7.80
12.	" " 36 "	" 76 "	7 " "	9.65

II. The Gardner Patent Portable Book Rack, Fancy Ends

(Like cut).

No. 13.	Size—Width 12 inches,	Height 12 inches,	2 Shelves—Price	$1.00
14.	" " 15 "	" 15 "	2 " "	1.30
15.	" " 18 "	" 18 "	3 " "	1.80
16.	" " 21 "	" 21 "	3 " "	2.15
17.	" " 24 "	" 24 "	3 " "	2.45
18.	" " 27 "	" 27 "	3 " "	3.20
19.	" " 30 "	" 30 "	3 " "	4.00
20.	" " 36 "	" 36 "	4 " "	5.50
21.	" " 34 "	" 48 "	5 " "	6.90
22.	" " 36 "	" 64 "	6 " "	8.25
23.	" " 36 "	" 76 "	7 " "	10.25

Portable Book Shelves,

Combined with Writing Desks.

III. The Patent Book Case and Portable Writing Desk,

Plain Ends.

No. 24. Width 36 inches, Height 66 inches, 6 Shelves—Price....................$11.75
" 25. " 36 " " 76 " 7 " " 12.75

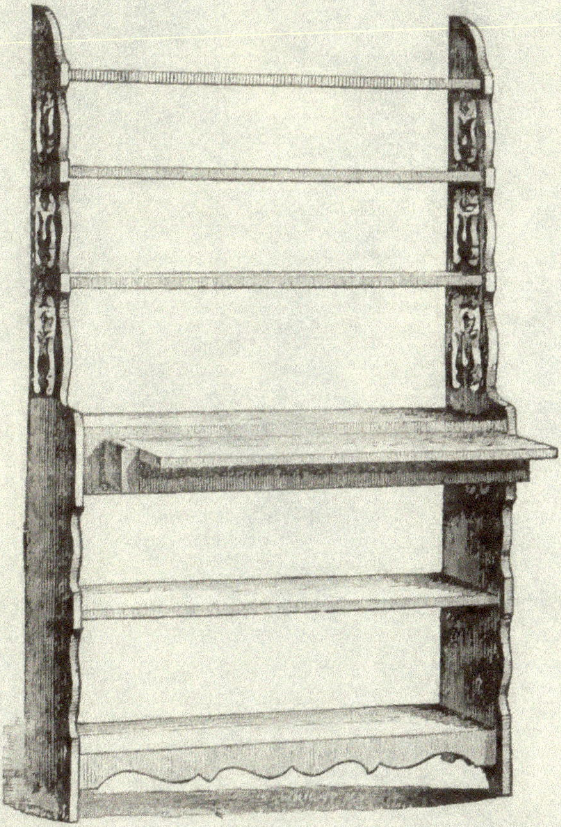

IV. The Book Case and Writing Desk combined, Fancy Ends

(Like cut).

No. 26. Width 36 inches, Height 66 inches, 6 Shelves—Price....................$12.50
" 27. " 36 " " 76 " 7 " " 13.50

WITH LOCKS, 50 Cents Extra.

They can be taken apart instantly, without turning a screw or drawing a nail, and can be packed as compactly for transportation as a few short boards. And again, they may be put up for use almost as quickly. For students, teachers, libraries, and many general uses, they must prove most acceptable. Teachers and students being migratory, will readily appreciate their advantages.

The Teacher's Lamp.

The studious, faithful teacher requires a faithful light to aid him in his preparation for his duties. We have found none equal to

THE SAINT GERMAIN, or GERMAN STUDENT'S LAMP.

It gives a superior, steady light, and with ordinary care will emit neither smell nor smoke. One-twelfth or one-eighth of a heavier oil—sperm, lard, or olive—mixed with kerosene, makes the best and safest oil. Pratt's Astral Oil is recommended for use in this lamp.

Professor Joseph Henry, of the Smithsonian Institution, Washington, D. C., considers "it the safest and pleasantest article of the kind he has ever used. It gives a brilliant, unwavering light, very agreeable to the eye. It is safe, since the vapor of the petroleum is entirely cut off from the flame, the reservoir being at a distance from the burning point, and the supply tube constantly filled with the liquid."

These lamps, being imported, may vary in price, depending upon the price of gold. We give prices for the present only:

No. **1**.—BRASS SLIDING LAMP, 13 line burner, 7 inch shade, and chimney complete, ... **$8 50**

No. **2**.—BRASS SLIDING LAMP, 11 line burner, 6 inch shade, and chimney complete, ... **7 50**

No. **1 a**.—BRASS SLIDING LAMP, double burner, 7 inch shades, and chimneys same as No. 1 single, ... **16 00**

No. **1 b**.—GERMAN SILVER SLIDING LAMP, 13 line burner, 7 inch shade, and chimney, ... **16 00**

Box and packing for shipment will cost $1.00 extra.

SCHOOL MATERIAL,—PART III.

PHYSICAL EDUCATION.

"Mens Sana in Corpore Sano."

Our Gymnastic Apparatus

Is made of well-seasoned wood, varnished and polished. Dumb-bells and Indian Clubs are made of maple; Wands of white ash or black walnut; Hand-rings are very strongly made of three sections—black walnut, cherry, and maple. Besides great strength, they have the merit of beautiful appearance.

		PRICE LIST.
Dumb-bells—four sizes:		
Nos. 1 and 2, for children	per pair,	**$0.60**
Nos. 3 and 4, for youths and adults	"	**.75**
Rings—two sizes:		
No. 1, for children	"	**.75**
No. 2, for youths and adults	"	**.75**
Wands—in required lengths, nicely turned	each,	**.30**
same, with metallic balls	"	**.75**
Indian Clubs—five sizes of short clubs:		
No. 1, weight about 2 pounds	per pair,	**1.25**
No. 2, " 3 "	"	**1.50**
No. 3, " 4 "	"	**1.75**
No. 4, " 5 "	"	**2.00**
No. 5, " 6 "	"	**2.50**
Six sizes of long clubs:		
No. 1, 7 to 8 pounds	"	**3.00**
No. 2, 10 "	"	**4.00**
No. 3, 12 "	"	**4.50**
No. 4, 14 "	"	**5.00**
No. 5, 16 "	"	**5.50**
No. 6, 20 "	"	**6.00**
Any size or style to order. Liberal discount on quantities.		
Kehoe's Book on use of Clubs, illustrated		**2.50**
Croquet, etc., etc.		

Gymnastic Apparatus.

APPARATUS is now regarded by educators almost as indispensable in physical training as agricultural implements are in successful farming. The demand, however, is not so much for the costly, fixed apparatus of the gymnasium, as for a few light and simple implements, which are cheap and easily obtained; which may be used with equal facility under cover, or in the open air—in a calisthenic hall, or in a bedroom; which may be employed by persons of all ages, either individually or in classes; and which insure generous emulation alike in the family, the school, and the gymnasium.

The four pieces of apparatus which most completely fulfill these conditions, and consequently are most deservedly popular, are **Wands, Dumb-bells, Indian Clubs,** and **Rings.** With these an almost unlimited number of varied, powerful, and graceful movements may be executed, bringing into play, under healthful conditions, every muscle, joint, and member of the human body.

How should this apparatus be constructed, with reference to form, size, and material? In answering this important question, let us bear in mind the fact that the *object* of gymnastic exercises is to secure beauty of form and grace of movement, as well as muscular strength; and that we aim not so much to acquire the power to bear heavy burdens—the power important for porters, hod-carriers, and coal-heavers—as for the qualities required in the more usual vocations of life, such as flexibility, poise, grace, ease, rapidity of muscular action, and a general diffusion of muscular vigor.

The primary object of gymnastic apparatus is not to serve as a test of strength, but to afford facilities for exercise. We employ it to secure greater variety and precision of movement, more rapid development, and prolonged interest.

The pieces here described are all made of wood, varnished with shellac, at least three coats, and well polished.

Wands furnish an extended course of beautiful and peculiarly effective exercises. For diversity in movements, as a promoter of digestion, and as a curative for dyspepsia, the wand, properly constructed, is not surpassed by any other piece of gymnastic apparatus.

The wand should be made of well seasoned white ash or black walnut, perfectly straight and smooth, *seven-eighths* of an inch thick for men and women, and *three-fourths* of an inch for boys and girls. When held vertical by the side, it should extend from the floor to the lobe of the ear, as in

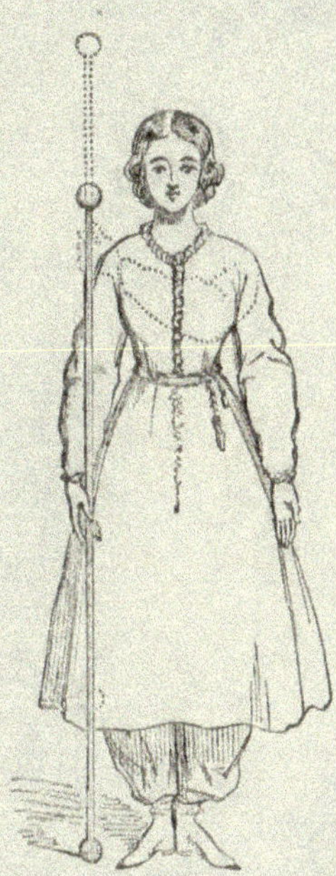

Fig. 1.

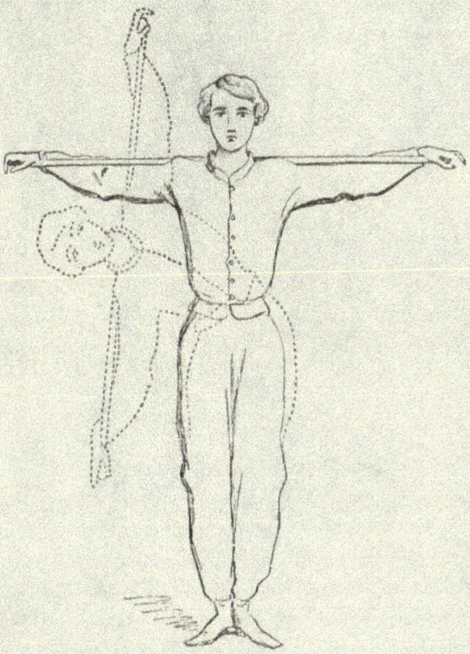

Fig. 2.

Fig. 1. It should be exactly of this length, as a large majority of the most valuable movements, as shown in Fig. 5, can not be well executed with a shorter one.

Fig. 3.

Fig. 4.

Fig. 5.

The wand is sometimes loaded at the ends with metallic balls—usually cast iron, well japanned. It not only affords an almost unlimited number and variety of movements by individuals, but also a most interesting and extended course of combined exercises for students, arranged in couples, as shown in Fig. 5.

Dumb-bells are regarded by many gymnastic instructors as incomparably superior to any other piece of apparatus, as a means of physical culture. Properly constructed, and in the hands of an adept, dumb-bells go beyond their usual province, and answer the purposes of Indian clubs, gymnastic rings, parallel bars, a wand, a foil,—in short, almost the entire apparatus of the gymnasium.

The dumb-bell most approved at the present time, is turned from wood. Fig. 6 will serve as a model. As will be seen, the handle has shoulders. It is long, bulged and beaded at the center, and well adapted to wrist movements (see Fig. 7), as well as affording every facility for free and easy motions of the hand, wrist, and forearm. The balls are moderate in size, beaded, and specially constructed with reference to the *ball grasp*, which adds greatly to the number and variety of its uses. (See Fig. 9.)

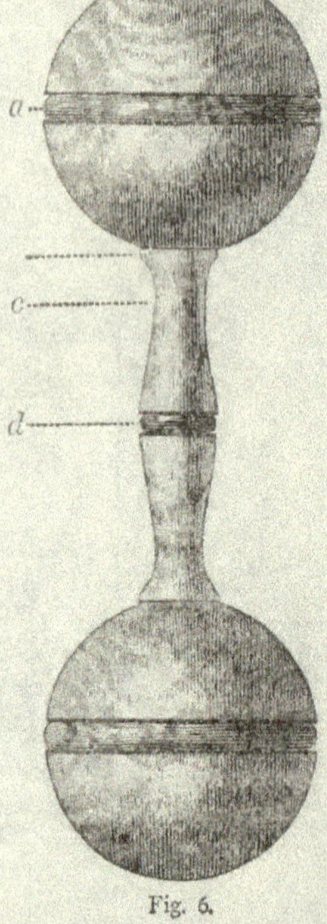

Fig. 6.

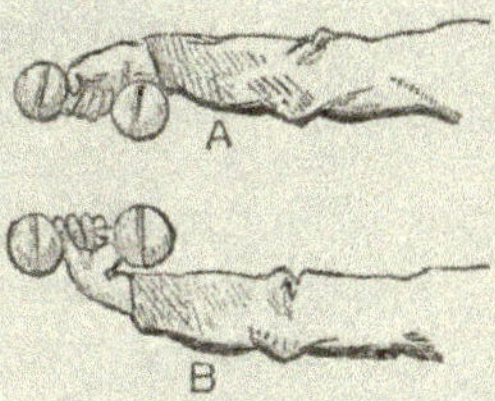

Fig. 7.

Fig. 8.

Indian Clubs, in our judgment, stand first in excellence. No other piece of gymnastic apparatus affords so many facilities for a marked, rapid, and systematic development—for so happy a combination of dash, daring, and skill: no other insures so absorbing and continuous an interest. While clubs enforce to a wonderful extent the simultaneous activity of the mental and physical powers, they are in the beginning accessible to the meanest capacity. The mastery of their alternate, reciprocating, and double movements, their beautiful devices,

Fig. 9.

Fig. 10.

and their endlessly varied and delicate combinations, would afford employment for the leisure hours of a lifetime: demanding the union of those superior, innate qualities which insure superiority in billiards and chess. No other piece of apparatus requires more skill in its construction. The poise should be so adjusted that, when in motion, the *central forces* may harmonize, requiring only the guiding will of the gymnast.

The model here given (Fig. 11) is believed to be superior to all others. As the manipulations in this exercise should be as perfect, and almost as delicate and complicated as those of a Thalberg, or an Ole Bull, much depends on the construction of handle. The club is sometimes held with the thumb and a single finger, sometimes with the whole hand, and sometimes it is guided merely with the tips of the fingers. In this model, there are, for practical purposes, really four handles: the entire handle from *a* to *d*, the space between *a* and *c*, between *c* and *d*, and above the shoulder at *e*.

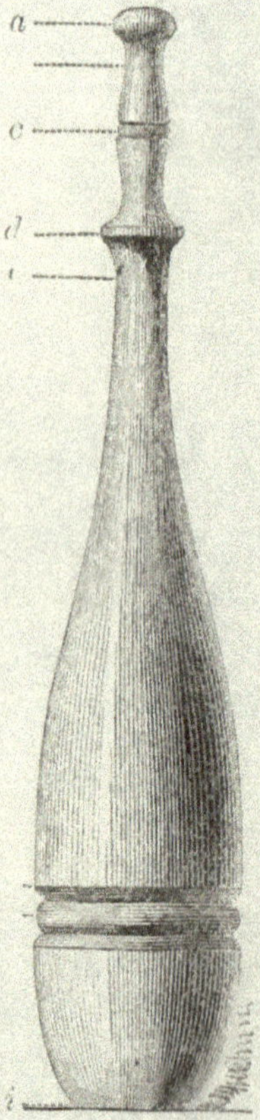

Fig. 11.

This model answers both for *long* clubs and for *short* ones. The *length* of the club is determined by the length of the arm. The long club, when held upon the arm extended horizontally, should reach to the point of the shoulder where the arm and shoulder join, as in Fig. 13. The short club in the same position should extend nearly two inches above the elbow.

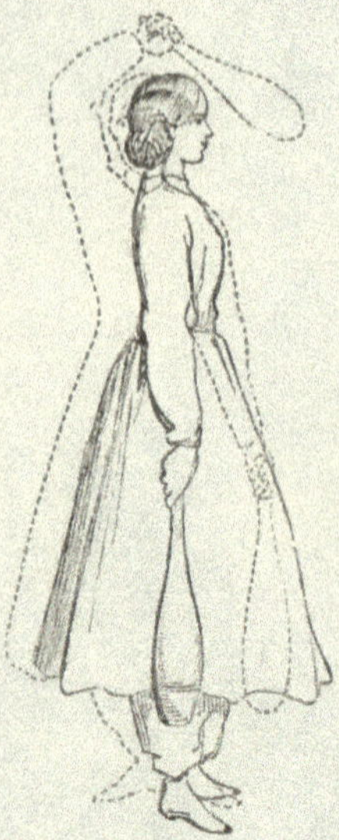

Fig. 12.

Rings afford opportunities for so many graceful positions and effective movements *in combination* for both sexes, and persons of all ages and degrees of

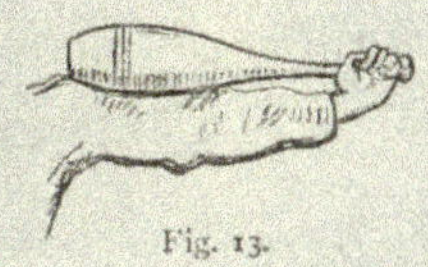

Fig. 13.

strength, that they are justly classed with the most desirable articles of gymnastic apparatus. The best ring is turned from three sections of wood glued together, the grain running in contrary directions. This makes them very strong. Light and dark colored wood in alternate sections, highly polished, make very handsome rings.

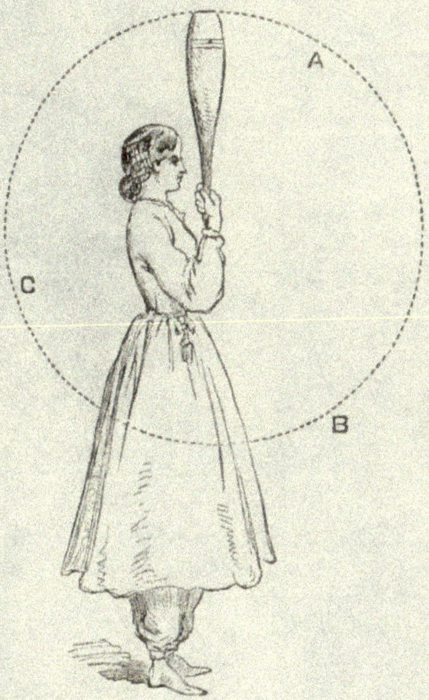

Fig. 14.

Our apparatus, devised by Prof. J. Madison Watson, has proved very satisfactory to our customers, and is having very large demand for schools and social clubs. Even more than dancing, light gymnastics—*social* gymnastics would be a better name—may be called the poetry of motion. Possessing none of the objectionable features of dancing, and liable to none

Fig. 15.

of its abuses, these exercises combine all that is desirable in that popular amusement—music, rythmic motion, and the exhilaration of muscular activity—with an infinitely greater variety of movements. They are at once enjoyable and healthful. The foregoing *illustrations* are from Prof. Watson's well-known "**Hand-book of Gymnastics**."—(*See Price List on 53d. page.*

Croquet—Field and Parlor.

FIELD CROQUET.

1.—Substantially good set for the school grounds—made of maple, in a neat and durable manner, plain finish. Eight balls and mallets, regular size, in a strong wood box, with book of directions.................price, **$4.50**

2.—Manufactured of rock maple, in a neat and durable manner, plain finish. Full size and number of parts, in a neat box........................ **5.00**

3.—Manufactured of rock maple, in a neat and durable manner, finished in oil. Bradley's patent sockets for bridges. Chestnut box............ **8.00**

4.—Rock maple mallet-heads, banded; rock maple patent indexical balls; plated bridges, with Bradley's patent sockets; record dials, polished; elegant chestnut box, oil finish.. **12.00**

5.—Boxwood mallet-heads, banded; improved linen plaited mallet-handles; boxwood patent indexical balls; plated bridges, with patent sockets; record dials. Genuine French polish. Elegant chestnut box, oil finish..... **20.00**

6.—Boxwood mallet-heads, banded; improved linen plaited mallet-handles; patent indexical rubber-covered balls; plated bridges, with patent sockets; record dials. Elegant chestnut box, oil finish.......................... **25.00**

CARPET CROQUET, for in-door use.

1.—**Youth's**; 4 mallets and 4 balls, turnposts and starting pins, 10 arches, clips, slate, and rules, in pine box.................................. **4.00**

2.—**Same**; in walnut box.. **6.00**

3.—**Maple**; 8 mallets, 8 balls, starting and return posts, 10 arches, clips, rules, and slate, in walnut box.. **10.00**

4.—**Boxwood**; best finish, and complete, with 8 mallets, 8 balls, starting and return posts, 10 arches, clips, rules, and slate, in walnut box........... **14.00**

This list of apparatus for Physical Education is necessarily very much abbreviated. We intend to supply all kinds of suitable apparatus for the amusement and exercise of youths and adults—believing that the proper development of the physical powers is no less important than the cultivation of the intellect.

Hence "books of sports," and implements for Archery, Base Ball, Cricket, Croquet, Quoits, and all other aids for out-door and in-door games and sports properly belong to this line of business.

Another catalogue, now in preparation, will also give illustrations of instructive toys for boys and girls.

SCHOOL MATERIAL,—PART IV.

GLOBES, etc.

CONTENTS.

Globes.

"A Good Globe is as essential in every school-room as an English Dictionary, or a Blackboard."

OUR NEW SCHOOL GLOBE.

Probably the principal reason why so few of our schools are supplied with a globe is that there has been no **good globe** to be obtained at a **moderate price.**

Our new five inch Terrestrial Globe will precisely supply this want. The map is **new**—clearly and finely engraved—prepared expressly for taking the place of the large and expensive globes. The "Grand Divisions" are boldly colored. The water is white, distinctly showing the principal Islands, Peninsulas, Capes, Gulfs, Bays, etc., etc.

It is mounted in a light and durable manner, strong brass mountings, inclined axis, on a neat black-walnut stand.

Securely packed in box with sliding cover. Price.............................. **$2.25**

A Hemisphere Globe (made by cutting a solid five inch globe through the Poles), showing also the two Hemispheres on a flat surface, will be found a great convenience to the teacher. The two parts are united by a brass hinge. Price... .... **$2.00**

Schedler's American Globes—12 Inches—Nos. 1, 3, 2.

Globes.

"**A Good Globe** is as essential in every school-room as an English Dictionary, or a Blackboard."

Schedler's School Globe, 20 inch. (4.)

Schedler's Globes took the First-Class Prize Medal at the Paris Exhibition in 1867, and at the American Institute Fair in New York, 1869.

They have been introduced in the Public Schools of New York, and many other cities, and are highly recommended by Dr. J. E. Hilgard, in charge of the Coast Survey at Washington; Prof. C. H. F. Peters, of the Litchfield Observatory of Hamilton College, New York; Prof. S. M. Capron, of the High School, Hartford, Conn.; Prof. R. Von Schlagintweit, the celebrated traveller, and many others.

These globes are superior in accuracy, durability, and in correctness and fullness of information. The latest geographical discoveries, territorial changes, etc., are laid down on the maps.

The mode of manufacturing the ball is Mr. Schedler's invention, secured by patent. It combines a perfect spherical form, with great strength and durability.

1. Schedler's 12 inch **Terrestrial**, plain iron stand..........	$15.00
2. Schedler's 12 inch **Terrestrial**, bronzed stand, full meridian, inclined axis..........	18.00
3. Schedler's 12 inch **Terrestrial**, low bronzed frame, with horizon, meridian, hour circle, and quadrant..........	25.00
4. Schedler's 20 inch **School**, bronzed pedestal frame, full meridian, inclined axis..........	50.00
5. Schedler's 20 inch **School** (extra), bronzed pedestal frame, 42 inches high, horizon, meridian divided in half degrees, hour circle and quadrant....	65.00

Globes.

"A Good Globe is as essential in every school-room as an English Dictionary, or a Blackboard."

Schedler's Library Globe, 20 inch. (8.)

Schedler's Scientific Globes, as well as his **Library Globes,** distinctly show the course of the Gulf stream, and other Oceanic Currents, Deep-sea Soundings, the lines of Equal Magnetic Variation, of Oceanic Communication, and of Submarine Telegraphs. These globes have met with the most flattering reception, and are well worthy the examination of all interested in the subject.

RECOMMENDATIONS.

I have examined your twenty inch Terrestrial Globe, and have no hesitation in commending it to the attention of all who desire a superior article of the kind, either for school or for a library.

HENRY BARNARD,
Late Commis'r of Education,
Washington, D. C.

As an object of art, Schedler's 20 inch Terrestrial Globe is really beautiful, and for the purpose of scientific study it could hardly be improved.

S. M. CAPRON,
Principal High School,
Hartford, Conn.

6. Schedler's 20 inch **Scientific,** bronzed pedestal frame, with full meridian and inclined axis.......... $60.00
7. Schedler's 20 inch **Scientific,** bronzed pedestal frame, 42 inches high, with horizon, meridian divided in half degrees, hour circle, and quadrant.......... 75.00
8. Schedler's 20 inch **Library,** fine bronzed pedestal frame, 42 inches high, with horizon, brass meridian divided in half degrees, hour circle, quadrant, and magnetic needle. It is a useful and beautiful ornament for the library or parlor.......... 175.00

Celestial Globes of same styles and same sizes, at same prices, are in preparation.

Packing boxes for shipping these globes are supplied for the 20 inch globes, each.......... 4.50

For the 12 inch, each.......... 2.50

Globes.

The Franklin & Joslin Globes have been long known, and highly esteemed. The 6, 10, 12, and 30 inch globes have been recently re-engraved, and the following important additions and corrections made.

Pacific Railroad; French Submarine Cable; Alaska, Sitka, and all territories of which the correct bounderies can be obtained; the present Russian, Prussian, and Austrian bounderies; important places, rivers, lakes, mountains, especially in Africa and New South Wales, and the correct names of countries that have been changed recently.

The 10 inch Terrestrial and Celestial Globes will be found of good service in schools and families, to illustrate Geography and Astronomy. The Terrestrial gives the boundaries in the United States and Territories, from the latest and best authorities, and exhibits the boundaries of other countries as laid down by the most eminent Geographers.

The 12 inch Terrestrial and Celestial Globes are the most popular for the larger Schools and Academies. They are not surpassed in accuracy and beauty of finish by any other globe of its diameter.

We believe that the use of globes in teaching has been undervalued. For example, many pupils get the idea *from the map* that Australia and New Zealand are at the two extremes of the earth, instead of learning that they are near neighbors, no farther apart than New York and Cuba. It is essential that every pupil should receive lessons from the globe, as well as the map.

Globes.

The Franklin 16 inch Globes (Terrestrial and Celestial), are especially valuable globes. They are very finely engraved, and are, unquestionably, more useful for daily reference than a map, showmg, at a glance, the relative positions of different countries, their boundaries, and theif latitude and longitude.

The Franklin 30 inch Globe (Terrestrial only) is very plainly engraved, and handsomely mounted on a solid Mahogany frame. It is the largest ever made in this country, and presents quite an imposing appearance; it is appropriate for public rooms, literary institutions, hotels, saloons of steamers, as well as for the large schools and colleges.

"FRANKLIN" GLOBE: SIZES AND PRICES.

6	inch wood frame (no quadrant)	per pair	$18.00
9½	inch wood, semi-frame (no quadrant)	"	24.00
10	inch wood frame (with quadrant)	"	36.00
10	inch bronze frame "	"	40.00
12	inch wood, semi-frame (no quadrant)	"	34.00
12	inch wood frame (with quadrant	"	44.00
12	inch low bronze frame "	"	50.00
12	inch bronze pedestal frame " (case and packing, *each* globe extra, $1.75)	"	75.00
16	inch wood frame " " " " " 1.50	"	80.00
16	inch bronze pedestal frame " " " " " 2.00	"	125.00
30	inch Terrestrial, quadrant and compass, on Mahogany frame, with casters, (case and packing, $8 extra)	"	275.00

Terrestrial and Celestial, separate, at half-price "per pair," and quadrant charged extra

Globes.

Perce's Magnetic Globes are peculiar in illustrating gravitation. They are metallic, and by the use of magnetized objects, representing Men of different races, Animals of different climes, Light-houses, Steamers, Ships, the actual living, moving world, with much of its most interesting and instructive phenomena, is presented in miniature to the mind of the pupil.

STYLES AND PRICES.

Five inches in diameter, plain stand..........	$6.00
Five inches in diameter, semi-meridian.......	8.00
Seven inches in diameter, plain stand........	12.00
Seven inches in diameter, semi-meridian......	15.00
Seven inches in diameter, full meridian.......	20.00
Twelve inches in diameter, plain stand.......	20.00
Twelve inches in diameter, semi-meridian....	25.00
Twelve inches in diameter, full meridian.....	35.00

One dozen magnetic objects, representing Men of different races, Ships, Steamers, Light-houses, and various Animals, and Mrs. Smith's Globe Manual, accompany each globe without additional cost.

They are securely packed for shipment.

Slated Globes are now finding a place, hitherto unoccupied, in every grade of school, from Primary to University. Their varied uses as "Spherical Blackboards," make them as much a necessity to intelligent teaching as common flat blackboards.

If for no other purpose than for laying a sure foundation for a right understanding of Geography, they are entitled to first rank in school apparatus. With them the teacher of Geography may begin objective instruction at the outset, showing the things themselves, not inaccurate pictures which the well-trained mind may *imagine* to represent them. Pupils thus learn not merely names of geographical lines, but what they are, what they are for, and how to draw them; and more, how to draw *by* them. Map-drawing becomes intelligent work, not mere mechanical transferring of unmeaning marks from one paper to another.

Multitudes of facts and phenomena can be illustrated and explained so simply and clearly that any child can understand them. The most obscure theorems and problems of Spherical Geometry, Trigonometry, and Navigation become, when studied in connection with the Sphere, perfectly intelligible.

As now made, these Globes, or Spherical Blackboards, are an improvement of the original invention of Professor Shepard. Sizes and prices:

No. 1.—	On handle, very convenient, size	4	inches	in diameter........................	$1.50
2.—	Brass meridian, wood frame,	6	"	"	5.00
3.—	" " "	9	"	"	9.00
4.—	" " bronzed frame,	12	"	"	15.00
5.—	" " "	15	"	"	20.00
6.—	High bronzed frame, with casters,	18	"	"	30.00

The Pocket Planisphere.

The simplest of all apparatus for "Easy Star Studies," is illustrated, full size, in the accompanying cuts.

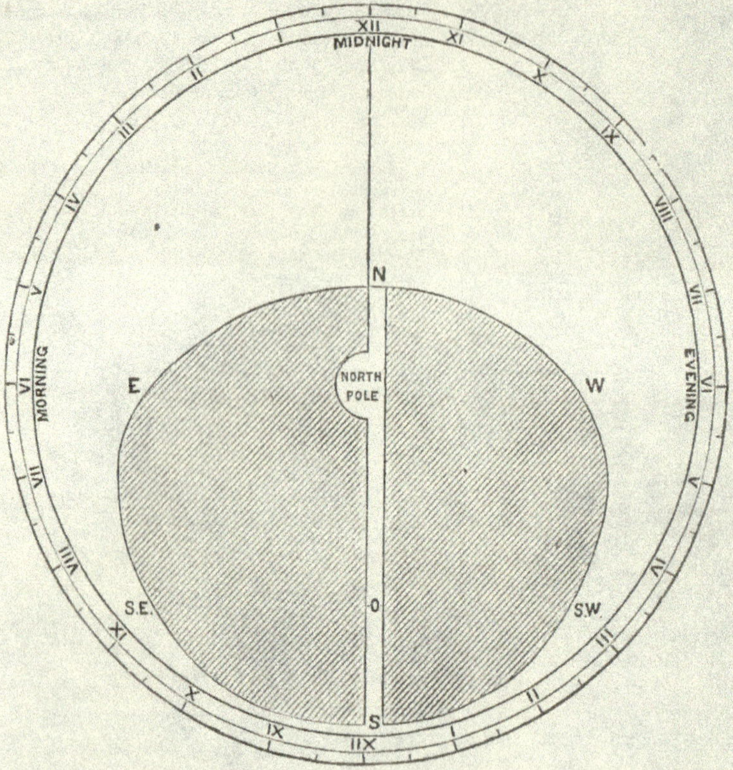

The Pocket Planisphere is the Cheapest and most convenient means ever devised for Identifying the Fixed Stars.

It consists of (*a.*) A light, strong card, about four inches square, carrying an accurate circumpolar Star-map, surrounded by a circle of the months subdivided for the days; and (*b.*) A smaller circular card, carrying the hours of the day, and an open space, representing the horizon. These two cards are attached at the centre, so as to turn one on the other.

This form—a simplification of BAUDIN's improvement of the original Planisphere invented by the celebrated astronomer BODE, in 1786—answers the same purpose as the large Planispheres, costing twelve times as much. In addition to cheapness, this Planisphere has the further advantage of being so small and light as to be easily carried in the pocket.

The **Pocket Planisphere** is used as follows: To bring to view the principal Stars visible at any given night and hour, turn the upper card so as to bring the hour of observation to correspond with the given time of year on the lower card. The open space will then exhibit the stars of the first and second magnitudes above the horizon at the specified time.

The Pocket Planisphere.

If the card be held face downward above the head of the observer, with the N. point toward the north, it will exhibit the stars in their positions relative to the real horizon.

The stars of the first magnitude are numbered on the Star-map, in the order of their brilliancy, from 1 to 15. The key to the identification of the stars is given on the back of the Planisphere.

Price.................Prepaid, by mail, 30 cents.

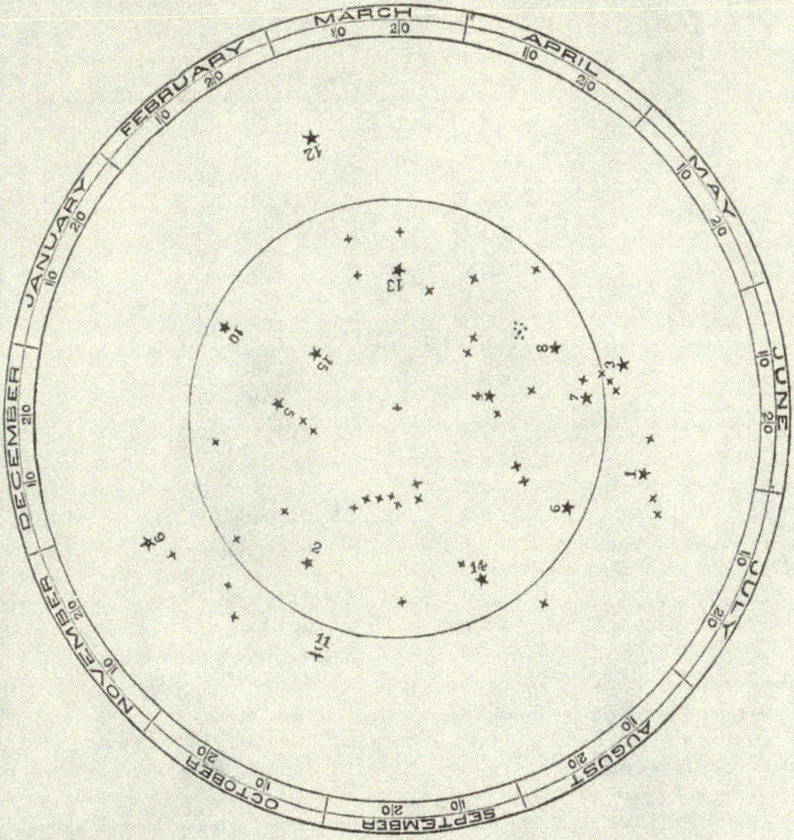

Maltby's Improved Correct Planisphere—diameter about 15 inches, mounted in a superior style—Imported—price, ... **$5.00.**

[The publication of the Pocket Planisphere induced a certain charlatan to demand from its publishers the payment of money for—say, an infringement of his fancied rights. His demands not being satisfied, he, aided by a peculiar affidavit from one Barnes, not unknown to fame (?), began suit for an injunction in defence of his "peculiar interests" in this little instrument, *nearly a century old*. Of course he got no "injunction"; but the court got some novel lessons in astronomy.]

Long's Patent Tellurian.

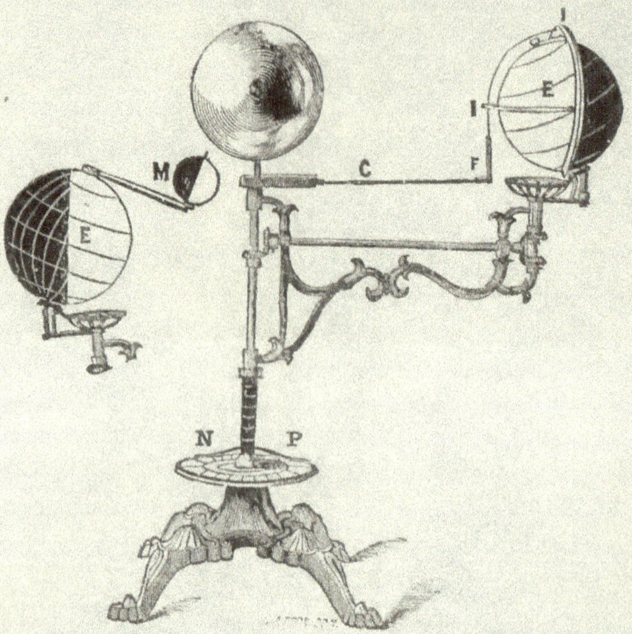

This apparatus took the first medal and diploma, at the great fair of the American Institute, in 1869, and has recently been adopted by the Board of Education, of New York.

Explanation.—S, represents the Sun; E, the Earth; M, the Moon; I, I, the Indicator, supported on the pivot arm; C, its connecting rod; F, its joint, which may be unscrewed; P, the Earth's pointer; N, the Sun's pointer.

It is calculated for every-day use in all schools where Geography is taught, and the relations of the Earth to the Sun and Moon need to be illustrated.

It will commend itself to the favorable judgment of teachers, because of the following considerations:

1. Size.—The Earth is represented by a five-inch globe, which makes all the illustrations on so large a scale, that they can be easily seen by a class. The Earth may also be used separately as a globe.

2. Accuracy.—It is operated by gearing, and moves regularly, and with certainty. The Indicator shows, not only the limit of day and night, but also the Meridian, the Plane of the Ecliptic, and the part of the Earth to which the Sun is vertical on any day, all with scientific precision.

3. Durability.—It has no appearance of a toy, or a fragile instrument. Every part is of good size and strongly made. It is, therefore, always ready for use at a moment's notice, and pupils may safely handle it to any reasonable extent.

A circular of the illustrations shown by it will be sent on application, with stamp

Price, best style brass mounting, boxed.............................. **$30.00**

A key, giving full description, is included without charge.

Bryant's Celestial Indicator.

THIS is a new apparatus for facilitating the study of astronomy. It is intended to illustrate clearly to children and to adults the various phenomena of the heavenly bodies: the motion of the earth around the sun, and the changes of the seasons; the earth's axial motion; the precession of the equinoxes; nutation; tides; eclipses, both solar and lunar; the change of the pole star; changes in the declination and right ascension of stars; the difference between the siderial and tropical years; the retrogradation of the signs of the zodiac; the revolution of the moon's nodes, etc., etc.

Accompanying the apparatus is a short Treatise on Astronomy, descriptive of the same, and illustrating how to use the instrument. An hour's time will enable the teacher to become familiar with the subject and with the instrument, and impart more information by illustration, with the **INDICATOR**, than is usually gained by pupils during their entire course.

The apparatus is made of brass; is simple and durable in construction; not liable to get out of order. It occupies about a cubic foot, and is carefully boxed for shipment to any part of the country.

PRICE,	**Lacquered,** - - -	**$30.00**
"	**Nickel Plated,** - - -	**40.00**

Among the many favorable opinions received, are the following:

"The Celestial Indicator, invented and constructed by Mr. Henry Bryant, is a simple apparatus which illustrates with great clearness many important astronomical phenomena. I am of opinion that it well deserves a place in our schools, where the elements of astronomy are taught and I know of no other similar apparatus, now in use, that contains such an amount of accurate illustration, at so small a price.

"JOHN BROCKLESBY,
"Professor of Mathematics and Natural Philosophy,
"in Trinity College, Hartford, Conn."

"I desire to recommend it, unhesitatingly, to the attention of all interested in astronomy, particularly teachers. Mr. Bryant's apparatus being quite unique, and different from all others, deserves a place in every good collection of scientific apparatus, on its own peculiar merits.

"S. M. CAPRON,
"Principal of H. P. N. S., Hartford, Conn."

Williamson's Concentric Celestial and Terrestrial Globes.

These Globes present to the mind of the learner a faithful representation of the relations of the earth to the heavens, while all the geographical and astronomical problems are solved with great simplicity and perspicuity.

The Celestial Globe consists of two hollow hemispheres of glass, held in position by a brazen equinoctial, which is graduated into degrees and hours. Within this hollow globe is an ordinary Terrestrial Globe, whose diameter is about one-half that of the Celestial Globe, both globes turning on a common axle and having a common centre, but so arranged that either may be revolved at pleasure, independent of the other, by means of milled heads at the Northern and Southern extremities of the axle.

On a platform attached to the tripod is a mariner's compass, by the aid of which the globe may be placed in its proper position.

On the inner surface of the Celestial Globe the stars of the first, second, third, and fourth magnitudes are gilded; the ecliptic, colures, meridians, and parallels laid down; and the outlines of the constellation figures, with their names, are artistically painted, not, however, so as to obscure the Terrestrial Globe within.

Price, with a "Manual of Problems on the Globes,"........................**$100.00**

Moore's Geoselenean.

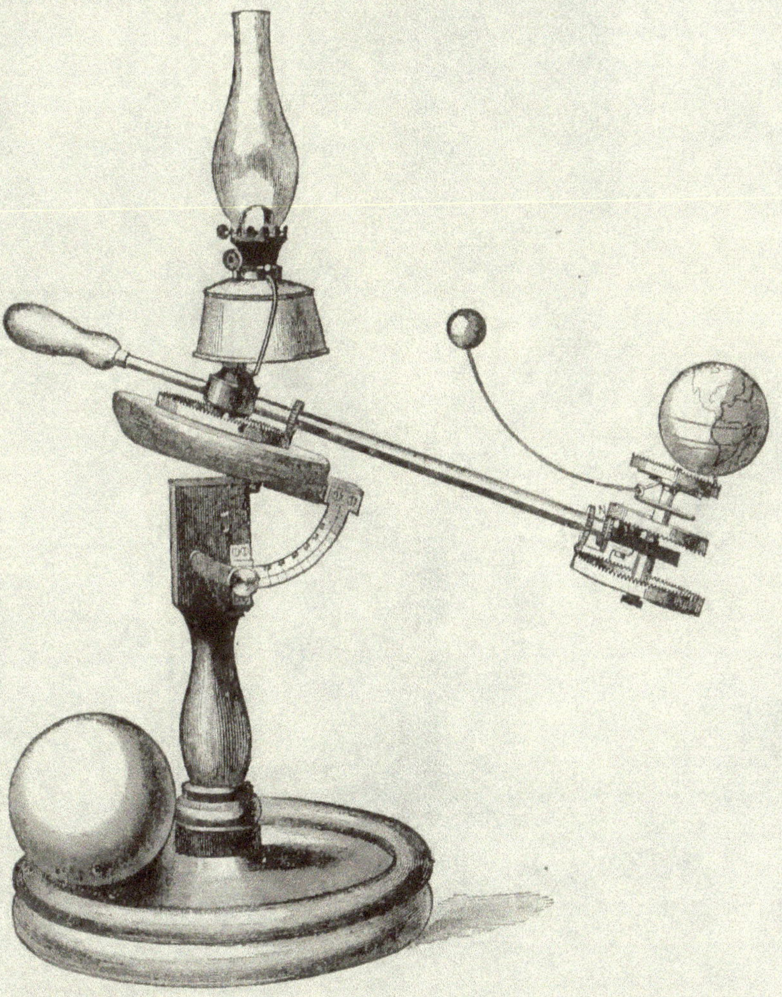

Moore's Geoselenean is a new instrument intended to illustrate the principal motions and phenomena of the Solar System much more perfectly, its inventor claims, than with the Planetarium or Tellurian. It is designed by John G. Moore, M. S., Teacher and Lecturer in Friends Central High School. A printed description of 18 pages accompanies each instrument. Price.......... $40.00

The Tellurian, or Season Machine, shows the Sun, Earth, and Moon, with the phenomena of the Seasons. Improved geared, brass, with compass and burnished Sun. Price.......... 25.00

The School Orrery, or Planetarium, represents the Planets in their regular order. Best, brass. Price.......... 17.00
Second quality material and finish.......... 15.00
Common, and wood in place of brass.......... 12.00

The Tellurion-Globe.

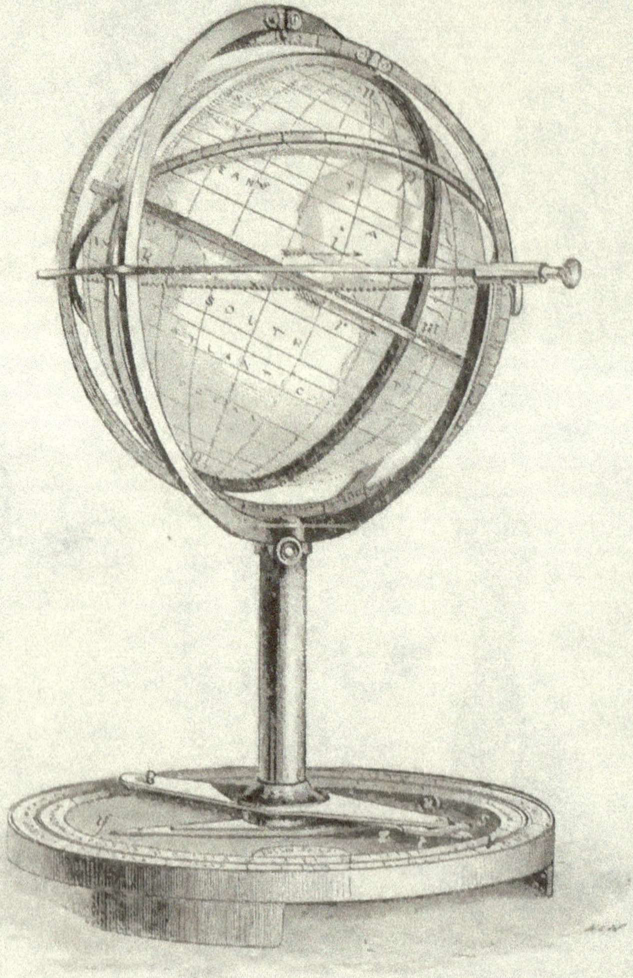

This instrument (the invention of J. L. Naish, B.A.) solves astronomical problems with facsimile illustrations, giving (with exact amounts), a complete analysis of the Equation of Time, and otherwise surpasses the ordinary globe both in facility of use and general scope.

EXTRACTS FROM TESTIMONIALS.—"Invaluable to lecturers and teachers."—SIR RODERICK MURCHISON, *Pres. of British Geographical Soc.* "Much more complete than any former means in use. The Equation of Time is made perfectly intelligible."—REV. DR. WOOLLEY, *Director of Education, to British Admiralty.* "Shows with clearness the solutions of geographical and astronomical questions."—COM. P. F. SANDS, *Supt. U. S. Naval Observatory.—Official Report.* "Has great merits; the two causes in the Equation of Time are very clearly shown."—LT. COMDR. J. A. HOWELL, *U. S. Navy, Head of Dept. of Astronomy and Navigation, U. S. Naval Academy, Annapolis.* "Admirable mechanical combination—simple but effective instrument."—PROF. SAMUEL MORSE. "Very beautiful and ingenious."—W. G. PECK, *Prof. Astronomy, Columbia College.* "A very ingenious invention, and elicited the admiration of all."—*Athenæum, May 9, 1868.*

Price.. **$80.00**

ATLASES, CHARTS, GLOBES, MAPS, ETC.

Adjustable Chart and Map Support, Price $10.

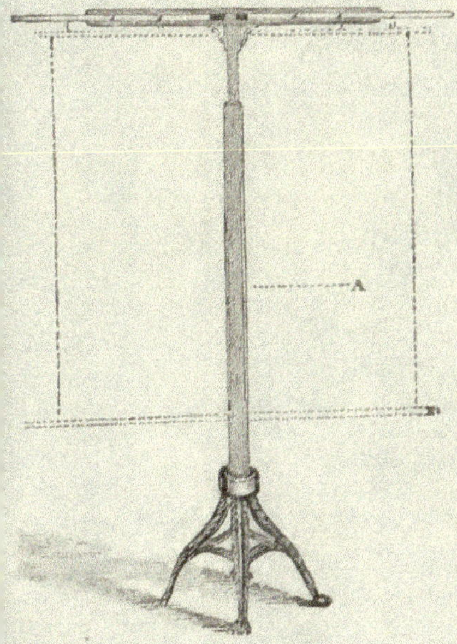

The cut pretty fully shows the construction of the support. The standard is grooved to sustain a movable "T," the cross-piece of which bears two sliding arms, provided with hooks, for sustaining the map or chart. The SUPPORT is raised or lowered by means of a knob, the position of which is indicated by the dotted line from A. This knob also governs a spring which holds the "T" in place. The cut shows the top raised one notch and the arms slightly extended to receive the large map shown by the dotted outlines. It will as nicely support the largest map as the smallest chart, and is so stiff and firm that some are using it for a blackboard support.

The merit of this SUPPORT cannot be considered relatively, for there is nothing else like it. It is the sole occupant of the field; and it answers its purpose perfectly. Setting aside its convenience, it must commend itself to every teacher on the score of economy. It will save its cost in a single year by preventing the necessity of subjecting maps to the soiling incident to their exposure on the walls.

ATLAS—COLTON'S—General, Geographical, Statistical, and Historical. 200 Maps and Plans. Imperial Folio. Cloth, morocco backs $20 00

MITCHELL'S—New General. 96 Maps and Plans, with valuable statistical tables. Folio, cloth, morocco backs 11 00

OF THE UNION, with all the States and Territories. States colored in counties—Railroads and principal towns located—Populations, etc 3 00

CHARTS :—WARREN'S PHYSICAL AND OUTLINE. 14 Plates on seven boards. The Set in portfolio, with hand-book 18 00

POLITICAL AND OUTLINE. For Common Schools. 8 in series, on muslin 10 00

GLOBES :—"FRANKLIN." Terrestrial or Celestial, separate, at half price "per pair," and quadrant extra.

5 in. Terrestrial, plain stand, new map		each	2 25
6 in. wood, semi-frame (no quadrant)		per pair	10 00
6 in. wood (full) frame do		do	18 00
9¼ in. wood, semi-frame, no quadrant		do	24 00
10 in. wood frame with quadrant		do	36 00
10 in. bronze, frame do		do	40 00
12 in. wood frame do		do	44 00
12 in. low bronze frame do		do	50 00
12 in. bronze pedestal frame do	(case and packing, *each* globe extra, $1.75	do	75 00
16 in. wood frame do	do do do 1.50	do	80 00
16 in. bronze pedestal frame do	do do do 2.00	do	125 00
30 in. Terrestrial, quadrant and compass, on mahogany frame, with casters (case and packing $8 extra)		each	275 00

GLOBES :—PERCE'S MAGNETIC, Terrestrial, each—

5 in. plain stand	$6 00	12 in. plain stand	20 00
5 in. semi-meridian	8 00	12 in. semi-meridian	25 00
7 in. plain stand	12 00	12 in. full meridian	35 00
7 in. semi-meridian	15 00	12 in. complete, high stand, hour circle, etc.	75 00

12 *Magnetic Objects*, representing the Races, Animals, Ships, Light-houses, etc., *free* with each Globe.

SLATE GLOBES. Invaluable in "OBJECT TEACHING," MATHEMATICAL GEOGRAPHY, &c.

No. 1.—On handle, very convenient,	size 4 in.	diameter		$1 50
2.—Brass meridian, wood frame,	6 in.	do.		5 00
3.— do. do.	9 in.	do.		9 00
4.— do. bronzed frame,	12 in.	do.		15 00
5.— do. do.	15 in.	do.		20 00
6.—High bronzed frame, with castors,	18 in.	do.		30 00

MAP OF AMERICA. Our whole Country, large scale, 72 in. × 80 .... $10 00
UNITED STATES OF AMERICA, from Ocean to Ocean, 21 in. × 37 .... 3 00

PHYSICAL AND POLITICAL. GUYOT'S NEW WALL-MAPS.

No. 1.—PRIMARY SERIES—on Muslin, in Portfolio. Sold in sets $18 00

United States in sections ...... size	48 in. × 60	Europe	24 in. × 36
Hemispheres do.	36 in. × 48	Asia	24 in. × 36
North America do.	24 in. × 36	Africa	24 in. × 36
South America do.	24 in. × 36	Oceanica	24 in. × 36
Central Europe do.	24 in. × 36	World (Mercator's Proj.)	24 in. × 36

No. 2.—THE COMMON SCHOOL SERIES. Packed in a neat box. Per set $25 00

	Length of Roller.	*Depth of Map.*		*Length of Roller.*	*Depth of Map.*
The United States	64 inches.	48 inches.	Asia	33 inches.	25 inches.
The Hemisphere	53 "	33 "	The World (Mer. Proj.)	36 "	25 "
North America	28 "	22 "	Central Europe	30 "	25 "
South America	28 "	32 "	Europe	36 "	25 "
Africa	28 "	32 "	Australia and Oceanica	36 "	25 "

No. 3.—INTERMEDIATE SERIES, on Cloth and Rollers, sold singly or in sets.

United States .... size	48 in. × 60	$4 00	Europe ...... size	48 in. × 60	$4 50
Hemispheres	60 in. × 72	7 50	Asia	48 in. × 60	5 00
North America	48 in. × 60	4 50	Africa	48 in. × 60	4 50
South America	48 in. × 60	3 50	Oceanica	48 in. × 60	5 00

No. 4.—LARGE SERIES, on Cloth and Rollers, sold singly or in sets.
The World, Mercator's Projection—size 72 in. × 120 .... $12 00

United States .... size	72 in. × 96	$8 00	Europe ...... size	72 in. × 96	$8 00
North America	60 in. × 72	6 50	Asia	72 in. × 96	10 00
South America	60 in. × 72	6 50	Africa	62 in. × 72	6 50
Central Europe	72 in. × 96	8 50	Oceanica	48 in. × 60	5 00

Key to Guyot's Maps 1 00

No. 5.—CLASSICAL, on Cloth and Rollers. ROMAN EMPIRE, 72 in. × 84 .... $15 00
ANCIENT GREECE (including City of Athens) 72 in. × 84 .... 15 00
ITALIA, including Map of City of Ancient Rome, 72 in. × 84 .... 15 00

OUTLINE MAPS.

CORNELL'S, 13 maps on muslin, in portfolio, and Key 15 00
MITCHELL'S New Outline, 7 maps on muslin, in portfolio, and Key 10 00
PELTON'S, 72 in. × 85, on cloth and rollers. Complete set 25 00
do. do. on heavy paper. do. 15 00
Key to Pelton's Outline Maps 75

HISTORICAL. Kiepert's large Mural Maps of Ancient History.

ROMAN EMPIRE, 67 in. × 103 .... $12 00
ANCIENT ITALY, 72 in. × 80 .... 11 00
ANCIENT GREECE, 70 in. × 84 .... 9 50
WORLD, at time of Persian and Macedonian Empire, 48 in. × 96 .... 8 00
THE ENVIRONS OF ROME, 38 in. × 45 (all on Cloth and Rollers) 4 00

BIBLE MAP. Map of the Lands mentioned in the Bible. 74 in. × 52 .... $7 50
Area embraced includes both New Testament and Old Testament countries, taking in Rome on the West, Egypt on the South, and the mouth of the Euphrates on the East. Lettering is bold and easily read from every part of a class-room. It gives ancient and modern names of towns, rivers, mountains, etc. Routes of St. Paul in his missionary tours are plainly indicated by distinct colored lines. All missionary stations are shown by spots of color, thus adding a very interesting feature.

MISCELLANEOUS.

Apgar's Geographical Drawing Book 94
Apgar's Map Drawing Cards. Complete set, in envelope 13
do. Superior quality 25
Guyot's Eureka Slated Map Drawing Cards. Complete set, in portfolio 1 50
Paper Map Drawing Cards. do. do. 75
Geographical Definitions. Illustrated, on chart, 34 in. × 44 .... 4 00
Geographical Cards (six sheets on boards), 24 in. × 31 .... 6 00
Geographical Dictionary: Lippincott's Pronouncing Gazetteer of the World 10 00
Historical Chart (Lyman's), and Key 2 50
Stream of Time, or Chart of Universal History, 32 in. × 43 .... 5 00

TEXT-BOOKS ON GEOGRAPHY, of all kinds, supplied AT THE PUBLISHERS' WHOLESALE RATES. Sent by Mail, postage prepaid, at retail prices.

SCHOOL MATERIAL,—PART V.

BLACKBOARDS, OBJECT-TEACHING AIDS, etc.

CONTENTS.

EUREKA WALL SLATES.

Ready made Standard Sizes, PERFECT Slate SURFACE, in neat ash frames :

No.	Size		Sq. ft. of Surface	Price
No. 1,	Size, 2 × 3 ft.,	finished on both sides (giving	12 Sqr. ft. of Surface)	$3 50
" 2,	" 2½ × 3½ "	" "	" 18 "	" 5 25
" 3,	" 3 × 4 "	" "	" 24 "	" 7 00
" 4,	" 3 × 4½ "	" "	" 27 "	" 7 75
" 5,	" 3½ × 4½ "	" "	" 32 "	" 9 50
" 6,	" 3½ × 5 "	" "	" 35 "	" 10 25
" 7,	" 4 × 5 "	" "	" 40 "	" 12 00
" 8,	" 4 × 6 "	" "	" 48 "	" 14 00
" 9,	" 3 × 6 "	neatly lined for Music		12 50

ANY SIZE MADE TO ORDER. Black Walnut frames Extra............. 1 00

They are so framed that they are free to shrink or swell without possibility of splitting or warping.

The utility of the blackboard is beyond discussion. It is an admitted necessity wherever teaching is to be done. The DAY-SCHOOL TEACHER, SUNDAY-SCHOOL TEACHER, LECTURER on Science, and PROFESSOR in college, each has constant need of it.

It being indispensable, the question is, What blackboard is *best?* The verdict of Science and testimony of teachers agree on the *EUREKA*. This surface is incomparably THE BEST. The most costly natural slates do not equal it. It is finer and harder and blacker than slate. It is also smoother, and yet it never becomes glazed, and marks upon it are perfectly legible from any direction.

The portable **Eureka Slate** is unrivalled. It is light, easily and safely handled, less liable than slate to breaks and scratches, more convenient to use, much cheaper, besides being safely transportable. The surface, though hard as flint, never checks or separates from the wood. This elasticity of the **Eureka Slate** is one of its peculiar and most valuable properties.

Blackboards, Spherical, or "Slated Globes."—Invaluable in "OBJECT TEACHING," MATHEMATICAL GEOGRAPHY, etc., six sizes......$1 50 to $30 00

Blackboard Easel—KENDALL'S. New and Perfect. Patented............ 3 00

Blackboard Support—HAMMOND'S, very substantial.
Size adapted to any one of our Standard Blackboards, $6; same, made of black-walnut...... 7 50

Blackboard Rubbers—8 varieties. See Special Circular. Per doz. $1 50 to 5 50

Blackboard Pointers—Lengths from 3½ to 5 ft. each.................. 30

Crayons—White, per gross..............30; Colored, per gross.................. 1 25
1 doz. White, in neat paper box..10; Do. colored.................. 20

Crayon Holders—Recently invented, neat and economical, each.............. 10.

BLACK-BOARD EASELS, SUPPORTS ETC.

Kendall's Black-board Easel is specially suited for class-rooms, lecture-halls, Sunday-schools, and places where economy of space is an object. When not wanted, it can be folded up in a moment, and put away like an ordinary board. Its portability, the little room it occupies when packed, and consequent cheapness of transportation make it a most convenient and economical Easel. It is Patented.

PRICE, Ash, ... *$3.00*

" Black Walnut, ... *3.50*

The Revolving Black-board Easel, for the Teacher's Desk or Table, has for some years answered a good purpose in the schools of New York City, and is now first offered to the public. The first cut represents it occupied by a Black-board, the second cut shows its construction. *Price, $5.00.*

Hammond's Black-board Support, Obviating the disadvantages of movable black-boards, has become deservedly popular. The iron feet are sufficiently heavy to insure stability. It is rigid and substantial. There are no glued joints; all the parts are firmly bolted together, and are taken apart for shipping. It has lock-pins for holding the board in position. It may be revolved either way—on horizontal or perpendicular axle—as shown in the cut. The board touches the Support only on these pins, and is noiseless. Beneath the board is a shelf for crayons, and for the falling particles of chalk. It is a serviceable and ornamental piece of furniture for the school or lectu e-room.

Size adapted to any one of our Standard Wall Slates, ... *$6.00*

Same, of black walnut, ... *7.50*

Black Board Rubbers, 8 varieties,..............Per dozen, **$1.50** to **5.50**

Eureka Wall Slates, neatly framed, 9 standard sizes.....Each, **3.50** to **12.50**

Slated Globes, for Mathematical Geography, etc., 6 sizes.... " **1.50** to **30.00**

Black Board Pointers, BLACK BOARD COMPASSES, Crayons, Crayon Holders, etc.

Blackboard Rubbers,

For Erasing Marks from Blackboards and Wall Slates of all kinds.

The dusty rag for clearing blackboards of marks, is disappearing with the slovenly teachers who were known in the past. No tidy teacher can permit the scattering of dust about the school-room, defiling the furniture, books, and dresses of pupils, besides damageing the health of teachers and pupils. To meet the increasing demand for Erasers or Blackboard Rubbers, we manufacture the following varied styles:

No. 0. Size 2 in. by $3\frac{3}{4}$ in. The block is ash or other suitable wood, properly grooved for grasping with the hand. It is covered with sheepskin, usually "Shearling." The skin is securely fastened to the block and bound with binders' cloth. Price, per doz. **1.50**

No. 1. Size 2 in. by 7 in. This is made in same manner and of same material as No. 0, differing only in length. Per doz..**2.40**

No. 2. Size $2\frac{1}{2}$ by $7\frac{1}{2}$ in. Is covered with first-class lambskin, having heavy and durable wool. The binding is leather. Per doz....................................**3.00**

No. 3. Is made of A 1 extra lambskin, having very fine long bleached wool, bound with red morocco. Per doz..**4.00**

No. 4. "Brussels." This rubber is made like No. 3, except that a good quality of Brussels carpeting takes the place of lambskin. Per doz..........................**4.50**

No. 5. "Tapestry." This is covered with fine heavy velvet Tapestry carpeting. It is a handsome and efficient rubber, highly esteemed in young ladies' seminaries and colleges. Per doz..**5.00**

No. 6. "California Rubber." Is made over an elaborate block, in three parts, screwed together, peculiar to this style. It is larger than regular size, and covered with superior heavy Red Plush. It requires no binding. Per doz..........................**5.50**

No. 7. "The Chamois Rubber"—*patented*—consists of a series of strips of Chamois skin, securely fixed in hard-wood block, properly grooved. It is so arranged that the series of Chamois edges come in snug contact with the blackboard, most effectually removing every particle of dust, gathering it up between the folds. When filled, the dust may be entirely discharged by rubbing two rubbers briskly together—thus all the wasted chalk may be conveyed out of the school-room. It proves durable and is *very highly appreciated.* Per doz..**5.00**

We claim that our Blackboard Rubbers are **the very best** manufactured. We will pay liberally for any new inventions or improvements on these articles.

The Chamois Slate Rubber.

"A GEM FOR THE SCHOOL-ROOM

It dispenses with sponge and water in erasing marks from the slate. No more need the teacher hear the frequent question, "Please, sir, may I go to wash my slate?" Nor need the child spit upon his slate to erase the marks.

It is made of wood and Chamois skin, arranged to bring a series of edges of skin snugly against the surface of slate.

Every teacher will recommend it because of its real convenience and neatness. Every pupil will buy it. It costs no more than a good sponge.

No. 1—size 1 in. by $1\frac{1}{2}$—price, per 100........................**5.00**

No. 2—size 2 in. square—per 100........................**8.00**

(Specimens, by mail, of No. 1, **10 cents**—of No. 2, **15 cents.**)

The Slate Pencil Holder.

The cut represents it about half size. It is made of wood, bored to receive a regular four-inch slate pencil—a six-inch pencil broken in halves answers the purpose. Its size obviates the difficulties of other inventions, which are too small for the regular slate pencils offered for sale. Its advantages are too manifest to require enumeration here. Every teacher knows how desirable it is to have a device which is large enough and long enough to prevent the irregular bits of slate pencils from cramping the childrens' fingers and injuring them for writing. The pencil is held securely in place on the same plan as the crayon in the crayon holder, fully illustrated below. It can be used as a pen holder.

(Specimens *mailed* for 10 cents.) **Price, each 5 cents.**

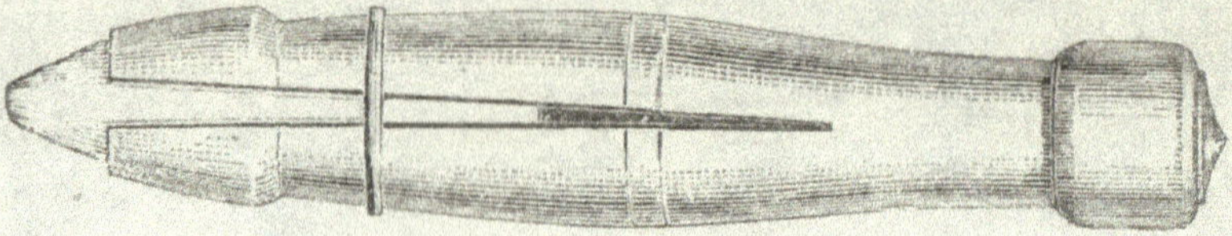

The Crayon Holder, Full Size.

Its length is adapted to receive an entire crayon (which should be inserted small end first). Its great merit, hitherto unattained, is that it is short enough to be held easily and naturally in the hand, as a crayon. It is light and pleasant to the touch, and cannot soil the dress and fingers. Being made entirely of wood, it will not scratch the blackboard. It will quickly save more than its cost in utilizing the small pieces of crayons which cannot be held in the fingers.

(Specimens *mailed* for 15 cents.) **Price, each 10 cents.**

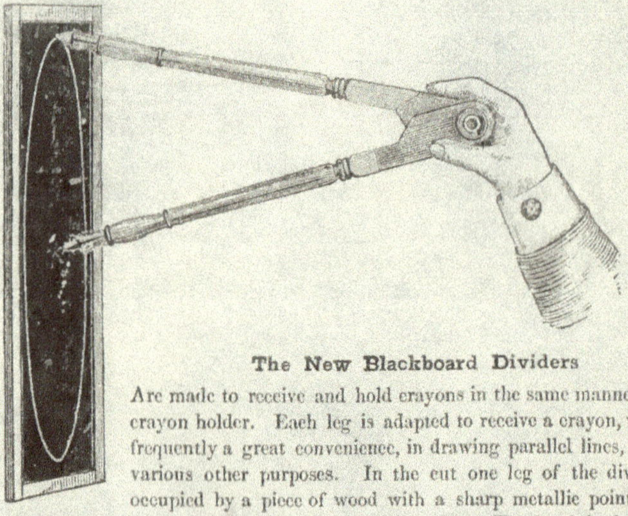

The New Blackboard Dividers

Are made to receive and hold crayons in the same manner as the crayon holder. Each leg is adapted to receive a crayon, which is frequently a great convenience, in drawing parallel lines, and for various other purposes. In the cut one leg of the dividers is occupied by a piece of wood with a sharp metallic point. This renders the length of the leg adjustable. The head is fitted with a strong set-screw, which cannot get out of order. These dividers have no equal, and are cheaper than the common articles. The same patent covers the slate pencil holder, the crayon holder, and the new blackboard dividers, or "crayon compasses."

Price, ... $1.00

Object Teaching Aids.

THE SPELLING STICK AND THE SENTENCE STICK.

The Spelling Stick consists of a piece of wood properly fashioned and grooved for holding the letters. It has a handle as shown in the cut. It is accompanied by letters on card-board—one set of CAPITALS, and a "three-a font" of lower-case letters.

Teachers of primary classes, with the aid of this simple device, will find it easy to fix the attention of their pupils, teach the forms of the letters, and how to combine them into words. By its use words and their spelling may be taught to a large class with less outlay of time and patience than is required for teaching a single pupil with the book alone.

The Sentence Stick has precisely the same construction. It is accompanied by 135 common words, on card-board. It is useful in teaching primarians to construct sentences, just as the Spelling Stick aids in constructing words. The first principles of grammar and composition may be pleasantly illustrated, and attention may be called to the common errors of speech. In the hands of a skillful teacher its uses may be greatly extended and multiplied.

These Simple instruments have been successfully tested by many teachers, and are highly esteemed for their practical utility. Their rank, as to efficiency in the school-room, is equal, or superior, to the *Numeral Frame.*

Spelling Sticks, or, "Word-making" Sticks for Primarians, each $0.25
Fonts of letters, on card-board, for same, in box 0.50
Sentence Sticks, for Primarians "to build up sentences" 0.25
Sets of Small words, on card-board, for same, in box 0.50

Alphabet Charts, 24 x 40 inches, heavy Manilla, with rollers:—
No. 1. Capital Letters and Arabic Figures (75 cts. each) ....
No 2. Small Letters, Points, and Roman Numerals (75 cts. each) } the pair 1.00

Alphabet Charts, Indestructible, 24 x 36 inches, with rollers, These are entirely **new,** being printed *on cloth, in oil colors,* by Dr. Johnson's patent process:—
No. 1. Capital Letters and Arabic Figures (75 cts. each) ....
No. 2. Small Letters, Points, and Roman Numerals (75 cts. each) } the pair 1.50

Alphabet Blocks, Hill's. No. 1, per box 0.25
No. 2, 35 cts.; No. 3, 40 cts.; No. 4, 60 cts.; No. 5, $1; No. 6 .... 1.25

Object Teaching Aids.

Color-Cubes, with direction for use..$1.25

This set of Color-Cubes comprises eight Cubes:—six of which contain six colors on each—red, orange, yellow, green, blue, purple. The other two Cubes contain white, black, drab, russet, citrine, blue, on each. The set is put up in a paper box, with a sheet of directions for use.

Kindergarten Blocks, au Froebel, per box..........................$1.00

Miss Peabody suggests that the teacher can find nothing better than these blocks to aid in conveying elementary ideas of FORM. They are easily susceptible of reduction to a great variety of forms, such as Arches, Arcades, Bridges, Castles, Chairs, Churches, Columns, Gateways, Houses, Sentry-boxes, etc., etc.

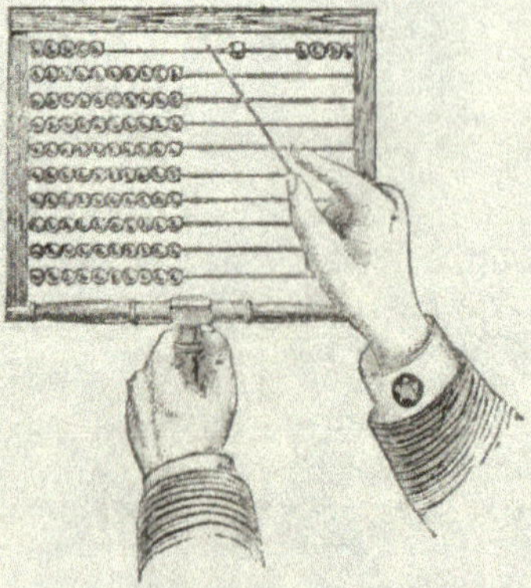

NUMERAL FRAMES

OF SUPERIOR STYLE AND WORKMANSHIP.

No. 1—With 100 Balls..........................$1.25
No. 2—With 144 Balls.......................... 1.50

The Abacus, or Numeral Frame, is now a very popular and almost indispensable aid in teaching children to count, and in giving them correct ideas of numbers, and of their first lessons in addition, subtraction, etc.

Valuable and ingenious hints for its use may be found in "Calkins' Classified List (illustrated) of Object Teaching Aids, for Home and Schools." (Price, **10** cents.)

MATHEMATICAL BLOCKS, DISSECTED.

1. **The Cube Root Block**—"To one place," in neat box.......................... $0.60
   This may be mailed (letter postage) for $1.25.
2. **The Cube Root Block**—"To two places".......................... 0.80

3. **The Cube Root Block**—"To two places, larger............ 1.00
   These are accurately dissected blocks, invaluable in illustrating the rule of Cube Root. One of them should be in the hands of every teacher who attempts to instruct pupils in that usually troublesome part of Arithmetic.
4. **Dissected Cone**—sections of different colored wood—for illustrating conic sections. Large size, 8 inches high, 4½ inches diameter at base.......................... 2.50

Melville's Complete Drawing and Building Blocks. Elaborate and very superior.......................... $15.00
For use in Art Schools, Scientific Schools, Colleges, Academies, and High Schools.

New Forms and Solids

FOR OBJECT TEACHING.

Containing sixty-four pieces—there being forty-eight Plane Forms, fifteen Solids, and a six-inch Rule, among which are several NEW Forms and Solids, not included in any other set.

Each Form is stamped with its Number in the List.

1. Equilateral Triangle.
2. Right Angled "
3. " " "
4. Obtuse " "
5. Curved "
6. Triangle—one curved side.
7. Isosceles Triangle.
8. Scalene "
9. Square.
10. Oblong.
11. Rhomb.
12. Rhomboid.
13. Trapezium.
14. Trapezoid.
15. Pentagon.
16. Hexagon.
17. Heptagon.
18. Octagon.
19. Nonagon.
20. Decagon.
21. Circle.
22. Semi-Circle.
23. Quadrant.
24. Segment.
25. Sector.
26. Ring.
27. Crescent.
28. Ellipse.
29. Oval.
30. Sphere.
31. Hemi-Sphere.
32. Prolate-Spheroid.
33. Oblate.
34. Ovoid.
35. Cylinder.
36. Cone.
37. Conoid.
38. Cube.
39. Square Prism.
40. Triangular Prism
41. Hexagonal "
42. Square Pyramid.
43. Triangular "
44. Six-inch Rule.

PRICE (neatly put up in substantial wood box), **$2.75.**

A complete *illustrated* description of these *Forms and Solids* appears in **Calkins' Classified List of Object Teaching Aids** (price **10** cents).

Geometrical Forms and Arithmetical Solids.

Each Piece is stamped with its Number, as in the List.

1. Sphere.
2. Hemisphere.
3. Prolate Spheroid.
4. Oblate Spheroid.
5. Pyramid and Frustrum.
6. Cone and Frustrum.
7. Cylinder.
8. Triangular Prism.
9. Square Prism.
10. Hexagonal Prism.
11. Cube.
12. Cube (Eight times No. 11).
13. Cube (Eight times No. 12).
14. Parallelopipedon.
15. Parallelopipedon.
16. Parallelopipedon.
17. Parallelopipedon.
18. Oblique Prism (3 pieces).
19. Parallelopipedon.
20. Parallelopipedon.
21. Carpenter's Theorem (4 pieces).

Twenty-six Pieces, in substantial wood box, **$2.50.**

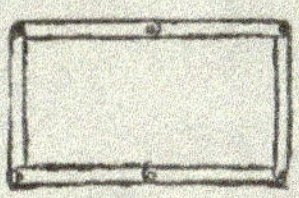

Parallelogram.

The Gonigraph is a small instrument resembling somewhat a jointed carpenter's rule, but made so as to bend in only two directions. It is made with several short rulers, or joints of iron or brass, fastened together by pivots. With it may be formed all the geometrical figures that consist of straight lines and angles, some of which are illustrated by the accompanying engravings.

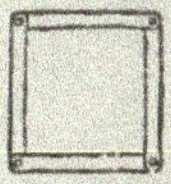

Square.

Rhomb.

Triangle.

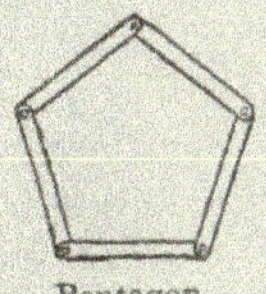

Pentagon.

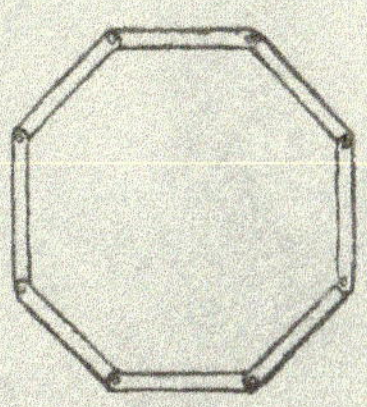

Octagon.

Price, in wood, 25 cts.; whalebone, 40 cts.; metal, 50 cts.

CALL-BELLS.

No. 1.

THE old-time School-master, emphasized his COMMANDS by heavy thwacks of a ruler—sometimes on the desks, and sometimes on the sconces of his terrified pupils. The Call-Bell is a better instrument, and has become as indispensable as the ruler or strap used to be—much to the relief of both teachers and taught.

The bells shown in the cuts are silver-plated, and of fine tone. The cuts represent one-fifth size.

No. 2.

No. 3.

No. 4.

No. 5.

No. 6.

No. 7.

No. 8.

No. 9.

No. 10.

PRICE LIST.

No. 11.

No. 1, Fancy Bronze Base	$ 90
" 2, Fancy Base	1 00
" 3, Fancy Bronze Base	1 10
" 4, Black Marble Base	1 15
" 5, Fancy Bronze Base	1 25
" 6, Fancy Bronze Base	1 45
" 7, Black Base	1 60
" 8, Bronze Base	1 75
" 9, Black Base	1 85
" 10, White Marble Base	1 95
" 11, Bronze Base	2 05
" 12, Black and Gold Base	3 50

No. 12.

Silver Plated Hand-Bells.

No. 1. Gong Shape. 70c. No. 2. 70c. No. 3. 50c. No. 4. 70c. No. 5. $1.70.

Hand-Bells of Pure Copper and Tin,

Warranted superior in tone; twelve sizes.

	Diameter.	*Height.*	*Each*
No. 1, Extra Polish,	2⅜ inch.	3⅞ inch.	*$0.20*
" 2, " "	2¾ "	4½ "	*.25*
" 3, " "	3⅛ "	5⅝ "	*.30*
" 4, " "	3½ "	6¼ "	*.45*
" 5, " "	3¾ "	6¾ "	*.65*
" 6, " "	4½ "	7½ "	*.75*
" 7, " "	5 "	8¼ "	*.90*
" 8, " "	5½ "	8½ "	*1.13*
" 9, " "	6 "	9½ "	*1.60*
" 10, " "	6¼ "	10 "	*2.00*
" 12, " "	6¾ "	10½ "	*2.40*
" 14, " "	7 "	11 "	*3.00*

Patent Spring Tape Measures.

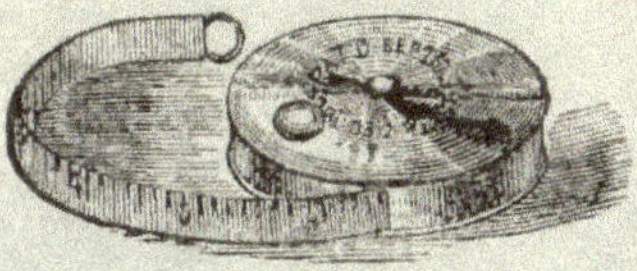

Three Feet Measures, in Silver Plated Cases,	Price,	45	Cents.
Five " " " " "	"	50	"
Six " " " " "	"	55	"
Three " " in Lacquered Brass Cases,	"	45	"
Five " " " " "	"	50	"
Six " " " " "	"	55	"
Three " " in Nickel Silver Cases,	"	65	"
Five " " " "	"	70	"
Six " " " "	"	75	"

School Clocks.

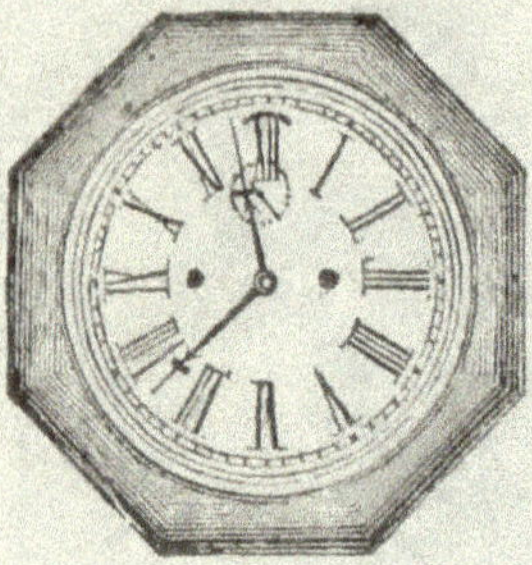

No. 1.

No. 1. Octagon Marine, one day, 6 in. Dial........................ $4.00

No. 2. Drop Octagon, Spring, Eight day, Height 25 in................ 6.00

No. 2.

In response to frequent calls from teachers and School Officers for clocks suitable for school use, the foregoing styles have been selected as best adapted for that purpose. These clocks are of the best American manufacture and are reliable time-keepers.

Timby's Globe Time Piece,

FRONT VIEW

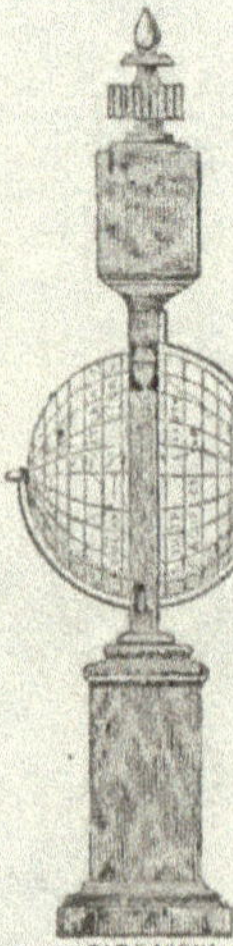

SIDE VIEW

For illustrating the relations of Longitude and Time.

The Time Piece consists of an eight-day clock, with a globe so mounted as to make one revolution every twenty-four hours, thus bringing each meridian directly under the sun (represented by a gilded ball), once a day; while the pointer, which shows on the moving dial *our* time, points constantly to that part of the earth crossed by the noon meridian. The time at every other part of the earth may be ascertained from the meridians. The Dial encircles the Globe, and revolves with it.

The globe may be turned either way without injury to the clock-movement.

The whole apparatus may be placed on its back or in any position desired for the study of the globe, or for illustrating the relations of longitude and time. The Clock is simple in consiruction, strong and durable, and is offered at a price but little greater than is asked for an ordinary clock of corresponding finish. The balance-wheel is set in jewels, and every care is taken to ensure a first-class Time Piece.

Price, (Box for packing 75 cts.) ***$25.00.***

Thermometers, Barometers, etc.

"The teacher cannot trust his own feelings to regulate the temperature of the school-room."

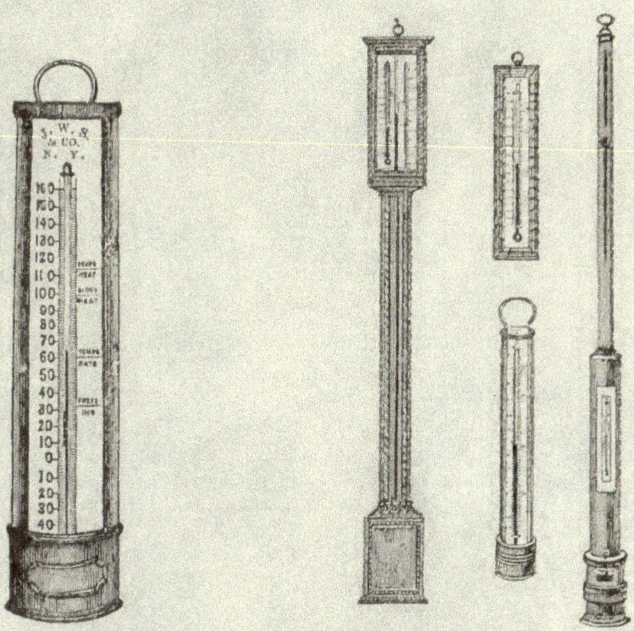

Our Thermometers are manufactured by one of the oldest establishments in the country, whose reputation is not surpassed by any in America or in Europe. These standard instruments are used by the Smithsonian Institution, at Washington, D. C.

List of sizes, styles, and prices.—Liberal discounts by the dozen.

7 **Inch, White Tube,** Tin Case	each,	0.50
8 " " " "	"	.55
10 " " " "	"	.60
12 " " " "	"	.75
8 " " " Mahogany Case	"	.80
10 " " " " "	"	.85
8 " " " Rosewood Case	"	.90
10 " " " " "	"	1.00

Standards.

10 **Inch, White Tin Case,** Single Degree Ruby	"	1.25
12 " " " " "	"	1.50
12 " " " Half Degree Ruby	"	2.25

Rain Gauge—the Smithsonian .... price, **5.00**

Glass Hydrometers, of usual styles, at manufacturers' prices.

Barometers, Aneroid and Mercurial, several styles, at usual rates.

Aids to Neatness and Cleanliness.

"Whatever may be requisite for the neatness and good order of a private residence, cannot be out of place, for the same purposes, in a School-House."

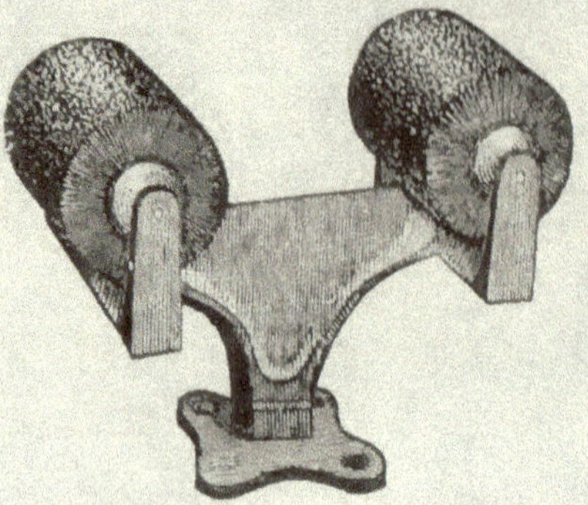

Shoe Scrapers, with Patent Revolving Brushes.

No. 1.—For fastening to wood steps, price, - - - - - - - - - **$2.00**
No. 2.—For fastening to stone steps, price, - - - - - - - - - **2.00**

No. 3.—Oval Pan Shoe Scraper, with Revolving Brushes, - - $2.50.

No. 4.—Square Pan Shoe Scraper, with Revolving Brushes, - - $3.00.

Door Mats...... Three Sizes,		17 in. by 25 in.;	18 in. by 33 in.;	19 in. by 36 in.
Jute,....................	each,	**$0.65**	**$0.75**	**$0.90**
Coir, ordinary............	"	**.90**	**1.10**	**1.40**
Coir, solid...............	"	**1.25**	**1.50**	**1.75**
Rope,.....................	"	**1.25**	**1.65**	**2.00.**

Modern School Officers require no arguments to convince them of the necessity for articles such as these **in every school. Live teachers** will see that they are constantly used when provided, and school children will acquire habits, through the use of these articles, which will adhere to them through their lives, and make better men and women of them.

Shades, Hat Racks, Dusters, and Sweepers.

"It is most important that the school-room be kept perfectly comfortable, cheerful, and clean."

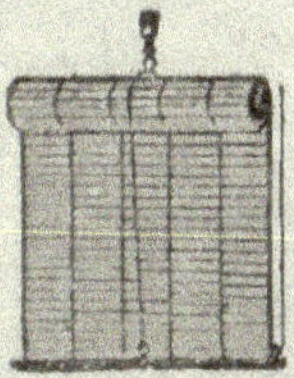

For School-room Windows the Rustic Shade is recommended on account of its **simplicity, durability, and cheapness.** It is furnished complete, ready to be put up with two nails or screws. They may be had **in any colors**—brown, blue, buff, pearl, green, or oiled walnut. The last two are generally required for school purposes. They are made for windows of any size. In sending dimensions for ordering the "Rustic Shades," give the full length and width of the window, allowing on the width about one inch over on each side.

Circular with prices, sent on application.

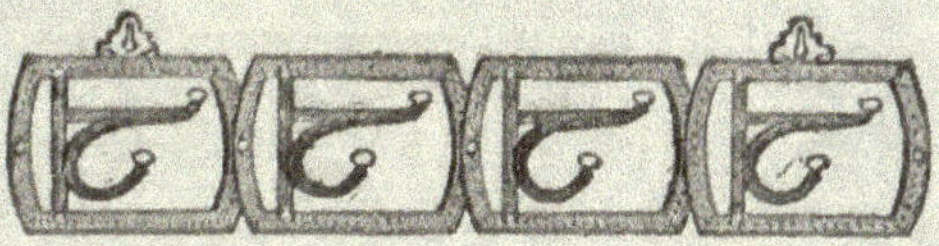

Hat and Cloak Racks. Four sizes, 4 to 8 hooks on each; price, **50 cts. to $1.00.**

The frames are made of black walnut, held together by screw rods; the hooks are iron, nicely coppered and well lacquered to prevent tarnishing in any climate.

School Furniture Dusters. 48 kinds, varying in size and color. Plain, each, 15 cents to $3.50;—Colored, 25 cents to $4.00.

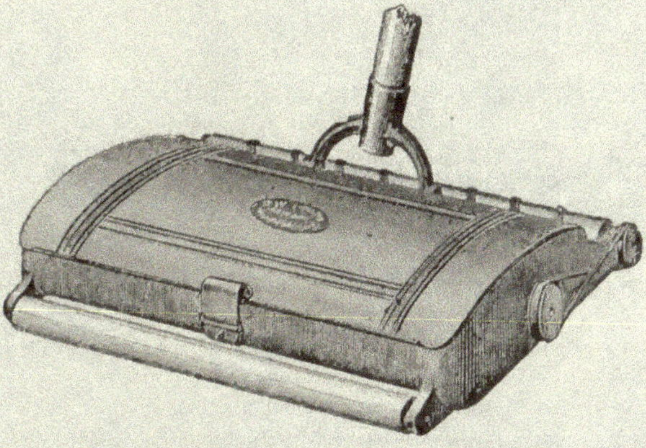

The Champion Dustless School-House Floor Sweeper, large size, price **$3.00.**

Aids to School Discipline:

A SUBSTITUTE FOR

School Records, Reports, and Prizes.

NEW AND APPROPRIATE DESIGNS, PRINTED IN COLORS.

An accurate register of deportment and scholarship promotes healthy emulation. Yet such a register is rarely kept. Teachers cannot record each recitation as it occurs, hence the record is neglected for the time, and afterward made from memory. *Perfect* accuracy being impossible, *confidence in the record is weakened and its moral force lost.* The **Aids** secure the good results of accurate records and reports, with less expense of time.

The **Aids** naturally and inevitably awaken a lively paternal interest, for the pupil takes home with him *the witness of his daily conduct and progress.*

The **Aids** may be used in various ways. This is convenient: In the morning give each pupil a **Card** (5 merits), representing a *perfect day*, to be forfeited for misdemeanor, or failure in recitation. **Single Merits** and **Half-Merits** are for pupils who fail to retain their **Cards** and yet are worthy of *some* credit. Five **Cards** held by any pupil are exchanged for a **Check** (25 merits), representing a perfect *School Week.* Four **Checks** are exchanged for a **Certificate of Merit,** representing 100 merits, or a perfect *Month.* These **Certificates** bear the pupil's name, and are signed by the teacher. The number held shows the pupil's standing.

If prizes or medals are awarded at close of session, there can be no mistake in determining to whom they belong: the decision being made by each pupil exhibiting his **Cards** and **Certificates,** no idea of favoritism can arise.

It is needless to discuss the value of proper incentives, for either children or adults. The use of Millions of these **Aids,** with the unbounded approval of Teachers, Parents, and Pupils, assures us that they are doing great good.

They are neat in design, printed in BEST Colors. The **Certificates** are prizes which pupils will cherish. Single Merits and Half-Merits are printed on card-board; Cards and Checks on heavy paper, and may be used many times—hence the system is **Cheap.** They are put up in sets of **500,** there being **80 Certificates, 120 Checks, 200 Cards, 100 Single Merits** and **Half-Merits.** **Price, per set (mailed) $1.25.**

Supplied separately (by mail):		**Half-Merits,** per hundred............	.15
Single Merits, per hundred..........	.15	**Checks (twenty-fives)** per hundred,	.40
Cards (fives) per hundred.............	.15	**Certificates (hundreds)** per hundred,	.60

The New School Medal

Is here shown, on both sides. It is made of a Superior White Metal, and will not easily tarnish. On one side, above the word "Excellence," is opportunity to engrave the *date* of presenting the Medal. On the other side, the pupil's name may be engraved on the *Scroll.* (The engraving costs, in New York, three cents a letter or figure; on receipt of the money, we will get it done at that rate. In most localities, some jeweller can be found to do it quite as well.) This is **the best School Medal** now made, and is highly appreciated. **Price, .25; by mail, prepaid, .35.**

The School Index, or "Roll of Honor."

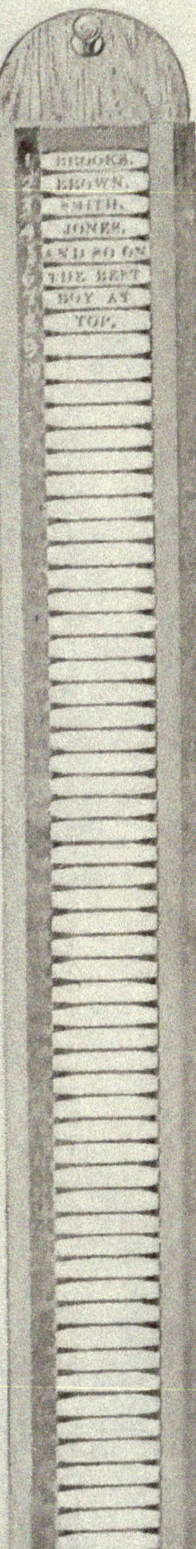

***"Honor and shame from no condition rise:
Act well your part, there all the honor lies."***

To teachers who keep a record of the work performed by their classes, and are weary of writing out, week after week, the names and relative merits of each of their pupils, the SCHOOL INDEX will be welcome, on account of the ease with which, by its aid, they can accomplish what has hitherto been an arduous task. Its construction is clearly illustrated in the accompanying cut. It consists of a frame in which are arranged small pieces of wood, on which the names of the pupils are to be written. These can be taken out and moved at pleasure. One side of the frame is hinged to admit of its being opened when any change in the position of a name-strip is required. On the other side, which is boxed, are numbers, as shown in the cut.

In connection with the **Aids to School Discipline,** the **School Index** furnishes an accurate and reliable means of showing the standing of every pupil. The "Aids" and the "Index" together, form a perfect System of School Records. At the expiration of a "quarter" or any specified time, each pupil produces his Cards and Certificates, and his rank being determined by the number of these in his possession, his name can easily be put in its proper place in the Index. If any error in arrangement is discovered, it can be easily corrected. In this respect, the superiority of the School Index over the ordinary Merit Roll is readily seen. Where the Aids are not used, the Index can be made to take the place of the "Merit Roll" or "School Record,"—the preparation of which has always caused a waste of much valuable time and effort.

The Index may be used to show the standing of each pupil as to scholarship alone, or scholarship together with deportment and attendance. As it is to be displayed in a prominent place, where it can be seen and examined not only by the pupils but by parents and others who visit the schools, it will necessarily have a beneficial influence on the conduct and diligence of the classes.

If desired, it can be used to show the rank of each pupil as to behavior alone, and in this case, will be a powerful aid in school government—BEING FIRST depending on BEING GOOD, every one will naturally strive to excel in good conduct.

The **School Index** is simple in construction; easily managed; can never get out of order, there being no "machinery" whatever about it; can be introduced without making any changes in the manner of governing or marking; is neat in design; and is light, portable, and *cheap.*

Wherever introduced, its use has been attended with **the happiest results,** and has called forth the praise of experienced teachers.

Price, plain, ... $2.00
Price, made of black walnut, . . . $2.50

Rogers' School Groups.

"Works of art are invaluable in educating the taste of the young."

The School Examination.—One of the School Committee has come to examine the school, and is pointing out, good-naturedly, on the slate, the mistake the little girl has made in her "sum," while the teacher stands by to encourage her.
Height, 20 inches.—Weight, when packed, 80 pounds.—Price............ **15.00**

Uncle Ned's School.—An old negro bootblack is keeping school, but one of his pupils, a mulatto girl, has asked him a puzzling question, while a lazy little boy is mischievously tickling his foot, which he feels, but is too much occupied to attend to it.
Height, 20 inches.—Weight, when packed, 90 pounds.—Price............. **15.00**

SCHOOL MATERIAL,—PART VI.

SCHOOL STATIONERY, etc.

CONTENTS.

Slates, Book-slates, Fancy Slates, Slate Pencils,

SLATE RUBBERS, Etc.

New Oval or oval edges with oval round corners.

Round Corner Counting-House Slates. Two Slates, united with brass hinges.

Size,	4 × 6 inches...price per doz.,	$1.30
"	5 × 7 " " "	1.50
"	6 × 9 " " "	2.10
"	6½ × 10 " " "	2.20
"	7 × 11 " " "	2.40
"	8 × 12 " " "	2.90
"	9 × 13 " " "	3.50
"	9½ × 14 " " "	4.80

Size,	6 × 9 inches, price per doz.,	$6.87
"	7 × 11 " " "	8.28
"	6½ × 14 " " "	8.90
"	8 × 12 " " "	10.68
"	7 × 15 " " "	11.75
"	9 × 13 " " "	12.75
"	8 × 16 " " "	12.75
"	9½ × 14 " " "	13.00
"	11 × 16 " " "	19.15
"	12 × 18 " " "	25.50

Contents of Assorted Cases of New Oval.

Sizes.	5 × 7	6 × 9	6½ × 10	7 × 11	8 × 12	9 × 13		Per Case.
No. 1	1½	2	2	3	3	0	DOZ.	$28.00
No. 2	3	2	2	2	½	½	"	22.40

Liberal discounts on quantities, and by the case.

Book Slates.—The following contain **three slates** each, hinged together, and covered with stiff covers, like a book.

Sizes in inches, 3¾ × 6½ .... price each, **$0.67**
" " 4½ × 7¾ .... " **.80**
" " 5¼ × 9 .... " **1.15**

Fancy Double Slates,—Superior quality and finish, set in fine wood panelled cases, polished and highly ornamented, brass hinges, imported. Eight sizes. Price (variable with gold) ....each, **.85** to **1.75**

SLATE PENCILS.—At lowest rates, which are variable with gold.

German.—Five, six, and seven inches, in wooden boxes........ per hundred,

Soapstone.—Four, five, and six inches, paper boxes........... " "

Composition.—Six inches, wooden boxes......................per gross,

SLATE RUBBER.—Chamois—"a gem for the school-room."

It dispenses with sponge and water, in erasing marks from the slate. No more need the teacher hear the frequent question, "Please, sir, may I go to wash my slate?" Nor need the child spit upon his slate to erase the marks.

It is made of wood and Chamois skin, arranged to bring a series of edges of skin snugly against the surface of the slate.

Every teacher will recommend it because of its real convenience and neatness. Every pupil will buy it. It costs no more than a good sponge.

No. 1—size 1 × 1½ inches..................................price per 100, **5.00**
No. 2—size 2 inches square.................................. " " **8.00**

(Specimens, by mail, of No. 1, 10 cents—of No. 2, 15 cents.)

School and Record Ink.

Our School Ink is specially put up for school use, and is better adapted to all school purposes than any other ink that we can get made. It flows freely, and flows jet black from the pen; it has no sediment; it does not "gum up" the pen and inkstand; it is unsurpassed in color, and it is cheap.

It is neatly and substantially put up, smallest size in glass cones; the half-pints, pints, and quarts in good glass bottles; and the half-gallons and gallons in square tin cans, for compact and safe shipment to any distance.

Price List of our School Ink.

Octagonal Cones, glass, per dozen,			$0.60
Half-pints, -	"	"	1.75
Pints, - -	"	"	3.50
Quarts, - -	"	"	6.00
Half-gallons, square tin cans, each,			1.00
Gallons,	"	" "	2.00

On Draught, $1.50 per gallon. Cost of keg or barrel to be added.

Congress Record Ink.

No. 1 Stands	per gross,	$6.00
No. 2 "	"	10.00
Half-pints	per dozen,	2.75
Pints	"	4.00
Quarts	"	7.00

(Two-thirds size.)

Arnold's Writing Fluid—all sizes. It being imported prices fluctuate with gold.

All other kinds of ink supplied at lowest rates when called for.

Ink-Wells, Ink-Well Covers, etc.

Glass Ink-wells are in very great demand. The points to be regarded in selecting them are few. First, it is necessary to secure **the largest possible capacity,** and yet have them fit the usual bore of school desks. Second, **good glass** is necessary, in order to **avoid waste from breakages, and consequent damage to books.** Such an ink-well is illustrated, **full size,** in the cut. It is shown beneath a cast-iron cover, japanned and hinged.

The New Brass Ink-well Cover is struck out of sheet-brass, and lacquered. Instead of having a hinge, it revolves on a screw, and is noiseless. It is very neat, and gives a bright and ornamental appearance to the desk. It must be admitted that whatever contributes to the good appearance of school furniture, is of advantage. We cannot do too much to make the school-room look pleasant and cheerful, and thus cultivate the taste of pupils.

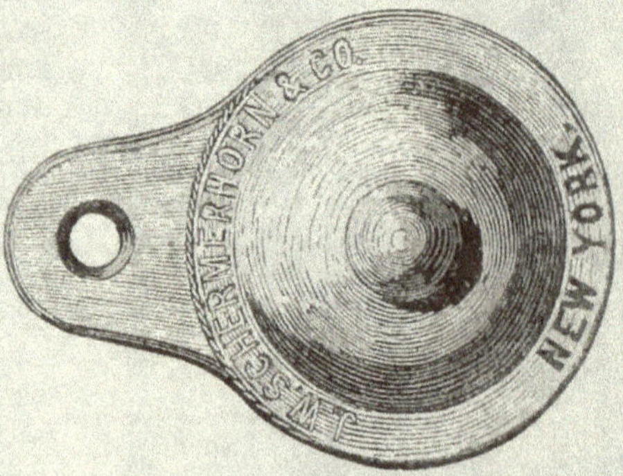

The Non-corroding Metallic Ink-well, shown, full size, in the cut, was invented in 1868. By a new process the interior is made insoluble by ink, securing all the advantages of glass, with increased capacity, strength, and durability. The loss and annoyance of breakage in handling and by frost is entirely disposed of.

The metal may be kept bright, giving an ornamental appearance to the desk. The cover is thoroughly secured with a brass hinge. It is made of standard size, to fit the usual bore of school desks.

Non-corroding Metallic Ink Sockets, being the same as shown in the cut **without the cover,** are supplied for use with the ordinary iron covers, or with the *new* brass covers. They are durable and economical. The size is adapted to the usual bore of school desks.

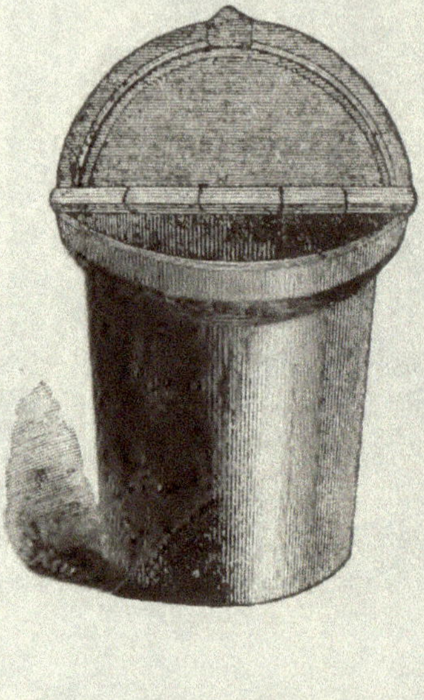

Ink-Wells, Ink-Well Covers, Ink Vents, etc.

The American Locking Ink-well Cover is a *new invention*, intended to supply the need of a *locking cover* for the common glass ink-wells, or any of the ordinary ink sockets. It is easily and readily fixed to any desks without the use of screws, letting in flush with the desk top. It is made of iron, and is japanned. The cut exhibits top view.

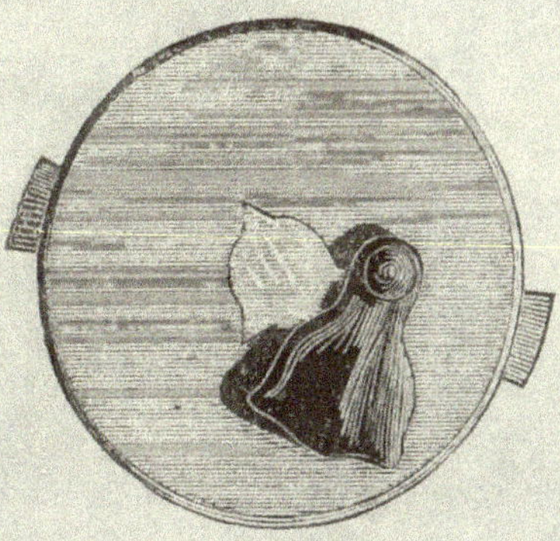

The opening in the top is sufficient for any size pen. It also admits the key for locking the cover securely fast to the desk. The size and peculiar shape of the opening is not liable to be fitted by any knife or other instrument which pupils are likely to have about them.

The pen opening is tightly closed by a little pivoted cover which keeps out the dust, and prevents evaporation of the ink.

In short, this device has more real advantages than any of the complicated and expensive "patent locking ink-wells;" it can be used with the glass ink-wells already on hand; and is *simple*, having no screws and no hinges; it is *durable* and it is *cheap*.

Scarlett's Ink Vent for filling Inkstands and Ink-wells.—With this vent, a steady stream may be poured, and cut off promptly. All overflowing inkstands and wells, and dripping of ink upon clothing and furniture, is thus avoided. The ink escapes at *a*. Should a drop cling to the orifice, instead of falling on furniture or floor, it is conducted back to the bottle, through the inclined gutter *c*. At *b* there is a small passage to the interior of the bottle. This is too small to permit perceptible evaporation, and yet admits sufficient air to cause the ink to flow from *a*.

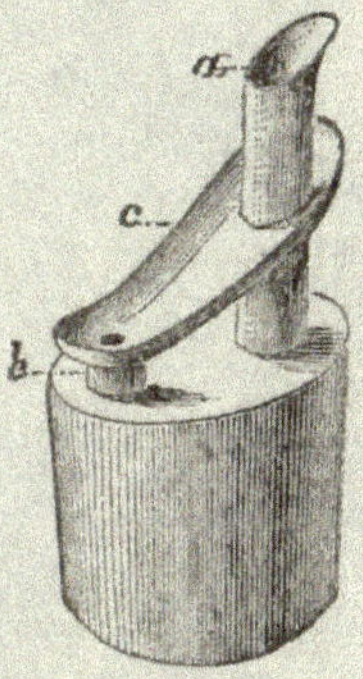

The convenience of this invention will be appreciated by all who have had experience in filling inkstands in the old-fashioned way. The cork is made tapering, to fit the mouth of *any* ink-bottle.

Specimens may be sent by mail for **25** cents.

PRICE LIST OF INK-WELLS, COVERS, VENTS, ETC.

Glass Ink-wells, or Sockets, shown in cut	per dozen,	$0.75
Iron Covers, japanned, with hinge	"	.75
Brass Covers, lacquered, new and extra neat	"	1.00
Non-corroding Metallic Ink Sockets	"	1.00
Non-corroding Metallic Ink-wells, wih covers	"	1.75
American Locking Ink-well Cover	"	1.00
Britannia Ink-wells, glass lined	"	2.25
Ink Vents, Scarlett's Patent, for filling Ink-wells	"	2.40

Teachers' Inkstands.

Reservoir Inkstand.

Calendar Inkstand.

Morgan's Patent Reservoir and Calendar Inkstands are well adapted for use in the school-room, on the teachers' desks. The dipping cup is constantly supplied with pure ink at a uniform depth. The sediment is prevented from flowing into the dipping cup by a bar between it and the reservoir.

A convenient calendar, and a tasteful pen-rack are combined with the **Reservoir Inkstand** (No. 1), to make the **Calendar Inkstand** (No. 2).

1.—Reservoir Inkstand	price each,	**$0.25**
2.—Calendar Inkstand, with calendar and bronze pen-rack	" "	**.90**
3.—Reversible Inkstand	" "	**1.00**

No. 3.—The Teachers' Reversible Inkstand consists of a glass pot with a ground shoulder, into which fits a water-tight funnel with a hollow stem and rim. The air which is forced down upon the ink causes it to rise the required height in the stem.

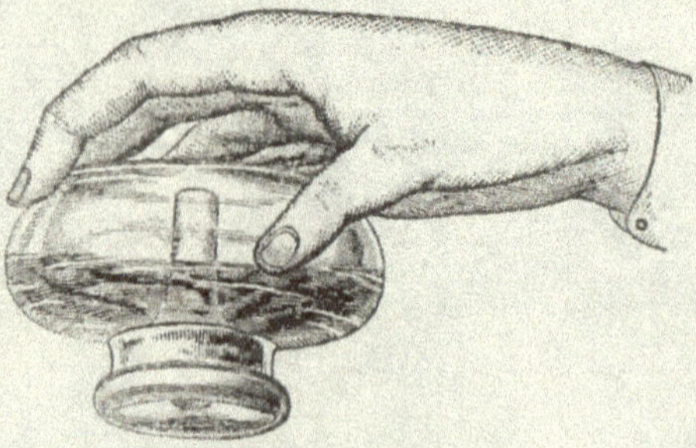

"THE INK CAN'T GET OUT."

When the stand is reversed, the ink that is already in the stem, *and no more*, will flow down into the hollow rim, where it stays till the stand is again brought to its upright position. Its chief points are: 1. The ink cannot be spilled. 2. The pen will always reach JUST enough to fill it. 3. The ink is protected from the dust and evaporation. 4. The entire funnel CAN BE REMOVED to replenish with fresh ink. 5. It is simple, being made entirely of glass. 6. It is cheap, costing but **$1.00**.

Fancy Inks.—Writing and Copying combined.

Violet, Perfumed, 2 ounce octagon cones	per dozen,	**$0.75**
Violet, square stands, flint glass	"	**1.25**
Carmine, superior, flint glass draped stands	"	**1.75**
Carmine, superior, flint glass draped stands, ground glass stoppers	"	**2.50**
Assorted, Twelve Colors, square stands, flint glass	"	**1.50**

The Celebrated Spencerian Steel Pens.

The well-known durability and perfect action of these pens, are owing to a peculiar process in carbonizing; and the main secret of their popularity is the fact that they are manufactured under the supervision of the **Original Inventor** of steel pens, whose great experience, combined with the aid of the **most skilled workmen in Europe**, enable us to offer an article as yet unsurpassed in all the qualities that are required in pens **adapted to every style** of writing. They are a nearer approximation to the real **Swan Quill** than anything hitherto invented. These pens *are indorsed*, and constantly used by the best penmen in the country. They are *used exclusively* in all the first-class Commercial Colleges in the United States and Canadas. They are more largely used than any other pens by Cashiers, Tellers, Book-keepers, etc., in the *principal banking houses* throughout the country. They are used by *all* who have given them a *trial*. They comprise fifteen numbers, viz.:

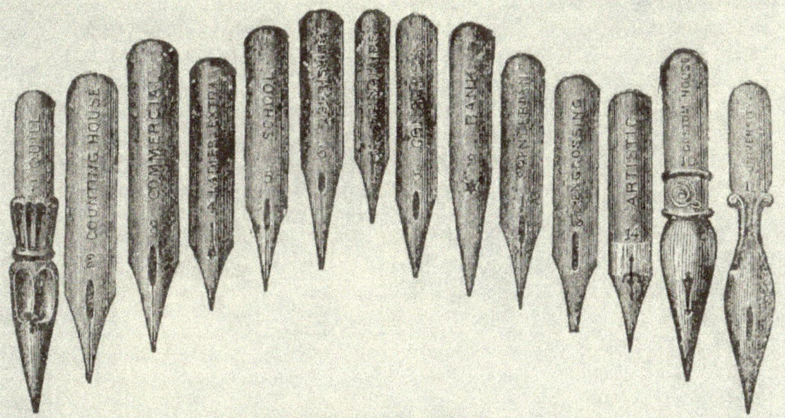

PRICES BY MAIL:

No. 1.	COLLEGE PEN. Point Fine; Action Perfect................	Price per Gross.		$1.25
No. 2.	COUNTING-HOUSE PEN. Point Fine and Flexible.........	"	"	1.25
No. 3.	COMMERCIAL PEN. Point Medium..........................	"	"	1.25
No. 4.	LADIES' EXTRA PEN. Point Extra Fine and Flexible.....	"	"	1.40
No. 5.	SCHOOL PEN. Point Fine, Medium in Flexibility..........	"	"	1.25
No. 6.	FLOURISHING PEN. Point Long, Flexible, and Medium in Fineness..	"	"	1.25
No. 7.	QUILL PEN. Point Medium, Quill Action..................	"	"	1.60
No. 8.	CONGRESS PEN. Medium Point, and very Flexible... ...	"	"	1.40
No. 9.	BANK PEN. Point Long and Flexible........................	"	"	1.40
No. 10.	CUSTOM-HOUSE PEN. Point Medium......................	"	"	1.60
No. 11.	UNIVERSITY PEN. Point Medium, very Smooth and Flexible	"	"	1.60
No. 12.	EPISTOLAIRE PEN. Point very Fine and very Flexible...	"	"	2.50
No. 13.	ENGROSSING PEN. Point Blunt and Smooth.......... ...	"	"	1.25
No. 14.	ARTISTIC PEN. Flexible, with Extra Fine Point..........	"	"	1.60
No. 15.	THE QUEEN. Point Extra Fine and Even..................	"	"	1.60

Caution.—We caution all who desire the genuine article against purchasing *any* "Spencerian" Pens, which have not the initials "I., P., B. & Co.," or, "Ivison, Phinney & Co.," on each Pen.

☞ FOR SALE BY DEALERS GENERALLY.

☞ **Sample Card**, containing all the **15 numbers**, artistically arranged and securely inclosed, sent by mail on receipt of **25 cents**.

The American Standard Penmanship.

Spencerian.

The Spencerian Penmanship was first published in 1848, and has worthily maintained its position since then as the most original and most practical system of writing extant. It claims superiority over other systems in analysis and method; in systematically and progressively arranged copies; in simplicity of style; in correct ruling; in its movement exercises; and in its adaptability to rapid and elegant business writing.

It is the *accredited source* from which the best penmen of the country have derived their knowledge and skill in the art. It is used in more *Normal Schools and Business Colleges* than all other systems combined. It is *more generally* used than any other system.

THE COPY-BOOKS are comprised in FOUR Distinct Series:—

I.—SCHOOL SERIES, Nos. 1, 2, 3, 4, and 5.

II.—BUSINESS SERIES, Nos. 6 and 7.

III.—LADIES' SERIES, Nos. 8 and 9.

IV.—EXERCISE SERIES, Nos. 10, 11, and 12.

INTERMEDIATE BOOK.

Retail Price, **15** cents each.

All the letters, small and capital, with twelve short sentences, are contained in the Intermediate Book. It is ruled to regulate the relative length of letters, and is undoubtedly the most practical and popular Copy-book published.

The Spencerian Key,

For the use of Teachers, Pupils, and Professional Penmen. Containing one hundred and seventy-six pages, and hundreds of Illustrations.

Price, by mail, in cloth **$1.50**
Cloth extra, tinted paper **2.00**

Spencerian Charts of Writing and Drawing.

SIX IN NUMBER.

Large size, 24 by 30 inches; on three cards.
Small size, 19 by 24 inches; on three cards.

☞ They are so printed as to present the appearance of SUPERIOR BLACKBOARD WRITING. The letters can be seen across the school-room.

A SERIES OF DRAWING LESSONS is also represented upon the Charts, which, with the Letters, make them by far the most attractive and instructive Charts ever presented to the public.

Large size, mounted, per express **$3.75**
In sheets, per mail **2.50**
Small size, per express **1.80**
In sheets, per mail **0.90**

Teacher's Guide

To the proper use of Spencerian Copy-books and Charts. In pamphlet form. 30 pages.

Spencerian Exercise Card, and Oblique Lines,

Containing Fifty Exercises for confirming the hand in correct positions, and imparting to it free movements. The oblique lines regulate the slant in writing. Price, by express, **50** cents per dozen; by mail, **5** cents each.

☞ Most liberal terms given on Copy-books furnished for Examination or Introduction.

Lead Pencils, Pencil Files, Holders, etc.

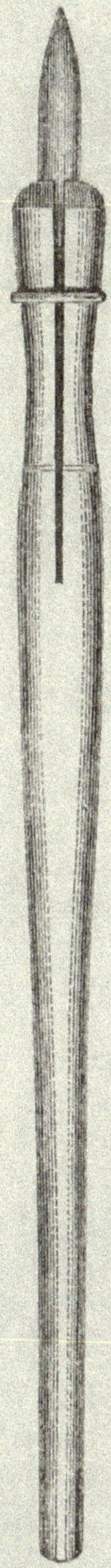

LEAD PENCILS, FABER'S.—All Grades.

Imported—prices variable with gold.

4 Grades.—Nos. 1, 2, 3, and 4, in paper box.

5 Grades.—Nos. 1, 2, 3, 4, and 5, in wooden box.

5 Grades.—Nos. 1, 2, 3, 4, and 5, with knife and rubber, in wooden box.

7 Grades.—Nos. 1, 2, 3, 4, 5, 6, and 7, in wooden box.

10 Grades.—Very finely graded, in wooden box.

Any grade in dozen or gross packages.

Eagle Pencils.—Nos. 1, 2, 3, and 4, and varied styles, in boxes.

Pencil File, with Dust Box.—Squires' Patent, for Lead and Slate Pencils. Price, **25** cents.

The New Slate Pencil and Pen-Holder

Is a **new device,** large enough to receive the regular slate pencils which are sold everywhere. It is long enough for a regular four inch slate pencil—the six inch may be broken in two. Every teacher knows how desirable it is to have the children use a regular handle or holder when they write with slate pencil or pen. The irregular bits of slate pencils cramp the fingers, and injure them for writing.

The cut illustrates it somewhat larger than regular size.

They are put up in paper boxes, 100 in each box. Price, **5.00**

Specimen sent by mail for **10** cents.

Propelling Pencils.

Red Wood, with German silver slide, - -	per dozen,	**1.75**
Black Wood, " " " - -	"	**1.75**
Red Wood, ivory tips, German silver slide, -	"	**2.25**
Black Wood, " " " " -	"	**2.25**

Stationers' Gum.

White Rubber.—4, 8, 12, 16, 20, 24, 30, 40, 60, 80, to the pound.

Black Rubber.—8, 12, 16, 20, 24, 30, 40, 60, 80, to the pound.

Artists' Materials of all kinds, at best rates.

Pen and Pencil Baskets and Racks, etc.

Style A.

Style B.

The Pen and Pencil Baskets are neat, light, and durable. They are imported.
Style A has three sizes. Price, each........................ **.75, 1.00, 1.25**
Style B, only one size. " **1.88**

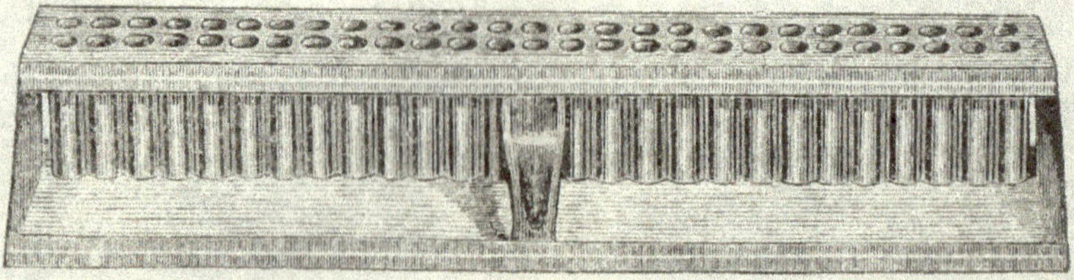

Squire's Patent Pen and Pencil Rack is intended for collecting, protecting from loss or injury, and distributing pens, lead pencils, and slate pencils in schools. Each pupil will get his own, without trouble or contention. It obviates the annoyance arising rom pupils having no pen, or a poor one—no pencil, or a short one. It is durably made of japanned tin.

Directions for use.—Let one pupil pass the rack for each pupil to put his pen or pencil in the hole whose number has been previously assigned to him. Distribute in similar manner. Price, by express (not mailable)........................ ...... **1.50**

Teachers' Pen Racks.

No. 1.

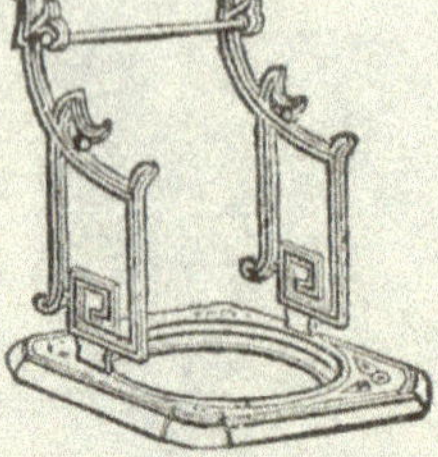

No. 3.

No. 2.

No. 1, Adapted to ordinary inkstands..................................each, .35
2, French pattern, single, heavy for paper-weight.................. " .40
3, Bronze, new style.. " .50

Many other styles to suit all tastes.

Writing, Exercise, and Composition Books,

AND COMPOSITION PAPER.

Blank Writing Books.—Superfine white paper, fancy paper covers, assorted colors.

No. 1.—American School, 12 leaves..........	per dozen.	**$0.75**
No. 2.—High School, 14 leaves..........	"	**0.95**

Exercise Books.—Superfine white paper, plainly ruled.

No 1.—Cap quarto, flexible covers, 16 leaves..........	"	**1.50**
No. 2.— " " 24 leaves..........	"	**2.25**
No. 3.— " " 36 leaves..........	"	**3.00**

Composition Books.—Superfine white paper, cap quarto.

No. 1.—Quarter bound, stiff cover, 24 leaves..........	"	**2.00**
No. 2.—Half bound, red sheep, morocco paper sides, 50 leaves....	"	**4.75**
No. 3.—Half bound, " " " 84 leaves....	"	**7.00**
No. 3x.—Full bound, " cloth sides, 84 leaves....	"	**7.50**
No. 3G.—Full bound, imitation morocco, gilt edges, 84 leaves....	"	**12.50**
No. 4.—Half bound, red sheep, morocco paper sides, 112 leaves....	"	**9.50**

COMPOSITION PAPER.—Rider's.

The teacher who would improve his pupils in "good English," has invaluable aid in Mr. Rider's method of correcting compositions. Under the old plan, weary hours are passed in *writing out corrections*, which may not be understood by the pupil, even if he take trouble to read them.

Rider's Composition Paper makes the pupil, *not the teacher*, correct the composition. At head of sheet is table of rules and laws which are usually neglected, each appropriately numbered. The teacher underlines errors, and places in margin a symbol directing pupil to proper item in table. The pupil can examine and analyze the principle violated and make corrections. Thus he inevitably becomes technically and thoroughly familiar with the requirements of the English language.

First Series is for beginners in Composition who may be careless in penmanship, in spelling, in use of capitals, etc. Its proper use will prevent little faults, easy to acquire, but difficult to mend.

Second Series reviews the greater points of the first, and attends to selection of words, grammatical construction, formation of sentences, paragraphing, condensing, etc., etc.

Third Series has reference to rhetorical correctness and elegance, and the cultivation of the best style of finished English composition.

As a time-saving invention it is most important, besides reducing composition to orderly method.

The tables are neatly printed at the head of letter-paper, properly ruled with blue and red lines.

Specimen sheets, by mail, pre-paid, **5c.** Price per quire, by express.......... **$0.30**

Our School Rulers.

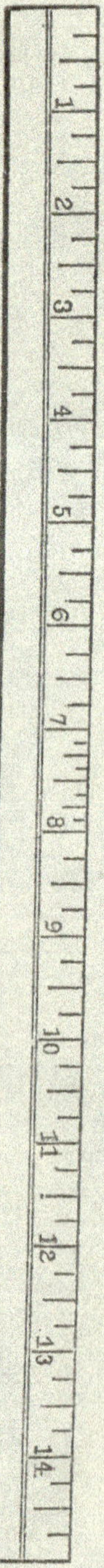

These Rulers are made specially for school purposes. They are well made of good, hard wood, polished. They are accurately marked in inches, half-inches, quarter-inches, and eighth-inches, stamped in black. One edge is properly bevelled. There are two sizes—one twelve inches long, and the other fifteen inches. The latter is recommended as most useful.

Price, each **$0.10**

(Specimen mailed, letter postage, 20 cents.)

Liberal discount on a gross.

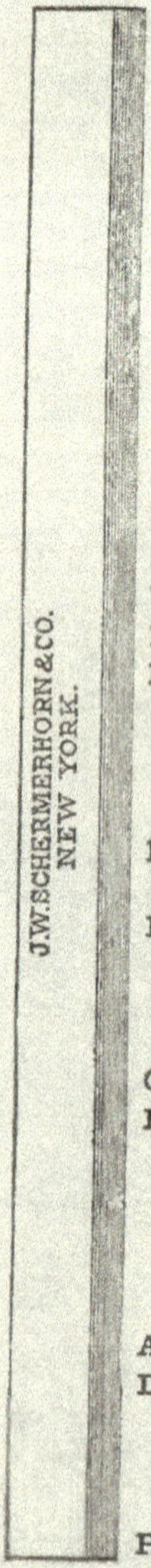

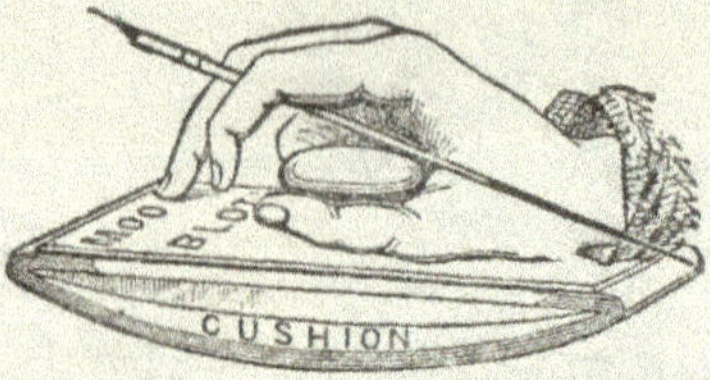

Moore's Cushioned Blotters.

Walnut, small, plain .... each, **$0.50**
Cedar, " " .... " **.60**
Rosewood, polished .... " **.85**
Paper, small, for each of above .... per packet, **.10**
Walnut, large, plain .... each, **.75**
Rosewood, large, polished .... " **1.25**
Paper, large .... per packet, **.10**

Blotting Paper.

Parker's Treasury, 80, 100, 120 pounds to ream, white or colored .... per quire, **1.20** to **$2.25**
Blotting Pads (12 pieces in packet) .... per packet, **.10**

Erasers.

Green's Patent Ink Erasers .... price per 100 pieces, **$5.00**
Erasing Knives.—Joseph Rodgers & Sons' wood handle, bone handle, ivory handle, imported. Price variable with gold.

Penholders.

Accommodation, steel tips .... per gross, **$0.60**
Double Conic, Cedar, small, steel tips .... " **2.20**
" " " medium, steel tips ...... " **2.67**
" " " large, " " ...... " **3.00**

Pen Racks of varied styles, prices each, **20** to **60** cents.

Papers—Note, Letter, Cap, Manuscript, Initial,

AND STATIONERY CASES.

The following are white wove, ruled, superfine, highly finished. They are neatly put up in manilla outside wrappers, with the numbers and weights marked on each package. The note and letter papers are in quarter-ream packages, and the cap papers in half-ream packages.

Octavo Note—3½ pounds to the ream	price per ream,	$1.25
" 4 " " "	" "	1.40
" 5 " " "	" "	1.75
Commercial Note—4 pounds to the ream	" "	1.40
" 5 " " "	" "	1.75
" 6 " " "	" "	2.10
" 7 " " "	" "	2.45
Letter Paper— 8 pounds to the ream	" "	2.80
" 9 " " "	" "	3.15
" 10 " " "	" "	3.50
" 12 " " "	" "	4.20
Foolscap—10 pounds to the ream	" "	3.50
" 12 " " "	" "	4.20
" 14 " " "	" "	4.90
Broad Bill Cap—10 pounds to the ream	" "	4.00
" " 12 " " "	" "	4.80
" " 14 " " "	" "	5.60
Legal Cap—10 pounds to the ream	" "	4.00
" 12 " " "	" "	4.80
" 14 " " "	" "	5.60

Manuscript Papers.

A carefully prepared set of rules for properly preparing manuscript for the press accompanies Nos. 2 and 3.

No. 1.—Students' Manuscript, size 3¾ x 8 inches, flat sheets for pencil, with three perforations at top for affixing to the eyeletted case—ruled on one side	per ream	$1.00
No. 2.—Editors' Manuscript, size 5 x 10 inches, flat sheet, with three perforations at top of sheet for tying them together in parts or chapters	per ream	1.20
No. 3.—Contributors' Manuscript, like No. 2, somewhat thicker	"	1.80
No. 4.—Authors' Manuscript, size 6 x 10 inches, flat sheet, otherwise like No. 3	"	2.25

Initial Stationery.

This is very handsomely put up in paper boxes, containing one quire ladies' note, with envelopes to match.

No. 1.—Everett, white wove	per box,	.25
No. 2.—Siddons, rose tint, ornamented box, perfumed	"	.30
No. 3.—Oriental, auburn tint, hinged neck box, ornamented with colored plates	"	.60
No. 4.—Offered and Accepted, lavender tint, ornamented with large colored plates,	"	.45
No. 5.—Galaxy, white wove, ornamented box	"	.30

This initial stationery will be mailed for **10** cents extra for postage.

Stationery Cases.

No. 1.—With three apartments; for letter paper, note paper, and envelopes	each,	1.56
No. 2.—With four apartments, and drawer for containing stamps, etc	"	2.50
No. 3.—With three apartments, and small trays for holding pins, stamps, wafers, pencils, etc	"	2.70

Paper Weights, Folders, Clips, Mucilage, etc.

Paper Weights.—Bronze, glass, iron—various styles and sizes . . . . each, **.20** to **$1.75**
Paper Folders, and Check Cutters.—Japanned tin, 2 to 4 inches wide, each, **.20**
Ivory Folders, and Paper Knives.—5, 6, 7, 8, 9, and 10 inches long, each . . . . . **.15** to **.75**

Letter Clips.

A variety of styles and sizes, each,
$0.15 to **1.25.**

Board Clips.—Cloth Sides.

Cap,	Iron	**$0.75**
Letter,	"	**.63**
Note,	"	**.52**
Cap,	Brass	**.80**
Letter,	"	**.70**
Note,	"	**.60**

These clips are supplied with the spring either on the side or on the end, as may be desired.

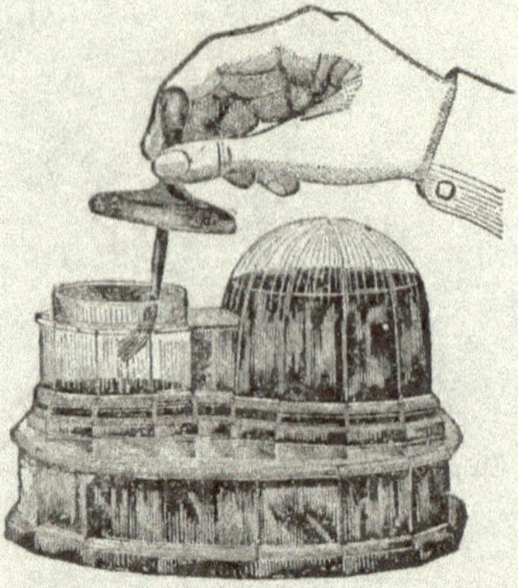

No. 1.

No. 4.

Morgan's Patent Reservoir Mucilage Stands.

No. 1.—	**Pressed Flint Glass,** with brush	each,	**$ 1.50**
2.—	**Flint Glass,** with brush	"	**.40**
3.—	**Flint Glass,** with brush	"	**.40**
4.—	**Pressed Flint Glass,** with brush	"	**1.50**

Stickwell & Co.'s Mucilage.—Made from pure Gum Arabic.

Three Ounce Cones, with cup and brush	per dozen,	**1.75**
Eight Ounce " " "	"	**5.00**
Pints, glass bottles	"	**6.00**
Quarts, glass bottles	"	**11.00**

Envelopes.—Letter and Official Sizes.

		Sizes. No. Pap'r	5 N. Gov.	6 $3\frac{1}{4} \times 5\frac{5}{8}$	6¼ $3\frac{5}{8} \times 6$	6½ $3\frac{1}{2} \times 6\frac{1}{4}$	7 $3\frac{3}{4} \times 6\frac{3}{4}$	8½ $3\frac{1}{2} \times 8\frac{1}{2}$	9 $3\frac{7}{8} \times 8\frac{7}{8}$
MANILLA,		115	$1 50	$1 70	$1 90	$2 20		$3 00	$3 00
		180	1 65	1 80	1 90	2 30	$3 30	3 20	3 30
	× ×	225	3 20	3 60	3 80	4 00		5 80	6 00
GOLD,		203	1 40	1 60					
		2758	1 90	2 20	2 40	2 90			
		3757	2 10	2 40	2 60	3 00	4 30	4 40	4 60
		1475	2 15	2 40	2 60	3 00			5 00
	×	475	2 35	2 70	2 90	3 40			5 30
¼ M's	× ×	2040	2 70	3 15	3 30	3 80			6 00
½ M's	× ×	5040	2 85	3 30	3 50	4 00			6 50
	×	3245	2 50	2 90	3 10				
	×	4245	2 70	3 15	3 30	3 80			
¼ M's	× ×	1575	3 00	3 50	3 70				
¼ M's	× ×	575	3 25	3 75	3 90	4 50			
LIGHT BUFF,		2068	1 90	2 20	2 40	2 90			4 50
		3776	2 10	2 40	2 60	3 00		4 40	4 60
	×	4545	2 35	2 70	2 90	3 40	4 80	5 00	5 30
	×	477	2 50	2 90	3 10				
½ M's	× ×	635	2 85	3 30	3 50	4 00			6 50
½ M's	× ×	563	3 00	3 50	3 70				
	×	4775	2 70	3 15	3 30	3 80	5 50	6 00	6 20
¼ M's	× ×	5635	3 25	3 75	3 90	4 50	7 00	7 50	7 50
¼ M's	× × ×	6600	3 80	4 40	4 60				
CORN,	×	495	2 35	2 70	2 90				
¼ M's	× ×	5030	2 85	3 30	3 50	4 00			
¼ M's	× ×	530	3 00	3 50	3 70				
	×	1495	2 50	2 90	3 10				
	×	4950	2 70	3 15	3 30	3 80	5 50	6 00	6 20
¼ M's	× ×	5725	3 25	3 75	3 90	4 50	7 00	7 50	7 50
¼ M's	× × ×	7700	3 80	4 40	4 60				
CANARY,		3036	2 10	2 40	2 60	3 00			4 60
		1045	2 35	2 70	2 90	3 40			5 30
	×	2045	2 50	2 90	3 10	3 60			
	× ×	1515	3 00	3 50	3 70				
	×	145	2 70	3 15	3 30	3 80	5 50	6 00	6 20
¼ M's	×	515	3 25	3 75	3 90	4 50			7 50
¼ M's	× × ×	5500	3 80	4 40	4 60				
ORANGE,	×	340	2 70	3 15	3 30	3 80			
¼ M's	× ×	504	3 25	3 75	3 90	4 50			
MELON, ¼ M's	× ×	595	3 25	3 75	3 90	4 50			
WHITE,		128	1 90	2 20	2 40	2 90			
		3136	2 70	3 15	3 30	3 80	5 50	6 00	6 20
	×	215	2 35	2 70	2 90				5 30
¼ M's	× ×	532	2 85	3 30	3 50				6 50
¼ M's	×	1340	3 10	3 60	3 75				
¼ M's	×	134	3 25	3 75	3 90	4 50	7 00	6 40	6 60
¼ M's	× ×	13	3 60	4 00	4 25				
¼ M's	× ×	106	3 75	4 20	4 40	5 00	7 20	7 80	8 00
¼ M's	× ×	1960	3 75	4 20	4 40	5 00			
¼ M's	× × ×	126	4 40	5 15	5 40				

Envelopes not designated as "¼ M's" are put up in ½ M's. For ¼ M's add 15c. per M. to price of ½ M's. Envelopes designated as "¼ M's" can be put up in ½ M's at 15c. per M. less.

NOTE.—" M." represents **one thousand.**

×'s are arbitrary marks, representing thickness of paper.

Post-office Boxes, Stationery Cases, and Calendars.

Post-office Boxes.

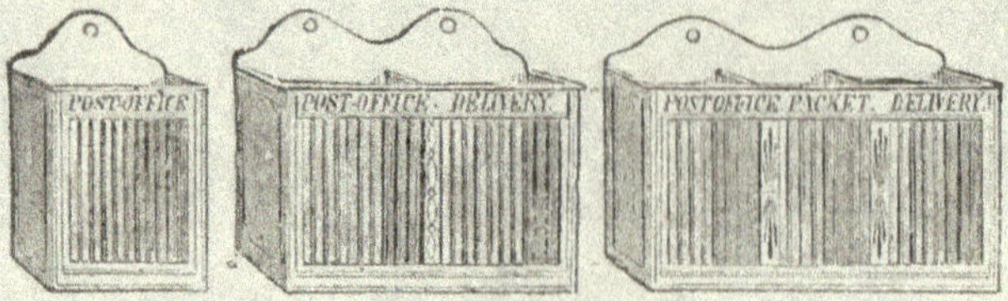

No. 1, One part, "Post-office,"....................................each, .84
2, Two parts, "Post-office and Delivery,"............................ " 1.20
3, Three parts, "Post-office, Packet, and Delivery,"................. " 1.50

Stationery Cases.

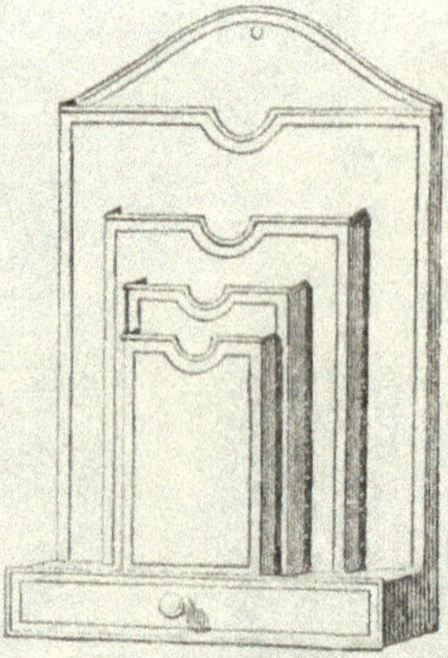

No. 1, Is a very convenient article for holding letter and note paper, and places for envelopes; also, with a drawer for containing stamps, etc., each 2.40

No. 2, With three compartments, for billheads or papers; also, contains small trays, for holding pins, stamps, wafers, pens, lead pencils, etc., each 2.60

No. 3, With three compartments, for letter paper, note paper, and envelopes ....each, 1.50

Calendars.

No. 1, Showing day of month.......................................each, .10
2, Showing month, and day of month.............................. " .50
3, Showing month, day of week, and day of month................. " .65

Drawing Papers, Bristol Boards, Drawing Books,

AND ERASABLE TABLETS.

Drawing Papers.—Whatman's English, imported. Prices variable with gold.

Cap,	14 x 17, rough or smooth,		Royal,	19 x 24, rough or smooth,	
Demy,	15 x 20, " "		Super Royal,	19 x 27, " "	
Medium,	17 x 22, " "		Imperial,	22 x 30, " "	

German Drawing Papers.—Variable with gold.

Cap,	14 x 17,	- - -	Royal,	19 x 24,	- - -
Demy,	15 x 20,	- - -	Super Royal,	19 x 27,	- - -
Medium,	17 x 22,	- - -	Imperial,	22 x 30,	- - -

Bristol Boards.—Reynolds & Son's Best. Variable with gold.

Cap,	two sheets thick.	- -	Medium,	two sheets thick.	- -
"	three " "	- -	"	three " "	- -
"	four " "	- -	"	four " "	- -
Demy,	two " "	- -	Royal,	two " "	- -
"	three " "	- -	"	three " "	- -
"	four " "	- -	"	four " "	- -

Drawing Books.—Interleaved with tissue paper.

No. 1.—Demy, 4to. printed covers, 8 leaves,	- -	per dozen,	$1.00
No. 2. " " " " 16 "	- - - -	"	1.40
No. 3. " " " " 24 "	- - - - -	"	1.75

First-Class Cold Pressed Drawing Paper.

Interleaved with tissue paper.

No. 1.—Cap, 4to quarter bound, 12 leaves,	- -	per dozen,	1.88
No. 2. " " " " 24 "	- -	"	3.75
No. 3. " " full cloth gilt, 48 "	- - - - -	"	6.00
No. 4.—Demy, " quarter bound, 12 "	- - - -	"	2.38
No. 5. " " full cloth gilt, 24 "	- - - - -	"	4.50
No. 6. " " " " 48 "	- - -	"	8.75
No. 7.—Medium, " quarter bound, 12 "	- - - - -	"	2.75
No. 8. " " " " 24 "	- - - - -	"	5.50
No. 9. " " half " 48 "	- - - - -	"	10.00

Erasable Tablets.—White.—(Use a soft lead pencil—erase with a damp cloth or sponge.)

Elementary Drawing Tablet,	- - - -	per dozen,	3.00
Progressive " "	- - - - - - -	"	3.00
Elementary Writing "	- - - - - - -	"	3.00
Leaf Tablet, size 4½ x 7 inches,	- - - - - -	"	1.00
Spelling Tablet, ruled for 40 words, size 5 x 8 inches,	- -	"	1.20

A variety of styles for the pocket and office.

Lunch Boxes, School Bags, etc.

The Patent Folding Lunch Box.

This is a novelty, and, doubtless, will be in brisk demand, because, when relieved of the daily rations, it is handy and compact. It folds up to only three times the thickness of the tin of which it is made

Price.. **0.50**

Liberal discount when quantities are purchased.

The French School Bags

are made of very light and durable material. There are two kinds—white and colored—four sizes of each kind.

No. 1, price..........	**0.65**
" 2, "	**.75**
" 3, "	**1.00**
" 4, "	**1.25**

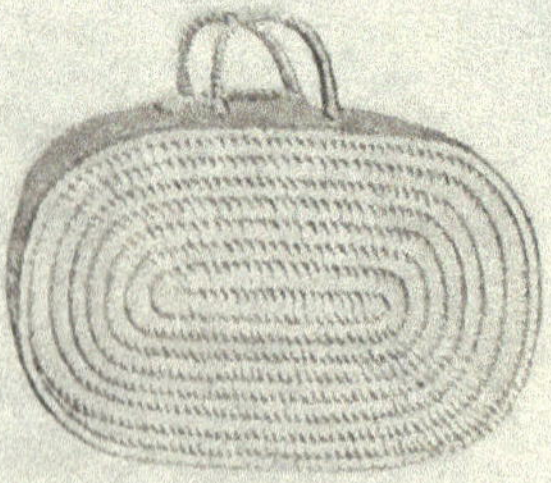

Oval Palm-Leaf School Valise..........	each,	**2.50**
Square Palm-Leaf School Valise..........	"	**2.50**

Book-Carriers, Easels, Rests, etc.

THE PATENT BOOK-CARRIER, for Boys and Girls

The damage which books receive between home and school is greater than their necessary wear and tear when in regular use. The common book-strap is a *convenience* in keeping books together; but is sadly destructive to the bindings.

The cut represents an invention to obviate this difficulty. It finds great favor with teachers, pupils, and parents, and is proving a success. The cut shows it partly filled with books and slates. It is simple and durable.

Price 0.50

Moore's Needle Gun Book-Clamp is a later invention for the same purpose. It winds up with a wheel, held by a ratchet under the handle. When operated it makes a peculiar "horse fiddle" noise, which is supposed, by some, to be music to the ears of school children.

Price 0.50

KENDALL'S BOOK-REST, for the Desk or Library Table.

The convenience of a well-adapted rest for the book, and the advantages of a proper angle for easy vision, are too fully recognized by all readers to require discussion here.

Kendall's Rest for the book *unites in one simple apparatus all the requisites of a perfect book rest*—for any size of book.

It consists of three standards united at the top by a metallic head, which allows the outside standards to open like the legs of a compass, while the middle leg turns back. To this tripod is attached the shelf which carries the fingers or springs for holding the book open. The whole can be "unshipped" in a second, and folded flat, as easily as a carpenter's rule. (Not mailable.)

Price 1.00

Rewards.

REWARD-OF-MERIT CARDS.

No.	Size				Price
No. 1,	size, $1\frac{3}{4}$ x $2\frac{5}{8}$,	in one color,	for day-schools,	per hundred	0.30
" 2,	" $1\frac{7}{8}$ x $3\frac{3}{8}$,	"	" "	"	.40
" 3,	" $2\frac{1}{2}$ x $3\frac{3}{4}$,	in two colors,	"	"	.70
" 4,	" $2\frac{1}{2}$ x $3\frac{3}{4}$,	"	" Sunday-schools,	"	.70
" 5,	" $2\frac{3}{8}$ x 5,	"	" day-schools,	"	.84
" 6,	" 3 x $5\frac{1}{4}$,	"	" "	"	1.12
" 7,	" 3 x $5\frac{1}{4}$,	"	" Sunday-schools,	"	1.12
" 8,	" $2\frac{5}{8}$ x $4\frac{1}{8}$,	illuminated,	" day-schools,	"	2.00
" 9,	" $2\frac{5}{8}$ x $4\frac{1}{4}$,	"	" "	"	1.50
" 10,	" $2\frac{1}{2}$ x 4,	in one color,	"	"	.67
" 11,	" 3 x $5\frac{1}{4}$,	"	"	"	.90
" 12,	" $2\frac{1}{2}$ x $3\frac{3}{4}$,	"	"	"	.72
" 13,	" $2\frac{5}{8}$ x $4\frac{1}{8}$,	illuminated,	"	"	2.22
" 14,	" $2\frac{1}{8}$ x $3\frac{1}{2}$,	in one color,	Snnday-schools,	"	.50
" 15,	" $2\frac{5}{8}$ x $4\frac{1}{8}$,	illuminated,	"	"	1.40
" 16,	" $2\frac{5}{8}$ x $3\frac{3}{4}$,	colored,	day-schools,	"	.95
" 17,	" $2\frac{5}{8}$ x $4\frac{1}{8}$,	illuminatea,	Sunday-schools,	"	2.44
" 18,	" $2\frac{5}{8}$ x $4\frac{1}{8}$,	"	"	"	1.70
" 19,	" 3 x $5\frac{1}{4}$,	colored,	day-schools,	"	1.40
" 20,	" 2 x $3\frac{1}{4}$,	in one color,	Sunday-schools,	"	.50
" 21,	" $2\frac{3}{8}$ x $4\frac{1}{8}$,	"	"	"	.72
" 22,	" $1\frac{5}{8}$ x $2\frac{3}{4}$,	"	day-schools,	"	.40
" 23,	" $2\frac{3}{4}$ x $3\frac{1}{4}$,	"	"	"	.62
" 24,	" $2\frac{5}{8}$ x $4\frac{1}{8}$,	illuminated,	"	"	2.44
" 25,	" $2\frac{1}{4}$ x $3\frac{3}{8}$,	in two colors,	Sunday-schools,	"	.64

The illuminated kinds are put up in envelopes, 10 cards in each envelope.

A discount allowed when ordered by the 1000.

TESTIMONIALS.—Appropriate Designs.

Neatly lithographed on heavy white paper.

No.	Size		Price
No. 1,	size, $6\frac{1}{2}$ in. x $9\frac{1}{2}$ in.	per dozen,	0.50
" 2,	" 8 in. x 10 in.	"	.60
" 3,	" 10 in. x 12 in.	"	.72

Special Testimonials or Diplomas to order.

CPSIA information can be obtained
at www.ICGtesting.com
Printed in the USA
LVHW030120210323
742063LV00002B/455

9 783382 127527